CRITICAL PRAISE FOR
HERBERT CROWDER

"Political intrigue and suspense . . . Crowder writes smoothly and with a flair for detail."

—*The New York Times*

AMBUSH AT OSIRAK

His riveting *New York Times* bestseller—the shocking novel of crisis and response in the fiery Middle East. . . .

"Excellent. Crowder skillfully blends a high-tech action story, a frighteningly realistic plot, and a fast-paced espionage thriller into a very enjoyable book."

—Dale Brown, bestselling author of *Flight of the Old Dog* and *Sky Masters*

"Absorbing . . . Diplomatic intrigue, incredibly fast-paced."

—*Toledo Blade*

"Exciting . . . brilliant descriptions." —*Cincinnati Post*

WEATHERHAWK

Crowder's shattering novel of government secrets, military intrigue, and criminal conspiracy. . . .

"Thriller fans will applaud!" —*Publishers Weekly*

"Superpowers, organized crime, and aerospace conglomerates clash!"

—*Kirkus*

"A crackerjack thriller!"

—W.E.B. Griffin, bestselling author of *Brotherhood of War*, *The Corps*, and *Badge of Honor* series

Also by Herbert Crowder

AMBUSH AT OSIRAK
WEATHERHAWK

SCIMITAR

HERBERT CROWDER

PUBLISHED IN HARDCOVER AS *MISSILE ZONE*

JOVE BOOKS, NEW YORK

This Jove Book contains the complete
text of the original hardcover edition.
It has been completely reset in a typeface
designed for easy reading and was printed
from new film.

SCIMITAR

A Jove Book/published by arrangement with
the author

PRINTING HISTORY
G.P. Putnam's Sons edition/March 1991
Jove edition/November 1992

ISBN: 0-515-10975-4

For Ibolya

ACKNOWLEDGMENTS

To George Crowder, for his extensive and painstaking research on this book and his perceptive critique of the finished manuscript.

To Marjorie Miller and my other fellow writers in her Westwood writers group, for their patience in hearing this book read chapter by chapter and for their many helpful suggestions: Susie Deutsch, Terry Gegasi, Sanford Holst, Larry Kurtz, Sheree Noble, Gudrun Stutz.

*For a fire is kindled in mine anger, and
shall burn unto the lowest hell, and shall consume
the earth with her increase, and set on fire
the foundations of the mountains.*

—DEUTERONOMY 32:22

SCIMITAR

Prologue

THE FIRST RAYS of the sun illuminated the stark landscape of the Jinquan test facility, its assortment of rude concrete structures thrusting long shadows across the sands of the Gobi Desert. The demonstration was scheduled for 7:00 A.M. In the distance a moving cloud of dust signalled the approach of a vehicle along the unpaved access road. It was traveling at a high rate of speed. A black limousine emerged from the dust cloud, its windows streaked with sunrise red and gold.

From the cluster of buildings, figures began to spill out of one of them as the limo neared, until an assemblage of perhaps a dozen Chinese, some in uniforms, the others in business suits, stood waiting to receive the honored guest, a prince of Saudi Arabia. But the man who stepped out of the limousine wore none of the trappings of traditional Arab attire. He was dressed like a western businessman, looking more urbane than most in his tailored three-piece suit, his black Vandyke goatee neatly trimmed.

Schooled in England and America, Bandar bin Sultan bin Abdul Aziz was accustomed to traveling the world at his king's behest. His field of expertise was weapon systems. As a jet pilot who had won his wings in Saudi Arabia's Air Force, Bandar had flown virtually every plane in his country's inventory, rising to the rank of general. He was a protégé of his uncle, King Fahd, who had delegated to him the conclusion of the impending weapons deal with the Chinese.

But this Chinese weapon lay outside his range of firsthand experience. His exposure to ballistic missiles had been minimal, which was the principal reason he had requested this morning's test firing. The Dong Feng, or East Wind, was one of China's older intermediate-range ballistic missiles, due for replacement with an upgraded version, which helped explain the government's willingness to part with it—for a not-inconsiderable sum of money. Old technology though it might be, it looked good to the Saudis, who had tried vainly to purchase IRBMs from America. The East Wind III had a much longer range than the U.S. Pershing—upwards of two thousand miles—and while its rocket engines were the outmoded liquid fueled variety, they were "storable," allowing the missile to operate even in remote areas such as the Mongolian border, where the Chinese had it deployed.

The impending purchase was a closely guarded secret. If Saudi Arabia's "special friend," the United States, were to learn about it, undue pressure would be brought to bear against the Saudis to back out of the deal. Bandar didn't relish the day when the Americans found out, but he would face that when he had to.

He had never witnessed a live firing of a ballistic missile. In the films he had seen, the vehicles had undergone preparation in immense gantries many stories high, the complicated and time-consuming checkout progressing through an agonizingly slow countdown as the volatile liquified gases that fueled the flight emitted ominous clouds of white vapor throughout.

But here at Jinquan there were no giant gantries. The DF-3 was a tactical missile, self-launched from its own trailer-erector-launcher. It was touted by the Chinese as a "mobile" missile, though Bandar wondered how mobile a liquid-fueled rocket of such immense proportions could be—twenty meters in length, two meters thick, and weighing thirty tons.

He was about to find out.

The missile was trundled up to the bunker in its trailer, towed by a giant sixteen-wheeled truck, moving at a slow but steady pace over the unpaved roadbed. Up close, it looked even more gigantic than he had imagined. It was painted a glistening white, with small black tail fins, encircled at several places along its lengthy fuselage by black rings. Curiously, its identifying label was not in Chinese characters but in letters of the Roman alphabet—large black letters stenciled onto its surface near the nose: DF for Dong Feng.

The tow truck and trailer with their ponderous load lumbered off toward the launch pad, a half kilometer away. Bandar watched the launch crew pile out of the truck and swarm around the missile, attaching cables, which he took to be electric, and hydraulic lines from the tow truck to the chassis of the trailer. Moments later the nose of the missile began to tilt upward, a hinged section of the trailer bed slowly raising it to an erect position. The missile crew began disconnecting cables and rolling them up. They climbed back into the truck and pulled away.

The Chinese spokesman tugged at Bandar's elbow. "It is time we moved inside the bunker. Launch will occur momentarily."

To the dismay of the spokesman, Bandar replied, "I have no intention of watching the proceedings from inside. I'll remain out here. I want to get a feel for the weapon my country is purchasing."

The officer relayed this to the others and an animated discussion ensued in Chinese. The officer repeated to Bandar again and again that it was unsafe, but their attempts to dissuade him were to no avail.

One of the delegation rushed inside the bunker and returned with two sets of headphones. "At least wear this," the spokesman said. "I will stay with you." Bandar accepted the headset and put it on, but adjusted it so that he could still hear, as the other members of the delegation repaired to the bunker.

The countdown, now proceeding by remote control, was nearing its final stages and was now picked up on the bunker's PA system and audible on an outside speaker. It was in Chinese, but Bandar's escort translated. "Five, four, three, two, one—"

A flash more brilliant than the sun made him turn away. A split second later, the earth shook beneath him and his ears were assaulted by an explosion like a hundred jet afterburners all kicking in at once. Bandar turned back to see the thickset missile rising smoothly and steadily from its vapor-shrouded launch pad as the arms of its mobile erector-launcher dropped away. The sustained, ear-splitting roar of its engine was inseparable from the continued shaking of the ground around him, filling him with an awesome sense of the vehicle's stupendous power.

It continued its majestic rise, picking up speed, incredibly graceful for the ungainly figure it had cut on the ground. The brilliance of its fiery plume seared its image across his retinas, but he remained transfixed and couldn't bring himself to shield his eyes. Upward it soared, toward a trajectory that would carry it hundreds of miles above the earth where nothing could disturb it or serve to impede its inexorable appointment with its target. The white-hot shaft of flame shortened to a disk, then diminished to a bright point of light, and still he watched, until there was nothing more to see.

He turned back toward the bunker, his eyes still dazzled by the missile's fiery departure, bright blotches of light persisting in his pupils. Time would erase them, but time could never erase the impact of this experience on his consciousness. He had been infected with the East Wind's awesome power. Its power had become his power. He would never be the same.

Nor would the Middle East ever be the same, once this power resided in the shifting dunes of Saudi Arabia's Empty Quarter.

1

CAPTAIN GUNNAR SIGURDSON was feeling mellow as he stood on the bridge of his ship, his back to the wind, watching the lights of Singapore Island fade into the distance. The brief stopover had been enjoyable as well as profitable. He had managed an evening ashore after overseeing the loading of his cargo and had just returned to weigh anchor following a five-course French dinner at the Meridien Hotel—a sumptuous and welcome break from the ship's fare that would have to last him until his return trip from the Gulf.

But it was the cargo previously loaded in Shanghai that contributed most to his state of mind. The Chinese were paying top dollar for the run to the Persian Gulf because of that cargo, affording a windfall for his company and a sizable bonus for himself. Munitions always commanded a premium, and these were very special munitions. Not that there was any real danger. He had been given ample assurance that the warheads were not armed. And the Chinese had even sent along an escort, one of their destroyers, to watch over their property.

The luminous dial on his watch read 11:30. The destroyer would be weighing anchor shortly, its crew back from their liberty in this favorite port for Chinese sailors, with its predominantly Chinese population. He wondered idly what kind of shape they would be in. His own crew had all reported back on time in high spirits, feeling their oats but with no one falling down drunk. A lifetime mariner, Sigurdson recognized that getting a little drunk on shore leave was part of the rites of passage.

His course was west-northwest through the Strait of Malacca, the passage that lay between the giant island of Sumatra and the Malay peninsula to its north. He had gotten a head start on the destroyer to save them a bit of time. With its faster speed, the Chinese warship would easily catch up to his ship before it was more than fifty or sixty miles into the strait. At this point it would have to slow down and proceed at the cargo ship's twenty-knot pace. Not that this was slow—it was better time than most freighters made. But then the *Oceania*, forty thousand tons, Liberian-registered with an all-Scandinavian crew, was quite different from most freighters.

She was a LASH ship—lighter-aboard ship. A form of container ship, if you wanted to look at it that way, which Sigurdson didn't; he was scornful of the container craft and considered them inferior to his own ship in many ways. Unlike his LASH ship, they carried no derrick equipment and were completely at the mercy of the harbor facilities for loading and unloading. He had watched contemptuously as more and more container ships stacked up in Singapore harbor, riding at anchor for hours that could drag into days, waiting their turn at one of the hideous orange monsters that had come to dominate the waterfront skyline in this busiest of all ports.

Meanwhile, the *Oceania*'s cargo was brought out to it, pre-stowed in the lighters—watertight steel barges sixty feet long and thirty wide—pushed into the LASH ship's stern by a tugboat, then hoisted aboard by the ship's own massive derrick on rails, which quickly deployed them to another part of the ship, where they were stacked neatly, side by side. One every fifteeen minutes, the entire Singapore cargo loaded in under five hours.

The *Oceania* was ideal for the China coast and numerous other ports in the Orient, where loading facilities were scant by western comparisons and where the freight often arrived at the port by river barge to begin with. And the lighters could hold a mammoth amount of cargo, several hundred tons, which gave them a big advantage over the smaller container ship modules. Take one of these Chinese missiles, for instance; it was far too big for a container ship, measuring more than sixty feet long and five feet in diameter. But laid diagonally across the bottom of a lighter barge, its nose cone removed and stored alongside, it fit quite nicely.

Ten lighters so loaded had been stored aboard the *Oceania* in Shanghai harbor; each of ten others contained a missile launch vehicle. Sigurdson could only visualize what they might look like; the missiles and launchers had been sealed inside the steel barges when the equipment left the factory that produced them, wherever in China that might be. All he really knew about the missiles was their Chinese name, East Wind, that they had been sold to Saudi Arabia, his destination, and that from their size alone, they had to be far and away the longest range weapons ever introduced into the Middle East.

Did they represent another escalation in the Middle East conflict? Well, that was none of his concern. It was the affair of the Chinese government, one of his best customers. He had been doing business with them for more than eight years. He had carried munitions for them before, on several occasions, but never on so grand a scale—and never with an armed escort. Why had they sent the destroyer this time; were they expecting trouble? Probably just a precaution. Despite the end of Desert Storm hostilities, the Persian Gulf was still a hazardous and unpredictable place. He would be glad when his cargo was unloaded at Dammam and he was safely out of there.

He glanced at his watch again. The Chinese destroyer would already be getting up steam, its crew making their way back to the ship. Their liberty expired at midnight. There would be stories swapped and raucous laughter and much bragging over whose philandering was most prolific. No matter what their nationality, sailors were sailors.

Four bells sounded on the bridge of the *Oceania.* It was 2:00 A.M. The captain exchanged looks with his first mate, who had the graveyard shift. Most of his crew had long since bedded down for the night. The captain had been waiting for the rendezvous with the Red-Chinese destroyer before turning in himself. It should have been here by now.

He left the bridge and walked through a short companionway to the radio room. On the LASH ship all the offices and quarters were located forward, on the single multistory island topped off by the bridge. The signalman looked like he was dozing off, but snapped to when he saw it was the captain entering his cubicle.

"Anything from the destroyer?"

"No, sir, no messages since we left port."

The captain frowned. "I want you to contact them, find out what's keeping them. See if they'll give you an ETA."

"Yes, sir. Shall I send it in English? The Chinese signalman turned in at midnight."

Sigurdson cursed. Everyone on his ship got to sleep except the captain. "Get him up, then. He can go back to sleep afterwards."

He walked back to the bridge and looked at the radar scope. Traffic in the strait was light this time of night, only a few blips visible and no sign of the destroyer within the range of his radar. The shoreline of Malaysia to the north was clearly delineated on the scope, as was Sumatra and its cluster of offshore islands to the south.

Eight minutes later the Chinese signalman reported to the bridge. He was from the destroyer's crew and had been placed aboard the *Oceania* to facilitate communications. His name was Chang and he spoke fairly good English. He saluted the captain smartly, his face flushed and excited.

"Sir, I regret to report a delay in the arrival of my ship. It has only just now weighed anchor. There was a slight problem in getting the crew back from their liberty."

"Slight problem? They're two hours late! What happened?"

"An altercation between some of our crew and some Taiwanese sailors. The police arrested them."

"They got thrown in the brig?"

"Yes, seven of the crew. My superiors had to bail them out. It took some time to get them released."

"What do we do now?" inquired Sigurdson. "Do they want me to heave to and wait for them here, or keep going?"

"My captain desires you to continue at your present rate of speed. It will save time. He expects to overtake you within four hours, somewhere in the vicinity of Melaka Island."

Sigurdson grunted. "All right. Dismissed." There was no point in staying up now. Escort or no escort, nothing was going to happen here; it was when they approached the Gulf that they would have to be on their toes. And besides, it wasn't as if they didn't have some protection aboard. Three Red-Chinese marines with automatic weapons had been placed on board the *Oceania* as an added safeguard.

He yawned and stood up. "I'm turning in, Axel. When Gunnar relieves you, be sure to tell him about the destroyer." As he passed the radar scope, something caught his eye.

"What's that up ahead of us?" He watched a few more blips bloom and fade out. "A small one, by the size of the blip, and slow. She can't be doing ten knots."

The mate nodded. "Malay fishing boat, probably. A lot of them in these parts."

"I don't see any lights yet." Sigurdson stepped outside for a better look. A faint glimmer was discernible on the horizon, and he delayed his departure for a few minutes more to watch the lights increase in brightness and move farther to starboard, signifying that they were overtaking the other vessel. He went back inside the cabin.

"There she is. We'll be abreast of her soon. Better give her a blast to let her know we're coming."

The mate complied. The LASH ship's whistle had an unexpected effect on the other boat. The captain and mate watched her lights slip gradually abeam, then remain there. She was picking up speed, as though she didn't want to be passed. And now her lights were getting brighter.

Sigurdson checked the radar scope again. The other vessel was directly abreast of the *Oceania,* less than a mile away now, still bearing in.

The mate had also noted the other ship's behavior. "What are they doing? Surely they must see our lights."

"They couldn't miss them unless they've gone blind." The first disquieting tremors intruded on Sigurdson's peace of mind. He picked up the phone and called the signal room.

"Larson, there's a vessel off our starboard beam, bearing in on us. I want you to send it a message via blinker to bear off. Immediately. Call the bridge when you've finished."

He returned to the radar scope. The other ship was continuing to close in. Now it was scarcely half a mile abeam.

"I didn't see any blinker response from her," the mate noted. "Shall I bear off to port?"

"Hold off for a minute." The phone rang and the captain picked it up. "You sent the message?"

"Yes, sir, twice."

"And there was no answer?"

"No, sir."

"Send it again. Keep repeating it." Sigurdson hung up the phone. "Left rudder ten."

"Left rudder ten," echoed the mate.

"Aye, sir." The helmsman spun the wheel. Sigurdson and the mate watched the lights of the other vessel. The captain checked the radar scope again.

"She's bearing in even faster! The bloody fools! What are they trying to do?"

"Shall I come farther aport?"

"No. I won't be run out of the channel by some insignificant fishing smack." The captain picked up the phone again and dialed a number. "Report to the bridge at once, on the double."

The boatswain's mate arrived shortly, out of breath. "Yes, sir?"

Sigurdson pointed to the lights off to starboard, looming alarmingly close. "Man the forward searchlight and direct it at that vessel."

The boatswain's mate ran off. A minute later the other ship, now barely a few hundred feet abeam, was illuminated from stem to stern by the LASH ship's brilliant searchlight. Sigurdson saw that their guess had been wrong. It was not a fishing boat but a tugboat—a rather large one, the seagoing type. There was no one on deck, no crewman to be seen. He trained his binoculars on it.

Her name and home port were painted on the bow, but he couldn't make them out. The letters were too faint, the paint eroded by the combination of salt and sea. Or had they been deliberately defaced?

The tugboat was now a scant hundred meters off his beam, in range of the *Oceania*'s powerful audio system. He seized the microphone and flipped the mode switch to external. "Captain of the LASH ship *Oceania* to the oceangoing tugboat off my starboard beam: You are too close! You are in violation of article 27. You will bear off immediately, understood? Bear off at once!"

There was no response from the tugboat, nor any apparent change in her trajectory. "Go wake up that Chinese signalman and get him up here again. Maybe they'll understand Chinese."

Before the boatswain's mate could respond, the cabin doors of the tugboat burst open. The deck was suddenly swarming with seamen. A powerful searchlight was trained on the *Oceania*'s bridge, momentarily blinding Sigurdson, who dropped his binoculars. On the tug's bow, crewmen wrestled a tarpaulin off a small deck-mounted gun. Moments later the bridge of the *Oceania* was rocked by an ear-splitting report as a shot screamed across her bow. As the echoes died away, a loudspeaker blared from the tugboat, an authoritative voice commanding the *Oceania* in English to heave to immediately.

Recovering from his shock, Sigurdson grabbed the phone to alert the Red-Chinese marines. That proved unnecessary; he saw them already scrambling up the outside ladder to reach the bridge.

Shots rang out from the tugboat, extinguishing the *Oceania*'s searchlight and throwing the tugboat into shadow. The beam from the tug's searchlight slid downward from the LASH ship's bridge to capture the three marines in its dazzling brilliance. The tugboat's loudspeaker voice commanded the Chinese marines to drop their weapons, the order repeated in Chinese by a different voice.

The Chinese marines ignored the warning, continuing their mad scramble for the bridge. Bright flashes of gunfire erupted from the deck of the tug, and the captain watched in horror as two of the marines, cut down by the sniper fire, lost their hold on the ladder and fell three stories to the *Oceania*'s deck. Their companion, wounded, swung around to return the fire, getting off a few wild bursts before the next barrage arrived. His weapon fell from his grasp and he pitched forward, one ankle catching in a rung of the ladder. He hung there, suspended head downward, as the fusilade of bullets continued to tear into his lifeless body.

"General quarters!" the captain shouted into the ship's address microphone. *"We are under attack!* Signalman, send out

a Mayday call, then call the destroyer and tell them what's happening!"

The intention of the other craft was clearly to board him. He considered his options. The destroyer was still too far away to help him, but perhaps some friendly ship was closer and would hear his Mayday call. In the meantime, he had to think of his crew. He had been badly shaken by the sight of the Chinese marines being gunned down. Without them, resistance was out of the question. He ordered the engine room to shut down.

The big ship took some time to slow down, its momentum continuing to carry it forward. As it coasted on, the tugboat maneuvered itself toward the LASH ship's stern, most easily accessible because of its lower freeboard. Grappling hooks were thrown over the side, followed by boarding nets, and a boarding party clambered onto the *Oceania*'s cargo deck.

Sigurdson watched them through his binoculars as they picked their way forward over the cargo of stacked lighters. They were a dozen or so, all armed with automatic weapons and dressed uniformly in blue dungarees, a swarthy bunch. Not Chinese, probably Malays. Except for two, who were Caucasian and appeared to be in command. One of the pair was limping noticeably, though managing to keep up with the others. The captain refocused the binoculars on the faces of the two Caucasians. They looked like Semitic faces.

Moments later, five of the Malays, led by the man with the limp, were standing on the bridge, their weapons trained on the captain, mate, boatswain, and helmsman. Sigurdson's sour look turned even more so. The automatic weapons pointed at him, he was not surprised to note, were Uzis.

"What is the meaning of this act of piracy? I demand—"

The leader placed the cold steel muzzle of his Uzi to the captain's throat, silencing him. His eyes had the piercing look of a bird of prey. "You are in no position to demand anything. Where is your radio room? Take me there—quickly!"

The captain led him across the bridge to the cubicle where the signalman was still tapping out a Mayday message. The leader raised his weapon. "No!" Sigurdson shouted.

A rapid-fire burst from the Uzi sprayed into the radio room. The signalman slumped over the smoking ruin of his equipment. The captain ran to him and raised his head, searching for a pulse. There was none. His crewman was dead.

He swung around furiously. *"Why—?"*

The smoking gun barrel contacted his throat again, hot enough now to sear his flesh. "There will be more casualties unless you follow my orders. Would you like to be next?"

"What do you want?"

"That's better." He lowered the Uzi but kept it pointed at the captain's stomach. "We are going to off-load a small portion of your cargo, Captain. Just two of the lighters. Then you can be on your way again."

"Unload cargo in this sea?" Sigurdson protested. "Impossible."

"No, Captain, not in this sea. We will proceed to the lee of that nearest island and anchor there." He motioned toward the port side of the ship. "You may start your engines now."

Fifteen minutes later the LASH ship dropped anchor in a small cove of one of Sumatra's coastal islands. It was a secluded place; no lights were visible on shore. On the way, the captain had noticed activity by the detachment of boarders who had remained on the cargo deck. Exploring the stack of lighters in the forward area of the ship where the Shanghai cargo was stored, they had scrawled giant *X*s on the tops of two of the huge steel barges. "Those are the ones we will unload," their leader now informed him. "You may proceed."

Sigurdson knew his cargo. One of the designated lighters contained an East Wind missile, the other a missile launch vehicle. How had they known? There were no external markings to tip off the contents. He hesitated, reluctant to give in so easily.

"If you don't comply, we will have no choice but to begin executing your crew," the man with the limp assured him. "One of my men knows how to operate your equipment. We will get our cargo one way or the other."

Sigurdson picked up the phone and gave the order. Before long the low-pitched droning of heavy electric drive motors was audible from the stern of the ship as the gigantic overhead derrick began to slide along its side rails toward the forward cargo section. It eventually came to a stop above one of the chalkmarked lighters and lowered an elevator-like platform into place. Vise-like jaws on the underside of the platform clamped onto sturdy steel lugs protruding from the four corners of the lighter, and the ponderous barge began to rise slowly from the stack.

The louder droning of the derrick drive motors was heard again as the mammoth structure reversed its direction, sliding back aft, where a notch in the stern of the ship permitted the lighter to be lowered into the water. The tugboat had meanwhile untied from the LASH ship and was waiting just astern. Before the derrick released its grip on the lighter, the tug had maneuvered its bow snugly against the steel cargo barge. With the lighter floating freely now, lashed to the tugboat, it backed away, then began pushing the lighter toward shore as the derrick retracted its lifting apparatus and began its sluggish progress forward again to retrieve the second lighter.

"There's no place to unload it around here," Sigurdson observed. "What will you do with it?"

The leader's lips curled in the semblance of a smile, but he made no answer. Together, they watched the tug and its cargo disappear around a point, a second tugboat emerging moments later around the same point and making for the LASH ship. It was considerably smaller than the other boat and not as seaworthy, Sigurdson noted. Assuredly, the cargo it held would have to be transferred to some other vessel before reaching the open sea. But what vessel? Where? How?

By the time the derrick had reloaded and moved back to the other end of the ship, the second tug was in position, awaiting it. The leader of the hijackers thanked the captain for his cooperation. "We'll take our leave now. Do not restart your engines until we are out of sight. After that, you are free to do as you wish. Do not attempt to follow us."

He was the last to leave the bridge, sending his men on ahead of him. Sigurdson watched them skip across the cargo stack toward the stern, where the second lighter was beginning to descend toward the water. At a command from their leader, the boarding party jumped onto the lighter, riding it down like an elevator. The leader waved to the bridge, then followed suit, surprisingly nimble for a man with his handicap. When the tugboat was firmly lashed to the lighter they clambered aboard, the derrick let go, and the tugboat headed for shore.

SCIMITAR

Sigurdson watched the tugboat draw away, its deadly cargo in tow, greatly relieved that the hijackers were gone, his ship and most of its crew and cargo still intact. He felt bad about the Chinese marines and even worse about his signalman. What a waste . . . It hadn't been necessary to kill poor Larson, either.

Despite the hatred he felt for the perpetrators, he couldn't suppress a grudging respect for the efficiency of the operation. It had clearly been planned with great care and finesse, right down to the last detail.

The third mate came running onto the bridge, out of breath. "Captain, look at this! Bergelin found it on the cargo deck. One of those pirates must have lost it."

Sigurdson squinted at the miniature artifact the mate had dropped into his hand. It was a replica of an antique sword, scarcely more than two inches long, with a curved, single-edged silver blade, its handle and hilt exquisitely rendered in intricate gold filigree. The symbol embossed on its blade confirmed his suspicions about the hijackers. It was a ram's horn, the ancient symbol since Biblical times of the tribes of Israel.

2

DAVID LLEWELLYN GAVE his wife a hasty peck on the lips and headed for the door.

"Not so fast." Hand on the doorknob, he turned. Daniella stood where he had left her, hands on hips, an impish smile on her face.

"So soon we've become 'old marrieds'?" She was still in her nightgown, her dark hair falling to her shoulders, tousled from a night's sleep. She had never looked more appealing.

"No way. We'll never be 'old marrieds.' " He returned and folded her in his arms, taking the time to kiss her properly.

"Mmm," she purred appreciatively. "More."

"Later. I've got to get moving."

"Just so you don't go on confusing me with the furnishings."

"Sorry. I guess I was already on the road to Jericho." He released her but she still clung to him.

"Why can't I go with you?"

"We've been over that."

She let him go, knowing the importance he attached to this assignment, sensing the excitement he must feel. "When will I see you?"

"No telling. But I should be back well before dusk. If it runs any later, I'll phone."

"Be careful."

He smiled back at her reassuringly, winked his eye, and was gone. Why had she said that, she wondered? Jericho was among the most trouble-free spots in the occupied territories.

The Palestinian uprising, the *intifada,* had barely touched it. Still, she was uneasy. She wished she were going along.

Still staring at the door her husband had just walked through, her eyes began to glaze over. She was back in the Sinai with David, speeding across the desert in a fifty-year-old open touring car, as a hail of bullets from a pursuing vehicle sought to snuff out their lives . . .

In those days, they had not been husband and wife. In fact, they had not even started out as friends. David had been summoned by the United States President to the Middle East because things were getting out of hand. He was sent in as a special envoy to Jerusalem, but his real mission had been to plug a security leak at the American embassy there. The assignment had come at a time in his life when he wanted out of the intelligence business, which he blamed for the loss of his wife, Katherine, to an assassin's bullet meant for him. It had happened in London, and it had taken David a long time to get over it.

Daniella smiled, thankful that he had come to the Middle East those days not so long ago. Then she had been Daniella Zadik, special assistant to the Israeli Foreign Minister. She always joked that she was really just a notch above a girl Friday, but it was only a joke. In fact, Daniella was a native Israeli who, after losing her family in the 1973 War, had gone on to become an agent for Mossad. An agent whose orders were to keep an eye on David Llewellyn.

When the Middle East heated up, so did their relationship. As Israel prepared an air strike on the rebuilt Osirak nuclear reactor near Baghdad, Daniella and David ended up working together, teaming up without the knowledge or blessing of their superiors. And what a team they'd been! Not only did David catch his embassy mole, but their joint efforts helped to thwart an Iraqi plot to bring down the Israeli government. In the process, they not only became friends, but lovers.

And shortly thereafter, husband and wife.

The Land Rover grumbled throatily as David Llewellyn shifted down for the turn onto Derek Yeriho, his mind on Daniella. Shortly after they were married they had decided she would resign her job and stay home to start a family. It hadn't worked out that way—the doctors couldn't say why. And now she was home, with little to do. She had been especially restless lately, was, in fact, climbing the walls. There was a void in her life, and he knew what it was—work.

Daniella had, like so many Israelis, an extraordinary work ethic. It had so impressed him when he had first set foot in this remarkable young-old country—this compulsion to contribute to the country's welfare and future, to make a difference by the dint of one's own labor, to share in the burden of keeping the country afloat in a sea of hostility surrounding it on every side. It was a special kind of zeal he associated with the spirit that made the kibbutz succeed. Granted, not every Israeli had it—far from it. But Daniella had it. Daniella had once been a kibbutznik.

Was he jealous of this in her, this part of her mind and heart that belonged not to him but to her country, that conditioned the way she looked at everything? Perhaps, in a way, even though he admired her for it. It would have been less difficult if he were not in the active employ of his own government, whose objectives and policies did not always line up with hers. Serving two different masters was a source of friction that put constant stress on their relationship. He had expected this to subside when she quit her government jobs. It hadn't.

Something had to be done. His attitude toward having a working wife had softened. Maybe she should get her old job back in the foreign ministry . . .

He passed the Garden of Gethsemane and began the climb up past the Mount of Olives toward the crest of the Judean hills, his thoughts turning to what lay ahead. He had been to Jericho only once before, though it was less than twenty-five miles from Jerusalem, a forty-minute drive. But the cultural separation between the two places could not be measured in minutes, or even miles.

Jericho lay in the West Bank, formerly a territory of Jordan, occupied by the Israelis now for more than twenty years, since the Six Day War. The ancient city's population of some seven thousand was still almost totally Arab, and an abandoned Jordanian refugee camp for Palestinians was still there, at the north edge of town. He remembered the strange, unsettling feeling it had given him, the sight of those hundreds of squalid, empty mud huts, whose occupants had mostly fled to Jordan across the nearby Allenby Bridge as the Israelis closed in.

Jericho. A magical name, a historic and symbolic place to Jews. For it was just across the Jordan River from the ancient walled fortress town, as recorded in the Book of Deuteronomy, that Moses, on his death bed, handed over the reins to Joshua, exhorting him to cross the river and lead the Children of Israel into battle to conquer Jericho and claim the Promised Land for his people. The ruins of the ancient city, the Tel es-Sultan, lay on the outskirts of the present town, the archaeological digs having uncovered layer upon layer of successive civilizations dating back to Neolithic times. Which, if any, of its excavated walls were the ones that had tumbled down for Joshua was still a matter of conjecture.

To Llewellyn the name Jericho had another unfortunate connotation. It was the appellation the Israelis had given to their intermediate-range ballistic missile, widely believed to be compatible with a nuclear warhead. The Jericho missile had recently undergone a major upgrade to extend its range and improve its accuracy. It was part of a pattern in the Middle East that had Llewellyn's government deeply concerned—the increasing proliferation of ever-bigger surface-to-surface missiles in the region.

The Middle East was turning into a *missile zone,* with virtually every country getting into the act. Syria, Iraq, Iran, Libya, and Egypt were all pursuing replacements for their obsolescent Soviet-made Scud-B missiles. Some time ago Egypt and Iraq had teamed with Argentina to develop a new five-hundred-mile missile, the Condor II, and Iraq was rumored to have their version already in production. Syria, after being turned down by the Soviets on their SS-23, was negotiating with China for their five-hundred-mile M9. And Saudi Arabia, the last to join the missile club, had more than made up for lost time.

The Saudis' secret purchase of East Wind missiles from China, revealed in 1988, had sent shock waves through the Middle East; with a range of over eighteen hundred miles, the East Wind dwarfed the other missiles in the region. And

19

Llewellyn had just learned through the State Department that a follow-on shipment of more East Winds to the Saudis was in the offing. Given the possible combinations of missiles and warheads—chemical, biological, nuclear—the prospects were chilling.

Was the Middle East headed for push-button warfare? How much time was left to find a peaceful solution? It was the U.S. President's determination to promote such a solution that brought Llewellyn to the West Bank. The peace initiative undertaken by the U.S. in the wake of the Gulf War had been floundering, the main stumbling block the question of who should represent the Palestinians, since the Israeli government refused to accept the PLO as a participant in the proposed peace talks.

But a recent development offered a possible way around the impasse. A new leader had emerged as a spokesman for the Palestinians, a man who was neither a terrorist nor a member of the PLO. A suspected activist in the West Bank resistance movement, he had been deported by the Israelis at the peak of the rioting, and had only recently been allowed to return to his home in Jericho. His support among the Palestinians, both in the occupied territories and abroad, was enormous. His name was Ibrahim Khalidy.

The Israeli Labor party had been instrumental in ending Khalidy's exile and pushing the government into accepting him as a negotiator. Those hard-liners in the government who had gone along on the assumption that the PLO would torpedo the deal anyway had been in for a surprise. Arafat had confounded the experts by agreeing to the arrangement. Though Khalidy had no direct ties with the PLO, expatriate Palestinians, Arafat included, appeared to regard him as one of theirs, a spokesman who would carry their interests forward in the emerging talks.

While elections of delegates for the peace talks had not yet been scheduled, this was the first ray of hope in a long time. Llewellyn had been instructed to seek out the new Palestinian spokesman, assure him of U.S. support, and offer his own services in whatever capacity could be helpful. Dissident elements on both sides had made threats against Khalidy; his continued good health was a primary concern of the President. Llewellyn was expected to size up the situation and advise his government in what way they might contribute to supplying some of the needed health insurance.

He had been pushing the Land Rover to its limit climbing up the Judean hills and hedge-hopping around the slower traffic. Now, as he crested the summit and began his descent toward the Jordan Valley, the traffic had thinned out and the landscape had undergone a remarkable transformation. He found himself in a wild, pastoral setting, not a house or any other structure to be seen. This was the wilderness of Judea; he knew that many Bedouin lived here.

Soon there were mountains on all sides of him, the road meandering between them, a sequence of tight curves in both directions. The road continued to descend sharply. As he neared the floor of the valley, the heat and humidity rose up to meet him. Jerusalem lay at 2,700 feet above sea level, Jericho 1,300 feet below, in the Dead Sea Rift. Fortunately it was still spring; in the summer here it could be stifling. The Land Rover was not air-conditioned. He cranked open the windows to let in more breeze. The road began to straighten and level out.

Something in the highway ahead caught his eye, still a long way off. Could it be a road block? You never knew when you might encounter one in the occupied territories. He slowed down. As he drew closer he saw that it was a dilapidated truck, parked half on the road and half on the shoulder. A crew of several men stood beside it, wearing the fluorescent orange tunics of highway maintenance workers. He swung the Land Rover into the opposite lane, giving them a wide berth. They watched him approach, staring insolently at his vehicle, and he caught the hostility in their eyes as he flashed by. The yellow Israeli plates on the Land Rover branded him as an outsider.

He reached the bottom of the grade and the arid reaches of the Dead Sea Rift engulfed him, the empty gray-brown landscape stretching unbroken to the distant horizon. Almost unbroken—far ahead, his eye picked up a tiny patch of green. He closed the distance rapidly.

Arriving in the lush, Biblical town, he followed a Jericho street plan acquired on his previous trip and had no trouble finding the address. On a quiet, shady street near the center of town, he pulled up in front of a modest, single-story white stucco residence almost indistinguishable from its neighbors on the same block.

Approaching the house, he was surprised to see no sign of the surveillance he had expected, having been informed that the Israeli army had promised to insure Khalidy's security. His knock on the door was answered almost immediately by a bearded man in Arab headdress and an ankle-length white robe whom he took to be a servant, a very big man whose figure filled the entire door frame, blocking his way.

Standing over six feet, himself, there were few men Llewellyn had to look up to. This one was a good half a head taller and sturdily built. At least Khalidy had some muscle in his household to protect him.

"I am David Llewellyn," he announced, hoping there wouldn't be a communication problem.

"I am Ibrahim Khalidy. Welcome to my humble home."

The handshake was firm. At the sight of the U.S. diplomat's discomfiture, a half-smile lit the aquiline features of the bearded face. "You were not prepared for my appearance. I often have this effect on people, I'm afraid."

He led the way to a small sitting room with a table and four reed-bottom chairs. It was a sunlit room, yet cool, light filtering down through a skylight. "I think we will be comfortable here. May I offer you some refreshment?"

David knew it would be impolite to decline the hospitality of the Palestinian's house. "Just coffee, please, if you have it."

"Of course."

Khalidy excused himself and disappeared momentarily, returning almost immediately. "We shall have our coffee shortly."

"I like your house," Llewellyn volunteered.

"Thank you. This has been my home for many years. I have lived my whole life in Jericho, except for my two years in exile. And my time at the university, of course."

"Could that have been Cambridge or Oxford? Your English is so—cultured." So British, he had started to say.

Khalidy smiled indulgently. "The West Bank may appear to be mostly desert, Mr. Llewellyn, but it is not quite a cultural desert. We do have universities here—five, to be precise. My bachelor's degree is from the largest, Bir Zeit."

David flushed. "I didn't mean to imply . . ."

The Palestinian held up his hand. "I understand. Please do not feel that there is a need to continue with small talk on my account. You Americans like to get right to the point, so why not start by telling me what brings you here?"

A young, black-haired woman in a brightly colored Palestinian dress appeared and set tiny coffee cups and saucers in front of them, affording a welcome break in a dialogue that Llewellyn sensed was getting off on the wrong foot. How could he best convey to this proud, stand-offish Palestinian his government's desire to help out in the peace process?

"I am here in my capacity as the President's special U.S. envoy to Israel to extend his best wishes and assure you of his support in the forthcoming peace talks. His primary concern at the moment is for your personal safety; we have heard some disturbing reports about threats from some of the dissident factions. Which reminds me—I was surprised there were no guards posted around your house. Where is all this protection the Israelis promised?"

"They were there, Mr. Llewellyn. You just did not see them."

"Oh?"

"The local garrison sent a squad of soldiers to my home, intending to position them around all the doors and windows. I threw them out. How would it have looked to my supporters?"

"But you just said—"

"That the soldiers are still there. They were apparently given orders to be more discreet. They are posted inside two empty houses on my block, watching my residence continuously. As long as they stay out of sight I can tolerate their presence."

David felt better knowing that Khalidy's house was under surveillance and said so. The Palestinian shrugged.

"There is really no threat to my safety here in Jericho, Mr. Llewellyn. I am well known here, and it is a peaceful enough place. Whatever danger there is will come on the trips I must soon embark upon to rally the support of my people in other parts of the territories and the refugees in other countries. On the day after tomorrow I travel to Hebron, the next day to Gaza. I am shortly scheduled to visit Ramallah, Nablus, and Bethlehem. It has taken a lot of time to persuade the Israeli authorities of the necessity of doing this, but at last I have their permission."

Llewellyn was aghast. The Israelis must be aware of the hazards in those places. What were they thinking of?

"Will they be sending soldiers with you?"

"I would not hear of it! I have my image to consider. I cannot appear to be either their prisoner or their puppet."

"But surely you must be planning some protection."

Again the Palestinian shrugged. "I am in the hands of Allah, who has chosen me for this mission. But I will have some of my own people with me, and I know enough to be careful."

They lapsed into silence, Llewellyn much disturbed by what he had heard. He was gravely concerned for the Palestinian leader's safety. He'd be sweating out every minute that Khalidy was out of the country. Unless—

"I've been instructed to offer you my services, in any capacity whatever, during the forthcoming peace talks and the preparations leading up to them. I could even accompany you on your travels if—"

"Are you volunteering to serve me as a diplomat or as a bodyguard?" Khalidy inquired with a straight face. "Mr. Llewellyn, I'm afraid your reputation has proceeded you, as, shall we say, a man of action. But now that you have seen me, I think you might concede that I am perhaps better equipped to be *your* bodyguard. I do not go looking for trouble, but if it finds me, I usually manage to get out of it."

"I'm sure you do," David concurred. "I wouldn't mind having you on my side. But seriously, I think I can be of help in other ways, preparing for the talks with Israel. I'm used to dealing with their government at the diplomatic level and know them pretty well, and I can also provide the American point of view."

"Yes, the American point of view. Which is exactly why I cannot keep you around me, Mr. Llewellyn. I spoke of my image problem. I must not appear to be a puppet of the Americans, either."

The Palestinian rose from the table, extending his hand. "It was good of you to come, Mr. Llewellyn. Please convey to your president my thanks for his good wishes and support. And please tell him that the peace process will be best served by allowing Palestinians to debate the issues among themselves and arrive at a consensus with a minimum of outside interference.

"And now it is time for my morning constitutional, which I observe religiously per my doctor's orders."

Llewellyn was unwilling for this to be the final word. "Mind if I join you? I could use the exercise myself."

Khalidy frowned. "I maintain a brisk pace. You may have trouble keeping up."

"I'm a fast walker, myself."

"All right, then. But if you fall behind, do not expect me to wait for you."

The Palestinian had spoken the truth; his long legs set a blistering pace. Llewellyn had to push himself to keep up. He looked up and down the block but could see no sign of the garrison of Israeli soldiers supposedly quartered in one of the neighboring houses.

"Where are we going?"

"In the direction of the tell. I take the same route every morning. It is two miles there and back."

The same route every day at the same hour? Llewellyn shook his head. If he were in charge of the Palestinian's security, there would be some changes made. But it wouldn't be that easy; Khalidy would probably not cooperate. The hardest kind of individual to protect was one who thought himself to be in no danger.

Except for the demanding pace, the walk was a pleasant one. After passing one short, busy stretch of shops and small restaurants, they found themselves once again on shady, tree-lined streets that were almost deserted. From the dusty, arid landscape traversed by the main highway one would never have known that this tranquil residential enclave existed.

25

Llewellyn used the opportunity to reopen the earlier discussion.

"I wish you would reconsider letting me tag along on your visits to Hebron and Gaza. As an observer for my government, I could do you a service by sending back favorable reports. You have my assurance that I would stay in the background and be totally unobtrusive. They won't even know I'm there."

"On the contrary, they *would* know you were there. Americans draw reporters like honey draws flies, particularly American diplomats. The subject is closed."

They were close enough to see the tell, now, the mountain of dirt created by the various excavations looming ahead. The street they were walking along dead-ended well short of the earthworks.

There was a truck parked at its terminus. It had a familiar look to it . . . like that road-maintenance truck Llewellyn had seen on the main highway on the way in. The two doors of the truck cab opened simultaneously and the laborers casually began to clamber out. They had discarded their bright orange tunics, he noted, as they reached into the truckbed for their tools. Maybe they were going to work in the tell on the excavations.

Wait a minute . . . Those weren't shovels in their hands, they were—

"Get down!" shouted Llewellyn, tackling the Palestinian around the knees and bringing him crashing to the ground.

Automatic-weapons fire shattered the silence of the peaceful spring morning, bullets whining overhead and ricocheting off the street on all sides of them.

Maintaining his grip on Khalidy's legs, Llewellyn rolled to his right, dragging the other toward the shelter of a low concrete wall that fronted the last house on the block. It was the only chance they had. Bullets were still flying as they reached the wall and crawled behind it, safe for the moment. But for how long? They were unarmed. If the gunmen charged the wall, there was nothing they could do . . .

The firing ceased, replaced by an exchange of voices shouting in Arabic. Llewellyn looked questioningly at his companion.

"They are arguing over what to do next," the calm voice explained. If Khalidy was frightened, he wasn't showing it.

David raised his head warily. A scant hundred feet away, the gang of assassins had made up their minds. They were advancing, cautiously but steadily, toward the wall.

"Here they come." Llewellyn looked around for a place to run. The nearest cover was the house enclosed by the wall. It was fifty feet away. They'd be cut down before they got halfway there.

His mind raced, trying to find a way out. If he identified himself as a U.S. diplomat, would it cut any ice with them? Who was he fooling? They almost had to be Fedayeen—Palestinian terrorists from some extremist group; next to Israel, America topped the enemy list of all such sects. If they were out to erase Khalidy, whose peace prospects represented a threat to their authority and continued livelihood, an American envoy wasn't going to stop them. Killing him would lend additional zeal to their efforts.

Khalidy gripped Llewellyn's shoulder in a huge, bear-like hand. "Come, my friend, let us face death on our feet, like men." My God! He was going to stand up!

"No!" Llewellyn shouted, grappling with the giant's legs, trying to pull him back down. Before he could do so, he heard the terrorist guns open up again. But wait! The sound was coming from *behind* him. How had the gunmen . . . ?

It took a second to sink in. *The Israeli guard detachment.* Then he was on his feet with Khalidy, watching the terrorists run back toward their truck, the pursuing squad of Israeli soldiers closing in, peppering them with a withering fire from their Uzis.

One of the terrorists didn't make it. The other three reached the truck and threw themselves inside the cab, starting the motor. Shifting the truck into its highest gear, they tried to run the gamut. The soldiers aimed at the tires. A stray shot found the fuel tank. The truck exploded into a brilliant orange ball of flame. The fire was too hot for anyone to even think of approaching it; the soldiers stood there, watching it burn. No one got out of it.

One of the soldiers walked over to the fallen terrorist and knelt to examine the body. From his reaction it was clear that the man was dead. The Israeli began to go through his pockets.

The squad leader strode over to the wall on which the intended victims were sitting, their faces still reflecting the shock of their ordeal. He appeared angry. Ignoring Llewellyn, he addressed himself to Khalidy. Some heated words were exchanged in Hebrew. Then the soldier's manner softened. He looked at Llewellyn, nodded, and saluted.

"What was that all about?" David asked.

"He was unhappy that the assassins were all killed. Now we may never find out who they were. We're to go back to the garrison with them for questioning. He was also angry that he had been given orders not to stay too close to me, per my wishes. He said it almost cost us our lives."

"Why did he salute me?"

"Because I told him who you were—and that you had saved my life."

A shout went up from the soldier who had been searching the body of the dead terrorist. The squad leader went over to see what was up. He bent down to examine something hanging around the dead man's neck, then removed it with the help of the other soldier. Returning to the wall, he showed Khalidy what he had found, putting a question to him. The Palestinian studied the object for a moment, shook his head, and passed it on to Llewellyn.

The amulet suspended from a gold chain was something out of the Arabian Nights, a miniature Persian scimitar, its handle and hilt encrusted with gold. The insignia emblazoned on its curved silver blade struck him as totally incongruous. It was the tightly spiraled horn of a ram—the shofar—used as a signalling trumpet by the Jews in battle from the time of Joshua, still blown in synagogues on the New Year and Day of Atonement.

Why on earth would an Arab terrorist wear a talisman inscribed with a Jewish symbol?

The soldier at the wheel of the army jeep screeched to a stop in front of Khalidy's house, unloaded his two passengers, and departed in a cloud of dust. Llewellyn couldn't wait to climb into the Land Rover and be on his way. They had been detained for hours at the army base, where a team of anti-terrorist experts had grilled them over and over again, looking for possible clues to the identity of the would-be assassins. On top of everything else that had happened, it had left him feeling utterly exhausted.

Khalidy appeared equally fatigued. He invited his guest to accompany him inside to refresh himself for his trip back, but Llewellyn respectfully declined. They shook hands, the Palestinian again asking him to convey his thanks to the American President for his support.

The Land Rover's engine caught with a gratifying rumble, and Llewellyn backed out of the parking spot and paused to strap himself in. Putting the Rover back in gear, he was about to start off when he saw the girl in the Palestinian dress who had served the coffee run out through the gate to intercept him. She handed him an envelope, then turned and ran back inside.

The note was in English. "If you are going to Hebron and Gaza with me, you must be at my house no later than 8:00 A.M. the day after tomorrow. Otherwise, I will be forced to leave without you."

3

THE SOLITARY FIGURE on the forecastle of the Lebanese tramp steamer stood motionless, clinging to the railing, as the bow alternately rose and fell beneath his feet in a heavy sea. The weather was very much to his liking, especially the low ceiling, the uppermost portion of the ship's mast disappearing into the cloud layer. No one was going to find them in this weather. Until it cleared and search aircraft were able to fly again, the *Beirut Victory* was just another blip on a radar scope.

Luck, some would say; without the cloud cover they might have been caught. Perhaps. But he had left as little to chance as possible, everything planned to the last detail and rehearsed beforehand. Like the specially designed sling that allowed the freighter to hoist a ponderous lighter barge aboard using two of its derricks simultaneously. The technique had been perfected in Beirut harbor before the ship embarked for the Orient. Now the two hijacked lighters with their lethal contents reposed snugly in two of the freighter's holds, hidden from surveillance by overflying aircraft.

From dawn till dusk of the first day after the hijacking, as the tramp steamer churned northwestward at her maximum speed of twenty knots, hugging the coast of Sumatra, they had seen only a handful of planes, and none had come anywhere near them. Before daylight the next morning—this morning— he had watched the starry arms of the Southern Cross move clockwise until the constellation lay just off the port beam as they rounded the tip of the huge island and turned westward into the Great Channel south of the Nicobars, heading for the vast reaches of the Indian Ocean. Shortly thereafter the stars had dimmed and disappeared and he had rejoiced as dawn revealed the protective layer of low clouds.

The sea was growing heavier. A wave crashed over the bow, drenching him, and he turned and headed back for the bridge, his limp more pronounced now, his left leg dragging painfully. It was always at its worst when he was tired, and it made him realize how much he needed to rest. Well, he could afford to sleep, now; there would be plenty of time for sleep. And plenty of time for working out the last few details of his plan. It would take the tramp steamer the better part of two weeks to reach his destination.

He found his stateroom, threw off his clothes, and fell on the bunk, using both hands to lift the prosthesis attached just below his left knee onto the bed. A souvenir of the 1982 Israeli incursion into Lebanon, inflicted during the savaging of the Scintilla refugee camp, his missing leg was a constant reminder of how much he owed them, a debt he had only begun to repay.

He eased back onto the pillow, thinking about the cargo lying in the *Beirut Victory*'s hold. Two more weeks. After that, his debt would be paid in full . . .

A sharp rap on the door of the tiny stateroom brought him out of his bunk, wide awake. "Who's there?"

"A message has come for you." It was the captain's voice. He opened the door.

A bearded man in a Lebanese merchant-marine uniform with four stripes stood there. Tall and portly, he had to duck his head to enter, a head that was hatless and almost hairless. The two had known each other for a half-dozen years, an acquaintance that had proven profitable for the captain, who was also part owner of his ship. He was used to being well compensated for the risks he took. And this would be the richest trip yet.

"We just received it. It was marked urgent. It is in that code of yours."

He handed the envelope to the man in the khaki skivvies, who tore it open and studied it for some time without registering any visible reaction. Then he frowned, crumpled the paper, and tossed it onto the bunk.

"Bad news?"

"Bad for some, good for others." A glance at the porthole told him it was still daylight outside and the weather unchanged. He picked up his watch and looked at it. He had been sleeping for only a few hours.

"I am about to have dinner," the captain volunteered. "Will you join me?"

"No," the other declined. "I think I will sleep some more."

But when the captain had left, he didn't climb back into the bunk. Sleep would be impossible now. He uncrumpled the message and read it again. *Disaster!* The Jericho operation had failed, his entire squad wiped out. He had planned it meticulously, personally supervising the dry run before he left.

What could have gone wrong?

If only he had been there, he thought, his plan would have succeeded. But he couldn't have set his priorities any other way; the shot at the Chinese missile was a once-in-a-lifetime opportunity. If his new backer hadn't demanded immediate action against Khalidy, the hit on the Palestinian chief negotiator could have been postponed until his return.

Well, they would get Khalidy the next time; a contingency plan he had prepared would be put into play at once by his chief lieutenant. It was as important to him as it was to his backer that they pull it off. For he and his benefactor shared a common objective—to derail the Arab-Israeli peace initiative.

Like his new silent partner, he considered himself a businessman, a trader in commodities. The commodity he brokered was terror, the demand for it in the Middle East exceeding the supply, which kept the price high. But a peace agreement could change all that. The mere announcement of Palestinian autonomy talks had already caused several of his former backers to suspend their monetary support.

The fools! And Yassir Arafat, going along with the peace talks, throwing the weight of the PLO behind them. It was the last straw. His contempt for Arafat was shared by leaders of other PLO splinter groups. The PLO chief's days were numbered. He would be replaced soon by a new leader. Why not one who had demonstrated all of the right qualities? The daring to conceive a bold stroke like the hijacking of the most devastating weapon ever to enter the Middle East, the brains to plan it, the resourcefulness to carry it out? His accomplishment was certain to be the talk of the Arab world.

It was the funding from this new silent partner that had enabled him to mount the costly venture. And the irony was that his new sponsor knew nothing of the hijacking operation. Were he to learn of it, the cash flow would cease abruptly.

The money was funneled to him through a process designed to protect the source from exposure. He had never met the man and did not know his identity. But he had to be something of an eccentric, the possessor of a weird, ironic sense of humor.

He fingered the gold chain around his neck—the chain that had held the amulet, lost somehow during the hijacking operation. The amulet had been his new sponsor's idea, the miniature swords suspended from chains supplied to him with the second installment of cash, with instructions that they be worn by the "soldiers" in his employ. Why not? The idea had appealed to his own sense of irony—an Arab sword inscribed with a Jewish shofar, symbolic of a cooperative effort between certain Arabs and Jews to defeat the Arab-Israeli peace process.

What could be more appropriate? After all, his new silent partner was a wealthy Jew from Tel Aviv.

The prim, gray-haired secretary knocked on the office door, then opened it a crack. Her boss was on the phone. He motioned her inside and went on talking without missing a beat in that machine-gun, non-stop style of his.

She stood awkwardly, waiting for him to finish, knowing he might run on for another five or ten minutes if she didn't forcibly interrupt. Undisciplined. That was the word for Mossad agent Baruch Shmona. Brilliant was another.

As always, his desk and conference table were littered with papers and reports stacked many layers deep. How she would have loved to get her hands on them. But she was forbidden to do any of his filing. Each night the piles of paper went helter-skelter into his vault, only to flop back onto his table again the next morning in the same state of disarray. It was a mystery to her how he ever found anything.

His personal appearance matched the disheveled look of his

office. That impossible, scraggly beard. And he would wear the same baggy suit for weeks at a time, until its creases and wrinkles looked permanent. With his bent-over posture he looked twice his real age, which was young enough to be her son.

If he were her son, she would take him in hand. First, the beard would go, and then—

He was hanging up the phone. Thank goodness. The intense brown eyes sought hers. "Yes, Rebecca?"

"The director would like to see you in his office, right away."

He frowned. "Something urgent?"

"His secretary doesn't confide in me, I'm afraid. You'd better hurry."

Few things made Shmona nervous, but being called to Mossad Director Mordechai Shilo's office was one. Shmona's section chief was there with the director when he arrived. Both were unsmiling as they greeted him and deadly serious. Oh, oh. Had somebody died?

The Mossad director's appearance gave no clue that he was one of the most powerful men in Israel. Middle-aged, myopic, and short of stature, only slightly taller than Shmona, he wore heavy lenses and a conservative dark blue suit. Mordechai Shilo was made to order for the low-profile organization he headed; he could blend into any crowd and not be noticed. His name never appeared in print and, like the location of Mossad headquarters, was unknown to the vast majority of Israeli citizens.

"Baruch," the director began, making it clear from the beginning that despite the wide disparity in their positions with the Institute they were still on a first-name basis—"we have what could be a major crisis developing, a serious threat to our national security. It requires an immediate investigation. Some first-rate detective work is called for, and it must be done expeditiously. We would like you to handle it."

Shilo paused, apparently waiting for his reaction. "Of course," Shmona responded, wondering why they were making such a big deal instead of going through normal work assignment channels. His section chief provided the answer.

"We're imposing special security on this one, because of its sensitivity. You'll understand in a moment. You won't be able to discuss the circumstances of your assignment with anyone else in the agency. They won't be cleared."

Now he was really intrigued. "Is this something to do with the thing at Jericho?"

The two Mossad executives looked at each other, the section chief deferring to his superior. "The 'thing at Jericho,' as you put it, may well be tied in with another development, the one that is of primary concern to us. There is some evidence of this, which I will get to in a moment."

The director got up from behind his desk and came around to sit at the conference table with the other two, his voice dropping several decibels. "You are doubtless aware of the purchase by Saudi Arabia of ballistic missiles from China. You may also be aware that a second installment of missiles and launchers were due to be delivered this month."

Shmona nodded again. The shipment of the Chinese missiles was common knowledge inside the Mossad, which had been tracking the operation since the controversial missile purchase was first divulged. A Mossad agent had been placed aboard the ship before it embarked from Shanghai.

"I don't think I need to tell you what a serious threat these missiles represent to our country," Shilo went on. "They are the most potent weapons ever introduced into the Middle East. Their range is sufficient to reach our major military bases and population centers from launch sites in even the remotest parts of Saudi Arabia, their accuracy as good or better than our own improved but shorter range Jericho missile. Mobile launchers are used, which gives them great flexibility in basing and makes them virtually impossible to pre-target. And these Chinese East Winds are compatible with all types of warheads—high explosive, chemical, biological, nuclear."

Shmona knew all this. The director had a tendency to be overly pedantic. He wished he would get to the point.

"Having such weapons in the hands of the Saudis is one thing," Shilo continued. "We are certainly not happy about it, but it is something we can probably live with. King Fahd insists that the purpose of the missiles is to provide a deterrent to Iran and Iraq, whose own extended-range missiles are a threat to Saudi Arabia. Besides, the Saudis are well aware that any missile launched our way would bring about swift retaliation from our superior air force."

Shmona's patience gave way. "Are you saying some other Arab country is also getting these Chinese missiles?"

"Not exactly . . ." The director stood up and began to pace restlessly. "The shipment of missiles and launchers from China reached Singapore three days ago, escorted by a Chinese destroyer. While the destroyer was still in port, the ship was accosted in the Strait of Malacca and boarded by a heavily armed party off a seagoing tugboat."

"The shipment was hijacked?" Shmona gasped.

"Not the entire shipment. Only one missile was off-loaded. And one launcher. But in the wrong hands, one of each is too much."

"But how—who?" Shmona was incredulous. Those missiles were gigantic. How could one disappear?

"The 'who' turns out to be easier to answer than the 'how.' Our agent aboard the ship provided us with a good description of the man who led the hijackers. A Palestinian with a physical impairment that makes him easy to identify, a pronounced limp. It seems he lost a leg in one of the refugee camps during our Lebanon campaign, when the Falangists overran those two South Beirut camps and went berserk. We don't know his real name, but he is known to his followers and fellow terrorists as 'al Saif'—the Sword."

The name rang a bell with Shmona. Like most of his fellow agents in Mossad, he had heard of al Saif, who had split with al Fatah over the PLO's disavowal of any further acts of terrorism to found a new sect, "The Sword of Islam for the Liberation of Palestine." In the three years this group had been in operation, it was believed to have been responsible for at least two assassinations, three kidnapings, and an aircraft hijacking. For the past year, al Saif had been on Mossad's most wanted list. He was a brilliant strategist and masterful planner, with a fanatical following. He also seemed to be well supplied with funds.

Shmona whistled softly . . . If al Saif was in possession of an East Wind, there was not much question as to what he might do with it.

"It can't be that easy to hide an East Wind," Shmona observed. "The missile's too huge. If they try to reach the Middle East with it, they'll surely be intercepted . . . Won't they?"

The director again exchanged looks with his section chief. "One would hope so. But it's a big ocean out there, full of ships, any one of which might have the missile hidden in its hold. We can't count on the terrorists being apprehended. We must pursue a contingency plan of our own."

"You mentioned a possible connection with the Jericho incident," Shmona reminded him.

"So I did." Shilo nodded at the section chief, who reached into his pocket and withdrew a trinket on a gold chain, which he deposited on the table. Shmona picked it up and examined it. The item attached to the chain was a miniature sword, a not-inexpensive piece of jewelry, Shmona judged, if the gold handle and hilt were genuine, which to his inexpert eye they appeared to be. The shiny silver blade was reminiscent of an old-fashioned scimitar, broad and single-edged. It had a Jewish symbol, a shofar, engraved on it.

Shmona put the piece back on the table. "So?"

The director left it to his section chief to explain. "This was found around the neck of a dead terrorist in Jericho two days ago, one of Ibrahim Khalidy's would-be assassins. It matches the description we received from our seagoing agent of another such article found lying on the deck of the cargo vessel hauling the Chinese missiles, believed to have been lost by one of the hijackers—matches it in all particulars, including the Jewish insignia."

So al Saif was also behind the attempt on Khalidy's life, mused Shmona. Palestinian against Palestinian; there was nothing new about that. Most of the deaths in the occupied territories since the *intifada* began were cases in which fanatical Palestinians had administered kangaroo-court-style justice to other Palestinians judged to be too cooperative with the Israelis. As chief negotiator designate for the forthcoming peace talks, Khalidy was a threat to die-hard terrorists whose motives were to perpetuate the strife.

"What do you make of this piece of jewelry?" he inquired.

37

"Why would a Palestinian terrorist wear such a thing around his neck?"

"That's one of the things we'd like to find out," the section chief responded. "We've run the piece by several of our experts on Arab and Palestinian cultures. The Arab sword is an almost universal symbol of defiance among Palestinians. It has come to signify the eventual return of the occupied lands to their 'rightful' owners. But the experts were uniformly mystified by its imprinting with the shofar, the mixing of Arab and Jewish symbology. We think the answer to this question and further knowledge on the origins of this piece might provide some leads that could help us close in on this Sword of Islam bunch."

He picked up the chain and pendant and dropped them into Shmona's hand. The bearded agent stared at his two superiors.

"What do you expect me to do with this?"

"The piece is of recent vintage. It almost has to have been a special order. We want you to go into the jewelry business, find out where it was made and by whom, trace it back to the person or persons who ordered it."

"That could take weeks . . ."

Shilo stopped pacing and fixed him with a penetrating look. "It had better not. We do not have *weeks*. Need I describe to you the blackmail potential of such a weapon in terrorist hands? The Scuds Hussein hit us with were puny by comparison. We must find these hijackers, and find them soon—before we run out of time!"

Shmona walked back to his office in silence, the gold chain with its cryptic amulet an almost oppressive presence in his inside jacket pocket. He knew next to nothing about jewelry. Where was he to start? The director had alluded to "some first-rate detective work." What that really meant was leg work, and a lot of it. Where was he to get the people? His small staff of field agents were otherwise occupied, some loaned out on assignments he couldn't terminate without providing an explanation to their temporary controls. And he was prohibited from doing so by the director's special security edict.

His secretary took note of his downcast expression. "Did they fire you?"

"Worse." He went into his office and closed the door, sinking into his swivel chair. His secretary was heavily into jewelry. If only he could talk to her about it, show her the amulet and chain, she might be able to at least suggest a starting point. But he would still end up doing the leg work. It went against his nature. A good control shunned field work; that was the job of the field agents under him. His job was to stay in the head shed and strategize, sort and evaluate their inputs, sifting facts and drawing conclusions. Better he should send his secretary out on the street. A woman would arouse less suspicion and—

An idea hit him and he grabbed the phone and dialed his section chief's number. "Yakov, you know how shorthanded I am. I'd like your permission to expand my staff."

"By how many?" came the guarded reply.

"Just one, for now."

"How will that help? You know how long clearances take."

"This one is already cleared. She's on leave of absence."

"She?"

"One of my best operators." Shmona grinned. "I trained her myself. She's a natural."

Daniella Llewellyn was very annoyed with her husband. It wasn't enough that David had barely escaped being killed by terrorist bullets on his last trip into the occupied territories. Now he was off again, headed for an even more hazardous sector: the Gaza Strip. She had pleaded with him not to go.

"I have to," he'd responded. "It's my job. Besides, nothing will happen to me. I'll be fine."

"Then take me with you," she had urged.

"Can't. Too dangerous."

Too dangerous? After what they had been through together in the past? Had he forgotten about the Osirak episode? She had pointedly reminded him of those days from not so long ago . . . he had still been adamant.

But even more disturbing was David's refusal to confide in her. She had had to drag the information out of him about the episode in Jericho, and he had told her next to nothing about this latest trip. They had always been able to discuss everything in the past, but now he was beginning to clam up. She told herself that he was doing it for security reasons or because he didn't want to worry her, or some of both, but it still bothered her. How could they continue to be a team—how could she help him—if he didn't tell her what was going on?

They couldn't. But that didn't mean she had to sit on her hands in their apartment worrying about him. She glared at the telephone. She had to put in a call to the Ministry of Foreign Affairs, asking for her old job back. The Foreign Minister was due to return her call.

When the phone rang, she pounced on it. "Hello?" The rapid-fire voice at the other end was immediately recognizable, but not the one she had expected.

"Daniella! Great to hear your voice! I've missed you. Listen, I need you back. It's an assignment that is critical to our national security, and you're the only one who can handle it. It's a highly confidential matter. You won't be able to discuss it with anyone, not even your husband. That part won't pose a problem, will it? Can you start tomorrow?"

He paused for breath at last, and she heard him inhaling and exhaling. "Daniella? Are you still there?"

"Yes, Baruch, I am still here."

"Well, what about it? When can you start?"

"Baruch, I'm going to make your day. I can start now. And about not discussing my work with my husband—that certainly won't be a problem."

She put the phone back down and smiled. Congratulations, she told herself, you're back in the action.

4

THE CHAUFFEUR-DRIVEN, U.N.-SUPPLIED Mercedes limousine left the main highway and turned onto a side road. "We are here," announced Khalidy. "Hebron—the city of Abraham, most revered of the Biblical patriarchs among Muslims. This is his burial place, and that of his son, Isaac, and his grandson, Jacob, and their wives. Later today you'll see the magnificent mosque constructed above their tombs. But our first stop is the city hall for a conference with the mayor and city fathers before I deliver my address."

The outskirts of Hebron looked peaceful enough, the streets virtually deserted. Llewellyn discovered why, when the Mercedes pulled up in front of a three-story concrete edifice that had to be the town hall. The walkway and stairs leading to the entrance were already crammed with spectators. There were no soldiers or police in evidence to keep order or clear the way, only a handful of Arab officials wearing some sort of arm band. It was a security man's nightmare.

The big Palestinian seemed totally unconcerned. A cheer went up from the throng as he emerged from the car and unfolded his hulking frame, waving his hand at them. Khalidy set out to push his way through them, the hard-pressed officials doing their best to clear a path for him. But everyone seemed to be pressing forward, reaching out to touch him, straining for a close-up glimpse of the man who would lead the crusade to regain their homeland.

As he reached the first step in front of the entrance, Khalidy tripped and almost went down under a surge of bodies. Llewellyn shoved his way rudely between a gaggle of robed admirers, straining to reach his side. Help came from the top of the stairs, a stentorian voice bellowing at the crowd, somehow parting them to create the semblance of a passageway. Llewellyn reached Khalidy and pushed him toward the opening, following him through as the crowd closed in behind. The crush was incredible.

The big voice at the top of the steps was coming from a tiny little man wearing a checkered *kaffiyeh* over a stout-size brown business suit, the bulging eyes set in a bloated face reminiscent of Peter Lorre in a Middle East movie scenario. Safely out of the crush, Khalidy seized his hand.

"Mr. Llewellyn, may I present my assistant, Halib Begassey."

So this was the "advance party" Khalidy had referred to. "A pleasure, Mr. Llewellyn. Permit me to congratulate you on your alertness two days ago. We are in your debt."

He turned back to his chief. "All is in readiness, Excellency. They await you inside."

"I'll wait for you by the speaker's platform." It had already been explained to Llewellyn that his attendance at the meeting with the mayor was not "required." Besides, he wanted to check out the site for the outdoor speech and train his practiced security eye on the surroundings. He watched the giant and his miniscule assistant disappear into the building. What a pair!

The mob at the front of the hall was beginning to disperse, flowing in a counterclockwise direction around the concrete structure. He fell in step with them, pausing at the corner of the building, then climbed up again to the top stair. Standing in the shade next to a large pillar supporting the roof overhang, he could observe the entire field of spectators and remain virtually unnoticed.

The first thing he looked for was a sniper vantage point. Weapons fired from where the crowd was assembled would not be a threat; too many bodies in the way. He was happy to see that there were no nearby buildings of sufficient height to furnish a sniper with an unobstructed line of fire. But the low wall that enclosed the quadrangle might present a problem.

He descended the steps and made his way back out to the street. It was crowded with vehicles and pedestrians arriving for the address. He walked along the street until he reached the corner of the wall surrounding the quadrangle.

A stand of thick shrubs stood directly behind the wall, perfect cover for a person with a rifle. He ducked into the opening between the wall and the bushes and went down on all fours, hoping no one on the street had seen him. Crawling on through the bushes, he straightened up slowly, peering over the parapet. Just as he had feared. Above the heads of the assemblage in the compound, he had a clear view of the rostrum.

As he crouched back down again, something very hard prodded him sharply and painfully in the small of the back. A guttural voice behind him unleashed a burst of Arabic that could have only one meaning. He raised his hands over his head and slowly turned around.

There were two of them, one holding a rifle pointed at his stomach. They wore no uniforms, their casual western dress, quite common here on the West Bank, giving him no clue to their identity. The one with the rifle said something to the other, who pushed him roughly against the wall and proceeded to search him. He made a very thorough job of it, muttered something, and extracted Llewellyn's billfold.

"American," Llewellyn said, indicating the wallet. "American embassy."

"American?" The man who had his wallet spat and began to examine it. It held his diplomatic identity card, but it was unlikely that either of his captors could read or speak English. He studied the rifle that was still trained on him. It wasn't very modern looking, not even automatic. And there was no telescopic sight. If they were here to gun down Khalidy, they weren't very well equipped for the job.

The man with the wallet found the identity card and showed it to his comrade. Now would be the time to jump them, while they were distracted!

"Well, Mr. Llewellyn, you certainly don't waste any time." At the sound of the booming voice, his two assailants spun around, saw who it was, and relaxed, the gun swinging back in Llewellyn's direction. Halib Begassey stepped out of the bushes and issued a sharp command in Arabic. The man with the rifle immediately lowered it.

"These are my men," the rotund Begassey explained. "Part of my advance work is to see to security. I presume you were doing the same?"

Llewellyn nodded, lowering his hands. He hadn't heard the little man approach. Either he was slipping, or Begassey moved like a cat.

"I wouldn't go poking about in the bushes, if I were you," Begassey advised, recovering his billfold and tossing it back to him. "My men are somewhat lacking in training and experience. They could just as easily have shot you without knowing who you were."

"I'll be more careful next time," Llewellyn promised. "It's reassuring to know that someone's looking out for Khalidy's hide. Where are the Israelis? Their soldiers are billeted just two blocks away. Why aren't they here, providing protection?"

Begassey smiled ruefully. "Their presence here would create a major disruption. His Excellency would not hear of it. To gain the support of the majority of Palestinians he is convinced that he must shun such protection and avoid any appearance of being propped up by the Israeli authorities. He is a very brave man."

"Too brave for his own good. What will it take to make him more cautious, another episode like the one in Jericho?"

The little round man shook his head. "He will never change. That is why we must provide his Excellency with protection in addition to the Israelis." He put a forefinger to his lips. "Not a word of this to His Excellency, please."

"Khalidy doesn't know about your security precautions?"

"I thought it best not to go into it with him. He might have said no. He believes that Allah will provide for his well-being."

"And you don't, is that it?"

A crafty look came into the bulging eyes. "Why, yes, Mr. Llewellyn, of course I do. Allah will protect him, through use of His various instruments here on earth. And are we not all His instruments?"

It was after eleven, the appointed time for the address to begin, and Khalidy had not yet emerged from city hall. The crowd, which now packed the quadrangle from wall to wall, was beginning to grow restless.

Llewellyn was back at his original vantage point next to the pillar at the corner of the building, in the shade, Begassey standing next to him. "They are all here," he heard the little man remark.

"What? Who are here?"

"All of the various PLO factions. I expected them to all send observers, even the more hostile ones. They are too curious to stay away."

He pointed his finger. "That is an al Fatah delegation down in front, Arafat's party. See, in the red-and-white-checkered headgear? And see the man standing just behind them, in the army fatigue hat? He is from Hamas, the Islamic Resistance Movement. Hamas is very strong in Gaza. We will meet many of their followers there tomorrow.

"The two men several rows behind and farther to his right, in plain white *kaffiyehs*—they are from Habash's PFLP, the Popular Front for the Liberation of Palestine. Despite the white hats they are very bad boys. They will bear watching."

"I'll say—they're Black September," Llewellyn snapped. "Known terrorists. Why does the government allow them here? Why haven't they been locked up, deported?"

"Many of their leaders have been. Dr. Habash lives in Damascus now. But it is simply not practical to arrest them all. Ah, here we go." Begassey nudged Llewellyn with his elbow.

Khalidy had just emerged through the side door of the building, accompanied by several others in traditional robes and headdress. There was a murmur from the crowd that quickly blossomed into a general ovation. Llewellyn glanced back toward the PLO groups Begassey had identified. Only the al Fatah delegation were applauding.

In a sunlit stall of a *souk* a few blocks away, two men in casual western attire sat sipping tea. They were the only customers in the shop, the market place and neighboring street deserted. Everyone else, it seemed, was attending the ceremonies at the city hall.

At a resounding cheer and burst of applause from that

direction their eyes met. "He is a spellbinder, that one," the taller of the two observed. "Have you heard him?"

His companion, an older-looking man with a salt-and-pepper beard, shook his head. "No, nor do I care to. The fantasy he weaves is an opiate to our people, turning their heads from reality. That is why he must be stopped."

"Indeed. Still, a great pity. He would have made a fine soldier for us."

The other snorted. "That one would not be content to be a soldier. He would want to be the general. And we already have one of those, the best of generals, who has decreed that he must die."

A thunderous and prolonged ovation, punctuated by the shrill, throbbing cries of Arab women, signalled the windup of Khalidy's address. The man who had just spoken consulted his watch, threw some currency on the table, and stood up.

"The parade will pass this way shortly, en route to the Mosque of Abraham for the midday prayer. There are those among them who might recognize us. It is time we left for Gaza."

The other drained his cup and rose from the table, as the boisterous accolade for Khalidy continued. "They are still cheering. He must have made a very good speech."

"Perhaps so," his companion acknowledged. "But he will not live to make another."

5

THE MEA SHE'ARIM SECTOR of West Jerusalem was said to be the world's last remaining example of the *shtetl*, the endemic Jewish community that flourished in Eastern Europe before the Holocaust. To Daniella, born and raised in the Israeli capital city, this insular enclave of Jewish fundamentalism was simply another face of her multifaceted home town, albeit a most unique and colorful one. Though not of the ultra-orthodox persuasion, she felt perfectly at home here, had been coming here since childhood to partake of its atmosphere and browse its shop-lined streets.

One of her regular stops was a tiny jeweler's stall on a small alley just off the main street. She had a speaking acquaintance with the silversmith; he did beautiful work, and his prices, if you knew how to bargain, were unbeatable. It was here that she had decided to launch herself on her new job for the Mossad.

Her purse held the miniature scimitar suspended from a gold chain, its blade bearing the image of a ram's horn. It was not just a trinket, by any means, for it was beautifully crafted of precious metals. Apparently a number of them had been produced, from what Shmona had told her. He hadn't told her much else, nor how he had come by it. But her Mossad experience had already taught her that field agents were often expected to work in the dark.

One thing about the Mea She'arim, she thought, as she made her way along Hayer Adam—it never changed. It looked now as it must have looked originally, its residents still dressed in the Eastern European attire of the eighteenth century, long-bearded men in black gowns and fur hats, their women in wigs and scarves, following the strict orthodox tradition. Even its youth conformed to the standard, the boys' pale faces framed by side curls and topped by wide-brimmed hats.

When he heard her enter, the silversmith stood up from his workbench and moved behind the counter, surveying her through his thick bifocals. Recognizing her, he unleashed a torrent of Yiddish, of which she caught only a few words. He always remembered her face but invariably forgot her name and that she wasn't comfortable in Yiddish. She answered back in Hebrew to jog his memory.

"Ah, Mrs., you come at an opportune time," he remarked, switching to Hebrew. "I have something exquisite to show you."

"Perhaps another time, Mr. Gelbfisz. I didn't come to buy today. I'm here for some information."

"Eh?" The eyes in the bearded face went blank. "I do not understand."

She opened her purse and withdrew a small cloth bag, which she emptied onto the counter top. The gold chain spilled out, with the scimitar attached to it.

"This item has recently come into my possession. I would like to find out who made it so I can have it appraised."

Frowning, the silversmith picked up the artifact and examined it curiously, then replaced his bifocals with a jeweler's loupe and continued to scrutinize it. "Yemenite workmanship," he observed, setting the piece back down on the counter.

"Yemenite? How can you tell?"

"The delicate filigree work on the handle and hilt of the sword. It is done with fine gold wire. Only the Yemenis do it thus."

"The handle is filigree? I thought it was solid gold."

"No, it is filigree. Solid gold would make it much heavier." The silversmith found a magnifying glass and handed it to her. "Look again."

The glass revealed that the handle and hilt of the sword were indeed porous, composed of an intricate latticework of crisscrossing gold threads. She marveled at the workmanship.

48

"Could this be from a local artisan? One of the Yemeni jewelers here in Jerusalem?"

"That I couldn't tell you. But there are a number of Yemenite shops not far from here, in the Sephardic neighborhoods, Zihronot and Nahlaot. Perhaps they can help you . . ."

She thanked him and slipped the pendant back into the cloth bag, turning to leave.

"But Mrs.—I have a new bracelet to show you. It was made for you. I give you a special price. Only eight hundred shekels."

"Mr. Gelbfisz, I enjoy bargaining with you, and I don't want to rush it. I haven't the time, now, to do it properly. I will come back. Good day to you."

He was still standing at the door as it closed behind her. "Seven hundred shekels," she heard through the glass. "My final, rock-bottom offer."

Daniella was not unfamiliar with the neighborhoods to which the silversmith had directed her. An orthodox community of Sephardic Jews from Yemen, Turkey, Morocco, and Iran abutted the Mea She'arim to the south and west. More Yeminis resided along the several narrow alleyways leading westward to her favorite market, Mehane Yehuda, where she often shopped for fruit and groceries.

She was soon out of the *shtetl,* the character of the street and the people in it undergoing a pronounced change. There were fewer Hassidim to be seen here, and the attire was more modern, though still modest, no bare limbs in evidence. Stores of all different kinds had replaced the predominantly religious shops of the Mea She'arim—barber shops, clothing stores, sandal makers—even a blacksmith shop. She spied her first jewelry store across the street and quickly crossed to it. Its sign didn't indicate that it was Yemenite, but her first glance into its display window did. The intricate gold filigree work in many of its brooches and earrings told the story.

The jingle of a bell as she entered brought a salesperson through the beaded curtain behind the counter. It was a young woman, and she was bedecked with Yemenite jewelry. "Yes, madame?"

Daniella showed her the sword pendant on its gold chain. "Can you tell me who made this?"

Squinting at the miniature sword, the girl slowly shook her head. "It is clearly Yemenite, a beautiful piece, but definitely not one of ours. We do not make such things."

"Do you know of anyone who does?"

"Not in this area. I have seen nothing like it. But my grandfather might know. Let me fetch him."

She disappeared through the curtain. It was minutes before she returned, Daniella's impatience mounting. The morning was almost gone.

An old man pushed through the hanging strips of beads, limping grotesquely, helped along by his granddaughter. "Shalom," he greeted her, picking up the chain and its attachment. "This is the item in question?"

Daniella nodded. The old man studied it for a moment or two, his face impassive, then brought it closer to his eyes. He turned it over several times and felt the sharpness of the blade's edge with his finger. "Where did you get this, if I may inquire?"

She supplied him with the cover story agreed to with Shmona. "It belongs to a friend. He wants me to trace it and have it appraised."

"And how did he come by it? How is it that he doesn't know its origin?"

That one stopped her. "I really couldn't say."

The old man noted her discomfiture. "I ask this because tracing this piece will be very difficult. Its owner would do better to make inquiries from the source from which he obtained it."

"Yes. But that apparently isn't possible."

He shrugged. "I can give you my own appraisal, if that is of any help." He placed a jeweler's loupe in his right eye and carefully surveyed the sword again.

"Firstly the value of this piece is between two thousand and three thousand new shekels. There are only a few more things I can tell you that might help you. The piece is, of course, Yemenite, but there are thousands of Yemenite shops in Israel. It might have come from any one of them. Or it might have come from Yemen.

"Secondly, and this may be of help, the piece is not old at all—it is, in fact, very new. The silver blade is untarnished, yet it has only the thinnest coat of protective material. I would estimate its age as a few months, at most. And thirdly, it was almost certainly a special order, so your chances of seeing one like it in a shop window are not very good."

"A special order? How can you tell that?"

"The shofar embossed on the blade. None of our artisans, no matter how religious, would have done this unless it was so ordered. It is not in keeping with the motif—it violates the artistic integrity of the piece."

He took note of her puzzled look. "The sword is clearly of a primitive Arabian or Persian style. The Jewish symbol is incongruous and detracts from its value. I don't quite know what to make of it."

He meditated for a moment. "I once filled an order for a somewhat similar item, back in the old country. Nothing as lavish as this; they were pins to go on the hats of lodge brothers in a fraternal society. Perhaps this is the same sort of thing, a symbol for some kind of religious fraternal order."

Daniella picked up on his words. Religious order . . . Possibly a fanatical sect? Well, maybe she *was* making progress . . . "Then you've never seen this sort of article here in Israel?"

She saw his eyes glaze over, and it was some time before he answered. "Once, perhaps. It was many years ago, and I cannot recall the exact place or circumstance. I used to do a lot of browsing through the jewelry marts to keep abreast of what my competitors were offering. There is a vague image in my mind of viewing a piece similar to this one. But it would not have been here in Jerusalem. It would have been in Tel Aviv."

It was growing dark, and Daniella was suddenly very tired. She had been on her feet all day. Now she understood why they called this leg work; her legs ached all the way down to her toes. She needed a place to sit down.

She must have been to every Yemenite jewelry shop in Jerusalem. And what did she have to show for it? Not a single concrete lead to the source of the article in her purse that would help her trace it to its buyer. What would she tell

Shmona? Her first assigned task on returning to the Mossad, and she had failed.

Working her way up and down the narrow, winding alleys of the Yemenite quarter, she had visited every jeweler's establishment she came across. She was approaching the western end of the last alley and was now in sight of the Mehane Yehuda marketplace. Its refreshment stalls beckoned. She was ready to collapse.

She prepared to cross the street, and stopped. There on the corner, just across from the market, the precious contents of a brightly lit display window glittered seductively. She couldn't bring herself to pass it up, no matter how bone-weary she felt.

The proprietor had begun to remove the trays from the window, but the sign on the door still said open. She went inside, thinking only of getting it over with quickly, resigned in advance to coming up empty again.

"Shalom, madame."

"Shalom." She placed the miniature sword on the counter and went through her spiel. Out popped a jeweler's loupe, the proprietor scrutinizing the artifact as the others had done. His comments were much the same as theirs. Yes, it was Yemenite workmanship. No, he hadn't seen one like it and could shed no light on where it had been crafted or by whom.

She thanked him and prepared to drop the amulet back into its wrapper. "May I examine the chain, please?" the proprietor asked.

"Of course."

Back went the loupe into the eye, as he studied the gold chain attached to the sword. "Yes," he said, handing it back to her. "Yes, I thought so."

"What is it?" she demanded.

"I buy all my chains; I do not make them. This is one of the better-made chains available in Israel. It is 14-carat gold. See how delicate the gold links are, and yet it is very sturdy. I buy and sell many of these."

"Where—where do they come from?"

"I always get mine from the same place—a wholesaler in Tel Aviv."

• • •

SCIMITAR

Thirty thousand feet above a solid layer of low clouds, a sleek white jet with the lines of a Boeing 707 banked into a shallow turn to the right. The green symbol painted on its side, crossed swords beneath a palm tree, identified it as a Saudi Arabian plane. An immense, ungainly looking black-and-white-striped saucer suspended above its aft fuselage rotated slowly in a clockwise direction. It was one of the five AWACS—Airborne Warning and Control Systems aircraft—purchased from the U.S. in the 1980s.

Inside its windowless main cabin sat rows of radar technicians in front of control consoles that featured sizeable vertical displays bearing green symbology, nine consoles in all. The technicians looked bored; there was nothing much for them to do. They were used to charting the positions and courses of large numbers of aircraft over the Persian Gulf region, a demanding task. The maritime patrol mission they were presently embarked upon was quite different. Instead of other aircraft, they were looking for ships. The ships were few and far between, their movement so slow that charting their positions presented no challenge.

The biggest challenge was staying awake. Some of the technicians were dozing on the job, their heads nodding. It was understandable; they had already been airborne for more than seven hours on this marathon seasearch mission that had taken them almost three thousand miles from their home base in Riyadh, having undergone an in-flight refueling along the way. Their assigned task was to perform a radar search of a half-million-square-mile patch of Indian Ocean west of Singapore, charting all shipping in the region. They would be up for another seven hours and two more in-flight refuelings. No one had told them why.

The man sitting at the first console looked anything but bored, busily manipulating the keyboard alongside his display, as a new surface target appeared. Swiveling his chair around, he stood up to stretch his legs. He was youthful, tall and slender, and dressed in a trim-looking one-piece flight suit that set him apart from the others, who wore bulky leather flight jackets over their flight fatigues. Richard Llewellyn had first come to Saudi Arabia several years before, when the AWACS planes were undergoing their final shakedown trials before being accepted by the Saudis. He was already there when his brother David was first sent to Israel. An expert on the AWACS radar supplied by his company, he had flown aboard the giant aircraft on numerous occasions to monitor the performance of his equipment.

On one such flight the defenseless AWACS had found itself under attack by a heavily armed F-15 fighter plane, as part of an Iraqi plot to cause an incident that would drive a wedge between Israel and the U.S. Alerted by a last-minute radio warning from his brother, who had learned of the plot, Richy had used his technical knowledge of the F-15's weapons to instruct the pilot on evasive tactics that saved it from the deadly missiles launched against it.

After an absence of several years, Richy was back for a second tour of duty on the Saudi AWACS, to implement and check out software for several new modes, one an improved Sea Surface Search mode. Today's maritime patrol mission had sounded like an ideal shakedown opportunity for the latter mode and he had enthusiastically signed on for it. He was glad he had. His new mode was checking out beautifully, performing well against a variety of different sea states.

Richy knew little more than the others about the purpose of the extensive sea search they were embarked upon. Some big flap, of which he had been told no specifics, had them out here looking for a needle in a haystack, a lone cargo vessel that could be virtually anywhere in a million square miles of cloud-enshrouded ocean.

They'd been given no description of the vessel, which didn't really matter, because they couldn't have identified it, anyway, through the heavy undercast. Their job was simply to detect and chart the position of all the shipping within the specified search zone. By checking with the various worldwide maritime authorities, Ground Control would later attempt to identify each ship by its location, eventually working their way down to the single vessel they were after—the one transporting the smugglers, or gun-runners, or whatever their nefarious crimes that made them such a high-priority quarry for the Saudi government.

The plan struck him as somewhat impractical and possibly even unworkable, but Richy's opinion hadn't been asked.

Their search cut across all the main shipping channels traversing the Indian Ocean. While there were few ships showing on the radar display at any one time—just four at the present—the total number encountered during the protracted search was bound to be a fairly big one. In the two hours they'd been at it, they had already detected eighty-one ships. At that rate, the total would be well over two hundred sightings today that Ground Control would have to sort out using maritime data or whatever. It seemed inevitable that a good number of ships would remain unidentified.

He decided to try out his new expanded raw video mode again and announced to the group of technicians that he would be switching over to it for a minute. When he entered the command, the five synthetic ship symbols on the display were replaced by large, irregular blips that bloomed onto the scope at the same locations, their intensity slowly decaying. All the ship signatures looked virtually identical, no way to distinguish between them.

He punched in the command for the new "chirp" mode. The images of the ships changed appearance, breaking up into clumps of higher-intensity and lower-intensity blobs along their length. There were now significant differences in the five ship signatures, but the detail was not sufficient to identify them or even classify them into freighter, tanker, or other categories without further research. He switched back to the original mode.

The radar was not going to be much of a help in identifying the unknown ships, he concluded. That would have to be done with overflights as soon as the weather cleared.

Whoever it was down there trying to keep their identity a secret had the upper hand, for the moment. They would be safe as long as their "smuggler's weather" held out.

At the droning of the plane overhead, the man with the limp interrupted his trip across the deck to crane his neck in the direction of the sound. The thickness of the overcast denied him even so much as a glimpse of the aircraft whose engines were so clearly audible. It sounded like a commercial jet. But he knew that his location was nowhere near any commercial air route. The plane was looking for him.

When the sound from its engines reached a spot where it seemed to be emanating from a point 45 degrees from vertical, he consulted his watch, noting the position of the second hand. He checked it again after the sound had moved overhead and back to the same 45-degree angle on the opposite side. Seventy-two seconds had elapsed. Assuming the jet was flying at the normal cruise speed of a commercial jetliner, he applied a rule of thumb, pegging its altitude at around ten thousand meters.

The speed and altitude were a perfect match for the AWACS mission profile. If the Saudis had pulled an AWACS aircraft out of its Persian Gulf assignment, they must be really desperate. He took this as a good sign. Hopefully, the Saudis were trying to track down their hijacked missile on their own, without undergoing the humiliation of notifying their friends and allies and asking for their help. The fact that the theft had not yet surfaced in the news media—he and the captain had been monitoring the broadcast bands—tended to support this assumption. The House of Saud must be keeping a tight lid on the story, as were the Chinese. This was just what he had hoped for.

He had nothing to fear from the AWACS; its radar could not spot the illicit cargo on the *Beirut Victory;* only the human eye could do that, and only if a boarding party came looking. All that the AWACS could do was report shipping contacts and try to check them out with the international maritime service. He and the captain were prepared for that. The *Beirut Victory* was on a legitimate voyage, its cargo holds containing heavy machinery loaded in Singapore and destined for Bahrain. The captain duly reported his position daily to his company, and the maritime reports would confirm all this.

But a picket line of American or British warships might be something else entirely. If the captain was ordered to heave to on the high seas, he would have little choice. Still, it was hardly practical to search every ship in the Indian Ocean. And in just a few more days they would make landfall on Sri Lanka. Once they reached the coast of India, they could proceed toward their destination inside Indian territorial waters, where foreign warships would have no jurisdiction.

A few more days of this ideal weather—that was all he

needed. Today's weather forecast had been encouraging—no clearing in sight for at least two more days.

He resumed his progress from the forecastle to the bridge for his lunch with the captain. As he struggled up the ladder, eight bells sounded. Twelve o'clock, time for the midday prayer. The ship's clocks were still set for Singapore time. In Mecca, the workday was just beginning. And in Gaza. A day that would see his soldiers atone for their failure of three days ago, one of the few failures in his meteoric career. A perfectionist, he agonized over such setbacks; only the euphoria over his successful missile operation had made this one tolerable. And the knowledge that there would shortly be another opportunity.

To fail again was unthinkable. His silent partner would withdraw his support and the indispensable gold seam would dry up. He had formed a mental picture of this man he had never met or even spoken to directly, a sneer of contempt written across the man's Jewish features. A man with whom he had but one objective in common—to torpedo the impending peace talks. Deadly enemies, he and this man were in league together, using each other. Such was the way in war. The alliance was but a temporary expedient. Now that he had the missile, judgment day for this one and his ilk would soon be at hand. But he needed the gold seam for one last vital acquisition.

It was frustrating to be bottled up here, unable to influence the outcome in Gaza. But he had confidence in his plan and in those who would carry it out. This time Kareem, his most able lieutenant, would be on hand to direct the operation.

Al Saif reached the captain's quarters reassured that he needn't worry. Kareem possessed a talent for this business second only to his own.

Kareem would not fail him.

6

THE DRIVE FROM Hebron to Gaza was a relatively short one. Less than a half hour after leaving the West Bank, the U.N. limousine slowed for an arterial stop, then swung left onto Route 4, the main highway from Tel Aviv. The Gaza Strip lay a scant twelve kilometers beyond.

It was at the suggestion of Khalidy's assistant, Halib Begassey, that Llewellyn was riding in the front seat, where he could converse by cellular phone with Begassey in the lead vehicle, several minutes ahead of the limousine. He had his two henchmen along to scout out any trouble en route. "We must be very much on our guard today," he had warned. "Gaza is the most dangerous and unpredictable of places."

Traffic on Route 4 was much heavier, and within scarcely a minute the procession of vehicles began to slow, the speedometer dipping below the twenty-kilometer mark.

"The checkpoint outside Gaza," the young Swedish driver, Ivar Hagstrom, explained. "This is happening more and more."

The break in the limousine's steady pace brought Khalidy, who had been dozing, around. "We have arrived? We are in Gaza?"

"Not quite," the U.N. chauffeur responded. "It will take us some time to negotiate the entry point. You may return to your slumbers."

"No, I have slept enough." The Palestinian stifled a yawn. "I need to stay awake and think about what I will say to them."

Traffic continued to slow. Llewellyn became absorbed in the countryside they were passing through.

"That cluster of buildings ahead, to the right—what is that?" he inquired of the driver.

"Yad Mordekhai. One of the oldest kibbutzes in Israel. It has a fascinating history. Have you heard of it?"

"No. Tell me."

"It was during the original Arab-Israeli war in '48, which the Israelis call the War of Independence. The 165 members of the kibbutz somehow held off a battalion of 2500 Egyptian soldiers. Though they eventually had to retreat and the kibbutz was captured, they bought enough time for the Haganah to regroup and save Tel Aviv. To dramatize the historic event, a realistic model of the battle was constructed on the site, complete with tanks, dummy soldiers, and weapons."

"Does it still operate as a kibbutz?"

"Oh, yes. It is one of the most popular, I understand."

The ringing of the limousine's cellular phone startled both of them. Llewellyn picked it up.

"Begassey here. What is your location?"

"We're a kilometer or so from the Gaza entry point."

"I'll be waiting for you there. Look for me. I will ride in with you."

Their pace slowed to a crawl as they approached the checkpoint. Armed soldiers wearing brown berets were scrutinizing the occupants of all cars with blue plates, checking their passes and inspecting their trunks. Cars with yellow tags were let right through. Begassey suddenly materialized, climbing into the backseat with "His Excellency" just before the limousine was waved on.

Llewellyn wondered what had become of Begassey's escort car. Presumably it still contained the bodyguards in his employ. He knew better than to inquire in front of Khalidy, who did not approve of some of his assistant's precautions. The little man was sweating some from the heat and his exertions, but otherwise calm and composed. Only his eyes hinted at his restiveness, taking stock of everything along the road ahead.

So far the Gaza Strip looked peaceful enough. Groves of citrus lined both sides of the road, stretching as far as the eye could see. But shortly the grove along the right side petered out, revealing an extensive, built-up area whose boundary looked to be no more than a few hundred meters from the road, devoid of trees or any other vestige of vegetation.

"The Jebaliya refugee camp," Ivar informed him. "The very worst of the lot. I can't begin to tell you how bad things are in there. Jebaliya is a cesspool, even its air polluted by the stench of burning tires. Israeli Army reservists dread being sent there. The soldiers are constantly taunted by rock-throwing Palestinian youths. There are frequent bomb explosions."

Llewellyn stared at the stark tableau. "How many live here in places like this?"

"In the Gaza camps?" Ivar considered for a moment. "Perhaps a quarter of a million. Roughly half the population of the Gaza Strip."

"So many? Good Lord, where did they all come from?"

"Most were born here. They've never known anything else, anything but military rule. Their parents or grandparents fled here from their homes in other parts of Palestine during the 1948 war. Gaza was under an Egyptian military governor at that time, though never a part of Egypt; migration to Egypt was forbidden them. They have been here ever since, their children born here for two generations. Some of the younger males run away to join terrorist groups and become Fedayeen. The rest are stuck here for life."

Llewellyn got only a hurried glimpse of the rude cinder-block huts inside the nearest corner of the wire-fenced perimeter, but it was enough to give him a feeling for the place. Gray, like a day without sun, like a life without hope. A gray past, a gray future.

Shortly, the citrus groves gave out altogether. They had arrived at Gaza city. Ivar made a right turn onto one of the main city streets. Suddenly there were crowds of people, walking the streets, congregating in front of buildings. They looked much like the people of the West Bank. But one thing was very different. The soldiers here did not stay out of sight. They were very much in evidence. And they seemed to be everywhere.

The limousine was approaching the city hall. As they drew up in front of it, Llewellyn gaped at the size of the crowd choking the entryway, blocking their path into the building. The near calamity in Hebron came back to him with a rush, when he and Khalidy had almost gone down beneath hundreds of trampling feet.

"Here we go again," he sighed.

A beat-up van, its once-white paint faded to tattle-tale gray, was parked in an orange grove, hidden from the highway by the heavy foliage of the trees. Four men dressed in fatigues and armed with Uzis watched through the rear windows of the van as a fifth man threaded his way through the orchard from the direction of the highway. He arrived at the van on the run and out of breath.

"He just went by. Right on schedule."

"You're certain it was Khalidy?" questioned the only man who was not clean shaven. His beard was the same color as the van.

"Positive. Dark blue limousine, United Nations tags. The same car you and I saw in Hebron yesterday."

"How many in the car?"

"Khalidy alone in the back, the driver, and that same other man in front, the one who was with him in Hebron."

"Probably a bodyguard. We'll make short work of him." The bearded one consulted his watch. "Now if Kareem would only get here."

"He'll be along," commented one of the others, giving the lookout a hand up into the van. "There is plenty of time." He yawned. "We have a long wait ahead."

"There is not all that much time," graybeard grumbled. "We need to run over the plan again. We may want to change some things."

"Why don't we let Kareem worry about that?" the other asked. "The man is a perfectionist. Meanwhile, I'm going to take a nap."

He moved deeper into the van and stretched out. He was soon snoring. "How can Hammud sleep at a time like this?" a younger-looking man with a baby face whispered.

"Ssh!" hissed the lookout. "There's a car coming!" He pulled the doors of the van closed and all but the sleeping Hammud stared out through the windows. A military jeep came careening through the trees, bouncing wildly over the

61

deep furrows of the citrus orchard. The solitary driver was wearing a green uniform and a purple beret.

"Israeli soldier!" warned the lookout, raising the Uzi to his shoulder.

"That's Kareem, you fool!" Graybeard yanked the automatic rifle out of his hands.

A lanky form unfolded itself from behind the wheel and stepped out of the jeep. The dark green uniform was not a good fit; too short at the wrists and ankles, it hung loosely elsewhere from a body that was exceedingly thin. A gaunt face featured a sharp beak of a nose and smoldering eyes that looked like they could burn holes through you. Kareem picked up a paper-wrapped bundle from the back of the jeep and carried it to the van, tossing it inside.

"The uniforms?" The man with the beard lost no time ripping the package open. "Are there different sizes?"

"They only come in two sizes," quipped the thin man, with no trace of a smile. "Too big and too small." The intense eyes fell on the prone man behind the others.

"Who's that sleeping—Hammud? Wake him up."

The one with the baby face shook Hammud awake. He opened his eyes and sat up. "Is it time?"

"Kareem is here," the bearded one advised him. "Get into your uniform." He reached for the bundle and saw that the wrapper was empty, the others already changing into the heavy twill tops and bottoms. "There is no uniform for Hammud. We are one short."

"Give him yours," Kareem replied. "You won't be needing it. You'll be staying with the van."

"What? Impossible. According to the plan, I am in the jeep. As we rehearsed it."

"I am changing the plan. The van now plays an important part. I need a good man in the van.

"Now listen, all of you," he continued, "I want to convey to you the instructions I have received from our leader. Our whole future as a fighting unit depends on the success of today's operation. Our backers were dismayed over the botched job at Jericho. We cannot afford another such failure."

Several voices were raised in detriment of the Jericho fiasco. Kareem raised his hand for quiet.

"You're right. It was a mistake to allow the operation to proceed without proper supervision. We will not make that mistake again. That is why I'm here.

"As you know, I have been away with our leader on a most daring and ambitious undertaking, which still occupies him. It has succeeded brilliantly, placing a most potent weapon at our disposal. When he returns, you will learn all about it. But until then, security demands that I say no more. Back to the operation at hand. Here are the changes I have made in the plan . . ."

The dark blue limousine weaved its way carefully through the mass of cheering spectators overflowing into the street, turned the corner, and picked up speed. Sitting in front again next to the driver, David Llewellyn experienced a profound sense of relief. There had been no trouble—not so much as a thrown rock or burning tire. Throughout the afternoon he had been expecting it, constantly on edge to remain alert to the first indication of violence. The prolonged tension, plus the heat and humidity, had taken their toll. He felt totally spent.

The effect on Khalidy had apparently been quite different. He was ebullient, effervescent. Everything had gone splendidly. His speech, reassuring the Gazans that he would uphold their demands for total independence, was applauded wildly. The closed meetings which had followed with the mayors and with various Palestinian factions had been relatively trouble free. Even the delegation from Hamas, the Islamic Resistance Movement, after some fiery rhetoric about the total overthrow of Israel, had acknowledged their grudging support.

His riding partner in the backseat, Begassey, listened with only half an ear. The feisty little assistant was also showing the effects of his long vigil, dark circles surrounding the usually energetic eyes, now dulled by fatigue. Mercifully, the exit from the Gaza Strip was more expeditious than the entry. Cars were being waved through the checkpoint with only a cursory search of their contents.

Begassey's interference-running sedan was waiting for him just beyond the exit point. Before climbing into it he instructed Ivar to give him a five-minute head start, also reminding Llewellyn to stay in touch via the cellular phone.

Llewellyn watched the green Citroën sedan pull away. Besides the driver and Begassey, there were two other men inside, the same two that had jumped him in the bushes at Hebron. He wondered where Begassey had found them. They had apparently not attempted to enter Gaza, a matter of improper credentials, he suspected. And in any case, they couldn't have entered with their firearms.

Khalidy was impatient to get started again. "Why are we waiting here?" he demanded. Llewellyn let the chauffeur answer.

"Instructions from your assistant, sir. We're to give him a little head start."

"To what purpose?"

"Security, sir."

"Begassey is security-mad," the Palestinian grumbled. "Let's get under way."

"Yes, sir." The five minutes were not quite up. Ivar put the limousine in gear and slowly rolled back onto the highway, taking his time about picking up speed.

They had traveled only a few kilometers, Llewellyn absorbed in the passing of the legendary kibbutz, Yad Mordekhai, on the left, when a flashing light up ahead caught his eye. "Another roadblock," he groaned.

"Looks like it, sir," Ivar replied, beginning to decelerate.

Llewellyn picked up the phone and dialed Begassey. "Another roadblock ahead, I see. Any problem getting through it?"

"What?" Begassey shot back. "It wasn't there when we went by . . . Make an immediate U-turn and go back. It could be a trap."

Llewellyn didn't think so. He could make out a jeep and the green uniforms and purple berets surrounding it. Begassey must be getting paranoid. "It's okay. They're Israeli soldiers."

"Don't assume so. Stop, I tell you! There's no reason for a roadblock there. Turn around immediately!"

Llewellyn didn't have to tell the driver. Ivar had heard Begassey's strident voice through the phone's receiver and slammed on the brakes. They were scarcely a hundred meters from the military jeep that blocked the road and the four armed soldiers beside it. As the limousine swung around into a U-turn, Llewellyn looked back through the rear window, past the head of the startled Khalidy, to view the reaction of the soldiers.

That response came almost immediately—a barrage of shots from their automatic weapons. "Oh, shit! *Get down!*" Llewellyn yelled at the non-plussed Palestinian, ducking his own head. Had the Israelis gone crazy? The shooting stopped; he raised his head and looked back. The soldiers were piling into their jeep.

"They're coming after us!" he shouted.

Ivar already had the accelerator floored, and the limousine shot back over the terrain it had just traversed. "We've got to get to the Gaza checkpoint ahead of them. The commandant knows who we are. He'll protect us."

"What's happening?" the cellular phone crackled. "Did you turn around?" Llewellyn had forgotten about Begassey. The phone was lying on the seat beside him, off the hook. He picked it up.

"We turned, but they fired at us! They're chasing us in their jeep!"

"How many?"

"Four, all with automatic weapons."

"Try to reach the Gaza checkpoint! We'll be there as fast as we can."

Up the road, there was more trouble. A dirty white van approaching in the opposite lane swerved across the road, completely blocking it. *"Everybody down!"* warned Ivar, just as flashes of gunfire erupted from a window of the van.

Ivar braked frantically and took the one option open to him. He spun the wheel to the right and the limousine shot off onto the dirt road leading to Yad Mordekhai. It skidded crazily on the gravelly surface and almost went out of control, tottering precariously on two wheels before Ivar got it back on track.

Ahead some quarter of a mile lay the buildings of the kibbutz compound, a possible sanctuary, thought Llewellyn, if they could gain admittance and quickly alert its occupants to their predicament. Kibbutzes were noted for their ability to defend themselves from armed aggressors, this one in particular.

The limo's tires found firm traction again on a blacktop road and it plunged through an open iron gate, then braked suddenly for a sharp left turn. Ivar floored the gas pedal and they rocketed ahead, past livestock pens and sheds to their right. They saw cows and sheep but no people. The cellular phone blared again and Llewellyn picked it up.

"Where are you? What's happening?" asked the frantic voice.

"An armed van cut us off, blocking the road. We had to turn into Yad Mordekhai."

"Try to find cover!" Begassey advised. "We're on our way."

Two hundred meters down the road, it veered right again and Ivar had to decelerate. Before they made the turn, Llewellyn looked back and saw the telltale cloud of dust at the Yad Mordekhai turnoff. The jeep with the bogus soldiers was gaining on them.

They passed a dairy on the right and farm buildings on the left with still no sign of the kibbutzniks that tended them. A signpost in English and Hebrew read BATTLEFIELD, pointing toward a large parking lot to the left of the road. Ivar wrenched the wheel to the left and the limousine skidded into it.

"What are you doing?" Llewellyn shouted.

"The road dead-ends up ahead," Ivar explained, accelerating on across the parking lot. "We'd be trapped. We can at least find cover here in the battleground."

The limousine screeched to a stop next to a small shack and the trio jumped out. Just beyond the building, a wide foot trail led toward the crest of a small hill, another BATTLEFIELD sign pointing in that direction. "Up the hill!" ordered Ivar. "It's our best chance!"

"Go ahead. I'll be right behind you." Llewellyn had spotted a man inside the shack, which appeared to be a refreshment and souvenir stand for tourists. He ran over.

"Call for help!" he pleaded. "We're being chased by gunmen dressed as Israeli soldiers. But they're not—they're Palestinian terrorists!"

The elderly man inside the stand stared at him, speechless.

"Get help—they're right behind us!" Llewellyn shouted, sprinting past the shack and up the hill.

The crest of the hill revealed the simulated battlefield re-created as a memorial to Yad Mordekhai's heroic stand against the Egyptian army in the War of Independence. Along the ridge that dominated the wide meadow stretching below it, the original slit trenches dug by the defenders had been preserved, some of the obsolete weapons they used still affixed to the revetments. Arrayed across the expanse of open fields below stood realistic life-sized figures of the advancing Egyptian infantrymen, complete with helmets and rifles, an assortment of tanks and artillery lined up behind them.

Ivar was already pushing the reluctant Khalidy down the slope toward the battlefield when Llewellyn reached the crest. The Swede had been right. The area afforded some excellent hiding places among the array of soldiers, tanks, and guns. Before descending, he turned back for a last look, hoping they might have somehow lost their pursuers. No chance. The jeep had come careening into the parking lot.

Llewellyn plunged down the embankment and caught up with the foot-dragging Palestinian. He shoved Khalidy past the first few rows of wooden soldiers.

"Over here, behind this tank! Quickly!" He succeeded in getting the big man under cover only seconds before the jeep appeared at the crest of the hill, having driven straight up the foot trail.

Llewellyn caught his breath and looked around for Ivar. There he was, crouched behind one of the wooden soldiers, a dozen yards to his right. The Swede put a finger across his lips and pointed toward the jeep, Llewellyn nodding to indicate that he had seen it. The terrorists were already climbing out of it, their weapons drawn.

Lying prone behind the tank, Llewellyn watched through its treads as the "soldiers" started down the hill toward the simulated Egyptian army . . .

Spread out across the battlefield, the purple-bereted terrorists reached the bottom of the hill and were approaching the first line of wooden figures. Still moving cautiously, they thrust the muzzles of their Uzis behind the structures and into the tall grass surrounding them. The tall man in the middle of the group gave an order and they moved on to the next rank of "Egyptian infantrymen." The tall man was clearly their leader; Llewellyn got a good look at him. He was exceedingly thin and had a haggard face. There was something strange about his eyes; from this distance they looked like hollow sockets.

Despite the odds, Llewellyn vowed to make a fight of it. The way the men were spread out was to his advantage. If they could surprise one soldier and overpower him—seize his weapon—they had a chance. He gripped the shoulder of the giant lying beside him, pointing to the advancing soldiers and making a choking gesture with his hand at his neck. Khalidy nodded, getting up on all fours, ready to pounce. Llewellyn found a rock and prepared to toss it at one of the other tanks when the time was ripe. The diversionary ploy was as old as the hills, but it could still work. A few more seconds, and—

A screeching of tires . . .

Another car entered the parking lot. The terrorists heard it too; two of them glanced nervously back up the hill, but the group's leader gave a sharp command and they continued to move forward. As they reached the next line of wooden figures, Llewellyn saw Begassey and his two men come over the crest of the hill, rifles in hand.

The commander of the terrorist squad saw them too, and unleashed a burst from his Uzi in their direction. The trio scrambled for cover, plunging into the trenches at the top of the hill. Almost immediately shots rang out from that quarter, and now it was the terrorists who were diving for cover, ducking behind the wooden figures for what shelter they could afford.

Flurries of bursts were unleashed by the pinned-down terrorists, answered by single volleys from the ridge above . . . Totally hidden from view by the earthworks, Begassey and his men had the same advantage shared by the Yad Mordekhai defenders against the Egyptians. They could move at will along the expanse of trenches; the terrorists had no way of knowing where they would pop up next.

But now the terrorists' tall commander initiated a tactic designed to chance the odds. At his signal, two of his party began crawling to their left on their hands and knees, the other two, including the leader, scrambling in the opposite direction. It was clearly an attempt to outflank the men in the trenches. The rate of fire from the top of the hill increased . . . A howl to Llewellyn's left announced that one of their shots had found its mark.

But to his right, the tall leader was on his feet, running, and had reached the cover of some trees. He headed for high ground, climbing toward one corner of the fortifications. In another minute or less he would be in position to look down along the line of trenches and rake them with fire from his Uzi.

Suddenly, the sound of a motor straining in low gear was heard, and a small truck poked its nose over the crest of the embankment, pulling to a stop alongside the jeep. A heavy caliber machine gun was mounted on its open bed, manned by two uniformed men. The gun was quickly trained in the direction of the approaching Uzi wielders and a burst fired over their heads. They promptly hit the deck.

A loudspeaker blared from the truck, the voice shouting something in Hebrew. Llewellyn caught enough of it to know that it was an ultimatum to cease fire, lay down their arms and surrender. It didn't seem that the terrorists had much choice. They couldn't retrieve their jeep; the truck with the powerful gun was parked next to it.

But then he saw the terrorist commander and his man begin rolling on the ground to their right, over and over, until they disappeared behind the ridge above the parking lot. The truck did not fire again, its gunners making no attempt to stop them.

"Don't let them get away!" Llewellyn ordered, jumping to his feet and running toward the embankment, forgetting for the moment that two other terrorists were unaccounted for.

"Fire! They're getting away!"

"We can't do that, I'm afraid," said a voice at his elbow. It belonged to a snowy-haired man sitting inside the cab of the truck, the same one who had been behind the counter of the refreshment stand.

"Why not?" he demanded. "They're not Israeli soldiers. They're terrorists!"

"They may be, but we're not soldiers, either. We're only

kibbutz security guards. Don't worry, they won't get far on foot. The police are on their way."

The terrorists reached the parking lot and were running toward the U.N. limousine and Begassey's sedan parked beside it. A third member of their party emerged from the trees on the opposite side of the lot and ran to meet them.

Llewellyn ran over and grabbed the Garand from one of Begassey's men, drawing a bead on the terrorist leader. He squeezed the trigger but there was no report.

"The magazine's empty," Begassey explained ruefully. "We used up all our ammunition."

Llewellyn cursed and watched helplessly as the same white van that had earlier tried to block the limousine's escape came tearing into the parking lot and skidded to a stop beside them, the trio piling inside. The driver gunned the motor and the van swung around in a wide arc, exiting the lot on two wheels.

In a matter of seconds it was out of sight and earshot. There was still no sign of the police.

The gray-haired man shook hands all around. "My name is Esser Harel. I am in my fiftieth year at Yad Mordekhai."

"Fifty years?" Llewellyn made a quick calculation. "Then you were here when—"

"That's right." Harel smiled broadly. "I fought the Egyptians from these very trenches when they tried to overrun us in '48. I've been here ever since."

The other kibbutzniks climbed down from the truck bed, and there were further introductions and handshaking. "We probably owe you our lives for coming to our assistance," Llewellyn observed. Khalidy's booming voice seconded the motion. He looked none the worse for wear after his ordeal, except for his traditional costume that was no longer snow-white in many places.

Llewellyn turned back to the gray-haired kibbutz veteran. "I didn't think you'd believe me—about the soldiers not being genuine. How did you know?"

Harel's grin appeared again. "The purple berets gave them away. You never see that color around here. Purple berets are only worn by the Golani Brigade. They have no units south of the Golan Heights."

• • •

After the police made their belated appearance in two cars and were brought up to speed, the search for the wounded terrorist began, Llewellyn joining in with some of the others. He had a pretty good fix on the point where the howl of pain had come from, and went straight to the spot.

He found the Uzi first, then the crumpled form of the terrorist in the Israeli army uniform in a patch of tall grass where he had managed to drag himself. The roots of the grass were stained red. He had lost a tremendous amount of blood, Llewellyn saw to his dismay. He had hoped to find the terrorist alive; they'd get little information from a dead man. But there was no sign of breathing and no detectable pulse.

"Is he dead?" Khalidy had come up behind him.

"Looks that way." Llewellyn slipped his hand under the collar of the green denim uniform.

"What are you doing?"

"Just checking." His fingers made contact with a fine metal chain, and he drew it from beneath the collar until a small article attached to it spilled out. He cupped it in the palm of his hand so that Khalidy could see it.

"Look familiar?" The miniature gold and silver scimitar glinted in the late afternoon sun, the ram's horn insignia on its blade clearly discernible.

7

AT MOSSAD HEADQUARTERS, after ten unanswered rings, a frowning Baruch Shmona hung up. Daniella must have already left for Tel Aviv. He was too late to intercept her.

Earlier this morning he had received her call, reporting on yesterday's attempts to trace the scimitar amulet in Jerusalem's Yemenite district and the double leads pointing to Tel Aviv. He had readily agreed to her suggestion that she proceed there directly to continue her search. But that was before he had learned of yesterday's new development. Another scimitar had been found, this one around the neck of yet another dead terrorist in a second attempt on Khalidy's life near Gaza.

She had to be warned about what she might be walking into. Conforming to his standard operating procedure with field agents, he had told her only what he thought she needed to know, holding back the information on how the scimitar pendant had come into his possession. The less his agents knew, the less they could divulge, unwittingly or under duress. Besides, it hadn't occurred to him that Daniella's assignment could be hazardous—until this morning.

The latest incident outside Gaza demonstrated that the Jericho assassination attempt had not been just another sporadic terrorist outburst. The Fedayeen wearing these amulets were members of a determined band of assassins, evidently well organized and well financed. Showing the amulet and asking questions in the wrong places might turn out to be hazardous to the health of his leg person. He owed it to her to at least warn her; he *had* gotten her into this.

It was unfortunate that his office had been saddled with the assignment to begin with. This sort of thing was really the job of Shin Beth. The Israeli counter-intelligence organization had jurisdiction over domestic operations, similarly to the FBI in the U.S. But the Mossad director had been understandably reluctant to hand over to the rival agency an investigation connected so specifically and crucially with the Mossad's legitimate job of tracking down the terrorists presumed to have possession of the hijacked Saudi missile. The jurisdictional lines between the two agencies, like those between the FBI and CIA, were fuzzy and often overlapped.

Shmona heaved a sigh of resignation. He would have no alternative but to follow Daniella to Tel Aviv and make sure she was properly briefed to proceed with all due caution. He reached for the phone again to advise his secretary, Rebecca, and have her reschedule today's appointments. It rang before he picked it up.

"You're to be in the director's office in five minutes," Rebecca announced. "Bring your Nineveh file. He wants to be briefed on it."

"Nineveh?"

"That *is* your baby, isn't it?"

"Yes, but—" Nineveh was the code for Iraq's ballistic missile research and manufacturing complex in Mosul. Shmona was controlling an agent in the area who supplied him from time to time with updates on its status. "What's going on, Rebecca?"

"Big flap brewing. The IDF Chief of Staff has just called a special meeting for this afternoon. At least that's what the secretarial grapevine reports."

"What kind of flap?"

"Don't know yet. Stay tuned."

He dialed in the combination of his safe and removed the highly classified file. Since Saddam Hussein's invasion of Kuwait, it had been receiving a lot of attention. The burgeoning ballistic missile facility near the northern Iraq city was also the site of a warhead manufacturing plant, packaging explosives, deadly chemicals, and biological weapons into self-deploying modules for installation in its various missiles. Shmona had no doubt that the plan also called for nuclear warheads in the not-too-distant future.

Poison gas warheads produced here from chemicals shipped from the manufacturing plant at Samarra had been used against Iran in the later stages of the Iran-Iraq War. Since the end of that war, instead of tapering down, the Mosul complex had undergone an ominous buildup. Now Shmona's man in Mosul had reported that a new capability had been brought on line to manufacture warheads utilizing the much-heralded binary weapons, designed to deliver an ultra-lethal nerve agent.

His curiosity thoroughly aroused, he headed for the director's office, the Nineveh file in hand. Hopefully, the briefing would not last too long. He would get back to Daniella as soon as it was over.

Daniella's green Simca turned north off Elat Yafo onto Allenby Road. She had made good time, the unpredictable traffic on Route 1, the major artery between Jerusalem and Tel Aviv, agreeably light this time of morning. For the entire trip she had been trying unsuccessfully to focus her mind on her Mossad business, but thoughts of David kept intruding.

Following a cryptic call telling her only that he would be late, her husband had arrived home the night before looking like death warmed over. Usually the possessor of a hearty appetite, he had barely touched the food she put in front of him. He was, in fact, on the verge of nodding off at the table. "What happened?" she had asked repeatedly. "More violence—another attack?" He kept putting her off, finally promising to say more about it in the morning.

"I won't be here in the morning," she had informed him, and gone on to divulge her reinstatement in her old job with the Mossad. She had planned all day just how she would tell him, anticipating a strong reaction. But he had shrugged it off, making no comment at all, had left the table and put himself to bed. When she had looked in minutes later, he was fast asleep. She felt cheated.

He was still asleep when she left this morning and she didn't disturb him. The news summary on the car radio carried an item about a terrorist attack near Gaza the previous afternoon in which another terrorist had been killed. Though no details were given and David's name not mentioned, she was certain it had involved him. A fresh wave of concern for his safety swept over her, and she had almost turned around to drive back and exact a promise from him to give up this insane assignment. But she knew it would be futile; he'd just say it was his job and he had to do it. Okay, he had his job—she had hers.

The Yemeni jeweler in Jerusalem had suggested she start her search in a district of small wholesale shops along Allenby Road near Magen David Square. She knew her chances of finding a parking spot along the street were not good. Her best bet would be the spacious parking lot that serviced the Shuk Ha Carmel, Tel Aviv's vast open-air market.

She parked and walked back past the market to Allenby Road. Within a two-block area, she'd been advised, there were close to a dozen jewelry shops fronting on Allenby that specialized in the wholesale trade. Her plan was to walk through the district first, before entering any shops, and peruse the display windows for anything resembling the scimitar pendant in her purse.

Painstakingly, she scrutinized their display windows, but there were no miniature swords, nothing remotely like the scimitar, though the workmanship on some of the pendants and brooches in one of the shops seemed similar. She memorized the proprietor's name, Yakov Bareesh, and made a mental note to return and show him her pendant if she came up empty elsewhere.

It was after eleven before she ran out of shops, her frustration and disappointment mounting, having seen nothing remotely resembling the sword pendant. Had the memory of the Jerusalem jeweler been faulty? Or perhaps it was just that the pendants weren't selling well and were simply not on display.

Seizing on the thought, she retraced her steps, returning to the Yemenite store of Yakov Bareesh. This time she stepped inside through the open door.

A heavyset man wearing a yarmulke raised his head from behind the counter.

"Shalom, madame. How may I serve you?"

Opening her purse, Daniella fished out the pendant. "I have

been told this was purchased here in the wholesaler area. Is it yours?"

She dangled the scimitar on the end of its chain for a moment, then deposited it on the counter, watching the man's eyes. Had she detected a fleeting note of alarm behind the thick glasses? His manner denied it.

"May I?" He picked up the pendant and examined it carefully. "A superbly crafted piece. Yes, a little treasure. No, I regret to say, it is not mine. May I ask how you came by it?"

"It belongs to a friend." She changed her cover story a trifle. "He wants to buy more. He asked me to try to trace it to its originator."

The proprietor put the pendant back on the countertop. "I am afraid I cannot help you."

"You've never seen one like it around here? The jeweler in Jerusalem was so certain—"

"Which jeweler was that, madame?"

She mentioned the name. "Yes, I know of him. But in this he is mistaken. This piece does not come from here. Now if you will excuse me, please. Unless there is some other business I can help you with?"

"No, nothing." Dropping the pendant back into its cloth bag, she popped it into her purse, thanked him, and left the shop. She fought off her disappointment. There was still the Yemenite Quarter to explore. There were several jewelry shops there. Maybe she would get lucky.

The phone rang exactly eight times before it was answered. "Identify yourself," the man's voice at the other end directed.

"I am Yakov Bareesh, a wholesale jeweler here in Tel Aviv. I was instructed to dial this number and report any inquiries concerning a certain piece of jewelry. I have just received such an inquiry."

"One moment."

A different voice came on the line. "You say there has been someone inquiring about a piece of jewelry? Be more specific, please."

The Voice was one he had heard before. "It was concerning the scimitar pendant. A young lady came into the shop and showed me one of them—one of those I made for you. She wanted to know if it came from my store."

"You didn't acknowledge that, I hope." The Voice became steel-edged.

"No, certainly not." The obese jeweler removed his yarmulke and wiped away the drops of perspiration forming on his forehead. "I remembered what you said. I denied ever seeing it before."

"When did this happen?"

"No more than five minutes ago. I phoned you immediately."

"You're certain that the piece was one of those you supplied to me?"

"Does a father not know his own children? Besides, it had the shofar emblem on the blade."

"Did this woman identify herself?"

"No, she did not."

"You should have tried to find out who she was." Again the edge came into the voice. "You should have told her you would make inquiries, obtained her name and address."

"It—it didn't occur to me. But it may not be too late."

"What do you mean?"

"I'm not sure she believed me. I think she is still in the area—I think she may be back."

"All right. Now here is what you do. If she returns, stick to your story. But get her to identify herself, using any pretext that occurs to you. Then phone me at once with the information. Is that understood?"

"Yes. Yes, I—" A metallic click in the receiver informed the jeweler that the other party was no longer there.

The man who had just hung up on the jeweler stared at the desk for a moment. Beneath the prolific head of snow-white hair, incongruous dark brows glowered menacingly. If the woman had one of his talismans in her possession, it could mean only one thing—she must be with the Shin Beth! The scimitar must have been found at the scene of one of the botched assassination attempts. They were trying to trace it back to the party who supplied it to the terrorists—back to *him*. The situation had suddenly become very dangerous. If she continued to inquire, he could be exposed.

The woman had to be stopped . . .

He swung the swivel chair around to face the other man in the small office, his trusted assistant.

"You heard?"

The other nodded. He was a younger man, wearing a fashionably tailored suit, with dark hair and a bookish look heightened by heavy horn-rimmed glasses.

"I want you to go immediately to the jeweler, Bareesh's place, on Allenby. Stay out of sight and watch for the woman to return. When she leaves, follow her. Find out who she is and where she lives."

"At once, sir." The assistant rose and picked up his hat. "Can he connect you, this Bareesh? Does he know who you are?"

"No. The pendants were purchased under a fictitious name. He has never seen me face to face. We have only spoken by phone."

"Still, phone numbers can be traced."

"Yes." He had no doubt that the Shin Beth could turn up the address of his office in short order from the number in the jeweler's possession. "We must prevent that from happening."

"If the woman returns, I will be there." The assistant left the office.

His employer stood up and began to pace the room. He was not a tall man, but his imposing shock of hair gave him a distinguished appearance. A successful man, by any of the conventional standards businessmen use to assess the standing of their colleagues; he had an eight-figure net worth. But conventional was not a word that could be even remotely applied to Nachman Malamud, self-styled tycoon, the extent of his unconventionality never dreamed of by the vast majority of his business associates. Some were no doubt aware of Malamud's personal ties with controversial right-wing figures in Israeli politics and with his connection to the Gush Emunim activist movement, which advocated colonization of the entire West Bank and helped organize and finance the Jewish settlers. But only a handful knew the extent of his investment in West Bank properties and construction. An investment that could ruin him if the West Bank were to become an exclusive Palestinian Arab domain under the threatened plebiscite.

The Israeli Prime Minister had been denounced as a traitor by Malamud's right-wing friends for proposing the peace plan and allowing the talks to go forward. Yes, he thought, they speak out against it, but what good are words? He had taken the bull by the horns, had done something about it. Or would have, once the charmed life of this Khalidy character, the Palestinians' designated spokesman, ran out. The peace talks would be derailed and there would be an end to the nonsense about self-government in the West Bank.

But though many would applaud this result, few would have approved of his methods, he realized. An alliance with the despised Fedayeen! He smiled, thinking how often he had used the technique in the business world, an alliance of convenience with an archrival, a detested competitor, to gain the upper hand in a lucrative business deal. This was no different. This was business, too.

Still, it would not do for the truth to come out. That could be a road to ruin of a different sort. Vanity, he reflected, had led to many a great man's downfall. Was it only vanity, his desire to put his personal stamp on the Khalidy operation, distributing his amulets to the "soldiers" who would carry out his orders? In any case, he must take steps to cover his tracks. He must take out some additional insurance.

He sat down at his desk again and picked up the phone, dialing a number that for security reasons was written in his memory and nowhere else. If the snooping woman proved to be, indeed, a Shin Beth agent, he would need a real professional to take care of her. And he already had a host of such professionals on retainer.

It was past noon when Daniella made her way up one of the tangled streets of the Yemenite Quarter. One of the oldest sections of Tel Aviv, its low-roofed houses and shops had a character all their own. Restaurants abounded, and the mouthwatering aromas given off were too much for her. She succumbed to an establishment named Shaul's Inn with flagstone floors, heavy wooden furniture, and a colorful mural of a Yemenite wedding on the wall facing her.

She had seen a jewelry store just opposite the restaurant and, after lunch, crossed over to it. A quick examination of the contents of the display window turned up no scimitars among the Yemenite earrings and brooches and necklaces. A bell tinkled musically as she entered the shop and a head popped up behind the counter.

"Shalom, madame." The young man looked to be scarcely in his teens.

"Shalom. Is your—is the proprietor about?"

"My father is having his midday meal. But I am well acquainted with the merchandise. May I wait on you?"

The youth was trying so hard to be grown-up and professional that she hadn't the heart to reject him. Perhaps the proprietor would return soon. She opened her purse and took out the pendant.

"I'm looking for another piece like this one." She slipped the scimitar and its chain out of its cloth bag.

The eyes of the proprietor's son shone as he picked up the miniature gold and silver sword and fondled it. He replaced it on the counter.

"I am afraid I don't have one of these in stock at the moment," he announced in a formal adult manner that made her smile. "But I can order one for you. I'm not sure of the price. How much were you expecting to pay?"

Daniella couldn't believe her ears. "Order it? Where?"

"From the wholesaler, of course. They are made right here, a few blocks away."

Was this just part of his playacting, or was he serious? "I was just there—in the wholesale district. I searched everywhere. I couldn't find one."

"It may not be on display at the moment. But I saw one there not a month ago."

"Which wholesaler?"

He hesitated, afraid of losing a sale. "They will not sell directly to you, unless you are a retailer. You may as well order it through me. I can get you the lowest price."

"All right," she agreed, "if I buy one I will buy it from you. Now tell me the name of the wholesaler."

"It is from the shop of Yakov Bareesh, a friend of my father."

The fat man in the yarmulke? She knew there was something fishy about his manner. Why had he lied? "Can you go there with me? I want to verify that it's still available."

"I cannot leave the store unattended. Why not just call him?"

"No, I must see the article." It would be too easy for the jeweler to put her off again on the phone. But face to face, with the boy there, he would have to admit his deception, the first step to getting the name of his customer.

The youth shrugged. "Perhaps when my father returns, if he gives his permission. He should be back any minute, now. He's lunching just across the street."

"Shaul's Inn? I just came from there." She resigned herself to waiting, passing the time chatting with the personable youth, whose name was Arik. He had been to Shaul's several times and bragged about the food.

The discussion had just turned to Arik's favorite desserts when the door tinkled and the proprietor stepped inside. He listened to his son's story and quickly gave his permission.

At first she thought that Bareesh's place was closed. The door was shut and the shades were pulled down. But this proved to be only a defense against the afternoon sun, which shone directly onto the storefront. Arik proceeded to the door and turned the knob. It was unlocked. Ever the young gentleman, he held it open for her.

The jeweler didn't look as surprised to see her as she had expected. But when Arik followed her in, his face lost its composure.

"Shalom, Mr. Bareesh."

"Shalom, Arik. What are you doing here?"

Now he knows he can't lie to me any more, she thought. She decided to let Arik do the talking. "This lady wants to buy one of your sword pendants," Arik explained. "I told her I would give her a good price."

"Which pendant is that?" Did Bareesh think he could brazen it out by playing dumb?

"The tiny curved sword with the gold filigree handle. Like the one I saw in your showcase last month."

"Oh, that one." The jeweler now saw that he would have to change his story. "I'm not making that item any more. I have none for sale. I have already so informed this lady."

A mystified look came over the boy's face. The lady had neglected to tell him this. But his main concern was seeing his potentially lucrative sale slipping away. "Couldn't you make one up for her special? I'm sure she can pay."

The jeweler shook his head. Arik was crestfallen. Daniella took his hand and shook it, depositing a small bill in his palm as she did so.

"Thank you, Arik, for trying. You may return to your father's shop, now. I would like to have a word with Mr. Bareesh in private."

"Why did you lie to me?" Daniella demanded after the boy had left. "You know you made those pendants."

"Why did you lie to me?" the jeweler countered. "You're not really interested in buying more of those pendants. Who are you? What do you want?"

"I want to know the name of the person who placed a large order for the pendants, and where you delivered them."

"Under what authority? I refuse to discuss the matter further until you identify yourself."

She took a deep breath. It was one of those special situations. Shmona would approve, she was sure. There was no other way.

"I am with the Mossad." She fished in her purse and found her wallet, flashing the Mossad credential at the jeweler, and told him the substance of what little information Shmona had imparted to her. "The sword pendant with the shofar was found at the scene of a heinous crime against the state of Israel."

"Oh, my God!" Bareesh appeared thunderstruck as he stared into the determined green-flecked eyes of the attractive brunette agent.

The Mossad! He had been somewhat intimidated by the lucrative customer who talked so imperiously over the telephone, but he was much more afraid of the Mossad. They could close you up permanently, put you out of business. He had no intention of getting crosswise with them.

"I don't know his name. He phoned in the order; cash was

delivered to pay for it, and it was picked up by the messenger."

"You've never seen the man?" Daniella's disappointment showed in her face.

"I have only spoken to him over the phone."

"And you have no address for him?" He shook his head.

She had a sudden inspiration. "Did you call him to warn him after I questioned you?" The jeweler flushed and averted his eyes. "The answer is yes, I take it?"

He nodded abjectly. "I was instructed to do so at the time of the purchase."

"In that case, you must know his phone exchange. May I have it, please?"

She had trapped him. He had hoped to get rid of her without yielding up the one key he possessed to the Voice's identity. The Voice would surely know where she had gotten it. But now he had no choice. He wrote the number down on a blank claim check and handed it to her.

"I hope you realize it would be very foolish of you to warn him again. You could be charged as an accessory. Is that understood?"

"Yes. I want no trouble. I had no way of knowing—"

"You're not to contact him again. This is a police matter now. You may be asked for a deposition."

She left the shop and headed back to the lot where her car was parked, feeling jubilant. There was a public telephone she knew of on the way, inside the market. In her euphoria, she failed to notice the well-dressed man in the business suit and hat detach himself from a group of window-shoppers in front of a nearby store and follow her up Allenby Road.

In the phone booth, Daniella resisted the urge to try the number obtained from the jeweler. Instead, she dialed Shmona's extension at Mossad headquarters. His secretary answered and she identified herself.

"He's been tied up in a meeting with the director all morning," Rebecca informed her, "preparing for a general staff summit meeting. They didn't even break for lunch."

"This is pretty urgent. I don't think it can wait."

"It will have to, I'm afraid. It could cost me my job to drag him out of Jehovah's office. You want to leave a message?"

"Yes. Tell him I'm on my way back from Tel Aviv, mission accomplished. Tell him—" How to phrase it? "Tell him I have a phone number he'll want."

The green Simca pulled out of the parking lot and slid into the heavy traffic on Allenby Road. Two blocks later it signalled for a right turn. Several cars behind, a silver Mercedes followed it into the right-turn lane, the well-dressed man with the hat behind the wheel.

As the light changed, a van crossed two lanes of traffic to reach the right lane, barely in time to follow the Mercedes through the turn. It bore Israeli yellow plates and its coat of dark blue paint looked new. But someone had done a sloppy job. They had neglected to pound out the many dents before painting it. In several spots its previous coat of paint, a dirty white, showed through.

8

THE SPECIAL MEETING of the Israeli Defense Forces General Staff had been set up hastily by its chief and chairman, General Yigal Tuchler. For this reason, and because it was not a regularly scheduled meeting, several of those who normally attended were absent.

Though his mane of yellow hair had gone white, Tuchler was still regarded as a lion by his associates. His easygoing style was disarming; if he thought one of his officers was dogging it, his claws could come out very fast, as they were all aware. Sitting at the head of the table, he rapped the meeting to order. The six general officers seated around the table gave him their immediate attention, as did the lone attendee in civilian clothes.

Tuchler's executive officer, Col. Elon, sat at the foot of the table taking notes. He was asked by the chairman to read the agenda and did so. The reading was a formality; those in attendence had all been pre-briefed on it and held a copy in their hands. What they hadn't been briefed on was the hidden agenda, of which only their chairman was aware.

The long-awaited retaliation against Iraq for the Scud missile attacks on Israel was at hand. The Israeli Prime Minister and his Defense Minister wanted Tuchler to prepare for an immediate military action against Sadam Hussein. U.S. restraints against Israel's direct participation in the recent gulf war, occasioned by the need to prevent breeches in the U.S.-led coalition against Hussein, no longer applied. And there was ample justification for preemptive action at this time. Far from abating, the threat from Iraq had escalated. Despite the devastation to Iraq's war machine and infrastructure by Desert Storm, the missile technology center at Mosul had come through it all virtually unscathed. Since the end of the war it had become a hub of activity, new missiles beginning to roll off the Mosul factory's assembly line that were far more menacing than the outmoded Scuds.

The Prime Minister, of course, had his own reasons for advocating a dramatic military strike against Israel's avowed enemy. His faction-ridden Likud bloc was torn with dissension over the handling of the *intifada* and the projected peace talks with the Palestinians. A strike at Hussein would provide belated fulfillment to every Israeli who had yearned, in vain, for such direct retaliation by their country during the Scud missile attacks and would give his government's popularity a much-needed shot in the arm.

The written agenda consisted of but two items. The first was a grabber:

1. GROWTH OF IRAQ TACTICAL MISSILE THREAT
   - TAMMUZ MISSILE STARTING PRODUCTION AT MOSUL
     - 1200 KILOMETER RANGE
     - 1100 POUND PAYLOAD
   - NEW BINARY WEAPONS ASSEMBLY UNIT ON LINE
     - VISCOUS NERVE AGENT VX DEADLIER DERIVATIVE
     - PRODUCING WARHEADS FOR TACTICAL MISSILES
   - ESTIMATED CASUALTIES IN TARGET REGION: 30 TO 50% OF POPULATION IN ONE SQUARE MILE AREA

Col. Elon made several pertinent comments as he read through item one. "The Tammuz missile, also known as the al-Hussein, is only one of several tactical missiles to be manufactured at Mosul. The factory sustained moderate damage during Desert Storm, but has been repaired and is back on line.

"The new nerve gas is reportedly the deadliest ever produced, as the casualty estimate reflects. If the target area were Tel Aviv, this could translate to half a million dead."

This elicited a gasp or two and some angry side dialogue:
". . . The Butcher of Baghdad is out for our blood again."

". . . Hussein needs another lesson from us like we gave him when we wiped out Osirak."

". . . He's asking for some more of our two-thousand-pounders up his ass."

Item 2 on the agenda sheet read:

2. ALTERNATIVE RESPONSES
  - PREEMPTIVE AIR STRIKE
    - MANNED AIRCRAFT
    - DRONES
  - SPECIAL FORCES COMMANDO-STYLE DEMOLITION
  - NO PREEMPTIVE STRIKE
    - RELY ON DETERRENCE
    - DEVELOP ANTI-MISSILE
    - ACCELERATE CIVIL DEFENSE

Col. Elon read through the alternatives listed, explaining that the situation called for "surgical strike accuracy" in order to destroy only those buildings targeted and spare the nearby compound where the workers lived. For that reason use of Israel's own tactical missile, the Jericho, was not considered viable.

"Let us consider the alternatives in the order listed," Tuchler began. "First, your reaction to the Osirak approach, a preemptive air strike. General Barkai, I know that your planners have been actively pursuing air-strike options against Iraq. If you were assigned that responsibility, how would you proceed?"

The Air Force commanding general, the youngest member of the general staff, was known to his colleagues as a charger. Short of stature—he had been a fighter pilot when the cockpits of the early jets were too cramped for a tall man to fit into—he compensated with a strength of purpose and aggressiveness that made him seem much taller. But his response on this occasion was out of character.

"I'm not sure I would." Noting the disbelief in their faces, including Tuchler's, he hastened to clarify.

"I don't mean to rule out a manned strike, but the Mosul facility is known to be heavily defended, both by missiles and fighter aircraft. I have discussed these defenses with our intelligence people and they are formidable. Contributing to the difficulty is the distance we would have to fly—more than a thousand kilometers each way—over hostile territory, Jordan, Syria, and Iraq, under constant threat of attack by their MIGs. In short, the chances are high that we would sustain heavy casualties."

"What about drones?" Tuchler interjected. "We've spent plenty on those drones over the last decade."

"Our drones are relatively short range. They would have to be transported to the Mosul vicinity over the same hostile air space, facing the same MIG threat. So it would still be a manned operation, in that sense. But in the terminal encounter I concur that use of the drones would save lives."

"Your preferred approached, then, would be a combined strike using manned aircraft and drones?" Tuchler pressed.

"If we go forward with this, yes. But I haven't mentioned my overriding reservation about doing so. Satellite photos show that some of the missile launch sites west of Baghdad, knocked out during Desert Storm, have been repaired and are back in business. We don't have a reading yet on which sites can launch this new al-Hussein, but even if we're only talking Scuds, these new chemical warheads change the odds. Before hitting Mosul, we would have to mount a preemptive air strike against these launch sites, and some are heavily defended by SAMs. Given the element of surprise, we have a reasonable chance of taking them all out before a missile is launched. But if we should fail—"

He spread his hands. "The last line of your first chart shows what the consequences could be."

The room began to buzz with verbal reactions to Barkai's sobering assessment. The chairman rapped for order. "So that would be your recommendation, General? A dual strike at Mosul and Baghdad, timed to destroy the missile sites before the factories at Mosul are hit?"

"I would prefer hearing a discussion of the other alternatives before committing myself."

"Thank you, General Barkai." The chairman turned next to the commander of Army Special Forces. "General May-dan, could we pull off a commando strike against Mosul?

Could you get your demolition experts in there, blow up those factories, and get them out again?"

"In my opinion, it could be done." The voice was strong and the eyes still steely-hard, but the commando-tough body had been overtaken by flab and a bulging midsection. The Entebbe raid which Ephraim Maydan had helped plan and execute had been a long time ago.

"But it would be touch and go. And there are some big 'ifs': Demolishing an entire factory would not be in the cards, let alone two factories. But if intelligence could supply us with a blueprint of specific areas which, if destroyed, would cripple each facility, we could concentrate on knocking those out and incendiarize the balance."

"What about that, Mr. Shilo?" Tuchler addressed his question to the lone civilian, the Mossad director. Though he attended many of the general staff meetings, Mordechai Shilo was not actually a member, reporting directly to the Prime Minister. Tuchler knew him as a cautious man and was somewhat surprised to see him nod affirmatively.

"I think we can give you some useful input on that. In the missile factory you should plan on knocking out the guidance unit fabrication and assembly bays. Without the sensitive inertial navigation components to direct it, a ballistic missile is essentially blind. Incendiaries in the rocket booster manufacuring area would also be productive and might even destroy the whole site in one glorious fireball. We are prepared to provide you the information on these locations."

"And the warhead assembly unit?" Maydan inquired.

"That is more difficult; I have little input on it at present. But that can be remedied. There is a good chance of getting this information for you."

"How would you get in and out?" Maydan was asked by the chairman.

"The element of surprise would be essential. We would need to go in while it is still dark, sometime before dawn, preferably on a Friday, the Muslim Sabbath. I would employ a single Arava military STOL transport, which needs only a few hundred feet for takeoffs and landings and can accommodate an entire commando unit plus the demolition team and their equipment and materials. We would also have to pack enough fuel for the return trip. Being able to pinpoint an appropriate landing area is another important 'if.' "

"There is a military airstrip close by," the Mossad director volunteered.

"How close?"

"Within two kilometers of both factories."

"Too far. Besides, military airfields are often defended by army garrisons. Finding a suitable cleared area for our STOL aircraft in the immediate factory vicinity would be a must. It can be a parking lot or a soccer field; it doesn't even have to be paved."

Shilo nodded again. "I'm sure we can come up with something."

"How would you get by the MiGs?" the Air Force commander asked bluntly.

"Low-level penetration."

"And getting back?" Barkai persisted.

"That would be more difficult," Maydan acknowledged. "In all likelihood Syria and Jordan will be alerted by the Iraqis, and there's not much chance of sneaking through undetected coming back. This, then, is my final 'if'—a squadron or two of F-15s or F-16s flying MiGCAP on our return trip."

General Barkai grinned. "My fighter jocks would love that. They've been spoiling for a hassle with some live MiGs instead of those canned ones in our simulators. And I wouldn't have to split my strike force. We could concentrate on getting the job done on the tactical missile sites around Baghdad."

Tuchler nodded. A coordinated commando action and air strike might be the way to go. "Let us move on, then, to consider the other alternatives listed. I shall now play the devil's advocate and state the question we would all be asked if a preemptive strike were to end in disaster: why take the risk? Why not simply continue to rely on deterrence, the demonstrated ability of our potent Air Force to lay waste to any enemy nation foolish enough to lob such missiles in our direction?

"When the Syrians fired seven Frog missiles at Tiberias in 1973, we retaliated by sending jets against military targets, including their headquarters in downtown Damascus. They got the message. That was the first and last time Syria launched missiles into our territory.

"So why not continue to rely on deterrence while accelerating our civil defense program as a hedge against some madman pushing the launch button? Meanwhile, we can pursue a long-term solution in the form of an anti-tactical-missile system."

As he had anticipated, a chorus of voices rang out in response to his tongue-in-cheek proposal. "What about Saddam Hussein?" Maydan protested heatedly. "Did the threat of retaliation stop him from launching Scud missiles at our cities?"

"That could be considered an aberration," Tuchler argued, enjoying the storm he was kicking up. "He knew our hands were tied by the Americans, that we couldn't strike back. He had nothing to lose."

"He'll find out how wrong he was on that score," Maydan snorted, "when we go in there and blow up Mosul." His observation was enthusiastically seconded by most of the others, with the notable exception of Barkai. Tuchler was still not sure where the Air Force boss stood.

"General Barkai, you are frowning. How say you to alternative number three?"

The diminutive general cleared his throat. "I'm afraid I don't have much faith in the long-range solution you speak of. Who knows when our Arrow anti-tactical missile system will be operational? Five years from now? Ten? Can we continue to rely on deterrence to protect us in the interim?

"I see two problems. First, deterrence, like beauty, is in the eyes of the beholder. As our enemies strengthen their defenses, they may come to believe that they have blunted our ability to retaliate, and may need to be reminded that it is still viable. That is why an occasional raid, such as the attack on the Osirak reactor, is almost a must.

"The second problem is that given enough time, our enemies will have stockpiled sufficient numbers of these missiles that a first strike will become attractive to them. Once they achieve nuclear warheads, they will have the wherewithal to wipe out all of our retaliatory forces in that initial strike."

"There is a third problem." All eyes shifted to the quiet

civilian, Mordechai Shilo. "Putting all our eggs in the deterrence basket would be playing into the hands of certain unscrupulous parties.

"Deterrence only works," he continued, "on responsible, civilized leaders whose concern for the welfare of their people outweighs all other considerations. But suppose one or more of these missiles were to fall into the hands of some unscrupulous terrorist sect? The threat of retaliation after their use of the missile against us means nothing. They have no population centers of their own to be concerned about; they could target our cities with impunity, could send us an ultimatum, demand anything! Without some defense against this kind of threat, we would be subject to the most heinous form of blackmail."

"Surely, Mr. Shilo, your hypothetical example is a very farfetched one," chided General Barkai with a condescending smile.

"On the contrary, it is neither farfetched nor hypothetical, as your chief of staff is well aware. Do I have your permission to continue, General Tuchler?"

The Chief of Staff considered, not certain how pleased he was with the direction his meeting was taking. It had been his intention to devote a separate session to the threat posed by the purloined Saudi-Chinese missile at a later date, when and if it surfaced in whatever hostile hands. He considered tabling the discussion. But it was a bit late for that—the matter was broached.

"You may proceed, Mr. Shilo."

"Some two weeks ago, a second shipment of Chinese East Wind missiles left Shanghai, bound for Riyadh. One of the missiles was hijacked from the cargo ship a week ago, near Singapore, along with its trailer-erector-launcher, by parties unknown. It was presumably transferred to another seagoing vessel in the Strait of Malacca. Thus far its hijackers have eluded all efforts to intercept them. Their whereabouts are unknown."

There were exclamations of surprise and shock from various attendees, including some expressions of indignation over not having been apprised sooner. Tuchler rapped for order.

"You would all have been informed shortly. We were waiting to see where the missile would turn up. There is still a good chance the hijackers will be caught. The Saudis have a massive search in progress. They are even using their AWACS."

His panel refused to be patronized. "What kind of warhead is in it?" demanded Maydan, the demolitions specialist.

"None, at the moment," Tuchler replied. "The missiles were shipped without warheads, which are transported separately. We have been assured by the Saudis that they are non-nuclear."

"Then the bloody thing isn't even armed!" laughed the Special Forces chief, looking relieved. The Air Force commander shot him a look.

"If they can steal a *missile* like the East Wind, Ephraim, I'm sure they can manage to steal a *warhead*.

"You mentioned terrorists," Barkai continued, addressing Shilo. "Is some known terrorist group in possession of this missile?"

"We have evidence that they are Palestinians, belonging to an al-Fatah splinter group," the Mossad director replied. "They call themselves 'The Sword of Islam.'"

Menachem Rafi, the Army Ordnance general, was shaking his head. Israel's own ballistic missiles, the Jerichos, were under his command. He was quickly recognized by Tuchler.

"Despite what you say, Mr. Shilo, I don't really see this as a major threat, even if the parties that hijacked the East Wind turn out to be hostile to us. Missiles such as these are extremely sophisticated and place heavy maintenance demands on their users. This would be even more true for the East Wind, with its touchy liquid-fueled propulsion. What terrorist group would have the technical know-how to deal with it, to say nothing of the facilities and support equipment? How would they get it properly deployed, prepared, programmed to hit a specific target? I seriously doubt that we have anything to worry about."

"Thank you, General Rafi," the Mossad director replied. "I will sleep better at night, knowing that. Of course, unlike the rest of you, I sleep in Jerusalem . . ."

"What are you implying?" Rafi demanded.

"Only what is obvious: Tel Aviv is almost certainly the target for this terrorist missile. They would hardly target Jerusalem, with its Islamic shrines and large Arab population. So, I urge you to take this threat seriously and concern yourselves with how you would counter it. The effort to locate these terrorists and this East Wind missile is being given a top priority in Mossad. It has been assigned the code name *Deuteronomy.*"

"Ma Salaami." Prince Bandar bin Sultan bin Abdul Aziz replaced the phone in its cradle and stared reflectively out the window of his Saudi Arabian embassy office at the rain-soaked verdure of Rock Creek Park. He had just spoken to Riyadh. Over a week since the hijacking and still no clue to the whereabouts of the culprits or their ship, despite the diversion of the AWACS to help with the search.

Using the AWACS had been his own suggestion and he still thought it a sound one. The radar plane had done a superb job of mapping the shipping in the Arabian Sea. Flying daily for four straight days, it had detected over two hundred ships and begun charting and updating their positions. The hitch was that there was no central "clearing house" with the capability of identifying these ships from their observed positions. Attempts to coordinate with various international maritime authorities had succeeded in establishing the identities of most of the ships observed, but that still left a considerable number of unknowns. Which one was the hijackers' vessel? Without a break in the weather to permit visual and photo-reconnaissance inspections from the air, there was no way of narrowing it down.

Bandar tugged at his stubby black goatee and wrestled with the decision he had put off, had hoped to avoid making. The acquisition of the Chinese East Wind missiles was a coup he had personally engineered, as everyone in the world was probably now aware. As his country's ambassador to the United States, this had put him in an awkward position. He had breathed not a word of the impending deal to his American diplomatic associates, even after the first load of missiles had been uncrated in Riyadh and installed in the vast Empty Quarter, some sixty miles south of the capital city of Riyadh.

The first inkling the U.S. had of the emplacement of the IRBMs had been from satellite photos, and the discovery had sent shock waves through the State Department. The U.S. had demanded the right to inspect the warheads of the newly emplaced missiles, a request to which King Fahd had not yielded, though giving assurances that the warheads were non-nuclear. Bandar's State Department colleagues had taken a dim view of what they regarded as sneakiness on the part of the Saudi ambassador. He had spent the last several years mending fences.

That fence mending had not involved the total candor for which his American counterparts might have hoped. Among other things, he had neglected to inform them that the deal with China had included a second installment of improved missiles. To go before them now, hat in hand, and admit to this further deception would be painful, to say the least, especially having to acknowledge that one of the giant missiles had been "lost" in transit. But he could see no alternative. Without the help of the U.S. Navy and their friends, the "Brits," with whom they cooperated, the missile's hijackers stood a good chance of getting away cleanly.

To what nefarious end might the stolen missile be employed? Whatever it turned out to be, he and his government would be blamed for it—would face world condemnation, in fact—unless they did everything in their power to recover the missile. There was only one way he could think of to insure that the thieves did not get away with their explosive cargo—a naval blockade. Saudi Arabia's own pitifully small Navy was not up to the task. He needed the Americans and the Brits.

The matter had been thoroughly discussed with King Fahd, who had given him *carte blanche,* placing the decision back on his shoulders. He had no choice. He sighed, picked up the phone again, and buzzed his secretary.

"Get me an appointment with Secretary of State Baker. I need to see him before the day is out. Tell his secretary that it's an extremely urgent matter. You can allude to a possible terrorist plot. That will get their attention."

9

ROUTE 1 BETWEEN Tel Aviv and Jerusalem, the most traveled highway in Israel, was also one of the most unpredictable, traffic-wise. On the bad days, the fifty-kilometer stretch from Ben Gurion Airport to the capital city could be stop and go all the way. If control-point road blocks were set up at or near the Latrun corridor, an eight-kilometer segment through West Bank territory, the delays could be even longer.

This was one of the good days, Daniella reflected, the speedometer needle holding steady at the ninety-kilometer mark. It had been like this since leaving Tel Aviv, and the West Bank stretch lay only a few kilometers ahead. If there were a roadblock, traffic would already be slowing. Her luck seemed to be holding; it had been quite a day.

She couldn't wait to set her new piece of evidence before Shmona and have the Mossad apply their tracing expertise to the phone number recorded on the slip of paper in her purse. Where would it lead them? Other than hinting at the momentous import of the assignment he had given her, her Mossad control had told her virtually nothing about what was going on. Perhaps now that she had proved herself he would.

She decided to go directly to Mossad headquarters instead of stopping at her apartment. David would probably not be there, anyway, would be back on the job despite his ordeal of the previous day. She had never liked the idea of her husband playing nursemaid to a Palestinian, even if he was, as David assured her, one of the "good ones." Like most Israelis, she had misgivings about any peace process that raised the prospect of an autonomous Palestinian state in her country's backyard. She could understand the resentment of many of her countrymen about being pressured by the United States to move in a direction contrary to their own best judgment and instincts. It should be their own decision to make; they were the ones who would have to live with it.

She and David had had words on the subject more than once; it was about the only thing they ever argued about. Being married to an American had its problems, especially one who was in the active employ of his government. He was so obsessed with his president's peace initiative that he couldn't see her point of view, couldn't understand that the way she looked at things was conditioned by a lifetime in the eye of the Israeli-Arab storm. Maybe if—

There was that same car again in her rear-view mirror. She had first noticed the silver Mercedes just after leaving Allenby Road, when it followed her onto the expressway, and had seen it several times since. It had crossed her mind that its driver might be tailing her, but she had told herself that she was letting her new cloak-and-dagger role go to her head. Now, however, she had to admit that he was acting somewhat suspiciously. He had drawn closer and had just followed her through a lane change.

She decided to test him, turning out of the fast lane and slowing down. He followed suit, pulling in behind her. She speeded up again, cutting back into the fast lane. Here came the Mercedes again, pulling up behind her even closer, as though the driver was afraid of losing her. In her rear-view mirror she could see him very clearly now, a well-groomed man with a young-executive look. If he is tailing me, she thought, he's not very experienced at it. It was an unwritten rule never to get close enough to make your quarry suspicious, let alone give him a good look at you.

How to lose him? She had an idea. Just ahead lay a major expressway interchange, where the road forked off in a northeasterly direction to the West Bank city of Ramallah. She would get into the right lane and signal for a turn onto the Ramallah off-ramp, then at the last second swerve back onto the Jerusalem expressway.

The Mercedes followed her into the right-hand lane, sticking to her like glue, its own right-turn signal blinking on and off. Her ruse worked like a charm. When she suddenly cranked the wheel left and accelerated, the Mercedes driver was too close behind her to recover in time and went plunging off onto the Ramallah ramp. He braked frantically, but it was too late, the heavy concrete divider separating him from the accelerating Simca. Watching the Mercedes, Daniella failed to notice when, even farther back, a battered van with a fresh coat of sky-blue paint came reeling back onto the expressway from the Ramallah turn lane.

While congratulating herself on losing her pursuer, she was disturbed by the incident. Who was in the Mercedes?; why was he tailing her? She searched her memory but couldn't recall seeing the man at or near any of the places she had visited today. Could Bareesh, the jeweler, have put him up to it? No, there hadn't been time . . .

The driver of the Mercedes was clearly not a professional at undercover work, which ruled out his being a fellow Mossad agent sent by Shmona to keep an eye on her. Nothing she could think of made any sense. Perhaps her control would be able to shed some light when she reported the incident to him.

The grade grew steeper as the expressway ascended higher and higher into the pine-forested Judean hills. She was approaching what had always been her favorite stretch of highway where the road traversed a scenic crest near the Arab village of Abu Ghosh, presenting a sweeping tableau of the countryside below. But drivers were well advised to keep at least one eye on the road; there were sheer drop-offs in many spots. It was here, several years previously, that a terrible "accident" had occurred when a Palestinian from Gaza seized the wheel of a heavily loaded bus from Tel Aviv, which subsequently hurtled over the edge. Fourteen Israelis had been killed, many more injured.

Daniella proceeded cautiously, staying in the slow lane and sneaking an occasional peek at the incomparable vista below. The late afternoon shadows were lengthening, the receding hills and valleys presented in gradations from deep purple to pale lilac. Her attention returned to the road, her eyes flitting up for a quick check of the rear-view mirror, and she saw a blue van bearing down on her. It was still some fifty meters behind but moving very fast in the same outside lane she was in, closing the distance rapidly. She eased over to the outside edge of the lane, giving it plenty of room to pass.

But it kept coming on in the same lane, showing no sign of pulling out to pass her, looming huge, now, in the rear-view mirror.

It was coming on her too quickly . . . At the last second, the van swerved onto the inside lane and drew abreast of her.

Her first quick, nervous glance revealed a driver with a gaunt, expressionless face that could have been chiseled out of stone, his eyes focussed rigidly ahead. She concentrated her own attention on the road, waiting for him to pass. Why didn't he go by? He had slowed to her own speed, remaining just alongside her.

She shot another glance in his direction. *His eyes! They were staring at her now. Eyes that looked cold. Dead.*

She hit the brakes a split second before the van driver spun the wheel. Instead of catching her broadside, the van only clipped the front fender as it came careening into her lane. But the impact was enough to send the Simca out of control, tottering precariously on the narrow shoulder of the road. For a sickening instant Daniella found herself staring off into empty space toward the valley floor hundreds of feet below, before she wrestled the car back onto the road. She pulled off the road and onto the shoulder and stopped, her hands shaking uncontrollably.

The blue van was not through with her. It screeched to a stop forty or fifty meters down the road and now began backing toward her, along the shoulder. Her own car had stalled. She tried frantically to start it. It wouldn't start and the van was picking up speed. The driver was going to ram her . . .

Get out of the car! But she couldn't get out of the driver's side; cars were whizzing by, precariously close. She threw open the door on the passenger side, grabbed her purse, and flung herself through the opening. In the next instant, the van collided with the Simca.

The impact sent the green sedan spinning over the edge of the embankment. It rolled over several times before reaching a point where the rocky terrain fell away precipitously, launching itself into space in an upside-down plunge that culminated in a brilliant orange ball of flame far below.

Daniella had meanwhile landed on the downslope of the shoulder, its loose gravel skidding out from under her feet. Losing her footing, she plunged headlong down the steep slope, tumbling in a runaway descent. She curled herself into a ball, still clinging fiercely to her purse with its precious clue inside.

Over and over she tumbled down the steepening bank in a bruising progression of somersaults down its rock-strewn course. One large boulder stood between her and the precipice that had claimed the Simca. Her head struck it and she blacked out.

Kareem stepped out of the van and walked around it to peer over the edge of the embankment. He saw the Simca resting upside down on the rocks far below, still burning furiously. The driver's door had not opened; she must still be inside. Mission accomplished.

He heard an approaching truck downshift and looked up to see a semi-trailer apparently preparing to pull over and investigate. Hurrying back to the van, he drove off quickly. It would be unwise for him to let anyone get a good look at him. If someone driving past had seen the van back into the car and knock it over the edge, they would likely report it. The van would have to go back to the garage for another new paint job.

He remembered the woman's face as he drove away. There was no mistaking her identity; she fit the description that the Voice had given him. A real beauty; too bad. But he felt no pity for her. She was Shin Beth, the Voice had said. His loathing for the Israeli secret police force knew no bounds, fed by countless incidents of brutality against his people.

He looked back at her car again, still engulfed in flames. Good. One more Zionist pig dead.

The sun had already set by the time David Llewellyn pulled the Land Rover into its assigned parking stall at his apartment house in West Jerusalem. He was surprised to see the Simca missing from the adjacent stall. Daniella should have been home by now. Her second day on the job, and she was already into overtime.

He'd been half asleep, still in the throes of the Gaza aftermath, when she'd informed him that morning that she had taken back her old job with the Mossad. Later, when it sank in, he had mixed feelings. It would give her something to do and make her feel that she was making a contribution to her country, which he knew was important to her. The danger was that a job like that could take over your life, if you let it. And he harbored a long-standing distrust and distaste for all spy organizations.

Out of sorts, he took the elevator up, let himself in, and poured himself a large Scotch. He was unaccustomed to being alone in the apartment; it seemed strange and empty without Daniella. What could be keeping her so late? The clock on the kitchen wall read 7:34. He needed something to distract him. There was still time to catch the evening news.

He had no sooner turned on the TV than the phone rang. Striding quickly across the room, he picked it up, expecting Daniella. Instead, it was a man's voice asking for her. The man did not identify himself.

"Not home yet," he answered curtly. "May I ask who's calling?"

There was a momentary delay before the man answered. "My name is Shmona, Mr. Llewellyn. I am one of your wife's business associates. May I inquire if you've heard from her since this morning?"

"No, not a word. I thought she was still at work. Is something wrong?"

"I shouldn't think so," Shmona replied smoothly. "Mrs. Llewellyn was in Tel Aviv today on business. She's probably just stuck in traffic. You know that expressway."

He not only knew it, he was staring at it. The TV evening news was showing pictures of it. Another wreck. *Wait a minute!* "Hold on, please—"

He dropped the phone and ran to the TV to turn up the volume.

". . . in the same precipitous spot where a red Egged bus from Tel Aviv plunged off the expressway in 1989, when a Palestinian terrorist seized the wheel. The auto, a Simca sedan, exploded in flames at the bottom of a deep ravine. An unidentified woman, thought to be its driver and lone occupant, was taken to Hadassah Medical Center in critical condition."

"Oh, God!" Llewellyn gasped, suddenly sick with fear for Daniella. He grabbed the phone, his head pounding, and managed to get out, "Hadassah Medical Center!" before sprinting for the door.

The medical center, part of Hebrew University, stood on a hilltop seven miles west of the center of town, normally a fifteen to twenty minute drive from the apartment. He made it in ten. The Land Rover screeched to a stop near the emergency entrance, and Llewellyn raced inside to the admissions desk.

"The lady who went over the side of the Tel Aviv expressway—where is she?"

The woman in the nurse's uniform didn't understand him. "Slower, please. My English—"

He tried again and finally got through to her. She directed him to the Intensive Care Ward in the north wing. "They may not let you see her," she warned as he ran off.

The Intensive Care receptionist was glad to see him. Her "Jane Doe" needed an identity. "You're the husband?"

He nodded, swallowing. "How is she?" he demanded.

"Still unconscious, but her vital signs are good."

"May I see her?"

"Sorry, it's against the rules."

"How can I be sure it's my wife if I don't see her?"

The receptionist considered. "All right, I'll take you in, but just for a moment. You can't stay."

He followed her through the door of the Intensive Care Ward, where there were two nurses on duty and a dozen or so beds, only a few of them occupied. The receptionist whispered something to one of the nurses, and he followed her and the receptionist to a bed in the far corner.

She was lying on her back, eyes closed, tubes sticking out of her, her head swathed in bandages. But he knew immediately that it was Daniella; there was only one face like that one. She looked very pale but appeared to be breathing normally. Tears sprang to his eyes. He thought of Katherine, his first wife, gunned down in London by a bullet meant for him. Losing her had been the hardest thing he'd ever faced. And now, Daniella . . . his other love. He couldn't—wouldn't—lose her, too. The thought was unbearable, the pain too great.

He bent over and kissed her lips and was promptly scolded by the nurse, who pulled him away. As the receptionist shooed him out, he stole a final look at Daniella before the door closed.

"She'll come out of it soon, won't she?" he asked quietly.

The receptionist took note of his moist eyes. "I'm sure she will. They almost always do." Almost? Almost wasn't good enough. Not for him, not for Daniella.

He was in the waiting room, filling out forms, when a short, bearded man walked in, wearing a rumpled suit that looked like it had been slept in.

"Mr. Llewellyn? I am Baruch Shmona." The handshake was firmer than David had anticipated, the eyes steady. "Have you seen her? How bad is it?"

He tried to sound more reassuring than he felt. "She's still unconscious but from what they've told me, in no immediate danger. No broken bones or internal injuries. 'Trauma to the head' according to the doctor's diagnosis. If she'll just regain consciousness they say she'll be okay." He couldn't quite keep the anguish out of his voice on the last note.

"How did it happen?" Shmona asked. "Was there a collision? Was her car struck by another vehicle?"

He shrugged. "All I know so far is what I heard on the newscast. Now I've got a question for you? Could this have something to do with her new job?"

The Mossad man colored slightly. "Why do you ask that?"

"Because, *goddam it,* Daniella's a good driver, a cautious driver, and she knows that route by heart. It's damn funny that something like this would happen right after she goes back to work for you. What kind of assignment was she on, anyway?

Shmona looked even more uncomfortable. "I can't discuss her work, not even with you." He changed the subject. "Did they find any of her personal effects, I mean besides clothing? Did she still have her purse?"

"I never thought to ask." Llewellyn walked out of the waiting room to the receptionist's desk, Shmona tagging along.

"Where would my wife's personal effects be?"

"I'll check." She disappeared and returned a minute later with a wire basket that she deposited on the counter in front of them. It appeared to contain nothing but articles of clothing.

Llewellyn sifted through them, Shmona watching intently. The coat of the green suit Daniella had worn to Tel Aviv lay on top, smeared with dirt and badly torn, the skirt beneath it in the same condition. Farther down were her stockings and lingerie. On the bottom of the basket was a single shoe; she must have lost the other.

"There's no purse here," Llewellyn complained to the receptionist. "Didn't they find her purse?"

"Probably not, sir, if it isn't in the basket."

Shmona was visibly disappointed. "May I look through the clothing?"

"Be my guest." David watched him go through the pockets of the suit. "Something particular you're looking for?"

"A note, intended for me. She phoned my secretary about it from Tel Aviv, left a message." He had turned out all the pockets and come up empty.

"What kind of note? What about?"

"Business," Shmona answered evasively.

Llewellyn was appalled. "You're a cold one, Shmona. Your colleague is lying in there unconscious, in a coma she may never come out of, and you're thinking about business?"

Shmona regarded him evenly. "That's unfair. I couldn't feel worse about what's happened to Daniella, but there's nothing I can do for her at the moment. Except to try to make sure that the breakthrough she achieved for us today on a crucial matter of national security doesn't go to waste."

"A national security matter, eh? I ask you again—was she in danger?"

The agent shrugged. "Danger goes with the territory."

"She was, wasn't she? And you probably didn't even warn her she was on a life-threatening assignment. I know how you people work—I was part of that scene for more years than I care to remember. You use people. And they're all expendable, aren't they? Even the most innocent. Especially the innocent," he added bitterly, thinking of Katherine.

"I tried to warn her this morning," Shmona protested. "I couldn't reach her."

"So it *wasn't* an accident. I knew it! Shmona, you had better get some protection over here. Until you do, I'm not leaving her side."

Shmona looked at the tile floor. "Someone will be here first thing in the morning. I'll stay myself until then."

Llewellyn wondered how much help the pint-sized agent would be in a real-life fracas. He probably wasn't even armed. Shmona was the cerebral type who stayed in the background while others took the risks, who manipulated the chessmen, sacrificing the pawns.

"It would help if you told me who's behind this. What kind of killers are we facing here?"

"I don't know. Even if I did I couldn't tell you. I've already said more than I should . . ."

The receptionist came in and told Shmona he was wanted on the phone. He returned almost immediately and turned on the television in the waiting room. Llewellyn went over and joined him. The late news was just coming on. The first film clip was a rerun of the earlier scenario Llewellyn had already seen, the burning sedan below the Route 1 highway, the commentary again reporting the unidentified woman driver's condition at Hadassah Medical Center as critical. But this time there was something more.

An eyewitness had come forward with the information that the auto that crashed and burned was deliberately pushed off the cliff by another vehicle. It was described as a blue van of uncertain make and vintage, with Israeli plates. No license number had been reported.

Nachman Malamud clicked the off button on his TV remote and the picture on the set built into his office wall faded to black. He snatched the phone off the hook and punched in a number. It went on ringing and ringing as his impatience mounted. Someone finally picked it up.

"Marhaba."

"Where have you been? I've been trying to reach you for hours."

"Doing your work, as you well know. And Allah's."

"Well, you botched it. The woman is still alive."

"Impossible! I saw her car burn up with her inside it."

"Wrong. She wasn't *in* it you idiot. She must have been thrown clear."

"How do you know this?"

"The late news. Didn't you see the TV news tonight?"

"No, I never watch it. It is filled with self-serving Zionist distortions."

His insolence rankled Malamud, but he ignored it. "This was no distortion. The woman was taken unconscious to Hadassah Medical Center in Jerusalem. She is in Intensive Care and said to be in critical condition."

"Then perhaps she will not survive."

"Perhaps is *not* good enough. Go to the hospital and finish the job. And do it before she regains consciousness and talks."

"As you wish. It would help if I knew the woman's name."

"The news didn't give her name. Apparently she hadn't yet been identified. I'm sure you can find her without it. And take care that you also find her purse. It may contain some damaging evidence."

"The purse will make things more difficult. It will take a little time to come up with a plan."

"It must be done *tonight!* We don't know how soon she will wake up. And one more thing—don't use your blue van. There was an eyewitness who saw it strike the woman's car and knock it off the cliff."

"The van is already being repainted. But I will do as you suggest."

"I will call again at eight in the morning. *Do not* disappoint me this time. Shalom."

"Ma salaami."

There were only the two of them in the Intensive Care waiting room. It was after two in the morning. Shmona had dozed off and was snoring softly. One of those fortunate people who could sleep anywhere, anytime, Llewellyn surmised. He had never been one of them. How could the man sleep, he wondered, after learning that the injury to Daniella had been no accident but a deliberate attempt on her life?

For his part, he was too charged up to even sit still. His

restlessness had sent him prowling the nearby corridors and alcoves looking for any sign of trouble, but never out of sight of the Intensive Care unit for more than a minute or so. Apart from the usual hospital sounds, the bell tones and paging over the PA system, all was quiet.

It was all he could do to stay away from the door to the Intensive Care Ward. He had been back once and been turned away, the nurse promising to call him promptly if there was any change in Daniella's condition. Returning to chat with the receptionist, he had found that she, too, was dozing at her desk. It seemed that the whole world was sleeping except for him.

Well, not quite . . .

As he watched through the open waiting room door, a woman came scurrying up to the reception desk and interrupted the receptionist's catnap. Her head was bound tightly in the dark shawl worn by religious Muslim women. The torrent of words she unleashed must have been in Arabic because the poor receptionist was shaking her head and holding up her hands to indicate that she couldn't understand. Signalling the woman to wait, she hurried to the Intensive Care Ward and returned with one of the nurses, who apparently did speak Arabic. A long exchange between them culminated in some emotional histrionics by the Muslim woman, who was finally led by the nurse to the Intensive Care Ward.

Llewellyn got up and sauntered over to the desk. "What's going on?"

The attendant smiled and shook her head. "I could hardly understand her. Apparently she is related to one of our patients who was brought in today—she showed me the name, written in Hebrew."

The nurse returned with the Arab woman, who was weeping distractedly, and helped her to a seat in the waiting room. Llewellyn walked the nurse back to her post. "Poor woman. She's been traveling most of the day to get here from Nablus. Her sister was brought in yesterday, suffering from a severe stroke. She, also, is still in a coma."

"I didn't realize you treated Arabs here at Hadassah."

The nurse raised her eyes. "Of course we do. And we have quite a number of Arab doctors, as well as nurses."

Arabs healing Jews, Jews healing Arabs. If only that spirit could spread outside the hospital. Opening the door for the nurse, Llewellyn sneaked another peek at Daniella. She looked like she was sleeping peacefully, but he knew that the coma still gripped her. He closed the door and walked back to the waiting room.

The Muslim woman was huddled sideways in her chair, partially facing the wall, attempting to isolate herself as much as possible from the strange surroundings. Her face was totally hidden by the tight shawl. Her arrival had apparently not disturbed Shmona's slumber. His desultory snoring continued.

When the day shift reported, at six in the morning, there was more commotion and the Mossad agent finally awakened. He sat up abruptly, rubbed his eyes and looked around.

"How's Daniella? Has she come out of it yet?"

Llewellyn shook his head. "Not yet. The nurse promised to let me know."

The Arab woman remained motionless in her chair in the corner of the room, apparently asleep. Shmona regarded her suspiciously.

"Who's that?"

"A Palestinian woman from Nablus. Her sister's in Intensive Care. She speaks only Arabic."

The receptionist came into the waiting room. "I'm going off duty now, Mr. Llewellyn. Good luck. I'm sure your wife will wake up soon and be just fine. Sorry about the purse. Perhaps someone will find it and turn it in."

David thanked her for her help and good wishes and she left. "That reminds me," Shmona observed. "I want to send a crew out to Abu Ghosh to look for it. The purse may be somewhere on that hillside. Can you describe it for me?"

Llewellyn frowned. "She was gone before I got up yesterday. With that green suit she wore, it would probably have been her green leather purse."

"What size?"

"Ample, but not gigantic." He held up his hands to show an average size purse.

The Mossad agent struggled to his feet, stretched, and ambled over to the reception desk to use the phone. But now he had to wait. While they'd been talking, the Arab woman had come silently to life and left the room for the same purpose. She now had possession of the phone and was speaking into it in a low voice just above a whisper. Shmona knew some Arabic but could catch no more than a word here and there. He drummed his fingers impatiently, waiting for her to finish.

The day-shift nurses arrived for the Intensive Care Ward and the two night nurses emerged, preparing to leave. The Palestinian woman hung up the phone and hurried over to the one who spoke Arabic, haranguing her in a whining voice. The nurse first shook her head, then finally caved in as the woman's persistence wore her down.

"She has to return home," she explained to the others. "She refuses to leave without saying goodbye to her sister." The nurse led the woman off toward the Intensive Care Ward while Shmona put through his call.

At that moment a new face appeared on the scene. It was the day-shift receptionist, young and fresh looking, wearing a smile as sunny as the morning that was dawning outside. Llewellyn introduced himself, explaining that it was his wife who had been brought in the night before.

"The woman whose car was knocked off the highway? What a dreadful thing! It was on the news last night. I was on duty when they brought her in. Such a beautiful lady, so unfortunate. She is still in a coma?"

He nodded glumly. She patted his arm. "Try not to worry. I saw the doctor's report. The prognosis is good. He expects her to regain consciousness within twenty-four hours."

She busied herself behind the desk. "I see you already have filled out a report. You'll probably be wanting your wife's personal effects."

He informed her that the night receptionist had already delivered them.

"And her valuables also?"

"Valuables?"

"A green purse, I believe it was. We looked inside, but there was no identification. I locked it in the safe."

Llewellyn was flabbergasted. "Why didn't the night receptionist—?"

"She's new. She probably didn't realize we lock up the valuables separately, and I forgot to tell her. I'll go and get it for you."

"What's that about a purse?" Shmona had put his call on hold.

"They've got Daniella's purse! It's been here all along, locked in a safe."

Shmona spoke a few more words into the phone and hung up, visibly excited. The receptionist was back almost immediately. "You'll have to sign for it. Right here."

While Llewellyn signed, the Mossad man eyed the purse hungrily. "May I—?"

"I'll do the honors, if you don't mind." He undid the catch and opened the purse, removing a comb, hairbrush, cosmetics case, compact, and a case containing a pair of sunglasses. There was no sign of her wallet; she must have had it out of the purse.

A small card spilled out and fluttered to the floor. Shmona pounced on it. It looked like some kind of claim check. He turned it over. There was a telephone number penciled on the back. What was it Daniella's message had said? "I have a phone number he'll want." This must be it!

Shmona's moment of triumph never registered on Llewellyn. He had removed another item from the purse, wrapped in a soft cloth bag, which he had emptied onto the desk. In trance-like disbelief he stared at the glittering article in front of him. It was a dead ringer for the two others he had seen, hanging around the necks of dead Fedayeen terrorists whose fanatical onslaught had twice almost killed him. What in the name of God was it doing in his wife's purse?

10

KAREEM HUNG UP the phone and left the booth near which he had been waiting since the wee hours of the morning. It had taken long enough, he reflected, as he climbed back into his car. But it had been worth the wait.

So there was no purse to worry about, after all. It had apparently been lost at the scene of the accident. That made things much simpler. He had directed his confederate to go forward with the plan. He would pick her up at the hospital's north-wing exit within the next five minutes. They would have another three minutes to clear the area.

Consulting his watch and mentally recording the count-down zero time, he started the car. This time there would be no slipups. This time the woman whose striking face he had glimpsed for one short moment would not survive. He had just now learned the name that went with the face, and it puzzled him. Llewellyn. It sounded British. He had assumed that the Shin Beth agent was a Jew.

David Llewellyn remained immobilized, as if hypnotized by the exotic piece of jewelry that lay in front of him. A hand reached over and captured it.

"I'll take charge of this if you don't mind." Llewellyn stared at Shmona as the explanation dawned on him. Daniella had been trying to trace it for Shmona, for the Mossad. She had uncovered something and now they were trying to silence her—the same killers he and Khalidy had tangled with in Jericho and Gaza . . .

He turned away from the desk, staggered by the discovery.

His eyes turned glassy, and they didn't see the Palestinian woman come out of the Intensive Care Ward and start down the hall. They were focussed on something infinitely farther away, that existed only in his mind's eye—the tall, rangy figure of the man he had seen near Gaza, an expressionless face and eyes set into it that were more dead than alive, that smoldered with murderous purpose. Was that the man who was after Daniella now? That man would not give up.

Slowly, his eyes, and the world, swam back into focus. The Arab woman was moving off down the corridor, having said goodbye to her sister and left the Intensive Care Ward where both the sister and Daniella remained in comas.

Something bothered him; something was wrong . . . What was it?

"Her purse!" he gasped. "She doesn't have her purse!" He sprinted toward the door of Intensive Care. "Stop that woman! She's—"

The woman heard and increased her pace without looking back. Now he *knew* he was right. He flung open the door to the IC Ward and plunged inside, startling the two day nurses who had just come on duty. "Sir, you can't—!"

"There's a bomb in here! We have to evacuate the patients. There's not a moment to lose!"

The nurses looked on in confusion as he hurried over to Daniella's gurney and began wheeling it toward the door. "Stop, sir! The IV stand!" The stand to which the intravenous tubes and other paraphernalia were attached was being dragged along and about to tip over. One of the nurses rushed to stop him.

"We have to evacuate, I tell you!"

"Do as he says!" echoed an authoritative voice. Shmona had just reached the ward, flashing an official-looking badge at the bewildered nurses. One of them complied, carrying the IV stand as Llewellyn hustled Daniella's gurney out the door and part way down the corridor.

He ran back into the ward as Shmona and the other nurse rolled another patient out the door. The bomb—he had to find the bomb!

He got down on all fours and spotted the large black purse next to the base of a pillar, partially hidden by it. It had been just under Daniella's head. Grabbing it by its handle, he raced to the far end of the ward and dropped it in the corner by the outside wall. He swept a mattress off one of the empty beds and draped it over the purse, seizing another mattress and another and piling them on. Shmona came running up.

"You found it? You found the bomb?"

"The mattresses may not help much, Shmona. We've got to get everybody out!" They helped the nurses roll out the last two occupied beds, rushing them down the corridor to the spot where the others were resting. Before they got there, the floor shook beneath their feet as though from a violent earthquake, as a heavy blast sent shock waves through the entire north wing. The overhead lights went out and the corridor was plunged into darkness.

Llewellyn groped his way toward Daniella's bed and found her hand in the darkness. It was like ice! He couldn't make out her face. He put his hand on her forehead. It felt a bit warmer.

"Are you okay?" The words popped out of his mouth before he remembered that she couldn't hear him, and he felt foolish. Something brushed his hand, a faint, fleeting touch. Had he imagined it, or was it . . . an eyelash? The light was abruptly restored as one of the hospital's back-up generators cut in. Daniella's eyes were wide open, staring up at him.

"David," she murmured. "Make them stop shaking the bed, David."

The general and the civilian sat on opposite sides of the long conference table in the Israeli Defense Forces War Room. There was no one else present in the vast room, dominated by a multicolored map of the Middle East, rear-projected onto a glass screen that covered most of the wall behind them.

Tuchler had begun by filling the Mossad director in on some late developments in the hijacking of the Saudis' East Wind missile. As usual, Shilo was several steps ahead of him, but pretended otherwise.

"It was Bandar who asked for the help of the U.S. Navy?"

The Chief of Staff nodded. "By way of the State Department, of course. King Fahd is apparently allowing Bandar to run the show. The missiles are his responsibility."

113

"He must have eaten a large dose of crow in the process," Shilo observed.

"Yes, I should say. Having to confess to a secret follow-on order for more missiles, after having been chastised by the Americans for not informing them of the initial purchase."

The pair had a good chuckle at the Saudi prince's expense before Tuchler continued in a more serious vein. "Now that the cat's out of the bag, it changes things for us, of course."

The other nodded. "How widely has the news been disseminated?"

"It's been pretty well contained so far, I believe. The British were told, of course; their Navy may participate in the blockade. We are apparently the only other government that's been informed, with Bandar's concurrence, I should think. Ambassador Arad was called in by the U.S. Secretary of State and apprised of the missile's hijacking, with a cautionary note about its possible appearance in the Middle East."

"Arad didn't let on that we already knew—?"

"No, no." Tuchler smiled. "He didn't know, himself. Your input was confined to the Prime Minister's closest advisors and the general staff."

"Well, it's only a matter of time, now, before word leaks out to the whole world, to the media. We'd better hope the hijackers are caught before that happens. Where will this naval blockade be established?"

"I have no information on that as yet. The AWACS has been searching a giant swath of the Indian Ocean between Sumatra and the Maldives."

Both men turned to look at the back-lighted map projection, Tuchler rising and striding over to indicate the sector of ocean under AWACS surveillance. "With every day that passes, of course, the search widens and extends farther west to allow for additional progress of the hijacking vessel."

"My God," Shilo muttered, "they can't blockade the entire Indian Ocean. The U.S. and Britain combined haven't that many ships."

"Precisely. That is why I believe we must play a certain card at this time—a card which only we hold. And I need your concurrence to do so."

Without comment, Shilo allowed the Chief of Staff to continue. "Thanks to your agency's discovery of the follow-on shipment of missiles and successful penetration of the merchant ship transporting them to Saudi Arabia, we have evidence of the connection between the hijackers and the Fedayeen. Evidence that strongly suggests that the hijacked missile is intended to pay us a visit."

Tuchler punched a code into a small control keyboard built into the wall alongside the giant map. A red circle appeared against the pale-blue background that defined the confines of Israel and the occupied territories amid its diverse-colored Middle East neighbors. The center of the circle was the city of Tel Aviv. The Chief of Staff continued to push buttons, and the circle expanded.

"Sixteen-hundred nautical miles. That is the nominal range, I am told, of this Dong Feng, the missile from China. I say nominal range, because I am informed by my experts that this range may vary somewhat, depending on the payload, the direction of launch, and the amount of loft in the trajectory. But let me set in the nominal range of sixteen hundred. There . . ."

The red circle had expanded to encompass virtually all of Saudi Arabia and Iran, passing just south of the entrance to the Red Sea at Aden and cutting across the Gulf of Oman to the southeast of the Persian Gulf. "To come within striking distance of our cities, the Fedayeen must deploy their weapon somewhere inside this circle. There are only two possible routes their ship could take—the Gulf of Oman and the Gulf of Aden. These are the spots where the naval blockade should be concentrated."

"So you propose to pass this advice along to the Americans?" At Tuchler's nod he pursed his lips. "That could get us into hot water. The first thing they will ask is to see the evidence, and we would be forced to admit that we have a spy aboard the ship transporting the missiles, have known about it all along, and haven't breathed a word of it to our American friends. And my agent is *still* on board. We would be placing him in jeopardy."

Tuchler frowned. "Really, don't you think the gravity of the situation warrants—?" The Mossad director held up his hand.

"There may be a better way. Approaching the Americans directly might take a lot of explaining. They have probably not even been told about the 'evidence'—the article lost by the hijackers. If the Saudis did show it to them, it would only have been to cast suspicion on our country as the likely perpetrators—the Jewish emblem on the pendant. In which case we'd have heard about it from the Americans. But we haven't, have we?"

The Chief of Staff looked mystified. "You're not suggesting we approach the Saudis with this? They would surely suspect a trick."

"No, we can't very well do that. But hear me out. Persuading the Saudis may be the key. And we can do that indirectly. I can pass the evidence along to my contacts in the CIA—a photograph of the sword pendant found on the dead Fedayeen terrorists and a statement of our suspicions that the same terrorist sect is responsible for the missile hijacking and our concern that the weapon is headed our way. I can arrange to have this information leaked to the Saudis by the CIA through their connections with Saudi Foreign Intelligence. Once they compare our photograph with the article found on the ship and see that they are identical, they're sure to reach the same conclusion we did."

Tuchler did some chin stroking of his own. "It could work. If it doesn't, we can always fall back on the direct approach. Agreed, then. You will inform the Prime Minister of your intent and get his blessing? Or shall I arrange a briefing through the Defense Minister?"

"It will be quicker if I do it. You can clear it through your boss in parallel." Shilo stood up, then sat down again, remembering some unfinished business.

"There is still the chance, of course, that despite the naval blockade, the terrorists will continue to elude their pursuers and get this weapon deployed within range of our cities. They have shown themselves to be extremely resourceful. If they are not caught soon and word of this threat leaks out to the press, it could create a panic. We will be bombarded with questions about the protection of our people. May I ask whether our previous meeting has borne any fruit?"

Tuchler erased the missile range circle and resumed his seat across the table. "I have asked General Rafi, under whose jurisdiction the anti-ballistic-missile mission falls, to perform a survey of in-house capabilities to deal with this terrorist missile and come forward with an emergency plan of action. He reports back tomorrow."

"Rafi, eh?" Shilo's faith in the Army Ordnance commander was less than total. Rafi was a plodder, inclined to do things by the numbers. What the situation called for was a crash effort to bring to bear the most innovative brainpower in the defense establishment on the problem. But Shilo had to be careful not to appear to be second-guessing the Chief of Staff. "Will there be others involved, as well?"

"Eventually there very well may. But I thought I would first see what Army Ordnance comes up with."

Tuchler had no trouble reading Shilo's meaning. He was aware of Rafi's limitations and had his own plan for dealing with them. He was already laying plans for a back-up effort by a separate agency to check out whatever assessment Rafi came up with.

A little competition could be very productive—if it didn't get out of hand.

"Captain! Come quickly! There is a patrol boat chasing us!"

The captain of the *Beirut Victory* shook himself awake and jumped into his clothes, expecting the worst. He might have known; things had been going too smoothly. After making landfall at Sri Lanka two days ago, his ship had moved into Indian territorial waters, plying its way up the Malabar Coast without incident. He felt comfortable in these waters, familiar to him from numerous prior excursions that had taken the tramp steamer to ports of call along its present route. And he knew that staying inside Indian territorial limits was his best safeguard against detection by ships and planes of other nations, which were not likely to violate the Indian boundaries.

Grabbing his hat, he followed the second mate out the door. It was an hour before dawn and still pitch black outside. The mate pointed astern, where the lights of another vessel were clearly visible, its blinker busily winking out a message. "See! It gains on us!"

The captain paused at the rail to read the blinker. It was an order to heave to, by authority of the Indian Coastal Patrol. He hurried to the bridge, considering his situation and options.

He had legitimate business in these waters, and his papers were in perfect order, including a bill of lading listing the cargo of heavy machinery loaded at Singapore and destined for Bahrain. The only real threat was the possibility that the Saudis had notified India to be on the lookout for the two hijacked lighter barges. That seemed unlikely, given what he knew about the strained relations between the two governments over the military alliance between Saudi Arabia and India's traditional enemy, Pakistan.

Reaching the bridge, the captain gave an immediate order to reduce speed and notified the signalman to answer the blinker and advise the Coastal Patrol vessel that his ship was complying with its instructions. "What's our position?" he inquired of the second mate, who was standing the graveyard watch.

"Fourteen miles due west of Bombay harbor." The mate pointed to the yellow glow along the horizon, off to starboard. Like Manhattan and Hong Kong, Bombay was an island city, and one of the busiest ports in the world. The captain had set a course running wide of the harbor mouth to avoid as much of the traffic as possible. Unfortunately, it hadn't avoided the Coastal Patrol.

The *Beirut Victory*'s progress through the light seas off the sheltered harbor slowed to a crawl as the patrol boat came swooping down on it from several points off the stern. A bright shaft of light reached out for them, finding the tramp steamer's bedraggled hindquarters and walking forward until its bridge was starkly illuminated. The captain squinted his eyes against the glare and watched the smaller vessel bear in on them from starboard and swing alongside.

A uniformed officer stood on its bridge, directing the action. He hailed the *Beirut Victory* over his public-address system, requesting permission to come aboard.

"Permission granted," the captain acknowledged over his own ship's address system. He saw no point in dragging his feet; any resistance would detract from the impression of a ship on legitimate business with nothing to hide. He gave

118

orders to have the boarding ladder lowered on the starboard side. A small launch detached itself from the patrol craft and motored across the gently rolling stretch of water between the two vessels.

The Indian officer was the first up the ladder. A seaman escorted him and his two companions to the bridge. He was polite, though rigidly formal as he introduced himself to the captain. "Where are you bound?"

"Bahrain."

"Your previous port of call?"

"Singapore."

"Why do you proceed through the territorial waters of India?" the officer inquired suspiciously. "There is a more direct route to the Gulf."

The captain was primed for the question. "We developed an engine problem off Sri Lanka. I thought we might have to put into Bombay for parts. But my machinist's mate was able to repair the damage."

The officer gave no indication of either believing or disbelieving the captain's reply. He asked to see the captain's papers and the ship's log, manifest, and bill of lading. After quickly perusing the first three and duly noting that the engine problem was recorded in the log, he concentrated on the bill of lading.

"Heavy machinery—sixty tons of it. We will need to have a look at your cargo."

"Is there something in particular you're looking for?" the captain inquired.

"What we always look for," the Indian replied. "Contraband. We will start in the number one hold and work our way aft."

The captain walked forward with the Indian contingent and accompanied them down the ladder into the hold. Sturdy wooden crates, some taller than a man and longer, were stacked neatly side by side. The Indian officer and his two assistants gave them only a cursory examination, thumping a few boxes and reading the information stenciled on their sides. "Let us move on to the next hold."

An array of boxes looking almost identical filled the number two hold. The inspection process here was even briefer.

"Let us move on," ordered the Coastal Patrol officer, apparently uninterested in the crates of machinery. It was as if he was looking for something specific. The captain began to perspire. It was the next two holds, numbers three and four, that held the two hijacked lighters. He rehearsed the explanation he would give as the party moved aft.

When the Indian officer caught sight of the huge metal barge sitting directly beneath the number three hatch, his eyes lit up. "What have we here? It looks like a standard lighter ship container. I don't remember seeing this on the bill of lading."

"Yes, yes—it is there." The captain helped him find the page on which he had had the entry of the two barges cleverly forged onto the original list.

"Oh, yes, I see it. There are two of them? Where is the other?"

"In the next hold—number four."

The officer frowned. "The contents are again listed as heavy machinery. The same as contained in the crates?"

"So far as I know."

"Then why are they in barges instead of crates?"

"It is my understanding that the barges are for a different customer. After being unloaded in Bahrain, they will be floated to their final destination."

The Indian's frown deepened. "I'm afraid I must ask you to open this one up."

The captain was aghast. "I can't do that! The barges are watertight. If I break the seal, they could sink in transit. And my company will be liable."

The Coastal Patrol officer was adamant. "I am empowered to inspect any article of cargo passing through Indian waters. I order you to open this container!"

The captain was equally obstinate. "I cannot do so. It would cost me my job."

Seconds ticked away as the Indian tried to stare the captain down. Then he barked an order to his men in a dialect the captain recognized as Hindi, though he didn't understand what was said. Was he being arrested? The two assistants were wearing sidearms.

But the pair didn't go for their guns. Instead, one of them

headed for the ladder leading up to the deck. "He will return presently," his superior explained. "Meanwhile, shall we move on to the next hold?"

The situation in the number four hold was similar, the giant lighter reposing directly beneath the hatch, blocking access from the hatch to the other cargo stowed around it. "Clearly, the barges were the last cargo to be loaded," commented the Indian. "May I inquire why?"

The captain's manner said the answer should have been obvious. "We had no choice. They are too large to be stowed anywhere else but in the space under the hatches."

As the officer was about to reply, the captain was startled to hear canine noises from the deck above, the excited whining and yelping of a dog. There were no dogs on his ship. He stared upward in surprise as a large police dog came plunging down the ladder, the man from the Indian Coastal Patrol, clinging to his leash, hardpressed to keep up with him.

The officer beamed. "Permit me to introduce Krishna, one of my most valuable assistants. He has a nose for his work second to none. Over here, Krishna."

The man who had been dispatched back to the patrol boat for the dog led it over to the immense lighter. Immediately, the sniffing began, the police dog working the barge, moving counterclockwise around it at a brisk pace, its tail wagging incessantly. The captain's initial amazement turned to amusement as the explanation dawned on him. He knew that dogs were widely used to sniff out narcotics and had also heard that their keen sense of smell could pick up the scent of explosives. The Indians were looking for one or the other or both. Fortunately, the lighter barges contained neither.

When the canine's circumnavigation of the lighter was completed without incident, the Indian officer gave a sign to the man at the end of the leash. Together, they scooped up the dog and lifted it atop the barge, a good two meters above the floor of the hold. Krishna whimpered a bit but then got down to business, crisscrossing the upper surface of the metal structure with his snout lowered, like a hound trying to pick up the trail of a rabbit. He returned a minute or so later, perched on the edge of the giant container, and jumped easily back down to the floor of the hold, coming back to lift his leg and christen the object of his attentions.

That, apparently, was his seal of approval. The Coastal Patrol officer, looking disappointed, returned the bill of lading to the captain with a perfunctory "thank you" for his cooperation and an apology for the inconvenience. Not at all, the captain told him, he had his job to do. He reached down and gave Krishna a pat on the head.

Minutes later, the Indian boarding party were back on their patrol boat and the relieved captain had given the order for full speed ahead.

Another relieved party had been monitoring the activity from the ship's forecastle. Watching the lights of the patrol boat recede into the night, the man with the limp descended to the main deck and made his painstaking way along the rail toward the bridge. The captain had led him to believe there would be no problem as long as they remained in Indian waters. It now appeared that he had been right. The boarding inspection was apparently routine, the appearance of the dog a sure sign they were checking for narcotics or munitions.

The coast of Pakistan, no more than a day's cruise ahead, might be an entirely different matter. If the Saudis informed any government to be on the lookout for their hijacked missile, it figured to be their fellow Sunni Muslim country, to whom they had awarded a lucrative military assistance pact. The captain, he knew, was planning to give the Pakistan coast as wide a berth as possible, avoiding its territorial waters entirely. The strategy was not without risk; it would expose the ship to overflights by planes of other nations and subsequent searches by their warships, if some sort of international blockade were to materialize. But there had been no indication as yet of any such cooperative effort. Every indication was that the Saudis had not yet gone public; there had been no breath of the missile hijacking on the radio news programs he and the captain listened to several times daily.

The stars winked down at him, incredibly bright out here on the ocean on a moonless night, reminding him that the weather, which had been such a faithful ally, was no longer on his side. The skies had been clearing since dusk the previous day. When dawn arrived shortly, the *Beirut Victory* would be exposed to the view of any aircraft that might be searching for it.

The thought was disturbing. There was no doubt in his mind that the Saudi AWACS had a plot of his ship's present position. It was the ship's identity the Saudis didn't know. But a closeup overflight in clear weather would establish that identity, not in itself a dead giveaway, since the tramp steamer had legitimate business in these waters. Its Singapore departure, however, might be found suspicious by the Saudis. It had been in the wrong place at precisely the wrong time.

He reached the ship's superstructure containing the galley, ship's stores, machine shops, crew quarters, and officer quarters, topped off by the bridge. It was almost time for the early morning newscast, a daily event that he and the captain always shared. Yesterday's broadcast had brought bad news—another failed attempt, near Gaza, on the life of Ibrahim Khalidy. What could have gone amiss in the execution of his painstakingly prepared plan, with Kareem there to direct it?

The information in the broadcast had been sparse. One "terrorist" had died, the others had escaped. He had expected an encoded wire from Kareem by now with the full story; it should arrive soon. Unless, Allah forbid, it was Kareem who had perished.

He climbed the ladder and made his way to the captain's cabin. The captain greeted him in good spirits, relating with amusement the activity in the hold, culminating in the dog's act of urination. "Dogs!" he chortled. "That's why I don't carry contraband anymore." His irony succeeded in coaxing a weak and fleeting smile from his laconic companion.

The news was just coming on. They listened with increasing impatience as the newscaster covered an earthquake in Bolivia, a plane crash in Italy, and a tour of America by the Prince and Princess of Wales. Not even a hint of the hijacking of the Saudi missile. But another item riveted the crippled man's attention.

"Violence erupted in Israel again early this morning, when a terrorist bomb exploded in Jerusalem's Hadassah Medical Center, severely damaging one wing of the structure. There is no casualty count available at this time, but it is reported that the famed stained-glass murals of Marc Chagall were undamaged. The bombing of the hospital, which serves both Jews and Arabs, is being universally condemned by Israeli and Arab leaders alike. This latest act of terrorism has been linked to the same terrorist group believed responsible for the recent attempts on the life of Palestinian peace-plan negotiators."

Kareem's work? If so, this was a venture he hadn't approved. Could Kareem be freelancing?

The captain switched off the radio. "No news is good news, as they say. Ready for some breakfast?"

"Yes, but first I must compose a message. Could I trouble you for pencil and paper?"

He scrawled out the text of the message to Kareem, encoded it, and tore up the uncoded version. "I'd like this to go out immediately."

"Fine," the captain agreed. "We'll drop by the radio room on the way to the galley. You expecting an answer?"

The other nodded his head. There had better be an answer. And it had better be a good one.

11

IT WAS MIDMORNING. High above the sparkling blue sea the stone-paved central plaza of Old Jaffa was already filling up with tourists as the unmarked sedan with red plates drove past the venerable lighthouse and climbed to the top of the hill. A short man with a beard emerged from the back, spoke a few words to the driver, and hurried up the cobblestone steps that led through a picturesque archway into the Artists Quarter. Inside, a maze of narrow alleys lined with shops, art studios and galleries meandered through the rebuilt stone structures of the Turkish occupation.

Baruch Shmona walked past a succession of show windows, turned right through another arch, then left down a connecting alley. Slowing his pace, he fell in step with a cluster of window-shoppers strolling languidly past the beckoning storefronts. He paused to inspect the window of an art gallery, then entered the shop, stopping in front of a large seascape that dominated the wall on which it hung.

He was immediately joined by a young lady in an artist's smock. "Exquisite, isn't it? It's by one of our most prominent local artists."

"Not my taste, I'm afraid. Where's Inspector Ben-Ezra?"

Her eyes did a quick reappraisal of him. "He's been waiting for you. This way, sir."

He followed her through a doorway that led to a back room. A solidly built man in plain clothes was standing on a chair, peering out a small window high up on the facing wall. Shmona had never met the man and was not overjoyed about having to work with the Shin Beth, the Israeli equivalent of the FBI. But sometimes it was unavoidable, particularly on domestic investigations where the Mossad was shorthanded. He had been involved in joint operations before. The problem was to avoid letting them take over.

"Ben-Ezra? I'm Shmona."

The man on the chair turned, nodded, and came down to shake hands. "Not much to report, I'm afraid. We've had the place under surveillance since 7 A.M. There's been no traffic in or out. I've got two men watching from the other side."

Shmona climbed up on the chair to have a look. Because of his short stature, he had to stand on his tiptoes to see out. The window looked out across a tiny courtyard onto the back of a row of shops on the next alley over. One building projected farther into the courtyard than the others, with a door and window opening onto it.

"That's the place—with the green door?"

The Shin Beth man answered affirmatively. So this was the address that corresponded to the phone number Daniella had obtained from the jeweler. There was no sign of life in the courtyard, and he could see nothing through the opposing window.

"Is it connected to the shop in front?"

"We can't be sure. They're separate addresses. The gift shop hasn't opened yet. There's a sign in the window that says it opens at nine."

Shmona consulted his watch. It was already after ten. "Have you interviewed any of the neighbors?" he asked, getting down off the chair.

"Not yet. Didn't want to tip off our presence in case the suspect showed up. Say, who is he, anyway, and what's he done? I didn't get properly briefed."

Shmona ignored the question. "We've waited long enough. Can you get me inside?"

"Sure, but I thought your priority was to place the suspect under surveillance."

"He isn't coming."

The inspector frowned. "If you knew that, why did you let us waste our time—?"

"I didn't know it until now." He saw Ben-Ezra's frown deepen. "The fact that the shop in front didn't open. The

126

proprietor probably knows the suspect, was warned to stay away. Either that, or he and the suspect are one and the same."

Ben-Ezra grinned. "Okay. I like to play hunches, too. So we go in right now?"

"Let's go."

The rear window was no more help from close up, not enough light inside to see by. Shmona hammered on the door. When there was no answer, he put his ear to the window and listened for a moment. "Not a sound. In we go."

"The lock doesn't look like much of a challenge," Ben-Ezra commented, inserting a plastic card between the latch and the doorframe to slip the bolt. He turned the knob, but the door refused to open. "Must be a deadbolt."

He produced a ring of keys and tried them all without success, taking refuge in a mild Yiddish curse. "I'd better get my lock expert. He's out front, watching the shop."

The expert had no trouble at all, using a small piece of wire to pick the lock. The door opened on a single large, vacant room, totally bereft of furniture. Their footsteps made a hollow sound on the bare limestone floor as they entered. Shmona found a light switch and flicked it on, using his handkerchief to preserve any latent prints. Wan light from a low-powered bulb in a recessed ceiling fixture illuminated the room.

His eyes panned across bare walls unadorned by pictures. "Looks like some kind of an office." There was a phone jack at either end of the room; the phones had been pulled. The room appeared spotless, as though recently cleaned. He bent down and ran his finger along the floor. No dust.

"Clean as a whistle," the inspector observed. "Somebody knew we were coming, for sure." Shmona crossed the room and pushed open a door. The closet behind it had several shelves. His finger test confirmed that they had been wiped clean. The only other door opened into a small toilet. It, too, looked immaculate.

"How soon can your crime lab people get here?" Shmona asked.

"Today—this morning. I've already alerted them."

"Good. Let's get them up here." The lab experts were magicians at finding evidence that escaped the naked eye. The trouble was, they took too long doing it. He needed something more immediate to go on; he couldn't afford to let the trail grow cold.

"Meanwhile, why don't we get your men to start interrogating the proprietors of the shops nearby. We're looking for names and descriptions of the occupants and any frequent visitors, or anything else they might have noticed out of the ordinary."

"It would help if I knew a bit more about this case," the Shin Beth man complained. "The division chief laid on a national security priority, but there was no explanation. What's going down here? Something to do with that Hadassah Hospital bombing last night?"

Shmona shrugged. "Search me. They didn't tell me much, either, except to put this place under surveillance and arrest the occupants. Must be tight security."

The inspector's look said he didn't believe him. Shmona ignored it. His best chance of maintaining the upper hand was to keep the Shin Beth in the dark as long as possible. He would feed them information only in dribbles, as necessary.

"While you're calling the crime lab, your men and I can start talking to the neighbors. I suggest we split up. We can work faster that way."

Shmona couldn't believe it. It appeared that none of the proprietors in the nearby shops had ever laid eyes on the occupant of the recently cleared-out office behind them. Its rear egress through the small courtyard between alleys made it possible for the occupant to come and go without passing their shops. None of the those questioned could remember seeing him.

There was one ray of hope—the gift shop adjacent to the office that had still failed to open its doors. One of the other shopkeepers had supplied the name of its proprietor and they had found a listing in the phone book, with a residential address at the north end of town. After a phone call had failed to raise anyone, Ben-Ezra had dispatched one of his men to the address.

Shmona motioned to Ben-Ezra to join him. "There's another possible tie-in with the suspect that needs pursuing—a jeweler over on Allenby."

He was starting to feel uneasy about the jeweler, Bareesh. He should have had the man picked up immediately for questioning. "Let's go pay him a visit."

It was only a ten-minute ride to the address on Allenby Road. At the sight of the steel security shutters across the shop window, Shmona chastised himself for not acting sooner. Another bird had flown.

He decided to have a look inside anyway. Ben-Ezra had his skeleton keys out. This time the first key the inspector tried opened the door. And why not? It had not even been locked.

Shmona pushed it open. "Mr. Bareesh?" There was no answer. They went inside.

It was instantly apparent that the place had been looted. Shards of glass were scattered across the floor from a display counter that had been shattered in several places. The jewelry cases inside were askew and mostly empty. Shmona shouted the jeweler's name again and pushed through an open door that led to the workroom in back of the store.

A man wearing a yarmulke lay on the floor, motionless, on his back. Shmona couldn't see his face. "Bareesh?" No response. He drew closer.

Behind thick glasses the eyes were wide open, staring. Whatever they had seen, in their last seconds as functioning organs, Shmona would never know. The man was clearly dead. If this was the craftsman of the scimitar pendants—and Shmona had no doubt that it was—he would not be identifying the customer who had placed the order. A customer to whom his silence was even more golden than the glittering pieces he created.

David Llewellyn sank into the familiar contours of his high-backed office chair and reflected on how infrequently he had occupied it during the preceding two weeks. He wouldn't have been here today if Ambassador Abrams, himself, hadn't tracked him down and called him at the hospital. "We need to talk," he had said bluntly. "I'd like to see you at the embassy as soon as possible."

Llewellyn had had some qualms about leaving Daniella's side, especially after all that had happened. But she no longer required intensive care and had been moved to a private room in another wing. She was sleeping peacefully and her nurse had assured him there was no reason for him to stay—after all the trauma, Daniella would probably be asleep for hours. In the wake of the bombing, Hadassah Medical Center was bristling with soldiers armed with assault rifles, and one of them was camped just outside her door. So he had left her in good hands.

His intercom buzzed and he picked it up. "The ambassador is ready for you now, Mr. Llewellyn." His secretary, a young American girl, had looked at him with awe when he showed up this morning. "We've been hearing all kinds of stories. I have a million questions to ask you. And a million papers for you to sign." For the office grapevine, the reports of his terrorist exploits would have been choice fruit. "Later," he told her.

The ambassador rose from behind his desk and came around to shake hands. Almost a head shorter than Llewellyn, Abrams looked him over with concern. "You don't look too much the worse for wear. A little puffy around the eyes, perhaps."

"I think I could sleep for a week, sir, if I had the time."

The ambassador motioned him into a chair and went back to his own. "How's Daniella doing?"

"Much better, sir, now that she's out of her coma. The doctor says she'll soon be on her feet. They're keeping her another twenty-four hours for observation."

"That was a close call. Dangerous stretch of road out there on Route 1. There've been some terrible accidents. The Israelis should really build some retaining walls along there."

"We both know it was no accident, sir."

"Yes, I daresay. A blue van, wasn't it? Any leads on its driver?"

"The police are working on it. Nothing yet, as far as I know." He didn't elaborate. Abrams wasn't supposed to know about Daniella's Mossad affiliation, though embassy security had probably learned of it and informed him. He changed the subject. "Any word from Khalidy?"

"As a matter of fact, I just spoke to him." The ambassador

smiled and shook his head. "The man is unbelievable. After those two close calls, he's still raring to go. He called my office in great distress. It seems that the Israelis have grounded him, at least until the threat from this new terrorist group subsides. He had excursions planned to Ramallah and Nablus. They've been postponed indefinitely."

Llewellyn was relieved to hear it. "What did he want from you?"

"He was hoping our government could pressure the Israelis into lifting the restrictions."

"You didn't agree, I hope?"

"Certainly not. He should have been grounded after that first incident in Jericho. If it hadn't been for your presence there, and at Gaza—" The little man's lips formed a grim line. "If the Israelis hadn't acted, I don't see how I could have, in good conscience, permitted you to accompany Khalidy again, no matter what the President's wishes on the matter. Until those terrorists are dealt with, it's entirely too dangerous out there. We can't afford to lose you. Good envoys don't grow on trees, you know."

Llewellyn sensed that the ambassador was leading up to something. "I know the last thing you need after what you've been through is another crisis, but unfortunately these flaps make their own schedules. This information is not to go beyond these walls, is that clear? If it got out, there could literally be panic in the streets."

Llewellyn nodded.

"The term 'loose cannon' comes to mind," Abrams continued. "But there has never been a cannon in the Middle East to compare with this one." The ambassador went on to give him the complete rundown on the hijacking of the Chinese missile and the Saudi failure to recover it.

"A Chinese ballistic missile? Part of that new shipment of East Winds the Saudis ordered?"

The ambassador nodded his head.

"But those things are huge . . . How could one be hijacked?"

"Unbelievable as it may be, it happened. The Saudis believe it was loaded onto another ship and is probably headed for the Middle East—may, in fact, already be in the vicinity. They've been looking for it with their AWACS. They finally decided to get help from the U.S. Navy. Their ambassador called the State Department and informed them. That's how I learned about it. State is afraid this may become a threat to U.S. nationals in Israel and wanted to alert us."

"Threat? I don't see—Do the Israelis know about this?"

"They were notified by us, with King Fahd's concurrence, as long as they pledged to keep the secret. The Israelis suspect that the hijackers are Palestinian terrorists. They think it's a blackmail weapon for use against Israel. The CIA thinks so, too."

"Blackmail? Has there been a threat? Do they have any evidence—?"

Abrams handed him a sheet of paper. "Do you recognize this? Yes, I see by your face that you do."

Llewellyn stared at the paper. It was a photostat of a photograph.

That same piece of jewelry.

"How could I not recognize it? It's the amulet found on the dead terrorist in Gaza. Or one just like it, that turned up on one of the dead assassins in Jericho." And, he thought, it's also just like the one in Daniella's purse . . .

"I got this photo from Hendrickson."

Hendrickson was the CIA man attached to the embassy. "So?"

"The CIA got it from their friends in Saudi intelligence. This particular piece of jewelry was found aboard the *Oceania*, the cargo ship carrying the Chinese missiles to Riyadh. It was discovered just after the hijackers left the ship. It did not belong to anyone on the ship's crew. It was lost by one of the hijackers."

By one of the *hijackers?* Llewellyn stared at the ambassador. That meant . . . the terrorists in Gaza, the ones in Jericho, and whomever Daniella was involved with were all connected . . . connected to a plot that was getting more ominous by the second! Some, or all of them, were in possession of a weapon that could raze an entire city!

"Does the missile have a warhead?" he asked, still reeling from the implications.

"Apparently not, thank God. The Saudis have assured us that their East Winds do not use nuclear warheads and that the missiles were shipped without warheads of any kind. But who knows what other resources these maniacs may have available? Even if they can't get their hands on a nuclear device, who's to say they can't latch onto one of the chemical or biological warheads being produced in Libya and Iraq? Can you imagine what the casualties might be if such a thing were lobbed into greater Tel Aviv?"

Llewellyn could. He could also imagine the panic that would ensue if word of the threat leaked out. "We'll have mass hysteria on our hands if this story ever breaks . . ."

"Indeed. That is why we must be ready. Do you know how many U.S. citizens there are residing in Israel? My estimate is at least fifteen thousand, not counting the tourists who are here for a few weeks or less. We've got to prepare for the worst. If this threat escalates and gets into the press, every available flight out of here will be booked. The airlines will be swamped. Americans will be beating down the doors of the embassy to arrange transportation out of here. And rightly so. They are our responsibility."

"We'd have to arrange a special airlift." Llewellyn was thinking out loud. "Both civilian charters and military transports, like the evacuation of Saigon."

"*Not* like Saigon, one would hope. They waited too long, and everything was compressed into a final few hours of total panic. We can't let that happen here. That's why I want you to take charge of the problem right now. Start laying plans, lining up charter flights with the airlines on a contingency basis. Check with the Air Force on the availability of some of their giant troop carriers."

Llewellyn was appalled at the suggestion. "Sir, do you think that's such a good idea? What reason could I give them? Even a hint of what's going on could start rumors, cause the story to break prematurely. And can you imagine the effect on the Israelis if word leaked out that the U.S. government was planning to evacuate all their citizens, like rats from a sinking ship?"

Abrams refused to back off. "Don't give them any reason, then; don't even hint at the real reason. Tell them it's just an exercise, to find out what their response time would be if another Yom Kippur War were to break out. I'm relying on you to find a way to do this without arousing undue suspicions."

It was clear to Llewellyn that putting his request to the airlines in a hypothetical light would destroy the credibility of their responses. The companies might promise anything if they thought they wouldn't have to deliver. But he could see that he would get nowhere arguing with the ambassador, whose mind was clearly made up.

"Sir, may I ask something? Does the White House concur in this?"

"Unquestionably. I spoke directly with the Secretary of State. It was his concern about possible danger to our citizens here that led him to call me. And I have no doubt that the President, himself, is fully aware of the situation."

"What are the Israelis doing about the situation? They have a much bigger problem that we do."

"I have no way of knowing, but I would assume that they're taking a hard look at their civil-defense preparedness and at any possible way of intercepting this missile, if worst comes to worst and it does get fired their way. And, like us, they're probably praying very hard that our naval blockade will turn up the ship carrying the missile before it gets deployed."

The ambassador stood up to indicate the meeting was over. "I'll let you get on with your new assignment. I will expect a report tomorrow morning on your progress."

Llewellyn returned to his office and flopped down in his chair, disregarding the entreating look on his secretary's face for some consultation time. What was he going to do? He couldn't refuse a direct order from his superior, backed up by the Secretary of State. But he felt in his heart that pursuing a plan to evacuate U.S. citizens from Israel would be a grave mistake. A wholesale exodus of Americans from Israel at a time of crisis, concerned first and foremost with their own skins, could destroy the very spirit of cooperation between the two countries he had worked so hard—risked life and limb—to promote.

He just hoped—prayed—that the U.S. naval blockade would snare the phantom ship and its deadly cargo before an evacuation became reality.

12

COMMANDER ABRAHAM LINCOLN "Greasy" Spooner, captain of the destroyer *Lawrence,* watched the bow of the ship climb over the crest of a towering wave and braced himself for the descent into the trough. Like an elevator suddenly dropping several stories, the bow fell back toward the sea, taking his stomach with it. Wham! The impact of the hull slamming against the water sent shock waves through the ship.

"Ease off a couple of points to starboard, Mr. Owens," he instructed the helm. The sea was running heavy. If he had his choice, he would have slacked off a few knots on his speed. But his orders were to proceed to his assigned station at flank speed. Not that he had any qualms about his ship; it was built to take a pounding. Its crew was another story. If the heavy going continued, there would be a lot of sick seamen aboard the *Lawrence* before the day was out.

The *Lawrence* and its sister destroyer, the *Comte de Grasse,* were part of the USS *America* Battle Group, assigned to the Indian Ocean. Included with the 79,000-ton carrier and the two destroyers were the Aegis cruiser *Mobile Bay,* the missile cruiser *Dale,* and the frigate *Joseph Hewes.* It was only the two destroyers that had received the crash orders to weigh anchor immediately and deploy to stations some five hundred nautical miles to the west, outside the Gulf. There they would kick off a new action, designated "Operation Chain Link." The remainder of the battle group would join up with them within forty-eight hours.

The new action was aptly named. A fence was, indeed, what FleetOps had ordered, one which would keep some renegade vessel from penetrating into the waters of the Gulf of Oman or on into the Persian Gulf. He wondered what kind of idiot had dreamed this one up.

The plan called for the positions of ships in the vicinity to be handed over to the destroyers by data link from the Combat Information Center aboard the carrier *America*. From a link with the Navy Ocean Surveillance Satellite the CIC could monitor ship positions in the vicinity and also derive speed and direction information. The trouble was that the satellite sensor's resolution was not adequate to do any sort of ship identification or classification, all ships looking pretty much the same to it. Nor was the destroyer's own radar much better. Having found a ship on its radar, the *Lawrence* would have to overhaul the vessel and do a visual identification. After passing the ship's name and registry back to the CIC, the destroyer would be advised whether or not to board and search a particular vessel.

It was clearly impractical for the two destroyers to intercept and search every merchant vessel bound for the Gulf. The CIC was relying on a hookup with the ground station controlling the Saudi Arabian AWACS to help screen out the majority of the ships. The Saudis, Spooner had learned, had already been working on the problem and had obtained information from worldwide maritime services on the names, cargos, and ports of call of much of the shipping in the area. Even so, the *Lawrence* skipper felt certain, it was going to be a crapshoot.

The destroyer continued to take a pounding from the heavy swell. Four more hours of this before they reached their station. Spooner hadn't been seasick since his plebe days, but his stomach didn't feel too good at the moment. He decided to go below for a nap.

"Take over, Mr. Owens. I'm leaving the bridge."

Three and a half hours later, the captain was back on the bridge. He had slept only fitfully, the wind having shifted to the point where the bucking of the destroyer in the still-heavy seas had turned into a half pitch, half roll, the worst combination for queasy stomachs.

Lieutenant Commander Owens was looking a bit green around the gills, himself, as Spooner appeared on the bridge.

His watch wasn't up for another half hour. "What's our position, Mr. Owens?" the skipper inquired.

"We're eight miles short of our assigned station. My ETA is 0932." Spooner looked at the ship's clock. Twenty-two minutes away.

"Any further input from CIC?"

"Four updated ship positions came in. Mr. Engel has them. He already has radar contact with two of them."

"I'll take the con, Ed. Go below and get some rest."

"Thanks, skipper." Owens gave him a wan smile of gratitude as he crossed the bucking bridge, clinging to the bulkhead to keep his balance, and disappeared through the open hatchway.

The captain peered over the helmsman's shoulder to check the compass heading, then walked over to the radar station, where Engel was bent over the hooded scope. He picked up the computer printout lying on the desk and scanned it.

"Four fucking targets. And twenty to forty miles apart! How the shit do they expect us to intercept all of these?" He flung the paper back on the desk.

Engel pulled his head out of the scope. "I was hoping you'd have the answer to that one, skipper," the communications officer observed with a smirk. He was young and relatively green and could be a pain in the ass at times with his sarcasm, but he knew his stuff. "I just got number three on radar. Take a look."

Spooner put his eyes to the hood opening. There were four blips showing. The closest one, off to port, would be the *Lawrence*'s sister destroyer. The nearest of the others was twenty miles away, 120 degrees to starboard, a fair-sized ship, judging from the intensity of the blip, which saturated each time the antenna scanned by. Another ship lay thirty miles beyond it, and a third, slightly farther to starboard, at a range of seventy miles, near the outer limit of the radar's coverage. According to the satellite data relayed by the CIC, they were all bound in a westerly direction, toward the opening to the Gulf.

"We'll make for the nearest one immediately." He saw no point in waiting until they reached the exact Lat-Lon in the redeployment orders. "Notify the CIC and the *de Grasse* that we're altering course to begin the chase."

"Aye, sir." Engel picked his way toward his communications station, steadying himself against the bridge's forward bulkhead as he went. Spooner sat down at the navigator's desk and plotted the new heading that would place the *Lawrence* on a collision course with the unknown ship, which was moving west-northwest at eighteen knots, according to the CIC input.

"Prepare to alter course. Come thirty-two degrees to starboard and come to a new heading of three-aught-six."

"Aye, aye, sir." The helmsman spun the heavy wheel in a clockwise direction, and the destroyer heeled to starboard, thrusting its bow more directly into the brunt of the surging sea. He spun the wheel back in the other direction, and the destroyer quickly assumed its upright position. "Three-aught-six degrees, sir," the helmsman sang out.

"Mr. Engel, give me the target azimuth reading off the radar."

"Fifty-eight degrees," the communications officer called back.

"What's the range, now?"

"Eight miles, sir."

The captain, peering through the spray-drenched window with his binoculars, thought it should be in sight by now, as big a target as it appeared on the radar. *There!* His eyes picked up something farther to the right than he had been looking. "There she is. I've got her."

He kept the glasses trained on the unknown ship's position, getting an update each time the destroyer's bow crested a fresh wave. He couldn't tell much about it yet, except that it wasn't a tanker; it was riding too high in the water.

"Four miles," Lieutenant Engel called out. He pulled his head out of the radar scope and had a look through his own binoculars. His eyes were better than the captain's. "Looks like a container ship. But what's that superstructure on her stern? It's taller than the bridge."

The captain chuckled. Engel still had a lot to learn; he hadn't been at sea that long. Spooner could make out the ship's superstructure quite clearly now. "That's a special kind of derrick, Mr. Engel. You're looking at a LASH ship."

"LASH ship, sir?" That was a new one on Engel.

"It stands for lighter aboard ship. You know what lighters are, don't you?"

"Those big metal barges? Oh, I see. She loads them off her stern, with the derrick. Look, sir, they've spotted us. There goes their blinker."

He concentrated on reading the blinker message. "Sir, she identifies herself as the *Oceania,* Liberian registry, bound for Dammam. Her captain's noticed we're on a collision course and requests that we bear off."

"Not until we verify her identity. Maintain present heading." Spooner kept his eyes on the ship, trying to read the name on the bow.

"They're re-sending the blinker message," Engel observed. "Do you want me to respond, Captain?"

"Hold on a minute. Put your glasses on her. Can you read the name?"

"Oceania, sir."

"You're certain?"

"Aye, sir."

"Port five degrees," Spooner commanded the helm. "Mr. Engel, contact the *Oceania* and inquire what cargo she carries."

Engel moved back to his communications station to carry out the order. The captain could make out the Liberian colors now, flying from the LASH ship's masthead. The ship was apparently what she purported to be.

It was several more minutes before the *Oceania*'s blinker began to wink out another message. It was a short one. Engels returned on the double.

"No comment, sir."

"What?"

"That was her captain's response to your question about the *Oceania*'s cargo. No comment."

Spooner swore. "Mr. Engel, we are going to report this to CIC, including the 'no comment' part. Send the following message to the *America:* "Contact established with LASH ship *Oceania,* registry Liberia, bound for Dammam. She refuses comment on our question regarding her cargo. Have *Oceania* in sight. Her position is—give the appropriate Lat-Lon. Await your orders."

Ten minutes later, as the the *Lawrence* continued to shadow the *Oceania,* the reply was received from the CIC aboard the *America.* "Good work. Break off contact with *Oceania* and proceed to contact with next unidentified vessel."

"She must be clean," Spooner commented, after reading the message. He had already plotted the course to the next nearest unknown ship, and called off the new heading to the helmsman.

"Glad we didn't have to board her," Engel observed. "Her freeboard would have been a real problem. Her deck must be seventy, eighty feet out of the water."

The captain grinned again and shook his head at the lieutenant. "The stern, Mr. Engel. You board a LASH ship from the stern, where they load the cargo. Piece of cake."

The captain had no way of knowing that this was exactly the way the *Oceania* had already been boarded—by hijackers whose haul represented the same very special "terrorist contraband" that the U.S. Navy's Operation Chain Link was designed to recover.

Some three hours and seventy nautical miles later, the *Lawrence* had identified three more ships, the *Shikoku Maru,* a Japanese supertanker, the *Nantucket Island,* a U.S. container ship, and the *Manitoba Victory,* a Canadian cargo ship. Spooner was relieved that none had to be boarded. The sea had slacked off some but was still running high.

He was getting tired of this silly game chasing all over hell's half acre to do a ship-identification job the carrier was far better suited for, with its complement of surveillance aircraft.

They had already penetrated deep into the Gulf of Oman, far beyond the originally designated picketline. They were almost to the Strait of Hormuz, leading into the Persian Gulf. And dusk was not far off.

When the *Lawrence* was finally ordered by the *America's* Combat Information Center to come about and return to her original picket station, it was getting dark. The *America* was in the process of weighing anchor in Karachi harbor with the remaining ships in her battle group and would join up with the destroyers the following day. Operation Chain Link would not recommence until dawn.

"Thank God," Spooner muttered, leaving Owens on the bridge and heading below with Engel for some much needed R and R. It would start with a double-size belt of Jack Daniel's.

Sixty miles off the coast of Pakistan, the captain of the *Beirut Victory* watched the darkness of night descend over his ship and rejoiced. The threat from snooping aircraft was suspended until daylight returned. By dawn his vessel would be two hundred miles closer to its destination, approaching the territorial waters of Iran. He had much less to fear from Iranis than from Pakistanis.

He was preparing to leave the bridge when the mate hailed him. "Captain, we are picking up all kinds of activity outside Karachi harbor. I think you'd better have a look at this."

The captain joined him at the radar scope and peered through the hooded enclosure. The harbor mouth was sharply defined by the radar return. Well outside it, a cluster of prominent blips marked the presence of a veritable flotilla. It was not immediately clear whether the ships had departed or were, in fact, approaching Karachi. He continued to watch as another scan painted fresh blips on the scope face . . . and another . . . and another. It required ten scans before he was certain.

"They're coming out—they're coming our way."

"Pakistanis?" the mate suggested.

"No, Americans. The Sixth Fleet, Indian Ocean Battle Group. Karachi is one of their liberty ports. They're putting back to sea."

He had known of the U.S. fleet's presence in the Pakistani port but had played down its significance in his mind. The Americans were not involved in this little game. Could that situation have changed?

The mate had his head back in the scope. "The big one in the middle—that's the carrier?"

"The USS *America*. One of their latest—and best."

"Are they looking for us?"

"Perhaps. We can't afford to take that chance. Order the engines to half speed. I want to give them as wide a berth as possible—let them get well out ahead of us."

The mate left to signal the engine room and the captain had another look at the radar scope. The equipment was performing well, the picture of the American force exceedingly clear. The trouble was, if he could see them, they could see him. But by dawn they should be far enough ahead of him to be out of radar range.

The mate returned just in time to receive another order. "You'd better kill the radar. Operate it in the low-power mode only. We will turn it back up only momentarily, every hour or so. I don't want them picking up a strobe off our radar and sending a plane over tomorrow to investigate."

Leaving the mate on watch, he went back to his cabin. The light was on. Someone was inside waiting for him.

His Palestinian customer was sitting at the table. "Why did you reduce speed?"

Without answering, the captain opened a cabinet, removing a bottle and two glasses, which he filled. He handed one to the man with the limp and sat down opposite him.

"My friend, we may have a slight problem."

13

DAVID LLEWELLYN COULDN'T believe it. He had gone directly from the embassy to Hadassah Medical Center, only to be informed that Daniella was no longer there, had already been released. No one could tell him who had called for her to drive her home. Who had signed out for her? What kind of security was that? Especially after the bombing incident. Unbelievable!

He rushed home, hoping, praying, she was all right. The elevator was in use when he reached the foyer of their apartment building, the arrow pointing to the top floor. He headed for the stairs, taking them two at a time. Calm down, he told himself, she'll be there. He reached the sixth floor and bounded down the hallway, his key ready to thrust into the lock. And then he heard her voice.

With relief he opened the door, thinking she was on the phone. But no, she was talking to two men, their backs to him. At the sound of the door latch, their heads turned, and he recognized Baruch Shmona. He'd never seen the other man before.

"David! I'm so glad you're home." Daniella hurried over to embrace him. The king-size bandage on the back of her head had been replaced by a smaller, daintier one.

"Shouldn't you be in bed?" he asked glaring at the two unwelcome guests. She was fully dressed, wearing the suit he had brought to the hospital for her.

"No, I'm fine. The doctor says I should stay up as much as possible and remain active."

"What are *they* doing here?"

"Baruch was kind enough to drive me home," Daniella said pointedly. "This is an associate of his, Sergeant Neff."

Llewellyn eyed Shmona. "Business as usual, eh? No rest for the convalescing?"

"David, you don't understand," Daniella admonished. "I *asked* them to come. I called Baruch from the hospital because I wanted to know what had happened on my investigation. It's bad news, I'm afraid. They traced the phone number but the place had already been vacated. And the jeweler who gave me the number—" Her voice trailed off. ". . . They found him dead."

"Murdered?" Both his wife's look and Shmona's said yes. "That settles it. I don't want Daniella involved any more, Shmona. It's getting too dangerous. She's been through enough."

Shmona spoke for the first time, his voice like velvet. "The last thing I want is to let anything more happen to your wife. But the best way to protect her is to catch the maniac who's trying to kill her. Sergeant Neff, here, is from the Shin Beth. He's an expert on creating artist renderings of suspects. Daniella was just starting to give us a description of the man in the blue van who forced her off the road."

Daniella squeezed his hand. "David, it's important." He nodded, realizing that he had intended to ask her about it himself. But he'd had so little time with her since she came out of her coma.

"All right, Mrs. Llewellyn," the sergeant said, "I'll turn on my recorder again, if I may. You were saying that you got a close look at this man as he pulled up alongside you on the expressway."

"A look I'll never forget. I can still see those eyes, burning with hatred and contempt. His face was bony and rock-hard, the mouth rigidly set—frozen is the word that comes to mind. He had a prominent nose that almost came to a point—"

"Like this?" The sergeant held up a flesh-colored rendering of a nose in profile.

"Sort of. Only less rounded on top and even sharper."

Neff replaced the drawing with another. "More like this?"

"Yes! Yes, that's it, exactly."

"You described the mouth as rigidly set. Something like this?"

"Yes, but thinner and wider. Thin lips."

The sergeant flipped to another mouth. "Closer, but it didn't turn down at the corners." He tried another one on her. "Yes, that's more like it. Yes, perfect."

They continued on, covering the suspect's other features: hair, forehead, eyebrows, and chin. Neff flipped to a composite of all the features described and held it up. "Are we starting to capture him?"

The likeness was so close it scared her. But something wasn't right. "Almost. But there's something missing. I can't quite put my finger on it . . ."

"Cheekbones," Llewellyn said, on his feet, staring at the face in the rendering. "Try some high cheekbones!"

Sergeant Neff flipped through a few more pages. "Stop!" Daniella gasped. "That's the man!"

"It certainly is," Llewellyn echoed.

Shmona shot an incredulous look at Llewellyn. "You've seen him, too?"

"Only once, and not up close. But once was enough. He was wearing an Israeli army uniform. You're looking at the leader of the terrorist bunch who ambushed us just outside Gaza in the second attempt to assassinate Khalidy."

He told himself he shouldn't have been surprised. The scimitar pendant in Daniella's purse had been the tipoff; her attempts to trace it had put her at risk with the terrorist sect that wore it as an amulet. A sect apparently headed by the man whose face now stared at him out of the Shin Beth's do-it-yourself facial features kit.

"I can fill in a few more details on this man's description for you. He's quite tall, well over six feet, and very thin—his uniform hung on him like a scarecrow's. He has a shrill voice, at least when he's excited. He's very cool under fire. And he's ruthless—a hardened killer."

"Yes, we seem to have ample evidence of that," Shmona observed. "Well, this is a stroke of good fortune. Did you get all that, Neff?"

"Got it." The sergeant switched off his pocket-sized recorder. "Two eye-witnesses was more than we'd hoped for.

This picture and description will be on tonight's late news and in all the morning papers."

Thinking about the pendant reminded Llewellyn of the drawing the ambassador had shown him earlier in the day and the revelation about the terrorist missile. He wondered if Shmona knew. But of course, he must. The Mossad would be involved up to their eyeballs in any such outside threat.

Addressing himself to Shmona, he sent up a trial balloon. "I'm sure you're aware that there's a lot more riding on this than catching a few terrorists."

Shmona glanced at him warily. "I'm not sure I catch your meaning."

"Don't you? Would you like me to elaborate?"

Daniella was looking at him questioningly. Her boss held up his hand. "Just a moment."

He said something in a low voice to the sergeant, who nodded, picked up his things, and stood up. "I'll wait for you in the car."

When he was out of earshot, Shmona spoke to Daniella. "Your husband and I need a moment together for a confidential talk. I wonder if you'd mind—"

"She stays, Shmona. You almost got her killed with that assignment you sent her on. Don't you think she deserves to know what was really at stake?"

"But I have no authority to divulge—"

"I'll assume the authority and take the responsibility, if that's what's bothering you."

Daniella had gotten to her feet. "I have no idea what you two are going on about, but I don't mind, really, David, if there's something I'm not supposed to hear."

"Please sit down, Daniella. He doesn't have the right to decide that. It's important that you know—*I* want you to know. Then maybe you'll understand what kind of fire they've had you playing with."

She resumed her seat slowly, her eyes intent on his face. "The ambassador informed me about it this morning," Llewellyn began. "He was warned by the Secretary of State about a grave threat to U.S. citizens in Israel—to all persons in Israel. It seems that a ballistic missile has been hijacked by terrorists and is probably headed for the Middle East. A link has been established between the missile's hijackers and the Palestinian terrorist sect behind the recent assassination attempts—the same group of terrorists led by this man who tried to kill you. In short, there's a good possibility this missile may be aimed at Israel, to blackmail the government into God knows what."

Daniella sat there, stunned, transferring her gaze to Shmona. "You knew about this?" He made no answer.

"He knew about it, all right. Did he tell you that piece of jewelry he had you carry around, trying to trace it to its origin, was found on one of the terrorists killed in Jericho? No, I didn't think so. Well, it also happens to be the link I mentioned, the evidence of a tie-in with the missile hijackers. It seems one of them wore an identical pendant, which he lost at the scene of the hijacking."

Daniella's eyes betrayed a hint of the horror that was beginning to dawn on her. "This terrorist missile—is it nuclear?"

"There was apparently no warhead in it when they stole it. But we have to assume the worst—that they have access to one, not necessarily nuclear. Chemical or biological could also wreak havoc on a population center."

"Oh, God," she said, suddenly feeling sick. "What are we doing? Our entire Air Force and Navy should be out looking for them. If this missile is as big as you say, it must be difficult to hide."

"It's apparently aboard some kind of ship. The U.S. Navy is setting up a blockade. Hopefully they'll intercept it before they off-load it. But we can't rely on that. That's why the Mossad had you trying to trace this amulet. They were hoping it would lead them to the terrorist masterminds and through them to the hijacked missile. Am I right, Shmona?"

The Mossad agent could see no further point in clinging to his posture of non-disclosure. "We're still hoping that it will. Now that we have a description of their leader, it should hasten the process. It was Daniella's fine detective work that got us to this point; she's a first-rate investigator. But she's been through a lot and I respect your desire to keep her out of it. I'll see that she's assigned to another case."

He got up to leave. "Please, not a word of this to anyone,"

he cautioned Daniella. "Not even at the office. Only a handful there are cleared."

She nodded her acquiescence, and he started for the door.

"Just a minute, Baruch." Daniella grasped her husband's arm. "David, I know you mean well, but you can't decide a thing like this for me. We're talking about a possible holocaust right here in my native country. If there's anything I can do to help prevent such a disaster, I've *got* to do it. Buruch, please disregard what my husband said. I'm ready to go back to work."

"Well, if you're sure—"

Llewellyn shot Shmona a look, certain that he'd been set up. But he knew there was no way of dissuading Daniella; her mind was made up.

"All right, then," Llewellyn sighed. "On one condition. I work with you on this. I never leave your side."

"What about *your* job?" she inquired, with a half frown, half smile. "Are you resigning from the American embassy?"

"My own assignment's on hold, for the moment. I have some time off coming. It's agreed, then?" He looked for a reaction from Shmona.

The agent shrugged. "I can't very well prevent you from escorting your own wife. However, I have nothing for her to do at the moment. Perhaps she should take a day or two to rest up."

"I don't need to rest," she protested. "I could go back to the address in Jaffa, go door to door, show them Neff's likeness of the terrorist. Someone should recognize him as the one who operated the office there."

Shmona looked at her with mild surprise. "No, no, my dear, I'm afraid you're under a misapprehension. The man who tried to kill you was *not* the one who ordered the pendants nor the one whose number we traced to the office in Jaffa. They are apparently two different people. The sergeant just informed me that the Shin Beth have succeeded in locating the proprietor whose shop backed up to this office—the shop that was closed the day we raided the place. He denies knowing the man or even his name, but admits to having seen him enter and leave his office on several occasions.

"His description is nothing like your assailant. This is an

older man with heavy black brows and a thick head of snow-white hair."

Saudi Arabia's ballistic missiles were deployed some hundred and fifty miles south of the city of Riyadh, amid the vast wilderness of shifting dunes known as the Rub' al Khali, or Empty Quarter. Inaccessibility to attack had been the rationale for selecting so remote and desolate a site, but that very inaccessibility was proving to be a major headache in the logistics and support department.

The nearest housing for maintenance workers was more than twenty miles from the launch site, at Jabrin, an oasis that was once a stronghold of the fierce Murrah tribesmen and was still frequented by Bedouin. The closest thing to an officers' club on the tiny Jabrin military post was the officers' mess. When meals were not being served, it was possible to sit at one of the tables and order an iced drink. As in any other Saudi military or government establishment, alcoholic beverages were, of course, unavailable. But if one brought his own bottle and poured from it, nothing was said.

It was Major Baroudi's habit to arrive just after the noon prayer, a half hour before the midday mess commenced, and have a gin and tonic. Baroudi was in charge of security at the ballistic missile base, and since he delegated the guarding and patrolling of the missile sites to his subordinates, he had little to do. On this Sunday, the first work day of the Muslim week, he had just replaced his flask in the pocket of his uniform and was stirring the gin into his drink when he became aware of someone standing behind him.

He turned his head and saw that it was the civilian manager of maintenance at the missile site—what was his name? Ibrahim Masri. He had met the man only once. What was he doing, sneaking up like that? He didn't belong here, in the officers' mess.

"What do you want?"

"A word with you. May I sit down?" Masri was scholarly in appearance and slight of build, in contrast to the major, who was neither.

Baroudi frowned. "I conduct my business in my office. I will be happy to see you there."

"I was just there. They told me I could find you here. It's a matter of some urgency." The major's hostility did not deter him from sitting down.

Baroudi took a sip from his drink and looked at him sharply. "Well, what is it then? What is so urgent?"

"Two of my crew are missing. They went to Riyadh for the monthly holiday and failed to return this morning."

"Is that all?" the major scoffed. "They could be ill or simply have missed the bus. There are many possible explanations."

"I don't think so. They have always been most reliable and punctual. They are Pakistanis. I have questioned their associates. None of the other Pakistanis who stayed at the same hotel saw them for the entire weekend."

The major took another long sip. "Why are you telling me this? You think something has happened to them?" His own question seemed to alarm him for the first time. "Did they know any secrets?"

"Secrets? Yes, I suppose you might say so. They are two of my best men, both graduate engineers with a lot of experience. One is an expert on inertial guidance systems for ballistic missiles, the other an authority on the handling of hypergolic rocket fuels. Between them they know practically everything there is to know about our East Wind weapons."

Now Baroudi was truly concerned. When Masri had mentioned a couple of workers missing he had been thinking in terms of simple laborers. He removed a pen and pad of paper from his pocket.

"Give me their names and descriptions. I'll make some inquiries."

"I brought them with me." Masri handed him two sheets of paper.

The major scanned the information. "Hamad Khan and Ishmael Khan. Brothers?"

"No, not related. Hamad, the taller one, comes from Islamabad, Ishmael from Karachi."

Baroudi drained his drink and got up from the table. "I'll get a missing-persons report on the wire right away." He studied Masri's face. "You think they've been kidnapped?"

The maintenance director shook his head slowly from side to side. "I doubt that they have."

"But you said—then why—?"

"There is one more thing I haven't told you. A certain piece of support equipment has also turned up missing—a very elaborate and expensive electronic unit, a hard one to replace. Fortunately, I have two others. They are used for reprogramming and realignment of the inertial guidance system whenever a missile is re-sited or a new target assigned. Hamad Khan had access to this unit and was an expert in its use."

"You think he stole it, then?"

"It certainly looks that way."

The sleek, cylinder-shaped IBM building was one of the newer landmarks in the VIP business section of North Tel Aviv, stretching some twenty stories above the nearby Ichalov Hospital. On the fourteenth floor the elevators opened onto a sizable suite of offices, on whose double glass doors was painted "MALAMUD ENTERPRISES" in both Hebrew and English.

Inside his opulently furnished office, Nachman Malamud stood with his back to his desk, unable to concentrate on work, staring down at the panorama of the city spread out below and the blue sea beyond. He was looking toward Jaffa, its Ottoman clock tower and Great Mosque minaret clearly distinguishable. What a close call it had been, clearing out the headquarters of his clandestine enterprise only hours before the authorities descended on the place . . . His decision, made months before, to keep the operation completely separate from his legitimate business practice had been a fortunate one. He was confident that the thoroughness of his housecleaning effort had eradicated any possible clue that might tie him to the vacated office. And there was no one in the vicinity who knew his true identity.

He turned back to the desk and looked again at the portrait prominently displayed on the front page of this morning's paper. "Do you know this man?" the caption below the portrait inquired. He could truthfully answer no to that question, having never met the man face to face who was identified in the accompanying text as the Palestinian terrorist responsible for the Hadassah Hospital bombing and for several prior assassination attempts. He couldn't even have commented on whether the portrait was a good likeness. They had only spoken on the telephone. Again, his precautions had payed off; the Palestinian didn't know him, either. If he was caught, there was no way that Malamud could be implicated.

His intercom buzzed and he flicked the on switch. "Yes?"

"There is a Rabbi Kochbar here to see you, sir. I told him not without an appointment, but he's very insistent. He says he knows you."

Kochbar? The name didn't register, but his settlement projects had put him in contact with a number of rabbis associated with the Gush Emunim movement. "Send him in."

As soon as the rabbi entered, Malamud was certain he had never met the man before. He wore the broad-brimmed black hat and long black coat of the Hassidim, the ultra-orthodox sect. Malamud had had no dealings with the Hassidim, who were generally anti-Zionist and opposed to colonization.

"Shalom. Have we met?" Malamud felt dwarfed by the rabbi, who was exceedingly tall, and he stood up from his chair behind the desk.

The rabbi gave no immediate answer. He closed the office door behind him and advanced a few paces into the room. Without a word he removed his hat, the long hair and side curls coming off with it. He stripped away his beard, revealing the grin beneath it.

Malamud gasped, and glanced back at the newspaper portrait for confirmation. It was the Palestinian, all right. Panic seized him. "Put those back on!" he ordered, hurrying to the door to lock it from the inside. The "rabbi" complied, replacing the hat with its attached tresses and settling his lanky frame into a chair beside the desk.

Malamud stared at him. "How in the name of—?"

"How did I find out who you were? We have known for a long time. It is best that the 'how' remain our secret." The voice had a familiar ring. There was no doubt in Malamud's mind that this was the man with whom he had been conducting business by telephone for the past several months.

"We were never to meet face to face! You shouldn't have come here. That was part of the agreement and you've broken it."

Kareem shrugged. "A matter of necessity. A strange voice answered when I dialed your old number."

"You could have phoned me here instead of—"

"I tried. They refused to put me through."

Malamud couldn't believe the man would be so brazen. It was outrageous. He wanted him out. "What do you want?"

"It is also a question of what *you* want, is it not? Do we not still have the same goal? There is much work to do, and we have run out of funds."

"Why should I give you more money? You've made a botch of it so far. The targets I assign you seem to survive despite your efforts."

"What a short memory you have. The last one didn't survive too well, did he—the jeweler? As for the others, they were incredibly lucky. That kind of luck is bound to run out."

Malamud wanted out. The media blitz on the Palestinian had been awesome. Every Jew in Israel would be looking for him. "I think we should call a halt for a while. It would be better if you stayed in hiding, or left the country until things cool off."

"We cannot afford to give up the fight now." The smoldering look came into Kareem's eyes. "I have just talked to my leader. He is adamant that we press on. He has instructed me to use any means at my disposal to persuade you to give us the funds."

Malamud recognized the declaration for what it was—a thinly veiled threat of blackmail. What could they prove, he asked himself? They had no evidence to tie him to any of the terrorist undertakings. He was a pillar of the community. Who would believe them? Still, they could make it unpleasant for him. The mere accusation would be troublesome. And he told himself not to underestimate them. They had proven that they were resourceful—resourceful enough to discover his identity. Perhaps the "rabbi" was right. Perhaps the luck of the Palestinian peace negotiator, Khalidy, was due to run out.

"What kind of funding do you need?"

"The same as last time will be satisfactory."

"On one condition. You are not to come here again—ever. Do not even call me on this line. I will do the calling, is that understood? You can still be reached at the old number?"

Kareem nodded. "I will not be there, but if you provide the password you will be given another number to call."

"And the password?"

The Palestinian smiled wryly. "It is an Arabic phrase—*ruch minhon.* Freely translated, it means 'get out of here!' "

Malamud wrote the phrase down on the notepad he kept in his suit pocket. He took a business-size checkbook from his desk drawer and filled out a draft for cash.

"Wait here while I take this to my bank on the next floor and have them fill it. And please don't touch anything." The last thing he needed was the terrorist's fingerprints all over his office.

When he was gone, Kareem got up and moved behind the desk, fascinated by the spectacular view extending from the southwest to the southeast, a full quarter circle. It was the clearest of days. His eye traced the coastline southward, past the harbor city of Ashdod, receding into the light haze that clung to the horizon. He could see far into the West Bank, his family's homeland, the heritage of his blood brothers, and imagined he could see all the way to Hebron and the sacred tomb of the patriarchs. In the same direction, far beyond Hebron, he visualized the holiest of holies, the Grand Mosque in Mecca, the Red Sea to one side, the Gulf farther off to the east. And not far beyond the Gulf, a ship—the ship carrying his leader.

He had spoken the truth to Malamud when he mentioned having just spoken to the leader. The hookup had been made via radio-telephone from his organization's safe house in the outskirts of Tel Aviv. The money was needed to pay for certain uncompleted tasks relating to the payload of the captured missile. He had been instructed to personally carry out the transaction.

Kareem smiled his mirthless smile. If Malamud only knew what his money was really going to buy . . .

14

MOSUL, IRAQ'S SECOND largest city, was situated on the west
bank of the Tigris in the northern part of the country, not far
from the Turkish border. It was here, near the ruins of the
ancient Assyrian city of Nineveh, that Saddam Hussein had
elected to construct a research facility and manufacturing
complex for advanced ballistic missiles. Its remoteness from
the gulf had helped to protect it from the all-out onslaught of
Operation Desert Storm, what damage it had sustained was
long since repaired.

A ballistic missile warhead production facility was also part
of the Mosul complex, packaging high explosives and some of
the more deadly chemicals produced at Samarra into self-
deploying modules to serve as payloads for the big missiles.
And not to be outdone in another death-dealing department,
Hussein had also recently augmented the facility to provide
biological warheads, utilizing the most virulent strains of
micro-organisms capable of wreaking pestilence on mankind.

On this particular morning the director of the Mosul weapons complex was in a panic. He had just learned that the dour
Iraqi President-Dictator was on the way here from the airport
for an unscheduled personal tour of the facility. There was no
time to roll out the red carpet in a proper way, barely time to
alert his key managers to the visitation. Gathering several of
them around him for moral support, he repaired to the front
steps of the administration building to greet Saddam Hussein
and his retinue.

The director had recently come under fire for lax safety
measures and was out to convince the head of state that he

was on top of the problem. He had a gas mask kit slung around his waist, as did all his managers, and an assistant bore additional kits that the visitors would be asked to strap on, prior to departing on the tour. He had recently instituted a gas drill every day at 11:00 A.M., at the sound of a siren, when each employee was required to remove his mask from its container and strap it to his face. Hussein would be present when the drill occurred, would in fact participate in it, and would hopefully be favorably impressed.

The President arrived promptly, dressed in his habitual green army uniform with the red epaulets and looking his usual forbidding self. Two of his cabinet were with him, the ministers of defense and finance.

The tour started in the ballistic missile factory, which boasted production lines for two different configurations of tactical IRBMs. It was the most impressive venue from a visual standpoint, and the director always began his tours here. Seeing the monsters in their various stages of progression, from bare metal rocket casings to the finished articles gleaming with fresh paint, complete with control surfaces, guidance and warhead segments, and nose cones invariably had a favorable impact on the VIPs he ushered through. Though they made few comments, the director concluded that the President and his party were well satisfied with what they saw.

The next stop was the warhead assembly area, where various chemical and biological modules brought in from the other factories were packaged into fuze-equipped disseminator vessels suitable for installation in the various ballistic missiles. The warhead facility was a particularly hazardous area and was in a separate building, isolated from the others. It was built like a blockhouse, with thick walls that had warning signs of all kinds posted on them. High explosives were handled here, the director explained, in addition to the other types of warhead ingredients. The facility had also been designed to handle nuclear devices, he mentioned, knowing that Hussein had never given up his hope of obtaining such, even though his own capability to produce fissionable materials had been wiped out when Israeli jets destroyed his Osirak reactor.

"How do the assembled warheads get back to the missile factory?" Hussein inquired.

"We use secure armored vehicles to transport them," the director replied. He led the party to an outer office with an exterior window and made a hurried phone call.

"You will shortly observe one of the transport vehicles exiting the loading dock in the basement of the building." He had arranged for the demonstration in advance. "There it goes now."

As the group watched through the window, a closed van with square sides resembling a Brinks armored car emerged from beneath the building and crawled onto the concrete strip that stretched toward the ballistic missile plant a half mile away. The van was just beginning to pick up speed when a siren went off somewhere outside and a loud clanging erupted inside the building.

Alarmed, Hussein looked at the director for an explanation, who looked in turn at his watch. Ten-thirty. The emergency drill wasn't to have been for another half hour. Oh, no! he thought, as the realization seized him that this was no drill but the real thing. Please Allah! Not with the President here!

"Our masks—" The defense minister spoke calmly. "Should we put them on?"

"Yes—yes, of course." The director fumbled with his own cannister pack, extracted the mask, and affixed it to his face. He noticed that the others had managed to do the same without his help. "There is no real danger," he mumbled through the mouthpiece of the mask. "Probably just a small leak somewhere. But it's best that we move outside the building."

"Does this happen often?" the President mumbled back.

"Not often, Excellency. But we have very sensitive detectors that trigger the alarm if they sense even the slightest trace of foreign substance in the air. It is better to err on the safe side."

He led the party down a staircase and through an exit door in the back of the building, as the alarm bell continued to clang. Somewhere a siren was still going off in the distance. The armored truck bearing its load of warheads had pulled to a stop halfway to its destination.

"My car!" Hussein exploded from the mouthpiece of his

mask. "Have my car brought here immediately! We are leaving."

"But—" The director wanted to protest that he hadn't completed the tour yet, but one glance at the menacing eyes behind the mask made him think better of it. "At once, Your Excellency." He dispatched one of his managers to take care of it. The limousine pulled up within minutes, and its driver, wearing a gas mask the motor pool must have provided him, sprang out to open the back door.

The director watched with mixed feelings as the limo sped away toward the main security gate. Had he gotten his message across? Perhaps better than he could have expected. He wondered if there had been casualties. Before the limousine was halfway to the gate, he saw an ambulance pass it, speeding in the opposite direction, its siren blaring.

The two guards in the security tower, high above the complex, watched the ambulance pull up alongside the armored van. Two gas-masked orderlies in white uniforms got out, carrying a stretcher. The van's driver, his own mask in place, jumped out and ran to the back of the van, unlocking its rear doors. He disappeared into the back of the vehicle, the stretcher bearers following. A minute or so later they reemerged, the van driver alighting to help the other two descend from the van with the heavy stretcher, now weighted down with the form of a portly man covered by a blanket. With some difficulty, they managed to get him into the back of the ambulance.

"Poor sod," commented one of the guards. "Must not have gotten his mask on in time."

The driver of the armored van had closed and locked its rear doors and now climbed into the ambulance. It sped away, its siren sounding again as it headed for the main gate. It occurred to one of the guards that the driver's behavior was a bit peculiar, abandoning the armored van like that. He voiced this concern to his colleague.

"Probably just worried about his friend," the other suggested. "Wants to find out if he pulls through. But to be on the safe side we'd better report it." He picked up the phone.

By the time the call went through the ambulance had exited

the gate and was speeding toward the main highway to the city, two miles away.

The ambulance attendant in the passenger seat swiveled his head around. "Let's have another look at the patient."

A brown blanket covered the body from head to toe. The van driver peeled it back. The enormous, swollen head proved to be a black, spherical-shaped object about a half meter in diameter. Extending below it on the stretcher were two yellow cylinders of about the same diameter, laid end to end, each almost a meter in length.

"Which is which?" inquired the man in the passenger seat.

"The two yellows are the nerve agent. The black ball contains the 'bugs.'"

"Which is more lethal?"

The van driver shrugged. "Depends on how fast you want to go. The nerve gas is fast-acting. The microbes work slower, but they're just as deadly, and the diseases are highly infectious. In time, they could wipe out an entire population."

He inserted an end of one of the yellow cylinders into the mouth of a heavy bag that resembled a body sack, struggling to wrestle the bag all the way around it. "Why don't you come back here and help me?" Between the two of them they completed the job, encasing the three heavy units in the waterproof containers and sealing the ends with duct tape.

Its siren still wailing, the ambulance skidded around the exit from the elevated highway and turned in the direction of the hospital. Three blocks later its driver turned away from the hospital toward the outskirts of town, slowed down, and switched off the siren. After another five blocks he braked and swung into an open garage. The door to the garage promptly shut behind him.

A few minutes later, a petroleum truck rolled out of the garage and turned back toward the main highway. Seated in its cab were the same trio, attired in the cold-weather mackinaws favored by drivers who had to negotiate the frigid mountain passes to the north and east of Mosul.

As the tanker approached the highway on-ramp with the BAGHDAD sign, three police cars came hurtling down it and shot off in the direction of the hospital, sirens shrieking. The heavy truck lumbered past the BAGHDAD on-ramp and turned onto the one accessing the highway in the opposite direction. Its sign read:

TAL KAIF
DOHUK
TURKEY, IRAN

It was late afternoon. The plane came from the west, directly out of the sun, which explained why none of the *Beirut Victory*'s crew saw it before they heard it. On the bridge, the captain trained his glasses on it and got a good look as it flew by less than a mile away. It had U.S. Navy markings and was off the carrier *America*, he assumed. It didn't seem to be carrying any weapons.

It flew beyond his field of view and he left the bridge to keep it under surveillance. It continued on its straight and level course, receding toward the horizon, and he began to think it might be on some mission that had nothing to do with him. But then he saw the glint of sun on its wings as it banked into a steep one-eighty, and he watched it float back toward him, slowing and dropping in altitude until it was at most a hundred meters off the water. It was headed directly over his ship.

In the forecastle, another pair of binoculars was trained on the plane, in the hands of someone better schooled than the captain on modern weapons of war. The Palestinian immediately recognized the carrier-based S-3B Viking, employed primarily in anti-submarine warfare, equipped with sonobuoys and a radar so sensitive it could detect a periscope in even the heaviest of sea states. But he knew that this Viking was not out looking for subs. It was looking for him.

The twin-engine plane roared overhead, so low that he could feel the deck vibrating under the soles of his shoes, and then it was gone, returning in the direction from which it had come—the direction of the USS *America* Battle Group. To the Palestinian, the message could not have been more explicit. It had been sent specifically to determine the name and description of this particular ship, a vessel that continued to appear on AWACS radar and satellite surveillance plots of shipping approaching the Gulf vicinity. The *Beirut Victory* had finally been identified.

He was puzzled. Why had they gone to so much trouble? The aerial inspection could not have determined anything about the ship's cargo. If the U.S. Navy was establishing a blockade of the Gulf, as now seemed apparent, why not just send one of their cruisers or destroyers to stop the ship and search it?

It made him wonder if there was any way their Navy could know the identity of the ship that had taken part in the hijacking. Had the *Beirut Victory* been sighted in the Strait of Malacca, after all, its presence there reported? If so, they could expect one of the blockading warships to come swooping down on them at any minute.

To come so close . . . only to have this happen. What could they do? Darkness was scarcely an hour away. Perhaps the American Navy would wait for daylight—perhaps there was a chance of slipping away. He had to consult with the captain right away.

He headed aft, moving swiftly despite the pitching of the deck and his own disability, oblivious to the pain in his crippled limb.

The captain was waiting for him in his cabin, looking calmer than he had expected. He had a chart spread out across the small table and was measuring distances off it with a scale and divider.

"Do I think they know the name of the ship they're looking for? No. They're just doing some screening. They don't have time to board and search every ship bound for the Gulf. They're trying to eliminate some."

"How can they do that?"

"Simple. They know the missing merchandise must be aboard a cargo ship of some sort. That eliminates tankers and passenger ships, for starters. They can also use maritime data listing cargoes, itineraries, ports of call, and dates. Vessels that were nowhere near Singapore at the time of the hijacking can be crossed off the list."

The Palestinian was troubled by this statement. "Such data would show that we *were* there."

The captain shook his head. "My ship's itinerary doesn't show up on any maritime list. Being a tramp steamer that picks up cargoes of opportunity where we find them, we don't file a 'flight plan' when we leave home port. On the other hand, the blockaders can't eliminate the *Beirut Victory*, can't be sure we weren't in the vicinity. I think we can expect to see a U.S. warship off our bow sometime after dawn tomorrow."

"No sooner?"

"I doubt it. I estimate that the nearest ships in the blockade are upwards of two hundred miles away. Even if they started now and steamed at flank speed, they wouldn't get here much before daylight. As you know, we've been proceeding at reduced speed to let them draw far enough ahead that we would be out of their radar range. But I had another motive in doing this—to set up a misleading track history, so that when we change course and resume maximum speed we can lose them for a while."

"What are you planning to do?"

"Make a run for it. Dump you and your cargo on the beach and put back out to sea before they know what's happened to us."

His finger found a spot on the map. "We're just over a hundred miles from your unloading site, your little inlet here on the coast of Iran. I had planned to go in tomorrow, by daylight, but that Navy patrol plane changes things. We'll steam for the coast at twenty knots and ride in on the high tide around midnight."

"What if they see us change course? They'll know what you're doing. They'll know where to find us!"

"How will they know? We're not presently under radar surveillance. We've been cruising on the same course for two days. With a bit of luck, they won't check our position again until morning. By then you'll be ashore and I'll be back out to sea. After that, if they board and search, I'm clean."

They would need more than a bit of luck, the Palestinian reflected. The U.S. Navy's Ocean Surveillance Satellite remapped the area at several-hour intervals. If it happened while the *Beirut Victory* was still unloading its cargo, it would pinpoint his location. But he would just have to chance it; he was out of alternatives.

"Let's proceed, then. We're wasting time."

"Right. I'm off to the bridge to give the order." The captain scooped up his chart and headed for the door. "You can wait for me here, if you'd like, and we can go over the unloading plan."

Unloading plan. The words had a beautiful sound. How long he had waited for this moment, now only hours away, when his massive weapon would be ashore, rolling off toward its secret site where it would remain hidden from the world until the time came to activate it. Would his crew be there? His orders had been quite explicit. They were to have been on site by yesterday, at the latest, and to remain in the vicinity day and night until the ship arrived.

He felt the ship's momentum change and the deck begin to tilt as it commenced a hard turn to starboard. The engine room bells chimed, a repeater installed here in the captain's quarters, as the command for full speed was signalled from the bridge. He had a sense of the ship gathering itself to plunge with its maximum force toward a landfall on the southern coast of Iran.

He could see it in his mind's eye. A barren and desolate shore it was, this southern coast of the province of Baluchistan, isolated from other parts of the province by a rugged coastal mountain range and sparsely settled by nomadic sheep and goat herders. He had personally explored the area to select the ideal spot. He had found it. It was made to order.

The Royal Saudi Air Force base adjoining Riyadh's King Khaled International Airport was the focal point for the country's ongoing effort to track down the ship bearing its missing missile. It was here that the Saudis' five AWACS aircraft were stationed, flying long shifts with American crews to maintain around-the-clock vigilance of the Persian Gulf and its environs. The well-equipped AWACS ground-environment facility served as a communications center and clearing house for the joint operation with the U.S. Navy, connected both by voice channel and data link to the USS *America*'s Combat Information Center.

AWACS aircraft were still being diverted south and east from their regular missions for periodic inspections of the shipping in the Arabian Sea approaches to the Gulf. One such flight had just landed, with Richard Llewellyn aboard. Now he sat in front of a giant vertical situation display in the ground-environment complex alongside one of his Saudi ground controller friends, looking through the list of ships so far identified by the Navy.

Since learning that the U.S. Navy had joined in the search, Richy had taken a special interest in the operation, which he had dubbed "The Hunt for Black September." He knew nothing about the actual cargo in question aboard the unknown, much sought-after vessel. It was listed as "terrorist contraband," which certainly took in a lot of territory. The way it had the U.S. Navy cranked up, it had to be more than a few popguns.

"There is another ID coming in now," the ground controller reported, monitoring the data-link printout.

Richy read the printout over the controller's shoulder. A Viking aircraft from the carrier *America* had identified a freighter at the listed latitude and longitude as the *Beirut Victory,* registry unknown. Some of its more visible features were also recorded: four cargo holds, five derricks.

"Which one is that?" Richy inquired, referring to the vertical situation display, on which all the ships detected by AWACS were shown in their various locations.

"That's our number seventeen," the controller responded, circling it with his grease pencil. Each ship for which AWACS had set up a track file had been assigned a number, which appeared on the screen of the display next to its position.

"Seventeen? We've tracked that mother all the way from Sri Lanka over the past week. Any maritime data on *Beirut Victory?*"

"I'll check." The ground controller typed the name on his computer keyboard. Nothing happened for a few seconds. Then the notation "no input" flashed onto the screen. "It must not be in any of the maritime reports."

"Hmm. So we have no information on its itinerary other than the part of the ocean we've tracked it through. It's been averaging eighteen knots until yesterday, when it slowed down some."

They'd been told that the ship they were looking for had

come from Singapore. He made a quick mental calculation. "Extrapolating backward from Sri Lanka, it could have been in the Singapore region two weeks ago. I think we'd better talk to the Navy."

The controller dialed in the call letters on the voice hookup with the USS *America*'s Combat Information Center. Richy asked for the officer he'd been interfacing with, Lt. Cdr. Harold.

"Harold, here."

"This is Richard Llewellyn at the AWACS Command and Control Center at Riyadh, Commander. I'm calling about the latest ship identification made by one of your Vikings this afternoon—the freighter *Beirut Victory*?"

"Yes, Llewellyn."

"Commander, we've been tracking this ship for over a week, all the way in from Sri Lanka. We think it could be the one you're looking for."

"Yeah? How's that?"

"First of all, there's no history on it before we picked it up, no maritime data whatsoever. That usually signifies that a ship is freelancing, bouncing from port to port picking up cargoes of opportunity—tramp steamers, they're sometimes called. It stands to reason that it could have picked up this 'terrorist contraband' along the way.

"Second, if you extrapolate backwards from Sri Lanka at the speed it was making, eighteen knots, it could have been in the Singapore region two weeks ago."

"Yes, I see what you mean. It looks like a prime candidate for our first board and search. All right, thanks for the input, Llewellyn."

"No sweat. Keep us posted. We have another AWACS flight at 0600 hours, Riyadh time. We'll get you an update then on *Beirut Victory*'s location."

It had been a much easier day for the captain and the crew of the destroyer *Lawrence*, Spooner reflected. No more chasing all over the ocean to eyeball unidentified ships. That job was being done now, as it should have been from the start, by planes launched from the *America*'s flight deck.

The *Lawrence* had been instructed to remain on station at

its present location in the Gulf of Oman and wait for further orders, in case a boarding operation was called for. There had been no such order. Spooner was about ready to call it a day. He watched the sun sink below the proverbial yardarm, the traditional signal for the shipboard cocktail hour to begin. It was a time-honored tradition he intended to uphold as soon as he left the bridge.

"Skipper, there's a call for you from the flagship."

Spooner picked up the phone and a Lt. Cdr. Harold from the *America*'s Combat Information Center identified himself. "We have a board and search for you. A freighter identified as the *Beirut Victory*, registry unknown." He read off the latitude and longitude and the ship's present course and speed.

Spooner immediately recognized that the ship was upwards of two hundred miles away, its longitude over three degrees higher than his own. But its course was westerly, in his direction. "Do we go after her, or wait for her to come to us?"

"The orders signed by the admiral call for 'immediate intercept of said vessel with all due speed.' We'll fax you a copy."

"Good enough. But before we board and search, I hope somebody tells me what it is we're searching for."

"As your original orders specified, you'll be given that information when the final order to board and search is confirmed. It will be sent to you in code, for your eyes only."

Spooner hung up the phone, wondering what all the secrecy was about. If the ship they were seeking was a gunrunner, as he suspected, why didn't they just tell him? He moved to his navigation station to plot the intercept.

The first cut didn't please him at all. If he interpreted "all due speed" to mean the *Lawrence*'s maximum thirty-one knots, the rendezvous with the *Beirut Victory* would occur several hours before dawn, assuming the other ship held to its present course and speed. He didn't relish trying to execute a boarding operation in the dark; that could be hazardous to his boarding party, especially if the seas continued heavy. It made more sense to cruise east at a reduced speed of around twenty knots, planning to intercept the other vessel at first light so that the boarding could proceed with good visibility. And his weary crew would get a better night's sleep.

"Mr. Owens, we've been given a board-and-search assignment. A freighter, the *Beirut Victory*. She's some two hundred miles east of us, making about ten knots in our direction. Come to a new heading of 097."

"097 it is, sir." The watch officer instructed the helmsman, who commenced spinning the heavy wheel.

"Engines all ahead two-thirds."

"All ahead two-thirds." The bell sounded the command to the engine room.

"I'm estimating intercept around 0600 hours, Mr. Owens. We should have radar contact two hours or so ahead of that. Mr. Engel has the midnight watch?"

"Yes, sir."

"Pass the information on to him, then. In any case, I'll be up for the 0400 watch. Take over. I'm going below."

15

MAKING LANDFALL AT night was not the captain's favorite way of doing things. Even with the light of a newly risen moon only a few days past full, he couldn't see a thing through his binoculars. Thank Allah for radar. It showed that the *Beirut Victory* was within two miles of the coast of Iran.

There was no point in approaching any closer until he found the inlet he was looking for. He could do that on the radar, which did a good job of mapping the shoreline. He ordered the helm to a new heading running parallel to the shore and stepped outside the bridge to have another look through the glasses in the lower-ambient light condition.

He felt a presence at his elbow along the rail and knew that the Palestinian had joined him. "So, we make landfall, at long last. Allah be praised."

"Allah be doubly praised," the captain echoed. "The moon and tide are also in our favor. According to the charts we will have ample clearance over the shoal that lies across the inlet. But I must get in and out rapidly or risk being trapped in the cove when the tide recedes. We must do our best to expedite the unloading process."

"I couldn't agree more, Captain. The more distance you put between us before they find you again, the less chance they will know where to look for us. As for the unloading, you already know in general what is required of you. Among the party awaiting me there are experts on the handling of the equipment who can be of material assistance."

The captain grunted acknowledgment. He had no reason to doubt his customer, having seen ample evidence of his flair for organization and preparation. But experience had taught him that nothing ever went precisely according to plan. There was no such thing as a voyage without glitches—there were only little glitches and big glitches. If they could just avoid the latter.

"I must return to the bridge to consult the radar again. We're approaching the spot where your hidden inlet lies." He left the Palestinian standing at the rail and went back to direct the delicate operation of threading his heavy freighter in the semidarkness through a narrow, shoal-filled channel that he had never laid eyes on.

Finding the inlet on the radar proved to be the easy part. He ordered the helm to a new heading that would aim his ship toward the position of the channel mouth indicated on the radar, reducing engine speed to ten knots. Then he ordered the running lights turned off.

All but invisible, the *Beirut Victory* pointed her bow at the shadowy land mass. The sea was quieter now than it had been in days. The captain kept his binoculars trained ahead, searching for the break in the shoreline that would mark the inlet entrance.

A silvery-white line materialized out of the void, formed by waves breaking on the shore and reflecting back the moon's pale illumination. The captain's practiced eye looked for a gap in the line and found it.

"Two points to starboard. Engines to one-quarter."

The big vessel slowed to the speed of a walking man as it groped for the mouth of the inlet. "Sixteen fathoms," called the boatswain's mate. "Fifteen . . . fourteen." Getting across the shoal was the tricky part. The captain's chart showed a minimum of eight fathoms at high tide. That would be cutting it close, and there was no guarantee that his chart was accurate.

"Twelve fathoms . . . eleven . . . ten . . ." the boatswain's mate sang out. The active sonar depth readings were shallowing at an alarming rate! "Depth down to nine fathoms . . . eight." The captain sucked in his breath and held it. "Eight fathoms . . . holding at eight . . . nine fathoms again."

A cheer went up from the bridge and the captain breathed

easier. They had passed over the shoal and were inside the inlet.

It proved to be a tiny cove, scarcely a mile across at its widest. The surrounding shore showed no sign of development or dwellings of any kind. There were no lights to be seen.

The captain checked his chart again. A penciled *X* on the western shore of the cove marked the position of the wooden dock the Palestinian had described to him—not the sturdiest of structures, he had been given to understand, but extending into deep water and robust enough for the freighter to tie up to. He couldn't make it out yet but ordered the helm to turn in that direction.

As the big ship inched around, he raked the shore with his binoculars, trying to pick out the dock. When a light from that direction suddenly winked at him, he was startled. *Someone was there!* A succession of long and short flashes followed.

Assuming it to be the International Code, he tried to read the message, but it made no sense. A knocking on the nearby window drew his attention, and he opened the door to the deck. It was the Palestinian.

"There seems to be some kind of reception committee on your dock," the captain advised.

"Don't worry about them. They're mine. The message was for me, saying it is safe to land."

Easy for them to say, thought the captain, back on the bridge, as he studied the ramshackle wooden dock through his binoculars. Safe was a relative term; there was nothing very safe about trying to snuggle a twenty-thousand-ton freighter up to a dock without the assistance of tugboats. One false move and the flimsy-looking structure would come tumbling down.

"Engines to one-quarter. I want continuous fathometer readings until we're berthed."

"Eight fathoms and holding, sir."

"If it goes below that, report immediately."

The *Beirut Victory* slid across the placid surface of the sheltered cove, her bow parting the moon-spangled waters to send waves rolling against the not-too-distant shore. The dock loomed ever larger in the captain's glasses. He could see quite clearly now the cluster of men standing on it.

"Come two points to starboard. Mr. Haddad, have the boatswain lower a launch and send it on ahead to prepare for docking. We'll need spring lines fore and aft."

"Aye, sir." Within minutes the ship's launch with three seamen aboard had been lowered into the water and was speeding toward shore. The captain watched as it reached the dock, one of the seamen scrambling up a ladder to receive the giant hawsers that the launch would ferry over from the freighter.

"Reverse engines!"

Propellers churned up white water around the stern, and the ship's progress through the water slowed. The freighter was almost motionless now. They were still forty meters from the dock. Close enough.

"Engines all stop."

The bow line was lowered to the launch, which set out for the dock. A light line attached to the hawser was tossed up to the waiting seaman, who hauled up the looped end of the heavy rope and wrapped it around the end of one of the pilings.

At a signal from the boatswain, a winch aboard the ship began to take up the slack. The pilings supporting the dock immediately began to bend under the stress, and the captain watched in alarm as the dock swayed dangerously, those standing on it scrambling for something to cling to. As he braced himself for the structure's imminent collapse, the resilient pilings recovered and stabilized, and the dock held.

The bow of the freighter moved steadily toward its intended mooring. But now the captain saw that a new problem was developing; the stern was swinging farther and farther away, abetted by a current that was carrying it in the wrong direction. They were making a botch of it! If the stern moved too far away before the launch could get its line to the dock, the line wouldn't reach.

"All ahead one-fourth!" he commanded. "Hard right rudder!" The powerful engines began to churn, arresting the runaway motion of the stern, which began to move back in the other direction. The launch rushed the stern hawser to the dock, where it was secured, the stern winch whining into action as the captain ordered the engines shut down again.

The big cargo ship was drawn closer and closer to the dock, its bulk dwarfing the other structure, the ship's deck looming a full two stories above the surface of wooden planks. Could its minimal construction possibly withstand the force of contact with twenty thousand tons of moving ship? The captain had serious doubts that the padding slung over the side of the *Beirut Victory* would be sufficient protection against the impact of her hull.

The bow made contact first, the groaning of the dock's supporting pilings audible aboard the ship as they deflected alarmingly. Braced in advance, this time, the party on the dock held on tightly as the surface they were standing on tried to move out from under them. It shuddered and seemed on the verge of collapse. But again the marvelous resiliency of the logs driven deep into the cove bottom won out, and the dock survived.

When it came a minute later, the impact of the stern was like an aftershock of an earthquake, not nearly as severe as its predecessor. The dock quickly stabilized again, the *Beirut Victory* held fast to its mooring.

The first one down the ladder was the Palestinian, his handicap barely noticeable as he clambered onto the dock and embraced the leader of his advance party. It was the Eurasian who had accomplished the diversion in Singapore of the crew from the Chinese destroyer. He had been sent directly here from Singapore to prepare the way.

"All is in order?"

"We are ready for you," the other beamed. There were three others in his group, and al Saif embraced them, one by one, calling them by name.

"The East Wind technicians are here?"

"The two Pakistanis? Yes, they arrived yesterday with their equipment. Come, I will introduce you."

"In a moment. First, tell me the rest. The surroundings are secure? There are no unwanted eyes around to witness what we are about to do?"

"No. As I said, all is secure. It is the off-season for the fishermen who use this dock. The shepherds who were operating nearby when we were here before have moved their flocks to new grazing lands to the east. There is no one else about. I have seen no Irani patrols of any kind."

"Excellent. I will meet my missile experts now. I want them to help supervise the unloading of the cargo."

Aboard the ship, the captain was anxious to dump his incriminating load and get out again before the tide left him high and dry. They would have to hurry with the unloading of the lighters.

The derricks on either side of the number four hold had already swung into action, the giant hooks at the ends of their thick cables in the process of being lowered into the hold. Waiting below was the lighter barge containing the trailer-erector-launcher for the East Wind and the tractor to pull it. Directly under the open hatch, the metal barge still rested on the heavy rope sling that had been specially designed to lift it into and out of the hold.

When they saw the lighter emerging through the hatch, the group on the dock let out a whoop, then held their breath as it swung over the end of the dock, dangling precariously several stories above before beginning its painfully slow descent. When it settled onto the dock, another cheer rang out, as two men scrambled atop it, broke the seals, and undid the lugs that held the huge cover in place. Stringing cables through the brackets welded to its surface, they attached the hook from one of the hold's two derricks to the cables and vaulted back down on the deck.

Up went the hefty metal lid, turning on end as it lifted away from the lighter, splashing into the water seconds later and immediately sinking from sight.

Meanwhile the crew on the dock had swarmed inside the lighter. They ran more lengths of cables around the axles of the long trailer. The derrick hooks were again lowered and attached. After a few false starts and subsequent adjustments, the heavy piece of equipment began to emerge from its seagoing habitat. It was a primitive-looking steel truss affair, the carriage set on relatively small, whitewall-tired wheels, a long steel wagon tongue folded back over its frame. It settled onto the dock and the derricks returned for the remaining contents of the lighter, and a powerful-looking tractor shortly made its appearance.

While the crew on the dock hitched the tractor to the trailer, the empty lighter was dumped into the sea. As he gave the order to start operations on the number three hold, the captain saw a puff of black smoke rise from the deck. The tractor's powerful engine coughed, caught, and came to life with the rough, low-pitched rumble of a diesel starting up. He turned his attention to the most delicate part of the unloading process—getting the missile itself from the hold of his ship to the dock in one piece.

Again the process in the number four hold was repeated in number three, the derricks on either side hoisting the lighter carefully out of the hold in its rope sling. It was rotated out over the dock and lowered cautiously onto a spot alongside the trailer, its cover removed and disposed of as before.

The dock crew swarmed inside. This time, instead of cables, they carried the components of another type of sling, this one designed to protect the sensitive skin of the East Wind and its rocket casing. Stout, wide straps were threaded underneath the missile body in several locations, the straps then converted into a harness by attaching their ends to a connecting boom. A hook from each derrick was attached to either end of the boom and the delicate lifting maneuver began, the crew helping to guide the missile out of its container without striking the sides.

Fascinated, the captain watched the long, incredibly fat missile emerge from its metal cocoon. The absence of a nose cone, which had been removed and stored beside it in the lighter, gave it an even stubbier, blunter appearance. The East Wind's gleaming fuselage, a midnight blue-black in this later version with three white rings encircling it, was more immense than he had imagined, projecting awesome power. He had been skeptical that such a single-stage device could carry a payload all the way to Israel from here. Now he no longer doubted it.

The ship's derricks began to lower the East Wind onto its trailer-launcher, one of the Pakistanis directing the operation from below, exhorting the tractor driver to jockey the trailer back and forth, until it was in just the right spot. Many hands helped to ease the missile into place, and at last the mating occurred. Attachments were secured that locked the missile to the transporting unit, which also served to erect the missile to its launch position.

Now the white nose cone and black fins, which had also been detached, were removed from the lighter, the dock crew setting about attaching them to the missile, again under the Pakistani's supervision. Finally the empty lighter was lifted off the dock like its predecessor and dropped unceremoniously into the water.

Al Saif scurried back up the ladder for a last word with the captain, handing him an envelope. "Your final installment. Well done, my friend."

The captain pocketed the envelope without looking inside, extending his hand. "Many thanks. I won't wish you luck; I know you never trust to luck. Nevertheless, we have been very lucky so far." He glanced nervously at his watch. "But my luck is about to run out if I don't get out of here before the tide drops any further."

He barked out the order to start the engines. The Palestinian saluted, turned on his heel, and went back down the ladder. As soon as his head disappeared, the captain opened the envelope and looked inside. The money was all there.

The lines were cast off and the *Beirut Victory* drifted slowly away from its mooring. Preoccupied with the business of getting underway, the captain's attention was drawn away from the scene on the dock. When he looked back, the awesome missile, looking even deadlier with its fins and pointed nose, was already moving along the dock.

Where would they stash it? He didn't know, didn't want to know. From this point on, he was out of it, back to the sea lanes with his fat fee and his cargo of machinery bound for Bahrain, as if nothing had happened . . . as if there had never been a special passenger with a special cargo, nor an unscheduled stop at a tiny cove in Baluchistan.

They moved without headlights or light of any kind except from the moon, now higher and brighter than before. The dirt road was more primitive than the Palestinian leader remembered it, apparently little used, overgrown by vegetation in places, deeply rutted and excessively bumpy elsewhere. His advance crew had repaired the worst spots but other areas were barely passable, the missile-bearing trailer with its high center of gravity constantly in danger of tipping over, its progress exceedingly slow.

Negotiating tight curves proved the most difficult problem for the twenty-meter-long trailer. On two occasions it got stuck, the only way of extricating it to back up and try again, going off the road to complete the turn. It had taken two hours to traverse less than four kilometers, but now they had almost reached their destination. Perched on the front end of the trailer near the missile's nose, the leader kept looking for the grove of saplings he remembered. It couldn't be much farther.

He had assigned one of his men, with a broom, to walk behind the trailer, sweeping away the tracks that the tractor and trailer had left in the dirt. When daylight arrived there would be no telltale signs to lead anyone to suspect that a piece of heavy equipment had passed this way. They saw no one along the way and he told himself that was a good sign that no one had seen them.

The trailer made its agonizing way around another tight turn. There—there in the distance! Those were the trees, he was certain, the land behind them rising abruptly. A rock quarry was carved into the steep hillside, long since abandoned, its entrance all but hidden by the grove of trees and other vegetation that had sprung up around it.

It seemed to take an eternity to reach the spot. Then he was down off the trailer directing traffic as the tractor left the road and turned through an opening in the trees and underbrush that had been cleared by the advance party.

They hadn't done a good enough job. The trailer and its unwieldy cargo teetered precariously over the uneven ground, at one point threatening to tip over. "Stop!" shouted the leader. He put a shovel brigade to work to level some of the high spots, and the tractor started up again. Moving at a snail's pace, it somehow got its payload across the toughest area and found itself on relatively level ground, the old road used to haul away the blocks of granite from the site.

Inside the quarry it was just as the leader remembered it, the walls of rock surrounding them an ideal screen to shield their operation from searching eyes. Even with the missile elevated to its launch position, it wouldn't be seen from outside the quarry.

The taller of the two Pakistanis, the guidance expert, approached him. "I must know the exact location of this spot, to an accuracy of one-thousandth of a degree. I will need the same accuracy for the target location."

"I have the numbers for you." He withdrew a slip of paper from his billfold and handed it to the Pakistani. On it was written two sets of latitudes and longitudes in degrees, minutes, and seconds.

Spooner was awake well before his alarm went off. He hadn't slept well at all, having had second thoughts about the "all due speed" directive and his decision to cruise, instead, at moderate speed to time the intercept for daylight hours. He dressed hurriedly and headed topside. Eight bells sounded 4 A.M. as he stepped onto the bridge.

Lt. Engel had the graveyard watch and was still on duty. "Anything yet?"

"No, sir. No radar contact as yet."

The ship should have been well inside their radar range by now. "You're in the long-range mode?"

"Yes, sir, in narrow-sector search about the predicted track. There are no blips showing in the sector."

"No further input from the *America?* Heading changes, position updates?"

"No again, sir. They must all be sleeping in the CIC."

"Well, we might have to wake them up. Our quarry must have changed course. Try expanding the search and see if you can pick her up."

Engel switched to a wide-sector search and peered down into the hooded scope. "Still nothing. Want a look?"

Spooner put his eye to the hood. The scope face was devoid of blips, the only thing visible an irregular phosphorescent line far out on the left extremity of the scan, marking the shoreline of Iran.

"What's our maximum range in this mode?"

"About fifty nautical miles."

"Hmm. When was your last Navsat update on our own position?"

"Less than half an hour ago. At 0340."

"May I have it?"

Spooner went back to his navigation table and reviewed his calculations of the previous evening. They were right on course, within a few miles of his prediction. The *Beirut Victory* should be less than forty miles ahead, if it had proceeded on the same course at the same speed he had been given. It apparently hadn't.

"Mr. Engel, see if you can raise the folks at CIC."

"Aye, sir."

When the call went through he identified himself and asked for Lt. Cdr. Harold. "He's sleeping, sir."

"To whom am I speaking?"

"Petty Officer Manning, sir. Would you like to speak to the watch officer?" Spooner answered that he would.

"Commander Spooner? This is Lieutenant Ayres. What can I do for you?"

Spooner was put off by the flippancy in his response. "You're aware, I assume, Lieutenant, that my ship, the *Lawrence,* is on an assigned intercept, board-and-search mission? I was to receive written orders and also updates on the target position, neither of which have come through. Where are they?"

He could sense the lieutenant snapping to at the other end of the line. "I don't know, sir, but I'll find out. Hold, please."

At least they didn't play music when they put you on hold, Spooner reflected wryly, still annoyed at the lax attitude CIC was projecting. Lt. Ayres was back in less than a minute.

"Captain Spooner, a copy of your original orders is being sent out right now. Sorry about the delay. Encoded board-and-search orders will also be sent when you have the *Beirut Victory* in sight."

"That's just the problem, Lieutenant. That ship is not where it's supposed to be. We should have it on radar by now. Either the data sent me was erroneous, or the ship has altered course. I need a position update."

"Just a moment, sir." He was back even faster this time. "Captain, I am informed that we do not have the *Beirut*

Victory under surveillance at the moment. I can give you our present estimate of her position, if you wish. It's based on an extrapolation of yesterday's sighting, using the course and speed data from the AWACS track files."

"That sounds like what I already have, but give it to me anyway." He wrote down the latitude and longitude. The position differed by less than five miles from his own estimate.

"Lieutenant, the *Beirut Victory* is not at this position—not anywhere near it. We have a real problem here. When do you expect to have a new sighting?"

"Just a minute." He could hear the buzzing of voices. Why didn't they put someone on who had some of the answers?

"Captain Spooner, they tell me there's a Saudi AWACS flight scheduled for dawn. We have a direct data-link channel open to them. We should have something around seven o'clock."

"That's three whole hours from now! What about satellite data? Aren't you hooked up to the Ocean Surveillance Satellite?"

"Not directly, sir. Our input comes from Norfolk. It's seven to ten hours old by the time we get it."

"Well, for Pete's sake, have someone check it anyway!"

"I understand we did that, sir. Our last input, taken at about 6 P.M. yesterday, showed the ship on essentially the same track we've been extrapolating."

Spooner was becoming exasperated. "What about your E-2 Hawkeye, the 'hummer'? Can't you send it up?"

"That would have to be the captain's decision, sir. We'd have to speed up and turn the carrier into the wind to launch. And the captain—"

"I know, I know. He's sleeping. Look, Lieutenant, this whole Operation Chain Link of yours could fall flat on its ass before they play reveille aboard that seagoing hotel of yours. I think you'd better start waking some people up, and let's begin with Commander Harold."

"I'll see what I can do, sir. We'll get back to you."

"You do that." Spooner slammed down the phone. Engel looked at him questioningly. "They dropped the ball, Lieutenant. They dropped the fucking ball."

Harold's call came within ten minutes, while Spooner was

back at the radar scope with Engel, having another look. The CIC officer sounded greatly concerned. "What's happened?"

"It's gone, Commander—it's not there. The *Beirut Victory* has disappeared."

16

WHAT WAS HE going to tell the ambassador? David Llewellyn put the question to the other David Llewellyn staring back from the mirror. It was Monday morning and his deadline was up, the time the ambassador had allotted him to perform an evacuation survey with the airlines and report back. He hadn't called a single airline, reluctant to do anything that might set off a rumor—sow the seeds of panic—hoping that news of the recovery of the hijacked missile would get him off the hook. But no such word had reached his ears.

He concentrated on shaving off the last bit of lather on the tip of his chin, which he always saved till last, the dimple requiring special care. When the doorbell shattered the early morning quiet he almost nicked himself. Toweling off his face and grabbing his robe, he wondered who would come calling at six in the morning. As he reached for the door knob, he knew the answer.

"Shmona!"

"Shalom, good morning." The Mossad agent walked in without waiting to be invited. "I have a bit of news. Is Daniella—?"

"Not up yet. We just woke up."

"Who is it, David?" She came bustling up, dressed in a fresh-looking frock, making a liar out of him. "Oh, it's Baruch. *Boker tov.* You're very early. Something has happened, yes? Something good?"

"Has the naval blockade caught the terrorists with the missile?" Llewellyn asked hopefully. That would have been the best news he could think of.

"Sorry to disappoint you. Nothing of the sort has been reported." Shmona wrinkled his nose. "Do I smell coffee?"

"David just made it. It should be about ready. Won't you join us?" She led the way to the kitchen and got out the cups and saucers as Llewellyn motioned Shmona into a chair by the table and sat down in another.

"So what is this news bulletin of yours, Shmona? Has someone finally identified the man whose picture was on page one of all the local papers?"

"Not yet, I'm afraid. We've had some false leads and the usual number of crank calls over the weekend. It's disappointing, but hardly unexpected. The terrorist is undoubtedly known to persons in the local Arab community. Clearly, they're protecting him."

Shmona paused to sample the fresh coffee Daniella had poured. "No, my news concerns the other suspect, whose phone number we traced to that rented office in Jaffa. I believe I mentioned that the Shin Beth had been successful in tracking down the shopkeeper whose place was next door—the one that was closed the morning we were there. It seems he and his wife were vacationing in Eilat. The proprietor stated that he had never met the man in the office behind him, didn't even know his name. The man apparently never showed himself and kept odd hours, coming and going through his back entrance. But the shopkeeper did get a glimpse of him on two different occasions and was able to describe him."

"The white-haired man with the dark brows," Daniella remembered.

"Yes." Shmona pulled a sheet of paper out of his coat pocket and unfolded it. "The gift shop proprietor spent an hour with Sergeant Neff. We now have one of Neff's inimitable portraits of your man of the famous sword amulets."

He spread the rendering out on the table. The face beneath the imposing head of snow-white hair was relatively smooth and unlined. In bizarre contrast to the hair, thick, dark brows gave a brooding appearance to the eyes staring out beneath them.

"Now we're getting somewhere," Llewellyn exclaimed. "That's a face you'd never forget if you'd ever seen it. Does the media have it yet? When will it run in the newspapers?"

"It won't."

Both Llewellyns gave Shmona a look.

"We can't afford to have the same thing happen that has apparently happened with the Palestinian. The news accounts put him on his guard, sent him into hiding. It was probably a mistake to publish his picture. At least we can learn from our mistakes."

Shmona gulped down the rest of his coffee. "I want this man to believe that he's safe, that he's successfully eluded us. My plan is to proceed with discreet inquiries in such a way as not to arouse his suspicions."

David frowned. "The Shin Beth aren't very good at discreet inquiries. If one word gets back to him that they're looking for him—"

"Precisely. That is why the Shin Beth are not going to handle this. *We* are going to do it."

"We?" Daniella questioned. "You mean the Mossad?"

"I mean us, the two of us. The gift shop proprietor's description indicates that we are looking for a businessman, one who wears expensive three-piece suits. This is further substantiated by fibers found in the office suite. He may be an Arab masquerading as a Jew; the name on the office rental agreement was Saul Sternberg. It's a phony—we checked it out.

"I've mapped out some territories. I propose that we start with the restaurants frequented by businessmen for the business lunch, an institution in Tel Aviv. I will take Jaffa and the westside streets: Ha-Yarkon, Ben Yehuda, Yermiyahu. You cover Dizengoff Street and the City Hall area—the City Garden and the cafes to the south along Ibn Gevirol."

Llewellyn could tell from his wife's face that there was no stopping her. "I suppose you're determined to do this?" She nodded. "Okay, then I'm going with you."

"Oh, David!"

"That's not a good idea, Llewellyn," Shmona protested. "Your presence could blow her cover."

"Which is?"

"Daniella will be posing as a relative—let's say a niece—of the man in the picture. She is trying to trace him. He left home years ago, came to Tel Aviv, and changed his name. She doesn't know his new name or address, has only the portrait to go by. An American in her company would only arouse people's suspicions, make them doubt her story."

"You're saying I'd just be in the way." They both avoided his eyes. Okay, he'd have to do it another way. "When do you propose to kick off this new joint venture?"

Shmona looked at Daniella. "Immediately. This morning, if you can be ready. I thought we could drive to Tel Aviv together, go over the plan en route."

"The sooner the better," Daniella pronounced. "I'm ready now. I'll get my purse."

"You haven't even finished your breakfast," David protested.

"I'll take a roll with me," she shouted from the other room. He selected one from the basket on the table and wrapped it in a paper napkin handing it to her when she reappeared. She popped it into her purse.

"Let's go."

Llewellyn took her in his arms and held her close. "Be careful."

"I will, David, I promise." She squeezed him back reassuringly, then was gone.

While dressing hurriedly, he watched through the window as Shmona's unmarked gray-blue Opel pulled out of the parking area. He memorized the license number, then picked up the phone and called his office.

"Good morning, Sheilah. Please give the ambassador my apologies and tell him I'm indisposed. I'll call him later today."

"Now that's desert!" Richard Llewellyn exclaimed. He was looking down at a sweeping array of windblown sand dunes illuminated by the newly risen sun that stretched as far as the eye could see. The AWACS was flying over the Rub' al Khali, Saudi Arabia's vast Empty Quarter, en route to the easternmost corner of the Arabian peninsula, where it would continue its search for shipping in the Gulf of Oman and northern Arabian Sea.

It was more than an hour's flight for the AWACS from its base near Riyadh. Richy was impatient to get there and resume the search. Shortly after takeoff he had spoken with the

Combat Information Center aboard the carrier *America* and learned of the disappearance of the freighter *Beirut Victory*. The *America* had not yet been able to launch its own surveillance aircraft, the E2 Hawkeye, and its satellite data had failed to shed any light on the freighter's whereabouts. The U.S. Navy's destroyer *Lawrence* was still in the vicinity, vainly searching for the ship it was sent to intercept. CIC was hoping the AWACS could find it for them.

Richy could think of several possible explanations for the apparent "disappearance." If the *Beirut Victory* was in fact the ship carrying the terrorist contraband, it was possible that the terrorists had gotten word of the naval blockade and turned back, or headed for some nearby port to wait things out. But there was another possibility. They might be trying to sneak past the blockade in Iranian coastal waters, with or without the cooperation of the Iranian authorities.

In any case, the suspicious change of course by the freighter made him all the more certain his gut feel had been right all along—that the *Beirut Victory was* the ship Operation Chain Link was set up to snare. And snare it they would. Eluding a destroyer's puny radar was one thing. But there was no way the freighter could hide from *his* radar. He grinned. The *Beirut Victory* was about to be had.

The mammoth black-and-white-striped radome carried piggyback on the Boeing 707's fuselage spun slowly in the gleaming sunlight, the antenna inside scanning its powerful beam across a three-hundred-mile swath of ocean. Richy watched the phosphorescent green trace replenish the image on the face of the king-size vertical display, mapping out the shoreline on both sides of the Gulf of Oman. Most of the gulf was spread out before him, from its southern Oman boundary to a portion of Iran that defined its northern shore. The green flecks of light sprinkled here and there over the expanse of water in between were ships en route to or leaving the Persian Gulf.

It required several minutes' worth of scans to build up a time history that would provide a vector of each ship's course and speed. Then he dumped the positions and vectors into the central processor that would perform the correlation algorithm he, himself, had programmed into it, comparing each input with the track files of the ships the AWACS had been observing over the past week and their predicted positions, updated from yesterday's sightings.

Numbers began popping onto the screen next to some of the blips, signifying that these ships had been identified. By referring to a computer printout, he could find the name of the ship corresponding to each numbered blip. He knew most of the names and numbers by heart. The *Beirut Victory* was number 17. There was no number 17 on the screen.

There were two possibilities. It could be farther to the east, in the north Arabian Sea, having slowed down or turned turtle. Or it could be farther north, beyond the range of the AWACS radar, in the portion of the Gulf he could not yet see. He decided to check that possibility first. He called the pilot and requested a turn to the north.

The 707 performed a shallow banking turn to the left and levelled out. With each successive scan of the rotodome, a bit more of the Iranian coast appeared on his display. But no new blips so far. He told himself to be patient. There was still a hundred-mile stretch of coastal Iran, from Cape Meydani to the Pakistan border, that he couldn't yet see.

It was shortly after the promontory he recognized as Cape Meydani materialized on his screen that he saw it—a faint blip about ten miles south of the cape, still not sharply defined because of its distance from the radar. After several scans it began to grow more prominent, and he punched the designator that would develop its course and speed. It was traveling due west and was making almost twenty knots. He called the radioman on his intercom.

"Sparks, I think I've got it! Put me through to CIC."

It was Lieutenant Commander Harold who answered. He'd been expecting the call. "You found our 'Black September'?"

"I'd bet a bundle on it! An unidentified ship in a new location, ten miles off the coast of Iran, near Cape Meydani. Westbound, doing twenty knots. Her location is 25 degrees, 12 minutes north latitude, 59 degrees, 6 minutes east longitude."

"Much obliged, AWACS. We'll launch a Viking immediately and check her out. If she is the *Beirut Victory,* we'll get aboard and have a look-see."

"Keep us posted, Commander. Over and out."

• • •

The call from the carrier *America* found the *Lawrence*'s captain perusing a message he had just decoded that had been sent "for his eyes only." It was the description of the "terrorist contraband" he was to search for on boarding the freighter *Beirut Victory*. The message left Spooner, if anything, more perplexed than he had been before reading it.

The terrorist cargo was described as "two metal lighter barges twenty meters in length, hijacked from another ship in the Strait of Malacca." There were no further details. The *Beirut Victory* was by all accounts not a LASH ship but a conventional freighter—a World War II victory ship. What would she be doing with lighters aboard; how could she load or unload them? What sort of contraband were the lighters supposed to contain?

From the *America*'s Combat Information Center, Lt. Cdr. Harold informed him that a ship believed to be the *Beirut Victory* had been resighted by the AWACS far north of its original course, and that his orders, as before, were to intercept her with all due speed and put a search party aboard. A jet from the *America* had been dispatched to verify the ship's identity, and that corroboration would be provided to Spooner as soon as received. He wanted to ask Harold about the lighters but knew he couldn't do so in the clear over an open-voice channel.

He took down the position, course, and speed information and signed off, hurrying back to his navigation station to plot it. The new location surprised him. It was about ten miles off the coast of Iran, which put it some fifty miles north and slightly east of his own position.

Was the terrorist ship trying to pull an end run, sneak by him in the shelter of Iran's territorial waters? Considering the known ties between Iran and some of the terrorist sects, it wouldn't surprise him if the Iranis were in on it. Well, if it was the terrorists, they weren't getting away with it.

He laid out the intercept. No pussyfooting this time; the freighter wasn't going to escape him again. He would highball to meet her at flank speed. He plotted a thirty-knot collision course and computed the heading and ETA. Even at this speed it was going to take upwards of two hours.

"Mr. Owens, order the engines to full ahead and come to a new heading of three-two-zero."

"Three-two-zero it is, sir." The watch officer signalled the engine room and ordered the seaman at the helm onto the new heading, then turned back to him. "They found her again, the terrorist ship?"

"We don't know for sure that it's the terrorists' ship, Mr. Owens. It may not even be the *Beirut Victory*. If it is, we're to go ahead and board her."

"Assuming that it is, sir—there could be armed terrorists aboard?"

"I have no information on that, Mr. Owens. But we will proceed under the assumption that there might be when we board her. The boarding party will be well-armed. Here are the keys to the armory. I want you to break out ten assault rifles and a dozen sidearms, with plenty of ammunition for both."

"Got her, skipper." Lt. Engel pulled his head out of the radar scope. "She's about forty miles off, forty-two degrees to starboard. Looks like your intercept course was right on the money."

"Tell me if her bearing starts to change, Mr. Engel." Spooner was relieved. There would have been hell to pay if the freighter had given him the slip again. A message from the *America* had just informed him that one of their Vikings had made a positive visual ID. The ship on his radar scope was, indeed, the *Beirut Victory*.

He turned his thoughts to the boarding operation, thankful that the heavy seas of the past few days had slackened. The conditions were almost ideal now, the highballing destroyer slicing smoothly through waters that were almost totally calm except for a modest early morning chop.

Spooner had never participated in the boarding of another vessel, let alone presided over it. The manuals he had dragged out weren't too helpful; they went into some detail on the protocol but were short on practical instructions, such as how to get your men aboard a ship whose captain and crew refused to cooperate. He would have to play it by ear—improvise—

188

and hope that the *Beirut Victory*'s captain would perceive the folly of resisting a U.S. Navy warship.

He would command the boarding party personally, of course. This wasn't something you could afford to delegate to a subordinate. He planned to take plenty of firepower with him, and had already ordered the boatswain's mate to select eight seamen experienced in the handling of automatic weapons. It would soon be time to brief them.

The message flashed to the *Beirut Victory* was short and sweet. "Heave to immediately and prepare to receive a boarding party." The *Lawrence* had reduced speed somewhat to remain abreast of the freighter, which had shown no sign of slackening its own pace and lay a quarter of a mile off the destroyer's starboard bow.

Spooner's first glimpse of the *Beirut Victory* had not been a reassuring one. The disreputable looking "tramp" certainly fit the description, with her rusty hull and weatherstained superstructure, badly in need of new paint. As he waited for her reply the captain had no trouble visualizing a horde of savage terrorists, armed to the teeth, hiding in wait in her forecastle.

After five minutes elapsed with no response from the freighter, he ordered the message sent again. Almost immediately the other ship's blinker began winking back a reply. No slouch when it came to reading blinker, Spooner didn't need the signal officer's help on this one. "Under . . . whose . . . authority?" he read aloud. "The United States Navy, you jerks!"

"Is that your reply, sir?" asked the signal officer.

"Yes, what else? Better leave out the jerks."

The next message received from the freighter was a longer and more formal one, protesting armed intervention on the high seas and citing passages from the international maritime code. The captain read it, then calmly gave the order to put a shot across her bow. He had arranged for this in advance. There was no point in expending a round from one of the destroyer's five-inch guns. The forward anti-aircraft battery would do nicely.

A long burst from the ack-ack battery sent seamen on the

freighter's deck scrambling for cover as tracer bullets flashed across her forecastle. Within minutes her speed had slacked off noticeably, and a message blinked from her stern. "Complying under protest." It was another quarter of an hour before she had slowed enough to accommodate a boarding party.

Spooner took Engel with him and left Owens in charge of the destroyer. Both strapped on sidearms before the launch was lowered into the water, the eight seamen aboard already armed with sidearms and assault rifles. The boatswain's mate steered the launch to the ladder draped over the side of the *Beirut Victory*. Spooner was the first man up the ladder.

The freighter's bearded captain was there to meet him and followed protocol by having him piped on board. They saluted one another. "I am Captain Philip Atawi, and my ship is of Lebanese registry, out of Beirut. What is the meaning of this outrage?"

Spooner was relieved that the other captain spoke English so well. At least there wouldn't be a communication problem. "I am Captain Abraham Spooner of the United States destroyer *Lawrence*. My orders are to inspect your cargo in search of war materials being brought unlawfully into the Gulf."

"What business is that of the United States?"

"We are acting at the behest of Saudi Arabia's government, which requested our assistance."

"Ah, so—Saudi Arabia." The captain's manner lightened. "Then there is no problem. The Bahrain city of Manama is my next port of call. The Saudis are perfectly free to inspect my cargo when I reach their territorial waters."

"My orders are to do so immediately," Spooner responded firmly. The freighter's captain looked askance at the armed seamen climbing aboard his ship and saw that Spooner wasn't going to be put off.

"I find your display of force excessive, Captain. We are an unarmed merchant ship, carrying no weapons or war materials of any kind. If you are determined to search my ship, I cannot stop you. So let's get on with it; I have nothing to hide. But this act of piracy will be appealed to the highest international court."

The captain had caved in too easily. Spooner looked around warily, suspecting a trick. But there was no sign of resistance on the deck, not so much as an armed sentry. Was he expecting help from the Iranis, the arrival of one of their patrol ships, perhaps, that would claim jurisdiction? There were no ships in sight in any direction.

"What cargo do you carry, Captain?"

"Heavy machinery, destined for Bahrain."

"And your previous port of call?"

"Singapore, where my cargo was loaded."

Singapore. That would place his ship in the vicinity of the Strait of Malacca, where some sort of hijacking had apparently taken place. "I'll need to see your bill of lading. Then we'll have a look in your cargo holds."

The captain dispatched the mate for the bill of lading and led the way to the number one hold in the forward part of the ship. Spooner left Engel and four of his seamen on deck and took the other four with him, climbing down into the hold behind the captain. It was filled with large wooden crates, stacked wall to wall. The hatch above did not look wide enough to pass one of the giant lighter barges and there was no such item listed on the bill of lading.

Hold number two was similarly crammed with the same kind of big crates. Its hatch looked no larger than the other. They moved on to hold number three.

This one had a wider hatch, he noted, as they began the descent into the hold. There was a derrick on either side of the hatch. Inside the hold, he saw that its floor was again covered with more of the hefty crates, though there appeared to be more space between crates than in the other holds. He looked for signs that they might have been moved recently. He couldn't really tell.

Hold number four, back toward the stern, was a carbon copy of number three. If one of the missing lighters had ever lain in this hold, there was no sign of it. They climbed back up to the deck. The search was turning out to be one huge fizzle, a four-alarm false alarm.

The captain spread his palms as if to say, "Satisfied?" Spooner wasn't. He still had some questions.

"Why did you change course so abruptly yesterday, veer off

toward the coast of Iran after our jet flew over your ship? This is not exactly the most direct route to the Gulf. And you speeded up; you were doing only ten knots up to then."

"We were limping along on a bad engine," the captain explained. "It's been plaguing us off and on since we left Singapore. It got so bad I thought we might have to put into port and wanted to be near land. But my machinist's mate managed to get it fixed early this morning. It's all in the ship's log. Would you like to see it?"

Spooner declined the offer. Log books could be cooked, like any other books. "You didn't put into any ports, then, since Singapore? For repairs—any other reason?"

The captain denied doing so.

"Would you mind if I questioned one of your men?"

"Not at all. Mr. Haddad!" The man with the three stripes of a first mate hurried over.

"Not your mate, Captain. One of your seamen, if you don't mind."

"Why should I mind? But I'm afraid none of my seamen speak English. That is why I suggested Mr. Haddad. His English is very good."

"What about French?" Spooner's French was passable. "Do any of them speak French? Or Urdu? One of my men is fluent in Urdu."

"Only Arabic, I'm afraid. But I would be happy to translate."

"I'll bet you would," Spooner thought. Taking stock of the situation, he told himself that he had carried out his orders— to ascertain whether the *Beirut Victory's* cargo included two twenty-meter lighter barges. It didn't. Thanking the captain for his cooperation, he turned to Lt. Engel. "Let's go."

His crewmen made their way down the ladder to the waiting launch, Engel following. Spooner was the last to leave. He saluted smartly and was piped off.

Fifteen minutes later, his message was radioed back to the USS *America*. FALSE ALARM. BEIRUT VICTORY CLEAN.

It was night time and a light snow was falling. The red tanker truck with the name emblazoned on its side in Arabic script had been standing in the same place for more than four hours.

It was one of a long procession of stalled vehicles waiting for the pass ahead to be cleared by snowplows. In spite of the heavy mackinaws they wore, the three men inside the cab were half frozen. It had been necessary to turn off the motor to conserve fuel, and they could only afford to restart it sporadically to thaw out the inside of the cab.

Ishmael, the Mosul factory worker who had engineered the theft of the warheads, was growing increasingly uneasy. The Iraq-Turkey border lay only a few kilometers ahead. They had made good time to this point, arriving here before dark, only to be confronted by the road block. Although the driver reassured him, Ishmael continued to fret. The snoring of the third man, the one with the beard, on the seat between him and the driver, irked him. How could Nestor sleep at a time like this?

"This confounded cold cannot be doing my cargo any good. I hadn't counted on having it cold-soaked for such a period of time."

"Is it the chemicals you're worried about, or the microbes?" asked the driver.

"The microbes, of course."

"I think you can relax. The oil bath they're resting in should serve as a perfect insulator. I doubt if they'll see as much as a ten-degree swing in temperature."

At long last there were signs of activity up ahead, as one vehicle after another could be heard starting its motor. "I think we're actually about to move," the driver observed, starting up his diesel.

There was silence between them for a time as the tanker truck continued to pick up speed, lumbering past one of the snowplows that had cleared the way. Now that they were finally moving, Ishmael felt better, his anxiety beginning to dissipate.

The procession of vehicles began to slow again. They were approaching the control point on the Iraqi side of the border. It took several more minutes of fitful stops and starts before they could actually see it, a pair of small wood frame structures on either side of the highway that were little more than huts. Two guards wearing heavy overcoats and sidearms were checking the vehicles as they filed through.

It wasn't long before their turn came, as the sedan in front of them was allowed to advance after only a cursory look inside its trunk. The driver handed the border guard all of their fake passports and the papers on the truck. He examined them under his flashlight. "All of you are Iraqis? Your departure point?"

"Kirkuk," responded the driver.

"You stopped in Mosul?"

"No, we bypassed the city."

"And your destination?"

"Van, Turkey, to dump our load of heating oil."

"They can probably use it. It's extremely cold there right now." The guard handed back the papers. "The key to the cap on your tank, please."

"It's not locked."

The guard climbed up the rungs on the side of the truck and uncapped the loading receptacle. Holding his flashlight over it, he peered inside. Satisfied, he resecured the cap and climbed back down, waving them through.

Less than a kilometer beyond they reached the Turkish control point on the other side of the border. The facility was less primitive than the Iraqis', with several more modern-looking buildings, and was manned by soldiers. "Papers, please," one demanded in good Arabic, as another peered in from the other side of the cab.

"Any Turkish citizens? No, you are all Iraqis, I see." He stamped each passport and handed them back with the vehicle papers. "Your destination?"

"Van," replied the driver.

"How long will you be in our country?"

"Just long enough to unload our fuel and return."

"Enjoy your visit." The soldier motioned them through. "Drive carefully. The road is icy in spots."

Ishmael felt a great weight leave his shoulders as the tanker rumbled forward and picked up speed. "You see, I told you," the driver sang out euphorically. "You worried for nothing. The snow storm was a blessing in disguise."

Progress was slow, the soldier's warning about icy conditions proving to be an understatement. By the time they reached the town of Hakkâri, deep in the snow-capped Hakkâri mountain range, dawn was breaking, revealing the lush greenery of alpine meadows whitened here and there with remnants of the last snowfall. Cattle were already up, grazing away, and they passed several isolated farmhouses, smoke pouring from their chimneys.

The driver turned off on a dirt road leading to a dilapidated farmhouse well off the highway. There was no smoke issuing from its chimney; it appeared to be deserted. He pulled to a stop next to an equally run-down barn, and they piled out of the cab, grateful for the chance to stretch cramped muscles. Ishmael and the bearded man walked behind the barn to relieve themselves. When they returned, the driver was on top of the tanker, working at its surface with a wrench-like tool.

Ishmael climbed up to join him. The driver was in the process of removing metal pins from the upper surface of the tank; the pins were disguised as rivets, their round heads just like all the other rivets holding together the plates that formed the tank. Completing the job, he lifted out a sizable aluminum panel that had appeared to be riveted in place, part of the outer surface of the tank. Its underside was slick with oil. He laid it on its dry side on top of the tank, rolled up his sleeves, and plunged his hands through the opening into the foul-smelling oil.

His hands emerged clutching a light chain. "I'll need some help with these."

Ishmael moved over to assist him as the third member of the party climbed up to join them. The driver and Ishmael succeeded in extricating the first bulky package, wrapped in its waterproof bag. Freed from the buoyancy of the oil, it became extremely heavy. With the assistance of the bearded man, they eased it down off the truck.

"Ugh! That stuff stinks like rotten eggs!" complained Nestor. "It's all over my clothes!"

"You'll be changing clothes anyway," the driver advised him. "You two are crossing the border dressed as farmers. Come on, let's get the others out."

When all three oil-smeared bundles lay on the ground beside the tanker, the driver opened the barn's large double doors, revealing a flatbed truck of ancient vintage loaded with bales of hay. He climbed into the driver's seat and cranked the motor. The reluctant whine of the starter brought a few wheezes from it and nothing more.

"It's just a little cold." He tried again with same result. He held the starter key down until the starter would no longer turn over. Cursing, he got out of the truck and opened its hood, reaching inside. "Now try it."

Ishmael got in the cab and turned the key. The motor coughed, sputtered a few times, and finally caught. The driver shoved in and backed the truck out of the barn. Leaving the motor in idle to warm itself, he hoisted himself onto the truckbed and climbed atop the load of hay.

The bales were sizable and very heavy. With a stevedore's hook he removed several bales from the top tier and stacked them on the sides. Then he set about hollowing out some of the bales on the next tier down. The other two climbed up onto the load to help him. When they were satisfied that the hollows were large enough, they used the discarded straw to wipe most of the oil from the three cumbersome bundles, then lifted them onto the truckbed and wrestled them into their nesting places inside the stack of hay bales. When the bales on the upper tier were replaced, there was no sign the load had been tampered with.

The driver handed the other two a bundle of fresh clothing. While they were changing, he threw a tarpaulin over the load and tied it down at the four corners.

"She's ready to roll. This is where we part company." He handed Ishmael a road map and pointed out the route to the Iran border-crossing point.

"There should be no problem at the border. The guards are used to local farmers traveling back and forth. And you have your Turkish passports."

Ishmael embraced him. "You have done well, brother. We are in your debt."

"It is all for the cause, brother. I wish I were going the rest of the way with you." He thrust his fist into the air in the Fedayeen salute. "To success!"

The other two saluted him back. "To success!" Ishmael echoed. "To our homeland! To a free Palestine!"

17

THE MOSSAD DIRECTOR was just leaving his office when the call came in on the red telephone, a crypto-secure direct line from Israel Defense Forces headquarters in Tel Aviv. He walked back to his desk to pick it up.

"Hello, shalom."

"Mordechai?" The voice was that of IDF Chief of Staff Tuchler. "Shalom. I wanted to make certain you'd be attending my general staff meeting in the morning."

"Yes, Shimon, I am planning to be there." He had already passed that word to Tuchler's secretary; there must be another reason for the call. "What's up?"

"A new agenda item that will interest you. And the Deuteronomy defense alternatives are also on the agenda, per your wishes. Anything new in that department?"

"The American Navy's fishing net hasn't caught anything yet, if that's what you're asking. As for our efforts to track down the terrorists from this end, we have a promising new lead, but nothing to report at this time, I'm afraid."

"No payoff on the portrait of the terrorist that was circulated?"

"Nothing so far. It looks like we may have driven him underground. What's the new agenda item?"

"It's actually an old item that's heated up again. You may have already got wind of it from the Prime Minister."

"No. No, I haven't seen the Prime Minister in several days." Shilo was somewhat miffed at the thought that he might have been kept in the dark. "What—?"

"The Nineveh business. The Defense Secretary passed the

word to me that they may want to go forward with one of the options we considered. We're to decide on a preferred approach and have it ready to present to the Prime Minister within the week."

"Is this for real, or just another fire drill?"

"It could be real, my friend. It could be very real."

"Then do me a favor, please. Put the Deuteronomy briefing at the top of the agenda. If you start with Nineveh and we get embroiled in those Mosul strike scenarios, we may never get to anything else."

The general staff was convened promptly at 8:00 A.M. by its chairman, Lt. Gen. Yigal Tuchler. A colonel from Aman, the Israeli Defense Forces military intelligence branch reporting to Tuchler, was called on by the IDF Chief of Staff to introduce the first agenda item by describing the threat. The room was darkened and a black-and-white slide flashed onto the screen. It showed an ungainly thick-bodied missile, white with black striping, blasting off from a launch pad, bereft of any visible external supports.

"The Dong Feng III, China's East Wind missile, is something of a relic," the colonel began. "It is a derivative of a Soviet intermediate-range missile designed in the early fifties—American designation SS-5—and using the same outmoded liquid fueling. Twenty of these Dong Fengs were deployed, starting in 1971. They are all in the process of being replaced by later-technology versions with solid rocket motors, like our own Jericho. In short, the Saudis paid China three billion dollars for a batch of outmoded hand-me-downs."

This elicited some chuckles from the general staff. The only man in civilian clothes, sitting next to Tuchler, wrinkled his nose in distaste. The colonel from Aman had a tendency to be overly dramatic, reflected the Mossad director. Was he implying that the Chinese missile was not a threat because it was old technology?

The colonel clicked his slide controller again and the vertical shot of the East Wind was replaced by a horizontal one. "This is the Dong Feng III on its trailer, which also serves as a hydraulically actuated erecting device for launching the misșile. It can be towed by a truck or an ordinary tractor. Its mobility is limited to the relatively level paved surfaces the unwieldy trailer can negotiate with its heavy load. The hypergolic liquid fuel is reportedly storable for long periods of time, but we've heard horror stories about some of the accidents they've had.

"As to the missile's lethality," the colonel continued, "the Dong Fengs that were deployed in China contained a single re-entry vehicle with a fifteen-hundred-kilogram nuclear warhead of one megaton yield. The United States has been assured by both the Saudis and China that the Saudi deal did not include nuclear warheads, and we have since verified this. The missiles deployed by Saudi Arabia contain conventional high-explosive warheads, the type that did minor damage and caused relatively few casualties in the missile exchanges between Iran and Iraq during their recently terminated war, even when lobbed into population centers.

"In summary, it is our assessment that the hijacked Dong Feng missile, even in the unlikely event that it should somehow penetrate the blockade and become deployed at a site within range of our cities, would not pose a very serious problem."

Oh, really? Shilo thought, feeling personally attacked. It was *his* Mossad that had obtained intelligence of the missile hijacking and alerted the Israeli defense establishment to the danger. Now the rival intelligence agency, Aman, was playing it down, pooh-poohing the threat to Israel.

"One question, Colonel, if I may." Shilo interrupted. "Would your conclusion be the same if we learned that the warhead of this hijacked missile contained a derivative of the nerve agent VX, one of the most deadly substances known?"

The colonel from Aman bristled. "If you have such information, why were we not informed?"

"I didn't say we *had* such information, but we certainly can't afford to overlook the *possibility* that the terrorists could come into possession of such a chemical warhead. There are several sources accessible to them. So answer my question, please."

The colonel's supercilious manner began to disintegrate. "Admittedly, that nerve gas is highly lethal. If the warhead landed in the middle of one of our big cities and conditions were unfavorable, there could be many casualties."

"How many would you say?" Shilo persisted. "Worst case?"

"According to our own survey, a third of the city's population."

A collective gasp went up from the general staff. "Did I hear correctly?" Tuchler inquired. "Did you say one-third of the entire city could be wiped out? A city like Tel Aviv?"

"As a worst case. The casualties might not all die, of course; some might recover. And if the city dwellers were supplied with gas masks and were wearing them at the time, the casualties could be much lower."

"Thank you, Colonel." The Chief of Staff exchanged looks with the Mossad director. "That should dispel any thought of treating this threat lightly. I'm sure you are all as anxious as I to hear an assessment of the ability of our anti-missile systems to deal with it. After this terrorist missile was first discussed at a previous meeting, I asked General Rafi to make such an assessment. General, could I ask you to summarize your findings for us at this time?"

"Certainly, General Tuchler." The Army Ordnance commanding general stood up and strode to the podium. A tall man with a fine head of sandy hair and upright military bearing, he cut an imposing figure. Taking the slide control device from the Aman colonel, he clicked off the last slide and turned to face his audience.

"Whenever the subject of ballistic missile defense comes up, there is a tendency to think of a ballistic missile as an irresistible force against anything but some far-out Star Wars defense system. But what we have here is nothing like a Star Wars scenario. We are dealing with a single intermediate-range missile with a single, presumably non-nuclear, warhead, targeted on one of our population centers, in all likelihood Tel Aviv. This is a classical point defense problem. The Army has two point defense systems. The Hawk missile system is operational, the Patriot soon to be."

He clicked his slide control and a new picture popped onto the screen, a single curve resembling a parabola with time ticks along it. "This is a time-line trajectory of a typical IRBM with a nominal fifteen-hundred-mile range, similar to the East Wind. What makes this threat more difficult than the other threats our point defense systems were designed to cope with is the tremendous speed of the missile—IRBMs typically attain re-entry velocities of Mach 14 or more. But note the rapid deceleration after nose cone separation and re-entry."

His pointer traced the path of the missile down a constant linear slope to the point where its descent began to curve more steeply downward. "By the time it descends to ten miles above the target, it is moving much more slowly, a thousand meters per second or less, its path becoming almost vertical. It will continue to slow to a terminal velocity of around three hundred meters per second, or just over Mach 1. The Patriot missile can cope with speeds of Mach 5 to Mach 6; even our older Hawk missile can handle threats up to Mach 3 or 4.

"Because we are dealing with a non-nuclear threat and are not concerned with a nuclear air burst, we are not forced to intercept at high altitude—the mission for which our Arrow anti-tactical missile is being developed. We can afford to wait and intercept the RV after it has slowed to speeds that our present defensive systems, Patriot and Hawk, can handle."

"A question, General, if I might." It was the Air Force's commanding general, Barkai, who interrupted. "Might not your present defensive systems include manned interceptors?"

"Possibly. The crucial question is one of response time. There is only about a thirteen-minute interval between IRBM launch and RV impact. If our early-warning systems can detect the launch and begin tracking the missile shortly thereafter, we can determine its trajectory, alert the appropriate point defense systems, and transmit to them continuously its updated position, altitude, and velocity, so that these systems' own sensors are prepared to acquire the re-entry vehicle once it comes within their range.

"So it is our conclusion that intercepting the re-entry vehicle with one of our Patriot or Hawk missile batteries is feasible. In fact, they should find the re-entry vehicle, which cannot maneuver laterally, a relatively easy target. But the timing will be critical. The Hawk batteries have relatively short-range radar. They will have twenty seconds or less in which to acquire the target after it comes into range and get their missiles off. The Patriots, with longer-range radar, are somewhat better off. And as for your manned interceptors . . ." Rafi made a point of looking in Barkai's direction " . . . the timing would be even more critical."

Tuchler threw in a question. "General Rafi, you say that we must detect the missile at launch and begin tracking it shortly thereafter. If the missile is deployed in an unknown location some fifteen hundred miles from here, how can we accomplish this? Is it even feasible?"

"The feasibility question boils down to the three Cs—Command, Control, and Communications. As part of the Patriot agreement, the Americans will supply us with early-warning data from their satellite systems operating in this vicinity. We will receive almost immediate warning notification and position data on any ballistic missiles launched within two thousand miles of our border.

"The more difficult problem is setting up a track on the missile while it is still a thousand miles or more from our border. We would have to rely on our E-2C airborne radar platforms being on station at the time, alerted by some sort of ultimatum or other heightened level of hostility. And we would also be dependent on intelligence inputs on the general location of the launch site, in order to advise them where to loiter."

"Hmm," mused the chairman, "it sounds like we have a few problems yet to solve. Unlike Patriot, the Hawk missile has not, of course, been tested in this role. I gather, General Rafi, that your first line of defense would be the Patriot?"

"Quite so, with the Hawk as a backup."

"Could you inform us of the Patriot status at this time?"

"The American Patriot Missile units that defended our cities during Operation Desert Storm were withdrawn some months ago. Our first Patriot Fire Unit, or battery, was received two months ago, but without any missiles. A Fire Unit consists of a radar, an engagement control station, a power plant, and up to eight launching stations, each with four Patriot missiles in their firing cannisters. American military experts arrived last month to assist with the training of our own personnel, which is being expedited. Our first four Patriot missiles were delivered last week. I expect to announce the first missile test firing within a week."

Tuchler had already known this but wanted the others to hear it. He now recognized one of the other generals, who had a question.

"General Rafi, assuming that one of these chemical warheads is in that re-entry vehicle when it is torn apart by your missile's blast fragmentation warhead a few miles above Tel Aviv—what happens when all that nerve gas is released? If it is heavier than air, as I suspect, won't it come sifting down on us anyway, spreading like a shroud over our city?"

Rafi hesitated, uncertain how to answer. It was the colonel from Aman who came to his rescue.

"If I might comment, Mr. Chairman? The chemical-warhead lethality studies I previously cited treat this very point. It is shown that if the winds aloft are four knots or more—a condition that almost always exists—the poisonous gases will be almost totally dispersed before reaching ground level. For a detonation as low as two miles in altitude, the residual fallout on the target area was predicted as less than a tenth of a percent, according to my notes. Of course, the higher the altitude of intercept, the better things get."

Tuchler heaved a mental sigh of relief. He had heard enough to persuade him that the threat from the hijacked missile was not as formidable as he had feared. There was not just one, there were two defense systems with the potential of dealing with it. The launch detection and early-warning part of the problem would bear further scrutiny, of course, and the entire plan of action would need to be refined down to the last detail and simulated with appropriate computer models to verify its validity. But at least he could now move on to prepare for the Mosul strike without being nagged by the notion that his country was all but powerless against a possible blackmail threat from the terrorists holding the Chinese missile.

"If there are no more questions we will move on to the next agenda item. But first let me direct you, General Rafi, and you, General Barkai, to work together on this early-warning, command-and-control problem and formulate a detailed plan from which we can gauge the probability of making a successful intercept. If modifications are necessary—software or hardware—they should be addressed immediately and put on the front burner. There is no telling when we may run out of time."

Shilo was not totally happy with the turn of events. He was far from reassured by what he had heard that the Army's defensive missile systems really had the capability to counter a ballistic missile threat; he had heard extravagant claims from that quarter before. Despite Tuchler's reference to the front burner, he could sense complacency setting in already, could visualize the Deuteronomy threat sliding to the back burner as the general staff became more and more swept up in the preemptive strike against Saddam Hussein's huge chemical warhead and ballistic missile production complex.

He resolved to personally make sure that, whichever burner it ended up on, the burner stayed hot.

It was early afternoon. Daniella had been pounding the pavement since 9:00 A.M. in search of the terrorist connection. She had started near the north end of Dizengoff Street and worked her way south, discreetly showing the police portrait of the man who had placed the order for the terrorists' scimitar amulets to proprietors, waiters, and waitresses of cafes specializing in the business lunch trade. Not one individual in the dozens of restaurants she had visited had recognized the man with the prematurely snow-white hair and glowering black brows.

Exhausted, disheartened, and ready to drop, she reached the intersection of Dizengoff with Ibn Gevirol Street. Some glamorous occupation, this spy business, she reflected. So far it had been ninety-nine-percent leg work. And her legs were about gone, to say nothing of her feet.

She forced herself to press on, turning north on Ibn Gevirol. Along the several blocks between here and the town hall there were more restaurants and sidewalk cafes. She passed up the large McDavid's establishment on the corner, the Israel equivalent of McDonald's, as not sufficiently upscale for the business lunch trade. On the next block an attractive restaurant with outdoor tables shaded by blue-striped awnings beckoned. Cafe Ministori. It was one of the ones on her list.

As she made her way between the tables, a well-dressed businessman sitting by himself looked up from his newspaper, and she had a fleeting impression that she knew him. But she couldn't place the face, and when he immediately returned to his reading with no sign of recognition she decided she had been mistaken.

Collapsing at a vacant table, she told herself that she had earned a respite and picked up a menu. She ordered a falafel and a large glass of iced tea. The waitress was back with her order almost immediately. "Will there be anything else, madame?"

"Just the check, please."

By the time the waitress had returned with the check, she had dispatched the pita sandwich and drained the iced tea. She handed the waitress enough shekels to include a generous tip. "Keep the change, please. And perhaps I could trouble you to look at this picture of a lost relative I'm searching for." She pulled the police drawing out of her handbag. "He may have come into this restaurant at some time recently."

The waitress came around to her side of the table as Daniella spread out the portrait on it. She removed a pair of spectacles from the pocket of her uniform and put them on, staring at the rendering.

"Why, I think I have seen him, or at least someone who looks a lot like this. I can't be certain that it's the same man, but he's been in here several times for lunch with other businessmen. I think he may have an office nearby."

Daniella felt a surge of excitement. "Do you know his name?"

The waitress shook her head. "I'm afraid I don't." Her face brightened. "But perhaps the customer sitting behind you can help you. I've seen them here together. Oh—where did he go? He was here just a minute ago . . ."

Daniella turned to look at the table where the well-dressed man had been sitting. The chair was empty, an untouched piece of strawberry cheesecake remaining on the table, a tenshekel banknote beside it. She jumped to her feet and caught a glimpse of the man hurrying off down the sidewalk. The waitress pointed. "There he goes."

Thanking her, Daniella grabbed the police portrait off the

table and took off after him. He looked back, saw her, and ducked recklessly into the street, which was crammed with fast-moving traffic. Horns blared and brakes squealed as he dodged between vehicles, reached the median barrier, and plunged into the lanes of cars moving in the opposite direction. She was certain he'd be hit, but he emerged unscathed and sprinted on up the sidewalk on the opposite side of Ibn Gevirol.

There was no interruption in sight to the steady stream of traffic. She lit out up her own side of the street, trying to keep up with him and keep him in sight. There was a traffic light at the next corner where she could cross when it changed. She was halfway there when she saw him reverse direction, dashing back the other way. There was no light to cross by in the direction he was now moving; she was committed. She reached the corner just as the light changed and plunged across. In the process, she lost sight of her quarry.

Running back down the other side of the street as fast as her legs would carry her, she got to the corner where she had last seen him. He must have ducked down the side street, but there was no sign of him. Panting for breath, she rushed up the side street to the next corner and looked along the street that crossed it in both directions.

He was gone.

She had lost him.

David Llewellyn had spent the entire morning and early afternoon shadowing his wife. Keeping tabs on someone as alert as Daniella for so long a time without letting her see him would normally have been a tall order, but Dizengoff Street, with its swarms of people and myriad shops and cafes, was made to order for the purpose.

The problem was that he had worked up a voracious appetite and an all-consuming thirst in the process, and she showed no signs of stopping for lunch. The mouthwatering aromas given off by the variety of eating establishments made his plight all the more painful, but he couldn't afford to stop and order something for fear of losing contact with her.

When he saw her finally flop into the chair at the Cafe Ministori and pick up a menu, he rejoiced. Crossing the street, he had grabbed a stool at a falafel stall where he could keep an eye on her. He asked for a large stein of the local Maccabee beer and "the fastest thing on the menu."

By the time he wolfed down his food, Daniella had finished her own sandwich and called for the check. She was showing the police drawing of the terrorist to the waitress. But what was this? A man seated at the table behind her had stood up and was looking surreptitiously over the shoulders of the two women as they scrutinized the portrait. In the next instant he took off.

Llewellyn jumped to his feet and fumbled in his wallet. He tossed the counterman a bill, watching the man in the business suit hightail it down the sidewalk. Then he saw Daniella bolt out of the restaurant in pursuit. What was going on here? The man saw her, too, and changed course, darting into the street choked with moving traffic. He kept going, plunging in front of a large truck, its brakes squealing shrilly. Then he was on the sidewalk, not fifty feet from where Llewellyn was standing.

Where was Daniella? He caught a glimpse of her, stuck on the other side of the street, watching helplessly as the man she was chasing took to his heels again. When she began running up her side of the street in pursuit, Llewellyn saw the man reverse direction. She would never catch him now.

Coattails flying, the man in the business suit ran past the lunch counter and Llewellyn got a good look at him. Youngish, neatly groomed and fashionably dressed in his pin-striped gray flannels, no one he'd ever seen before. There was a desperate look in his eyes. He's scared to death of something, thought Llewellyn. Let's find out what, and why.

Picking up his change from the counter, he began walking rapidly in the direction the runner had taken. The man in the pinstripes reached the corner, looked back briefly, and turned down the side street. As soon as he was out of sight, Llewellyn sprinted for the corner and peered around it. His man was halfway down the next block, still running, but not as fast. He appeared to be tiring.

If he saw someone running after him, he would know he was being followed. Llewellyn had to be content with a brisk walk, staying as much as he could in the shadow of the buildings lining the sidewalk. The runner peered behind him, then loped across the street and disappeared down the crossing street.

Again Llewellyn broke into a run, reaching the corner to peek around it. His quarry had slowed to a fast-paced walk. The block was a short one. Llewellyn stayed under cover on the corner, waiting for him to reach the end of it, anticipating that he would "check six" again before committing himself. Right again. The dapperly dressed man took a long look around, saw nothing, and slowed down some more. Walking normally, he crossed the street and turned left down busy King Saul Street.

No need to hurry, now. Llewellyn reached the corner and merged with the other pedestrians meandering along King Saul, providing perfect cover for his trailing operation. Gray Flannel Suit stayed on King Saul for another two blocks. Then, in a move so sudden Llewellyn almost missed it, he disappeared into a building to his left.

Llewellyn sprinted to the spot. It was the entrance to the IBM building, towering some twenty stories above the street. He plunged inside, finding himself in an arcade-lined lobby choked with people. There was no sign of the pin-striped gray flannels.

He spotted the bank of elevators at the far end of the crowded corridor and pushed his way toward them. The light blinked out above one that was just starting up, and he arrived in time to see the floor-indicator arrow above the elevator entrance stop at number 7. As he continued to watch, it stopped again at number 9, number 12, and number 14 before descending.

Dapper Dresser could be on any of those floors; it would be out of the question to reconnoiter that many offices. But he couldn't stay up there forever. His best bet, Llewellyn decided, was to wait in the lobby and watch for the man to come down again. He settled onto a bench near the elevators for what he realized might be a long wait.

"It was that Llewellyn woman—the Shin Beth agent, or whatever she is—the one who went over the cliff on the road to Jerusalem. I recognized her immediately."

Malamud's impeccably dressed young assistant was looking uncharacteristically dishevelled after his post-luncheon workout. He lit up a cigarette, his hands shaking.

"A police portrait of me? My God! How did they get it?" The white-haired businessman had gotten to his feet behind his desk, his dark-browed eyes registering alarm. "Did you get a good look at it? Does it look like me?"

"It's not the best of likenesses, but it was close enough for the waitress at Ministori's to remember seeing you there. Unfortunately, she also remembered seeing me with you."

"She told this to the Llewellyn woman?"

His assistant nodded. "That's when I took off. She would have questioned me."

Malamud's concern increased. "She didn't follow you?"

"She tried. But I cut across traffic and lost her. You're safe, for the moment. None of the people at that cafe know who we are."

"Safe?" Malamud shook his head bitterly. "If that waitress could recognize me, then so could plenty of others. Once that picture hits the newspapers, I'm dead!"

"Maybe they don't intend to publish it," the assistant suggested. "If they were going to the media with it, why would they be canvassing restaurants and the like?"

"You have a point." Malamud considered briefly. "I have to make a private call. Wait outside. While you're at it, go back down to the lobby and make sure you weren't followed."

When his assistant had closed the door behind him, he picked up the phone and dialed a number. It rang and rang, a dozen times. He was about to hang up when a voice he didn't recognize answered.

"Marhaba."

Malamud recited the Arabic password the Palestinian had given him at their last meeting. *"Ruch minhon."*

"One moment." The voice spoke English this time. After a brief pause it came back on the line with the phone number elicited by his password. He wrote it down, hung up, and dialed it.

This time the call was answered immediately. It was the voice Malamud had expected.

"I am calling because I need your help again. That same accursed woman you were sent to dispatch is back in circulation again. That portrait the police did of your face? This agent has somehow got one of mine and she is taking it around and showing it to people. We've got to stop her!"

The ironic laughter at the other end of the line began before he had finished. "So the shoe is on the other foot. How does it feel? Shall I remind you of the advice you gave me when my own picture was published a few days ago? 'Get out of the country,' you told me. It so happens that I am about to follow your suggestion."

"You can't desert me like this!" Malamud protested. "I just paid you a small fortune!"

"So you did. And I will, of course, honor the obligation. Can you tell me where the Llewellyn woman is conducting this 'art exhibit'?"

"She is apparently working the restaurants in this neighborhood. She was at Cafe Ministori on Ibn Gevirol. But there's no guarantee she is still there."

"We will find her. Unfortunately I cannot attend to this personally. But I will send someone I trust.

"In the meantime, let me give you the same advice you gave me. Get out of the country. At least get out of Tel Aviv. It is no longer a healthy place to be."

18

ON THE GROUND floor of the IBM building, hiding behind a newspaper, David Llewellyn was having second thoughts about his decision to tail the mysterious young man in the pin-striped gray flannels and wait around for him to come back down on the elevator. He should have followed his first impulse and tackled the guy when he had the chance.

He was worried about Daniella, out there on the street with no protection, poking around for a lead on the terrorists. He shouldn't have left her. If only there was some way to contact her, let her know what was happening. She could join him here, question the man when he turned up again. She would probably be furious with him for interfering, following her without her knowledge. But in the long run she would understand it was because he loved her.

He knew she would be checking in with Shmona again; he had watched her telephone twice during the morning from restaurants along the way. They must have a central exchange to pass messages between them. If he could just get a message to Shmona— The only Mossad number he knew was Daniella's office in Jerusalem. She had given him strict instructions never to use it except in an emergency. He decided this qualified. Maybe the Jerusalem office had a way of contacting Shmona. It was worth a try.

He was heading for a phone booth he'd passed on the way in from the street when he saw the man in gray flannel emerge from the elevator, walk a few steps, and look around cautiously, his eyes sweeping the entire lobby. Llewellyn froze, then gradually relaxed. The man didn't know him; he was looking for Daniella. He strode back toward the elevators. The man he had tailed had turned around and was apparently waiting to go back up. This time Llewellyn wasn't letting him out of his sight.

He got there as the elevator door was closing and stuck out a hand just in time to trigger the automatic retraction feature. The door opened again. The only passenger was the man in gray flannel. Their eyes met, and Llewellyn managed a smile.

"Just made it. Eighteen, please." The other man was standing in front of the floor-selection panel and punched it for him, the light behind number 18 blinking on. He saw that number 14 was also lit. Now he knew the right floor, at least.

They stood side by side, not looking at each other, eyes straight ahead, waiting for their floor. Llewellyn could sense the other man's edginess. He considered getting off with him on the fourteenth floor, under some pretext. But his man would immediately be suspicious. He'd have to find another way to pin down which office he was in.

The elevator reached the fourteenth floor and Gray Flannels got out. Llewellyn punched 15 just in time to avoid going any higher, hit the door close button, and punched 14. When the elevator opened there was no sign of his man. He got off and walked into the suite of offices opposite the elevator. The lettering on the glass door read "MALAMUD ENTERPRISES."

The receptionist, a cute blonde, was sitting just inside the door and had a clear view of the elevators. "Shalom—may I help you?" she inquired in English, having apparently already sized him up as an American.

He had to chance it, he decided. He gave her a winning smile. "I'm looking for the gentleman who just got off the elevator. A young man in a gray pin-striped suit."

She eyed him suspiciously without smiling back. "You're not acquainted with this gentleman, I gather. Otherwise, you'd know his name."

"No, I'm afraid I'm not." He managed to maintain his smile while trying to think of what to say next.

"Then why, may I ask—?"

"He dropped something, you see, when we rode up together on the elevator. I wanted to return it to him."

"Why not just give it to me and I'll see that he gets it."

So she *did* know him. He shook his head. "I'm afraid I can't do that, miss. It's not that I don't trust you. But you see, it was a hundred-shekel bill that he dropped, and I'd like to return it to him personally." He removed a banknote of that denomination from his wallet and showed it to her.

The receptionist looked impressed. "I see." She considered briefly, then rose and walked over to another desk occupied by an older woman. A whispered conversation ensued, Llewellyn averting his eyes, effecting to be interested in a territorial map hanging on the wall next to him. He could feel their eyes on him and knew that he was being scrutinized.

Something unusual about the map registered in his consciousness and he inspected it more closely. It was a map of the West Bank, pins of various colors stuck into it, large clusters of them in half a dozen different locations. Malamud Enterprises apparently did some kind of business in the West Bank—a lot of it, judging by the number of pins.

The blonde secretary was back, eyeing him curiously as he tore his gaze away from the map.

"Mr. Zilbert—that's the gentleman you asked about—is in conference with Mr. Malamud. Mr. Malamud's secretary is going to buzz him."

"Perhaps we shouldn't disturb them. I could—"

Too late. The secretary was already talking on the line. She hung up and motioned him over to her desk.

"Mr. Malamud said to send you in, Mr.—?"

"Chalmers." He pulled an old alias out of his memory bank. "George Chalmers."

She opened the door to the office and thrust her head in. "Mr. George Chalmers, Mr. Malamud. Go right in, Mr. Chalmers."

Zilbert, in his pinstripes, was standing in front of the desk, staring at him fixedly. The chair behind the desk was vacant. There was no sign of the man named Malamud.

"Mr. Malamud is in the lavatory," Zilbert volunteered. "He'll be back momentarily. You have something for me, I understand?"

Llewellyn produced the hundred-shekel note. "I found this on the floor of the elevator, after you got off. It's yours, I assume?"

"Of course. How careless of me." He accepted the bill and pocketed it. "And how honest of you to return it." He held out his hand and shook Llewellyn's. "Mr. Chalmers, is it? Please sit down, Mr. Chalmers."

"Well, I really should be getting—" His first inkling of Malamud's return was something very hard poking him in the small of the back. He raised his hands instinctively.

"Yes, *do* sit down, Mr. Chalmers," said a strong voice behind him. Llewellyn eased himself into the chair and turned his head to look at the man holding a gun on him. His years of training as a counterspy had taught him to shield his inner reactions from others, but the sight of the black-browed eyes and prolific head of white hair sent shock waves through his system that it didn't take a seismograph to pick up. The reaction wasn't lost on the other two.

"I didn't lose any hundred-shekel bill!" Zilbert thundered. *"Just who the hell are you and what are you up to?"*

"Get his wallet," Malamud instructed. "And while you're at it, make sure he doesn't have a weapon. Stand up, please, Mr. Chalmers, and raise your hands higher."

Zilbert found the billfold in his trousers pocket and tossed it to Malamud, patting down the rest of him. "He's unarmed."

"You can sit back down now, Mr. Chalmers." A gasp went up from Malamud as he perused the contents of the wallet. "Llewellyn! His name's Llewellyn, same as that Shin Beth bitch! He must have been with her, must have followed you here! Wait a minute, what's this? He has American Department of State credentials. He's a U.S. envoy!"

Shock registered in the face of the man in gray flannels. He lapsed into Hebrew, and some hot words flew back and forth between the pair that Llewellyn wasn't able to decipher. But the sense of it was clear to him. Zilbert knew that he was out of his league. He didn't want any part of an action that would bring about the kind of retribution messing around with a high-level American diplomat was sure to invoke.

Llewellyn set out to exploit the situation, addressing Zilbert. "Call the American embassy. Let them know where I am. I'll clear you of any involvement. I'll—"

The sharp blow to the back of his head caught him by

surprise and he tried to stand up, but his legs had turned to petrified logs. The room and its furniture and the man in the gray suit swam together in a reddish-purple haze. In the split second before he lost consciousness he had a single thought: At least I wasn't shot . . .

After her futile pursuit of the dapper man in gray, Daniella re-crossed the street and returned to the Cafe Ministori. Her purse was still on the chair where she had left it, being watched by the waitress.

"Were you able to catch up with him, madame?"

"No. He was too fast for me. Is there a telephone nearby?"

"Just inside the door, to your left."

She picked up her purse, went inside, and found the phone, entering the number of the exchange Shmona had set up so they could stay in communication during their sweep of business lunch restaurants. Her message was taken; Shmona was due to check in within the next half hour and would call her back at the Cafe Ministori number.

Returning to her outdoor table, she ordered coffee and advised the waitress that she was expecting a call. She was still flushed over the exhilaration of the chase and excited by it. There was now clear proof that the drawing in her purse was a good enough likeness to be recognized.

The man who had run away had to be in on something with the white-haired man. Daniella felt certain she knew what: a link with the sect of gold scimitar terrorist assassins. The same terrorists who now possessed a weapon that could threaten her country with unspeakable devastation.

She had to convey this development to her Mossad control, get the wheels turning in the Mossad and local enforcement agencies to close the trap on the white-haired malefactor before he could get away. He was somewhere close by. She *could feel it.* The man who had run away would warn him. They had to nab him fast; he was their best chance of identifying the terrorists and locating the hijacked missile.

Time dragged by while she waited for Shmona to return her call. She was on her second cup of coffee when the waitress finally returned. "Your call, madame." She dashed to the phone.

Shmona was excited over her report, she could tell by the way he tried to sound calm and totally in control. He told her to slow down and asked her to repeat her story a second time.

"Okay—Daniella—here's what I want you to do. Wait for me there at the Ministori. I'll get there as fast as I can. We're going to continue working the restaurants in that neighborhood; it sounds like our man may have an office nearby. If so, it's likely he's been in some of the other places in the vicinity, as well. One of their proprietors or help may know who he is."

Daniella was disappointed. "But Baruch, while we're doing this he may get away. The other man will warn him. Why not arrange a police dragnet, cordon off the area?"

"That would take too much time, Daniella, and when he saw what was happening it might hasten his departure. As long as he thinks we don't know who he is or where he is, he may stay put for a while. This is the best way. Trust me. I'll be there as soon as I can."

Baruch Shmona had called Daniella from the Dan Hotel, where he had intended to show Sgt. Neff's latest creation to the personnel in its two upscale restaurants. He remained at the telephone, punching in the local number of the Mossad. Identifying himself, he reported a "code red" and requested that an unmarked car with two armed agents be dispatched immediately to the Cafe Ministori on Ibn Gevirol Street. They were to park nearby and remain out of sight until he contacted them on their car radio. There was ample evidence that these suspects knew how to play rough, the dead jeweler on Allenby the latest proof. Would they come after Daniella again? He felt certain of it. This time he'd be ready.

Hurrying out the hotel lobby and down the steps, he crossed the street against the light and turned down Frishman Street, where he had left his car. As he sped away from the curb, he felt a pang of conscience over using Daniella as bait like this. But it was justified, the situation warranted it. Locating the terrorist missile was paramount; countless lives in this very city could hang in the balance.

The traffic on Frishman was pokey, as usual. He followed the sluggish procession of cars across the Dizengoff intersection, staying on Frishman. Slow as it was, there was no more direct route. He leaned on the horn, cursing the slowpokes ahead of him. When they didn't respond, he gunned the motor and pulled around them, narrowly escaping back into his lane and causing an approaching car to slam on its brakes to avoid him.

His concern for Daniella's safety increased. She wasn't even armed. For that matter, neither was he. Until his reinforcements arrived, there wouldn't be much he could do to protect her, except to get her away from there.

He ran another light. Five or six more blocks to go. In another minute or two he'd be there . . .

Daniella came out of the ladies' room and headed back to her outdoor table to wait for her boss. Resuming her seat, she saw that a sidewalk hawker had moved in to work the patrons in the open-air part of the restaurant. They were quite common in the touristy parts of the city, but it was unusual to see one here.

"Kaffiyehs!" he shouted, making his way from table to table, waving an Arab head kerchief like the one he was wearing, under the noses of the diners. "Best quality!" The tray he carried was filled with the checkered cloths in a variety of colors, with head cords to match.

The waitress emerged from inside the restaurant, saw him, and hurried over. She exchanged words with him, Daniella watching with amusement. It was apparent she was telling him to move on, but he ignored her. She gave up and went back inside, no doubt to inform the manager.

Daniella's attention was diverted by a disturbance in the street. A van was double-parked in front of the restaurant, blocking one lane of traffic. Cars were honking, accompanied by angry shouts from their drivers. The driver of the van just sat there, waving to the cars to go around him.

Wait a minute—that van, windowless, its panels full of dents. It was green, not blue, but could it be the same one—? She couldn't make out the driver's face, but a sudden vision came to her of another face that had leered at her as the blue van was about to knock her off the Jerusalem expressway.

The Arab peddler reached her table, blocking her view of the van and its driver. *"Kaffiyeh,* Mrs.? All colors, very nice."

"No, thank you." She waved him aside, trying to see the face of the man in the van. But he didn't discourage easily.

"This one is especially nice." He pulled a folded kerchief out of his tray, a purple one.

"I said no. Please!"

She craned her neck to see around him. With a sudden, swift motion he seized her by the hair, pushing the cloth to her nose. The odor of chloroform was overpowering. She gasped and choked, clawing at his hands, trying to get to her feet. But he jerked her head back painfully, holding the cloth to her nostrils. She fought for breath against the suffocating vapor, until all the fight went out of her. She had the sensation of going under, of drowning in an unpenetrable sea of bubbles. Her body went limp and she fell to the floor.

The van driver jumped out and ran to help his confederate, now brandishing an automatic pistol to discourage bystanders from any thought of interfering. With one taking her feet and the other her shoulders, the pair lifted Daniella's unconscious form and carried it to the back of the van. Moments later, the battered green vehicle sped off down Ibn Gevirol.

The stunned spectators in the sidewalk cafe gaped after it, as the manager ran inside to phone the police. "Soldiers, on and off duty, all over town, carrying their guns," remarked a middle-aged woman with orange-red hair. "But when you really need them, where are they?"

When Baruch Shmona drove up and saw the gawking crowd in front of the Cafe Ministori, he feared the worst. There was no sign of Daniella among them, and it was clear that something had just happened. He peered down the street in the direction they were staring but couldn't make out what it was they were focussed on.

He was preparing to pull over and ask what had happened when he saw a speeding green vehicle a block ahead of him pull out of traffic and veer around several slower cars, then run the red light at the busy King Saul intersection. Could Daniella be inside? If he stopped to make inquiries, he would lose the vehicle.

He floored the gas pedal and took off after it. Jockeying around several cars, he accelerated toward the intersection, counting on the light to turn green before he got there. It did, and he shot through on the one open lane.

He caught several more glimpses of what looked like a green panel truck as it continued to weave in and out of traffic. Then it was stuck behind three clogged lanes of traffic waiting at another signal light, and he was gaining on it. Now he could see that it was not a truck, but some kind of van.

A windowless van with no markings. A van had been used in several earlier exploits. He got on the radio, reporting his position and the suspicion that the occupants of a vehicle he was following, a windowless green van, might have taken a Mossad agent hostage. Acknowledging the message, the Mossad dispatcher informed him that the two armed agents he had requested were two minutes away from the Cafe Ministori.

"Have them do a quick check on what happened there, then follow me. If those suspects are in the van, I'm going to need all the help I can get."

He was almost close enough to make out the numbers on the license plates when the light changed and the van took off again, dodging around another vehicle and momentarily out of view. They were approaching the south end of Ibn Gevirol, where it branched into three other streets. The van was now in the left lane, apparently planning to turn onto the left-branching street, Carlbach, in the direction of the expressway to Jerusalem. If it got on the expressway, they could bottle it up with road blocks at the appropriate spots. But suddenly the van swerved back into the right lane and made a hard right turn, careening onto the right-hand fork.

Caught in the left lane, Shmona hit the brakes, but was not quick enough to negotiate the right turn. He ended up on the middle fork, cursed, and sped to the next intersection. Were they onto him? They must have seen him gaining on them. Doubling back, he got back to Marmorek, the street the van had taken.

There was no sign of the van up ahead. What had become of it? To his right was the vast parking lot for the Habimah Theatre and Mann Auditorium. More out of desperation than anything else, he pulled into it.

The lot was half filled with parked vehicles, a matinee apparently in progress. Searching row upon row for a green van parked among them would be too time consuming. Instead, he drove to a spot where no cars were parked, halfway between the entrance and exit, and reported his whereabouts to headquarters. "I lost contact with the van when it turned west on Marmorek. It may have continued on or it may be hiding here in the parking lot. I'm watching the exits."

The dispatcher had some news for him. "Agents Namir and Lev are on their way to join you. They called in to confirm the abduction of a woman answering the description of agent Llewellyn."

"How about getting a police helicopter?" he questioned the dispatcher. "It could search the parking lot from above or spot them getting away on one of the side streets."

"One of their choppers is down for repairs. The other is being diverted from another job. It can't reach you for another fifteen minutes."

Fifteen minutes? Unless they were bottled up here in the lot, it might as well be fifteen hours. They could be halfway to the West Bank before—

Suddenly the green van shot out from between two rows of parked cars, streaking for the exit. Then it altered course and headed straight for his unmarked car. He had made the mistake of exposing himself. Now that the terrorists were certain he was following them, they were taking steps to put an end to it. Put an end to *him!*

He threw the auto into gear and turned toward the only other way out of the lot, the way he had come in, flooring the accelerator. It was his only chance. Exploiting its initial speed advantage, the van closed on him rapidly. As he neared the exit it was right behind him, and bullets began to fly, his rear window shattering. He ducked his head and kept going.

When another vehicle suddenly materialized directly ahead, entering the lot in the opposite direction, there was no time to think. His reflex action spun the wheel left as he hit the brakes simultaneously. His car went into a violent skid, tottering precariously on two wheels and threatening to roll, before its progress was arrested by a heavy chain-link fence. Almost simultaneously there was a sickening cacophony of screeching tires and colliding metal as the incoming auto and the van met head-on.

In his dazed condition Shmona had but one thought. He hauled himself out of the undamaged left side of his auto and lurched toward the smoking, demolished van. Its front seat no longer existed, the engine of the other vehicle now occupying that space. No one sitting there could have survived. The occupants of the sedan the van had collided with seemed to have fared somewhat better. He could see someone moving inside it, and it occurred to him for the first time that these were the two agents sent to assist him.

He would see to them later. He hurried to the back of the van and tried the doors. They didn't appear to be locked, but the distorting force of the collision had jammed them. He tugged as hard as he could, first on one door, then the other. The second gave a tiny bit.

Still grasping its handle in both hands, he pulled himself up onto the rear bumper, braced both feet against the other door, leaned backwards, and pulled with all his might. It yielded suddenly and he fell to the ground, landing painfully on his back.

Staggering back to his feet, he peered into the back of the van. On her back, bound and gagged, Daniella was spread-eagled across its floor. She couldn't speak because of the gag, but her wide, gyrating eyes told him she was not only alive, but conscious. Stout ropes pinioned her hands and feet to the four corners of the truckbed. The ropes had saved her life.

19

ICHALOV HOSPITAL, IN the center of Tel Aviv, was only a few blocks from the Cafe Ministori, where Shmona's pursuit of the terrorist van had started. It was here that an ambulance had brought the two badly injured Mossad agents, with Daniella and Shmona following in a police car. The doctor in the emergency room had taken one look at them and insisted that they admit themselves for immediate attention.

By the time they were examined and released with a clean bill of health, it was dark outside. Shmona was depressed; he had just been informed that one of the two terrorists, after being extricated from their demolished van and brought to the hospital, had been dead on arrival. The other was in a coma and could not be questioned. Another promising lead on the location of the terrorist missile down the drain. Or was it? If he could establish the identities of the two men, then maybe not. He decided to stay and get the crime lab started on it. He ordered a taxi to take Daniella home.

Daniella's first thought after being dismissed from the emergency ward was to call her husband. But instead of David's voice, it was her own voice on the recorder that answered. "Where are you?" she asked after the beep. "Working late again? I'm still in Tel Aviv. I'll be home in an hour or so."

Disconsolate, she hung up, craving the reassuring sound of his voice. She considered calling him at the embassy, but thought better of it. Her voice sounded shaky to her, and there was no point in alarming him. She knew she would be fine with a little rest, the rest the doctor had just prescribed. Her story would keep for a while, until she could talk about her experience calmly and unemotionally.

"Are you sure you're all right?" Shmona asked solicitously.

She nodded, trying to make her tight lips form a convincing smile. It didn't quite come off.

"Go home, rest, don't even think about work," he told her. "I'll look in on you in a day or so."

She was touched by his evident concern. Since the first day when she had been introduced to the cerebral little man who was to be her Mossad control, she had been in awe of him. Now, with the distressed look on his face and the patch over the cut on one eyebrow, he reminded her of a little boy after a nasty fall, on the verge of tears.

She kissed the bandaged eyebrow. "Thanks for my life."

He watched her walk down the stairs to the waiting taxi, a tear in each eye. The same inner voice that had scolded him for putting her life on the line spoke to him again. "Shmona," it said, "you're going soft on me."

A scant block away, in the office building that towered over the five-story hospital, two men were entering the freight elevator on the fourteenth floor, supporting a third man who could not walk and appeared to be unconscious. As they exited to the basement-floor parking area, the taller man propped between them, they were accosted by the night superintendent.

"What's wrong with your friend?"

"Nothing serious." The white-haired man supporting the unconscious man's right side grinned at the superintendent and winked. "He just became a father. Did a little too much celebrating and passed out. We're taking him home."

"Why are you using the freight elevator?"

"We didn't want his business associates to see him like this. It could damage his reputation."

David Llewellyn's first sensation on returning to consciousness was that of coming out of a blissful sleep into a harsh outside world that he was not all that eager to enter. It was a dark, cold world and also, he discovered, on his first attempt to relieve the cramped muscles in his legs and back, an extremely painful one. He couldn't move them, and the effort to do so set off an explosion in his head.

He lay still, waiting for the pain to abate, remembering the blow to his skull and the circumstances leading up to it. Where was he now? He began to take stock. He was lying on his side, tied in such a way that he was almost totally immobile, his legs bent behind him, his feet tied to his hands. His mouth was dry and uncomfortable. Something was stuffed into it, a piece of cloth. He tried to spit it out, push it out with his tongue, but he couldn't. Another piece of cloth was tied across his mouth, behind his neck.

It occurred to him that he might also be blindfolded, which would explain the darkness. But he had no sense of a bandage across his eyes. Then he noticed a pinprick of light. It was coming from a tiny hole that appeared to be just above his head, and it flickered. He was in a closed space, a very cramped space. And it was moving. The trunk of a car!

Now it all fit, the feeling of motion, the droning and vibration from the motor. He began to pay attention to the other noises, occasional rushes of sound, the passing of other autos. They were infrequent. He must be outside the city, on a road with little traffic. How far had they come? How long had he been out?

His muscles ached to be relieved, but every time he tried to move against the restraining bonds, the pain in his head became worse. Little by little, he managed to work himself into a more comfortable posture. The cramps in his limbs and back eased, giving him a chance to think. He had to get his mind working. He had to find a way out of this.

He felt the vehicle begin to decelerate from its steady pace, the motor winding down. It slowed to a crawl. Were they stopping? Had they reached some destination?

A voice. The voice of the driver. He was asking something, asking directions. That must mean—

"Smolah." Another voice, telling him to turn left. So there were two of them. The same two? He couldn't be sure.

As the car began to pick up speed, the driver spoke again, asking how much farther they had to go. It sounded like Zilbert, the man in the gray suit.

"Esser." It was Malamud's voice, he was almost certain.

Ten kilometers farther. Wherever the pair were taking him, they were almost there.

It was only an hour after dawn, the quiet residential street deserted, as the two men emerged from the sprawling ranch-style house. They were no longer in business suits, both now attired in slacks and sport shirts open at the neck. Malamud's snow-white mane was topped by a plaid Ben Hogan-style cap.

They lit up cigarettes and strolled over to the late-model silver Mercedes parked in the driveway. Malamud rapped on the trunk. There was no sound from inside.

"Could he still be unconscious?" Zilbert wondered aloud.

"Let's find out." Malamud unlocked the trunk and raised the lid slowly. The bound man inside did not stir. Zilbert was alarmed.

"You don't think he suffocated?"

"Don't be ridiculous. The trunk isn't sealed. He has plenty of air." Malamud thrust a hand in front of Llewellyn's face and held it there.

"I can feel his breath on my hand." He gave the face a stinging slap. There was no response. "He's still out."

Malamud slammed the trunk closed. "I'll drive." They got into the car and drove off.

"You didn't sleep, did you?"

Zilbert shook his head. "Too keyed up, I guess."

"Not me. I could have slept another couple of hours, but I wanted to be out before Rachel was up. She asks too many questions."

"Where are we going?"

"To the club. We'll have breakfast there, and we can talk without being overheard."

"What about—him? If he comes to, he might make some noise, attract someone's attention."

"The way he's trussed up? He can't even move. But to be on the safe side, I'll park away from the lot in a spot where nobody will come near him."

The Mercedes pulled off onto a dirt road and followed it into a grove of pines. Malamud stopped the car and turned off the motor, and the two men strode toward the large, rustic club house a hundred meters beyond. Inside, the kitchen was doing a brisk breakfast trade.

They selected a remote corner booth and ordered bagels and eggs. The worried look on Zilbert's face persisted. When the waitress was out of earshot, he heaved a heavy sigh. "What are we going to do? How are we going to get out of this?"

His mentor gave him an exasperated look. "Get hold of yourself! You know very well what we're going to do. Our Palestinian friend had the perfect solution—some acquaintances of his in the hostage business—the Hezbollah. A high-ranking American diplomat dropping into their lap is an answer to their prayers. It's all arranged. They take him off our hands today, and that's that. Once he's tucked away in one of their safe houses in Lebanon and they announce his capture, his disappearance will be explained and the blame will fall on them."

"Yes, but what about the Llewellyn woman? She and her husband must have been working together."

"Didn't I tell you? Our friend sent some of his people to take care of her. We should be rid of her by now."

"But the authorities still have that picture of you. When they discover that we've run away—"

"They still don't have a name to go with the picture. Even if someone recognizes me from it, they can't prove it's really me. That's one reason I'm staying out of sight for a while, so I won't be available for questioning if that happens. And we didn't 'run away.' You saw the note I left for my secretary; we're just getting away for a few days to work at home on a special project. I'll be in touch with her by phone. If anything threatening occurs, she'll warn us."

"But—"

"No more buts. Haven't I always taken care of you? Try to relax. Here's your breakfast. Enjoy."

Zilbert took a bite of bagel and poked at the eggs with his fork. The bagel was dry and he couldn't swallow it and had to wash it down with coffee. He put down his fork, unable to eat.

There was one more question he wanted to ask his boss. It concerned the superintendent who had seen them leaving the building the night before. Llewellyn's picture was certain to be spread all over the news media. If the superintendent recognized it and went to the police, they were dead meat.

Llewellyn had purposely played possum so that his captors would feel free to talk. It had worked, as far as it had gone. He had tuned into their conversation but hadn't learned much. Malamud had spoken of a "club" where they would breakfast. What kind of club? Where was it?

The mention of it had offered him hope, the chance that there would be people around, whose attention he might find some way to attract. But that hope was all but dashed when they decided to park in this remote spot. He hadn't heard a voice or a footstep since they left the car.

It might not have worked, anyway. Try as he might, he couldn't get rid of the gag in his mouth and had been unable to loosen his bonds sufficiently to get a knee or elbow within striking distance of the trunk lid. If he couldn't find a way to make some noise, it was hopeless.

A sudden noise riveted his attention. It was the sound of a twig breaking; someone was approaching. More crackling sounds reached his ears and the crunching noise of heavy shoes on rocky soil. He redoubled his efforts to get onto his back, and succeeded. Sensing that his forehead was close to metal, he began rocking back and forth.

The impact of his head with the trunk roof was more painful than noisy, but he gritted his teeth and kept it up. Over and over . . .

He stopped and listened, holding his breath. A voice rang out, not far away, and another voice responded, closer still. He couldn't make out what they were saying. He banged his head several more times, then stopped to listen.

Click! It was a sound he recognized instantly, a sound familiar to his ears. *"Tov! Tov!"* shouted the first voice he had heard. He banged his head against the top of the trunk again—eight, nine, ten times. He stopped. The crunching footsteps had started again. They were receding. There were no more voices. They hadn't heard him.

Nursing his aching head, he listened to the noisy footfall until it was out of earshot. The noise made by a certain kind of shoe, a shoe with metal spikes. The loud click had been the unique sound of a wooden club making contact with a small, hard white ball.

At least now he knew where he was. There was only one golf course in all of Israel. It was in the heart of a playground for the affluent, a burgeoning area of luxury homes located near the ruins of the splendid city Herod the Great had built to honor Augustus Caesar. He was in Caesarea.

By the time Shmona's *sherut* reached Jerusalem, the sun was already up. He envied it. It had been to bed; he hadn't. No point in going home now—he had an early morning meeting. He directed the driver to stop at a street corner and set out to walk the several remaining blocks to Mossad headquarters.

The night's mopping-up work in the aftermath of the latest brush with the terrorists had left him depressed. Identification of the two terrorists was going to take time. Neither had carried any papers that could shed light on their identities, addresses, or affiliation. The lab personnel had gone over the demolished van with their customary thoroughness, lifting fingerprints and sweeping up fibers and other minutiae. They would attempt to trace the vehicle and check out the prints and dental records of its occupants, a time-consuming process at best.

He winced, anticipating his director's reaction when updated on this latest development. "Do you expect the terrorists who have this missile pointed at our throat to postpone their countdown until your plodding detective work pays off?"

He knew that Shilo had another concern. Operation Doublespike was heating up, the strike on the Iraqi ballistic missile and chemical warhead complex at Mosul. Once it received the green light, it could take over and push the hunt for the terrorist-held missile onto the back burner. As manager of Project Nineveh, the intelligence-gathering operation in Mosul, Shmona feared that his own time would shortly be dominated by the strike planning. His meeting this morning was with his deep-cover agent in Mosul, who had been called in for consultation on Operation Doublespike.

When he walked into his office the phone was already ringing. It was seven in the morning; Rebecca wouldn't arrive for another hour. He picked it up.

Daniella's voice was frantic. "Baruch, thank God you're there! David didn't come home last night. He didn't leave a message on the answering machine, which he would have done. I just know something's happened to him; I'm sorry to be bothering you but I didn't know who else to call . . . The police would only ask me a lot of questions I couldn't answer and end up telling me not to worry."

Shmona had been on the verge of telling her the same. "Have you contacted the American embassy?"

"They don't answer. No one's there yet."

"Okay, Daniella, I'll do what I can from this end. We'll check out all the places where someone would be taken after, God forbid, an accident. But there's not much else we can do until you talk to the embassy. They may know where he is. If not, we need to know when they last saw him, where he was going, whom he left with, and so on, so we can pick up his trail. Call them and get back to me, please."

"Baruch," she said with trepidation, "you don't think . . . You don't think he's been kidnapped, do you? I mean, he *is* a diplomat and . . . well, after his run-ins with those terrorists . . ."

"I don't think any such thing, Daniella. He's probably just off on an assignment and there's some logical explanation why his message didn't reach you. So try not to fret, and keep trying the embassy. Call me back as soon as you've talked to them."

She murmured her thanks and he hung up the phone, only half believing what he had told her, not wanting to believe the worst. An American envoy snatched by terrorists inside of Israel proper? It had never happened before. Still, there was always a first time . . .

Shmona found the directory he was looking for in his secretary's bottom drawer. It listed the phone numbers of all of the hospitals in the vicinity. It also contained the unlisted numbers of the morgues. He was on his fifth hospital call when the knock came on his office door. The middle-aged man who entered was of medium stature with a homely, nondescript face that would get lost in any crowd. His most distinguishing feature was his spare frame, on which hung a rumpled business suit that appeared at least one size too large. He was Salman Nadwa, Shmona's field agent from Mosul, Iraq, known to his colleagues as "the scarecrow."

"Shalom, Salman." Shmona hung up the phone and rose, mustering one of his rare smiles. He hadn't been face to face with his deep-cover agent for the better part of a year. He shook his hand warmly.

The warmth was not returned. Nadwa was clearly disturbed about something. He lost no time in getting it out on the table.

"Why was I left in the dark? Why was I not consulted, not even informed?"

"Salman, take it easy . . ." Nadwa was good, but occasionally he had to be stroked. Shmona guessed now was one of those times. The man was probably upset over Operation Doublespike. Most likely he'd gotten wind from the Mossad grapevine that the strike on the Mosul facility was moving forward. "Look, Salman, you were going to be told. It's the reason we brought you in. To inform you, consult with you."

"A little late, aren't you?" Nadwa sneered.

Shmona shook his head. "Not at all. The plan is still being put together. The fact is that Doublespike isn't even a definite go, as yet."

"Doublespike?" The scarecrow shook his head exasperatedly. "I'm referring to the 'triple snatch' you pulled off—the grab of those three warheads out of Mosul under the very nose of Saddam Hussein. You might have at least warned me. Hussein has turned the place upside down. I came this close to getting swept up in the aftermath! It's been a bloodbath—and I had no warning."

Shmona's deliberately calm exterior gave no clue to the adrenaline suddenly released in his veins. "Three warheads, you say? Chemical warheads?"

"Two chemical, one biological—as if you didn't know. It's an open secret that Israel was behind it. If I hadn't learned about it from one of my own sources . . ."

"It wasn't one of ours, Salman. It wasn't an Israeli operation."

The Iraqi deep-cover man stared at him. "Don't try to con

me like I was some reporter from the Jerusalem *Post.* I know all about plausible deniability."

"Salman! Hear me, and hear me well. Our country had *no* part in such an undertaking. If you had bothered to check in with us, reported this event through the designated channel, you'd have discovered this. And we'd have had the information that much sooner. Now, when did this theft take place?"

Nadwa blinked. "Yesterday. Yesterday morning. I didn't hear about it until late afternoon, as I was leaving for the airport. There wasn't time to contact you; I had to run for it. And I knew I'd be seeing you this morning."

He bit his lower lip, his whole demeanor transformed. "If it wasn't Israel, then . . ."

"Who? I have a pretty good idea." Shmona was certain his superiors would reach the same conclusion; he was impatient to get word to them. But he knew that neither his section chief nor the director would be in their offices for another half hour.

He removed a cassette recorder from his desk drawer and switched it on. "Okay, Salman, start at the beginning. I want you to tell me everything you've learned about the theft of these warheads—the type of warhead, the time, the place, the circumstances, the modus operandi. Don't leave anything out, not even the smallest detail."

Lockjaw Logan, as his nickname implied, was a man of few words. When it came to a lucrative charter, for which the pilot had been paid half the fee in advance, he was also a man of few questions. He landed his vintage Aero Commander at the Urmia airport in Iran's West Azerbaijan province a few minutes ahead of schedule. Taxiing to the private plane side of the airport, he parked in front of the small reception building and went inside to await the arrival of the two petroleum engineers from Turkey. An hour later he was still waiting.

Lockjaw broke out a fresh pack of cigarettes and lit one up, hoping he hadn't been stood up and counseling himself to be patient. He had long ago learned that waiting was part of the game here, where nothing ever seemed to proceed on time.

Logan considered himself an old Iran hand, having flown for a British firm that had pulled out with the coming of the Ayatollah. When his colleagues fled, he had decided to stay

231

on, reasoning that experienced pilots would be in short supply and job opportunities plentiful. He had managed to weather the firestorm of Islamic revolution that followed, though there had been two lean years in which he hardly worked at all before the madness began to taper off. His skill and knowledge of the country eventually paid off, and in a few years he had saved enough to purchase the somewhat antiquated but eminently flight-worthy Aero Commander and start his own charter business.

"Mr. Logan? Mr. Aloysius Logan?"

Lockjaw hadn't seen the man approach. Wincing at the mispronunciation of his despised given name, he got up and turned to look at the speaker.

"I'm Logan, mate. And you'd be—?"

"Ishmael Halevi. I believe you were expecting me." They shook hands briefly. "My partner is outside with our equipment. Is your plane ready to go?"

Lockjaw nodded, sizing the man up. He had hauled a lot of oil men around. If this was a petroleum engineer, he was the Queen of Sheba. The passenger's attire was early twentieth-century bucolic; you rarely saw overalls any more, even on a farm. One thing was sure—he was no farmer, either. His hands were too soft.

"Let's get your gear loaded. There's a front moving in." He led the way outside. Another man in overalls, this one with a beard, was waiting beside three baggage carts that each held a bulky object encased in an oil-stained canvas bag.

"This is my associate, Nestor Rishad. Mr. Logan, our pilot."

Another soft hand with an even limper grip. Lockjaw examined the equipment, hefting an end of one of the parcels. He could barely lift it.

"What is this bloody stuff? It weighs a ton. I'm not in the freight hauling business."

"Special motors, sealed in cannisters," answered the smooth-shaven one, who seemed to be in charge. "For installation on Platform Fourteen off the Strait of Hormuz. Together they weigh precisely two hundred and forty-six kilos. Is there some problem? I understood that you could—"

"They won't fit in the bloody baggage compartment,"

Lockjaw grumbled. "I'll have to stow them in the cabin." At least it wasn't narcotics, he reflected. Too heavy. That would have been all he needed, getting caught in one of the customs inspectors' impromptu spot checks with a load of hash smuggled in from Turkey.

"Let's go, then." He walked beside them as they rolled their equipment toward the twin-engine plane. "I've filed a flight plan that calls for refueling stops at Isfahan and Shiraz, en route to Bandar-Abbas. I understand we will take on another passenger at Shiraz?"

"Correct, Mr. Logan—a very important passenger." The man called Ishmael smiled. "He is the one with the money to pay you the balance of your fee."

20

"GOODBYE, MRS. LLEWELLYN, and try not to fret. Nine times out of ten there's some perfectly harmless explanation for these apparent disappearances; take the word of an old hand in these matters."

The U.S. ambassador to Israel hung up the phone and sat for a moment frowning at it. His bravado had been for Daniella's sake; he was a lot more concerned about her husband than he had let on. Llewellyn hadn't come to the embassy at all the previous day, had called in and left a message that something pressing had come up and he was taking the day off. No one at the embassy had seen him or heard from him since; Abrams had just finished checking. Of course, that in itself was no proof of foul play, but this *was* the Middle East, where high-ranking diplomats were like trophies to certain types of hunters. And given his special envoy's recent history . . .

Well, he thought, consoling himself, Llewellyn, of all his staff, was a man who knew how to take care of himself. True, Llewellyn was inclined to be independent and unpredictable. But hadn't he just survived two brushes with terrorists? The ambassador sighed. Maybe there was a simple explanation. Maybe Llewellyn was up to something he didn't want the embassy, or his wife, to know about . . .

Khalidy? Llewellyn had been instructed by Abrams to steer clear of Khalidy until the present terrorist threat subsided. If he *had* decided to pay the Palestinian a visit, it would explain why he hadn't informed the embassy, perhaps also why he had neglected to inform his wife, who might likewise have been against it.

Abrams phoned Khalidy. Unfortunately, Khalidy reported, Llewellyn wasn't with him.

"No. No, I have not seen him or spoken with him in several days. Do you mean to say that he is missing? That is bad news, indeed. You have no leads to his whereabouts?"

"None whatsoever at the moment, I'm afraid. Any ideas?"

"Nothing specific, but given all that has happened recently, one can hardly rule out anything. I assume that the appropriate authorities have been notified?"

"They're looking for him now, but quietly. We're trying to keep it out of the news media, at least for twenty-four hours."

"A wise decision. With your permission, I will make some inquiries of my own, discreetly, of course. I have channels open to me that are not open to you, nor to the Israelis."

Something of an understatement, reflected the ambassador; Palestinian channels from Gaza to the Galilee. "Of course, Dr. Khalidy. Any help you can give us—"

"I will get back to you. Let us pray that no harm has befallen David Llewellyn. I have the greatest regard for him. He is my brother. I owe him my life."

In a meeting with the director? Daniella slammed the phone down angrily, frustrated over not being able to talk to her control, having expected him to be standing by for her call. Patience, a calmer inner voice counseled; Rebecca will get your message to him as soon as she can.

She urgently needed to tell Shmona that no one at the embassy had seen her husband or had any idea of his whereabouts. Her mind reeled with all the horrible possibilities, but she tried to concentrate on *finding* David and worrying later.

The ambassador had promised to pursue the matter through his own channels, but had sounded far too complacent to suit her. She couldn't just sit here, waiting for Shmona to call back. What else could she do? Whom else could she ask for help? It was family that counted at a time like this, family that would reinforce one's own concern, pull out all the stops to do something about it. And she had no family.

But David did! She seized the phone again and punched zero. "How do I put through a call to Riyadh, Saudi Arabia?"

It took over a half hour for the call to go through. The operator finally rang her back. "I have your party, miss. One moment, please."

"Hello. David?" The signal was weak and the voice barely audible, but it brought tears to her eyes.

"Richard, it's Daniella. David's not here. That's why I'm calling." She fought to keep her voice under control. "Your brother didn't come home last night, and there's been no word from him. No one has seen him since yesterday morning. He's disappeared. After all the recent trouble with the terrorists, I'm really worried. I'm afraid he may have been—" She couldn't finish the sentence.

"Kidnapped? Daniella, is that what you're saying?"

"Yes." It was half spoken, half sobbed.

"Take it easy, Daniella. Davey's been getting in and out of scrapes as long as I can remember. He knows how to handle himself. And with all his connections, I'm sure every policeman and undercover agent in Israel must be looking for him."

"But that's the problem—they're *not!* Everyone seems to be marking time, hoping he'll turn up. I can't get them to move, and I'm afraid that by the time they do . . . it may be too late."

There was silence on the line, and she was afraid she had lost the connection. "Richard? . . . Richard?"

His somewhat subdued voice came back in her ear. "Okay. I'm coming up there, Daniella. I'll get the first plane out of here. I'll call you before I board and let you know my arrival time. And Daniella—"

"Yes?"

"Keep your chin up."

She hung up, feeling a great sense of relief—and just a trifle foolish. What could Richy really do when he got here? Had she summoned him all the way from Riyadh just to hold her hand?

She walked to the bathroom, found a tissue, and blew her nose. She felt better, having unburdened herself, having shared her misery with the other person closest to David.

Back at the phone, she rang Shmona's number again. His

secretary answered; her boss was still in conference with the Mossad director.

This time, Daniella decided to confide in Rebecca. She told her the whole story.

Mordechai Shilo's expression was grim. "There can be no doubt as to who is behind this brazen theft of the Iraqi warheads. My friends, Deuteronomy has just escalated to catastrophic proportions. Unless we can locate this missile, our country could be facing its darkest hour."

Shmona and his section chief were taken aback by the doomsday tenor of the Mossad director. "It's not as if we hadn't anticipated this might happen," commented Yaakov Avidan, the section chief. "It was your own initiative that brought this threat to the attention of the general staff and persuaded them to look into viable countermeasures. Wasn't there a consensus that both the Patriot and the Hawk had the capability to perform a successful intercept of the missile's payload?"

"Conditionally, yes." Shilo's face retained its grave demeanor. "The condition being that Deuteronomy be detected soon after launch and accurate track data forwarded to the intercept systems. General Barkai had expressed confidence that this could be accomplished by the Air Force's Hawkeye radar planes. But General Tuchler called me late yesterday. It appears that Barkai and his surveillance specialists are having second thoughts. It's not an easy problem for them. They will have to maintain their E-2C Hawkeyes on continuous air alert, cycling planes back and forth and using in-flight refueling, an extremely costly operation."

"How can they even think about cost?" broke in Avidan angrily. "We are talking about the loss of our *biggest* city and *half* its population."

Shilo held up his hand. "To be sure. But let me finish. Even if they mount this continuous airborne surveillance operation, they have concluded that they cannot guarantee the timely detection and tracking of Deuteronomy unless we can pin down the location of its launch site within, say, two hundred miles."

Shmona shook his head. *"Two hundred miles?* Right now

we couldn't place it within a thousand miles! Nobody knows *where* it is."

"Correction." The director turned his eyes on Shmona. "The terrorists know where it is. The men in possession of the ordnance stolen from Mosul must know its location, else how will they deliver those warheads? I want you to try to pick up their trail."

Shmona had been halfway expecting this. "That won't be easy."

"No, it won't. But there are only so many ways that ordnance can be smuggled out of Iraq and transported south for a mating with the missile. I suggest that you conduct an immediate survey of possible routes and means of transportation from Mosul to the Gulf region and get some of your field people in position to intercept and trail the individuals moving these warheads."

"I have only one field agent in the area, our man in Mosul," Shmona protested, "and he's here for the Doublespike briefing."

"Then send him back," snapped Shilo. "The Doublespike planning can wait. If we don't survive Deuteronomy, there won't be any Operation Doublespike. Now, get moving."

Shmona's secretary was waiting just outside the door of the conference room as the meeting broke up. She got her boss's attention and drew him aside.

"Mrs. Llewellyn has called several times trying to reach you. She sounded very distressed this last time. She asked me to inform you that the American embassy hasn't seen her husband since the day before yesterday and has no idea of his whereabouts."

Shmona smote his brow; he'd temporarily forgotten about Daniella. "Okay, Rebecca, here's what you do—call her back and tell her I'll speak to her as soon as I set some wheels in motion. And Rebecca—not a word of this to anyone."

He dashed after his section chief and director. "Yaakov, Mr. Director—there's another development I need to fill you in on. One of my agents—the wife of the American special envoy, David Llewellyn—called this morning to inform me that he's missing. His embassy hasn't seen him since two days ago.

"There's more than an outside chance that he's been abducted by the same group that has Deuteronomy."

The waiting was finally over. Inside his dark, oppressive cubicle, Llewellyn heard the crunch of two distinct pairs of feet approach and stop nearby, then the sound of a key in the car door lock.

Every bone in his body ached and his ankles and wrists were swollen from the tight bindings. The inside of his mouth felt like the Sahara Desert, and his bladder was bursting. Surely they would let him out for a minute to relieve himself and at least give him some water.

Then again, maybe not . . . the springs creaked and the chassis wobbled as first one, then another body ensconced itself on the front seat. The motor started immediately and the car began to move. How much longer could he hold out? The motion of the auto continued slow as it bounced and jostled over the rough surface beneath it. Then it stopped again, giving him renewed hope.

He heard the doors on both sides open and the occupants step out. The sound of a key, again, this time in the trunk lock. Huzzah!

After his long confinement, the sudden influx of light blinded him. "He's awake." Malamud's voice. "Let's get him out of there."

Undoing the bonds on his feet but leaving his hands tied, the two men lifted him out of the trunk and set him down on his feet, propping him against the trunk of a tree. With its support, he could barely stand up; one foot had gone to sleep. He moved it up and down, trying to restore the circulation, looking around as his eyes adapted to the light. He was in a pine forest, the area remote and deserted. There was not even a dirt road visible. Malamud was holding a revolver.

"We're going to remove your gag so that you can drink some water and eat something. Don't try to cry out or we'll cram you right back into the trunk. There's no one around to hear you, anyway. Take the gag out of his mouth, Zil."

The oppressive handkerchief was withdrawn from his mouth. "My hands." Llewellyn spoke in a harsh whisper. "Untie them, please. I have to urinate."

Zilbert looked at Malamud for guidance. "Go ahead." When the assistant had complied, Llewellyn turned his back and emptied his bladder against the tree.

Zilbert handed him a paper cup. The water was warm but he wouldn't have cared if it was boiling. He swallowed greedily until he had drained it. "More."

"Later." Malamud took the cup from Zilbert and produced a paper plate with some food on it. Llewellyn wolfed down the remains of Zilbert's breakfast, his eyes taking in the vehicle he'd been riding in for the first time. A late-model silver Mercedes 560 SEL with yellow Israeli tags. He memorized the license number as he finished his breakfast.

"Put the gag back in his mouth and tie him up again," Malamud ordered.

"Wait a minute . . ." His voice was stronger now. He had planned what he would say to them if he got the opportunity. "There's something you don't know. Those terrorists you thought you were using have really been using you. Your money has financed the hijacking of the most powerful weapon in the Middle East, an intermediate-range ballistic missile that dwarfs anything Israel has. They're ready to wipe out half of your countrymen, unless you help us find them. You've been used. Badly."

The two men looked at him as if he had lost his marbles. "Shut up!" Malamud spat out. "Put the gag back in his mouth."

"How do we know he's not telling the truth? Is it possible . . ."

"Oh, come on—in his situation, he'd say anything. A ballistic missile hijacked?" Malamud snorted. "He's been in that hot trunk too long."

Llewellyn concentrated on Zilbert. "Do I sound delirious? I can give you particulars. It's a Chinese East Wind missile, hijacked off a ship bound for Saudi Arabia. It's somewhere in the vicinity of the Gulf right now, aimed at Tel Aviv, ready to start its countdown. And your Palestinian acquaintance, the man whose picture ran on page one, knows all about it."

Malamud flushed, remembering his last conversation with Kareem. *Get out of Tel Aviv. It is no longer a healthy place to be.* Was it possible? No . . . it was totally inconceivable! The

American was a clever trickster, trying to talk his way out of trouble.

"Enough! Back in the trunk with him!" Malamud took the gag from Zilbert and stuffed it back into Llewellyn's mouth. "Put your hands behind you!"

While Malamud held the revolver to his head, Zilbert retied his hands behind his back. The white-haired man pocketed the pistol and grasped Llewellyn beneath the armpits.

"Grab his feet." The two men lifted him over the rim of the trunk and dropped him into it. He landed with a thud, his head banging painfully against the spare tire. A rope was looped around his feet and drawn tight, then tied to the rope around his hands. A moment later he was re-incarcerated as the lid of the trunk slammed shut.

The Mercedes moved off, bumping and jouncing for some distance until its tires found a smoother surface. As it picked up speed, Zilbert's voice broke the silence.

"What if he's right? What if he's telling the truth?"

"Don't be ridiculous. How could you believe such a thing? He's just trying to trick us into releasing him."

"But why would he make up such an implausible story? If he was going to lie, wouldn't he have told us something more believable? And he had specifics—the type of missile, the circumstances. He couldn't have—"

"Lower your voice! I don't want him tuning in on us." Malamud's voice dropped to a few decibels above a whisper. "If there were anything to his story, don't you think we'd have gotten wind of it before this? You couldn't keep something like that a secret for long."

"I don't know about that . . . His information may have come through secret diplomatic channels. The Americans have close ties with the Saudis. We should have questioned him some more. Why don't we stop again somewhere and—?"

"We'll do nothing of the kind. We're going to continue on and follow through with our plan."

Zilbert was silent for a time, apparently beaten down. "What happens when we get to Acre?"

"The people our Palestinian friend contacted are to meet us there and take him off our hands."

"Hezbollah?"

"I would doubt that they are Hezbollah. I expect they are middlemen of some related homegrown sect of Islamic fundamentalists. Their job will be to get him into Lebanon and hand him over to the Hezbollah."

"How will they do it—get him across the border?"

"Who cares? That's their problem. I have no intention of even asking."

Zilbert sighed. "I hate dealing with such people. Can we trust them?"

"We don't have much choice, do we?"

Curled up in the trunk, Llewellyn strained his ears to hear, but could pick up no more than an occasional word of the conversation, the road noise drowning out the rest of it. He had understood most of what was said before they lowered their voices and had taken heart at the argument that had ensued between the two.

The seed he had planted showed signs of germinating. But would the browbeaten Zilbert assert himself enough to interfere? Interfere with what? He had no real clue to whatever it was that Malamud had in store for him, other than the probability that it was something terminal.

Weak though he appeared to be, Zilbert seemed his best chance. Perhaps his only chance.

The ancient city of Acre, situated on a promontory at the northern end of the Bay of Haifa, commanded a sweeping view of the towering Mount Carmel across the bay and Israel's third largest city built on its slopes. The chief port of the area under the Crusaders, Acre had relinquished that distinction to Haifa not long after the Turks had built their own city atop the ruins of the Crusader town. Four mosques within the walled confines of the Old City bespoke an Islamic heritage still reflected in its predominantly Muslim population.

The midday call to prayer was ringing from the colorful Old City's several minarets as the silver Mercedes sedan approached. But instead of following the flow of traffic inside the wall, the Mercedes made a right turn and entered the newer section of town. Passing the bus station, it turned left, passed a park, and swung right again. Two blocks later it slowed, turning into a driveway that led to the front of a four-story building, and pulled to a stop, its driver honking the horn twice.

A door opened and a man's head appeared. Then an overhead garage door in the side of the building began to raise itself. The sedan pulled inside and the door closed behind it.

Malamud followed the ramp down to the next level, where a number of vehicles were parked, and pulled into a vacant slot. He shut off the motor and got out of the car, Zilbert following suit, peering around anxiously.

"Where are they?"

"They'll be here. It's barely noon; the *azan* is still sounding."

"Before they come, why don't we at least open the trunk and hear him out. He's—"

Malamud stopped him with a finger to his lips. He drew his companion off to a corner of the garage, where they conversed in hushed voices.

Inside the trunk, Llewellyn speculated on who "they" might be. Some other parties had apparently been called in by Malamud. Some of his terrorist bedfellows? They'd had two cracks at him already. Would the tall Palestinian with the high cheekbones and fierce eyes come out of hiding for one more shot?

Two short beeps from an auto horn sounding just outside suggested that he wouldn't have long to wait for his answer. There was a sharp click and then a buzzing sound as the garage door opened again, and he heard the low throbbing of a motor in idle as another vehicle slid down the ramp and stopped nearby.

The motor was turned off and he heard two car doors slam. There was the sound of feet shuffling across a cement floor and words were exchanged in subdued voices from some distance away. He couldn't make out what was being said.

Footsteps approached and the trunk lid flew open. Malamud's mane of white hair appeared, Zilbert behind him. Llewellyn could not yet see the others. A new voice spoke. "Be so good as to blindfold him before we remove him."

Zilbert reached in and wrapped a folded handkerchief over his eyes, tying it behind his head. Then several pairs of hands were lifting him, carrying him, and there was a rolling sound he recognized as a van door sliding open.

"One moment." That same new voice again. He felt fingers probe the bonds on his wrists and ankles before he was thrust rudely inside onto a bare metal floor.

The sliding door clanged shut behind him and he heard the front doors on both sides open and close again as the driver and passenger climbed in. The motor revved to life and the van backed for a short distance, then moved off up the ramp.

Llewellyn's spirits took a nosedive. His attempts to sway Malamud's wavering accomplice had gone for naught. Malamud had dumped him, handed him off to his executioners, lacking the stomach to do it himself.

He was being taken for a ride, gangland style. The type of ride where you didn't need a round-trip ticket.

21

THE SPECIAL ANTI-BALLISTIC missile study group convened by
General Tuchler had been in session for two days. Impatient
at the lack of progress being made by his own people on the
critical early-warning and trajectory tracking phase of the
ballistic missile encounter, the general had decided to bring
things to a head by subjecting the problem to the scrutiny of
outside experts. He had arranged to have it hosted by the
prestigious Weizmann Institute of Science at Rehovot, near
Tel Aviv, a two-hundred-acre complex of futuristic buildings,
green lawns, and sub-tropical gardens that was home to some
eighteen hundred researchers and doctoral fellows.

In addition to those participating from the Weizmann Institute, Tuchler had assembled some of the best technical minds
from all parts of Israel to focus on the ballistic missile defense
problem. There were attendees from Haifa's Technion, the
MIT of Israel, as well as various equipment supplier experts
from Israel's not-inconsiderable defense industry, among
them Israel Aircraft Industries, Ltd., Rafael Armament Development Authority, and Elta Electronics Industries, Ltd.,
the radar specialists from Ashdod. And the general had
brought along a number of his own military hotshots.

To act as chairman, Tuchler had selected the Weizmann
Institute's Dr. Ephraim Bar-Tel, a world-acclaimed scientist.
Bar-Tel was an old friend of his, whose counsel he had sought
on a number of occasions.

Personally briefed by Tuchler on the terrorist missile situation and the need to keep the story from getting out, he had
helped draft a cover statement that focussed the study effort

on the specific answers desired by the general without divulging that the threat was real. For "purposes of specificity" the Saudi East Wind III missile, armed with a highly lethal chemical warhead, was projected as the threat to be addressed.

By the second afternoon Bar-Tel was armed with a briefcase full of results, and hurried to the office where Tuchler was waiting for a summary of the study group's findings.

Anticipating a one-on-one session, Bar-Tel was surprised to find another attendee in the company of the general. "I think you know Dr. Tessler."

"Yes, of course." The two scientists nodded at one another. Tessler was an American, formerly the civilian director of ABMDA, their ballistic missile defense agency. Bar-Tel had met him once at a strategic weapons symposium the American had chaired. He had left the government years ago and was now a high-powered consultant, the Israeli Defense Forces among his clients. He seemed to know everyone in the business.

"I've asked Elliot to sit in and comment," the general explained. "You needn't pull any punches—he's aware of the East Wind hijacking and the immediacy of the threat." At Bar-Tel's raised eyebrows, the general hastened to add that Tessler had been let in on the secret by the U.S. Department of State, which had been apprised of the hijacking by Saudi Arabia.

"I've already briefed Elliot on the study ground rules and objectives. Give me your results and conclusions first; then we can backtrack, if necessary. What did you decide? Do our existing weapon systems have the potential to cope with this East Wind threat, or don't they?"

"They have the potential, without question," Bar-Tel responded. "My panel decided that several of our existing systems have the ability to encounter this non-nuclear threat with a high probability of success, provided that they receive *early* warning and tracking data on the incoming target. But that is a big 'if,' and—"

"In the case of the Patriot missile I would concur," the American, Tessler, interjected. "But what are these other systems?"

"Our first-line air defense missile systems—the Air Force

Hawk missile and the Navy's Barak Point Defense System. We also found, surprisingly, that manned interceptors would have some capability against this threat, if they could be appropriately pre-positioned."

"But these systems were designed to work against aircraft targets," Tessler countered. "How can they handle the much higher speed of a re-entry vehicle?"

"By waiting for it to slow down, a tactic we couldn't afford to employ if we were dealing with the nuclear threat of your classic ABM systems, where a nuclear explosion in the low atmosphere could be catastrophic." Bar-Tel pulled a drawing from his stack of material and spread it on the table in front of the other two.

"This is a typical trajectory of an IRBM like the East Wind. It reaches a burn-out velocity of around fourteen times the speed of sound, achieving an altitude of several hundred miles. As it re-enters the atmosphere, it begins to experience a heavy deceleration when it is still forty to sixty miles above its target; this deceleration can reach forty times the effect of gravity. The re-entry vehicle slows rapidly. A blunt-nosed RV will be decelerated to around a thousand meters per second by the time it descends to ten miles above its target; a more pointed body, like the East Wind nose cone, might reach an altitude of five miles before it has slowed that much.

"It will eventually slow to a terminal speed approaching the speed of sound, say three hundred to four hundred meters per second. These speeds are in the regime of airborne targets our point defense weapons are capable of handling."

"I see," Dr. Tessler nodded. "Then I think you have also answered my next question, how you would discriminate the true target from the re-entry 'junk'—the burnt-out rocket motor and parts that break off from it on re-entry, as well as decoys purposely released. This has been something of a bugaboo for previous ABM systems. But you have the luxury of waiting until the junk is all burned up before you engage the target."

"Exactly." Bar-Tel was beginning to feel some rapport with the American expert. "It gives us a big advantage in the terminal encounter. But this is assuming we can provide our point defense systems with adequate early warning and mid-course

247

tracking data on the target. In these areas we have our biggest problem, because we are almost totally dependent on outside agencies."

"How so?" the general grunted. "What about our Hawkeye radar planes? They have the ability to spot a missile lifting off and track it with good accuracy and are equipped with a long-range data link to send the information back."

"The E-2C Hawkeyes are an important asset," Bar-Tel acknowledged, "that may, indeed, play a role in this engagement, though probably not in launch detection and early warning. That job entails maintaining a continuous vigil over an area some fifteen hundred to two thousand miles from where the planes are based. En route, the Hawkeyes would have to fly most of the distance through Saudi air space, as would the in-flight refueling tankers required to keep them on station.

"Even if some arrangement could be worked out with the Saudis, it would be impractical to maintain such an operation for very long with only the four existing E-2C aircraft. Of course, if we could count on a heightened state of alert such as might be brought about by an ultimatum, for example, it might not be out of the question."

The general shook his head vigorously. "We are dealing with barbarians. Who knows what kind of warning they may give us? Perhaps none at all. We've got to be prepared for *any* contingency, including the possibility that these terrorists are engaged in an act of pure vengeance."

". . . Which would preclude any reliance on the Hawkeyes for early warning."

"What are the other alternatives?"

"Satellites. Unfortunately, the launch of our own surveillance satellite is still months away. There are, however, a number of American satellites that focus on this part of the world. The newest, specifically designed for ballistic missile launch detection, is their DSP—Defense Support Program Early Warning Satellite.

"One of these DSPs is in geo-synchronous orbit over the Indian Ocean as we speak. It employs a dual-wavelength infrared telescope to detect the sudden flare-ups of large rockets igniting and lifting off, the data transmitted directly to the North American Air Defense headquarters."

The general was frowning again. "Our own air defenses are linked to NORAD, but I don't recall ever seeing such data. It was supposed to be part of the Patriot deal. Are we receiving it?"

Bar-Tel shook his head. "Apparently not. The information is highly classified and closely held." His face formed a wry smile. "The DSP, of course, monitors our own Jericho test launches, among others."

The general turned unsmilingly to the American. "This could be an action item for you, Elliot. I want you to coordinate with NORAD through the appropriate chain of command and arrange for us to get this launch warning data. If you run into difficulties, your U.S. State Department should give you all the authority you need."

Dr. Tessler nodded without comment, pulling at the battered pipe that never seemed to leave his mouth as he made a note on a small notepad.

"What happens next is crucial," Bar-Tel resumed, pointing again to the drawing that still lay in front of his audience. "Notice the time ticks on this missile trajectory. *The entire flight occupies less than fifteen to twenty minutes.* From the time the nose cone begins re-entry some sixty miles away, the terminal defenses have *less than a minute* to achieve intercept. If their guidance radar is faced with a time-consuming search, the interceptors will never make it. The point-defense radars must know exactly where to look for the target. So we're forced to acquire the target much earlier with mid-course tracking equipment and hand its position off to the terminal defense systems. And the sooner we can acquire it, the better our chances of success."

"The better our chances?" the general objected. "You make it sound like the spin of a roulette wheel. We're talking about the possible loss of Tel Aviv!"

"Unfortunately, nothing is one hundred percent, sir. Still, acquiring and tracking the incoming missile during its mid-course phase—and reporting its trajectory to the waiting interceptors—will get us as close to one hundred percent as possible. Failing this, we would have to fall back on picking up the incoming missile with our air defense radars, whose range is limited to, say, between one hundred and two hundred miles. I'm not saying this couldn't work, but it's cutting it too close for comfort."

"Is this where the Hawkeyes come in, then?" asked the general. "You would use them to acquire the target sooner?"

"Our study group advanced that possibility. But that would entail placing the E-2Cs on continuous airborne alert to assure having one already orbiting somewhere downrange when the missile is launched—on the basis, say, of having received some warning or ultimatum. And you, yourself, seem to have already ruled that out."

The American, Tessler, spoke up. "Why not utilize some existing downrange radars? We could link you up with the Peace Shield radars in Saudi Arabia."

The general's initial reaction was almost violent. "What? Rely on an *Arab* country on a national security matter? The government wouldn't hear of it! The Saudis have been bankrolling our enemies for decades; we're technically still at war with them. It's their fault we're facing this terrorist threat to begin with. If they'd taken better care in shipping their infernal missiles—"

"Precisely why I believe they'd bend over backwards to cooperate," Tessler said pointedly. "And don't think of it as a joint venture with the Saudis; you'll be dealing with us. Peace Shield is an American network, manned and supported by American personnel. We can handle the whole show."

"But how would we get access to the Peace Shield radar tracks?" Bar-Tel threw in. "There's no existing data link between us and Saudi Arabia."

"Oh, but there is." Tessler smiled broadly. "AWACS is tied in with Peace Shield. The AWACS data link is compatible with your own air defense network; our NATO AWACS planes have accessed you on any number of occasions. One of the AWACS aircraft is constantly in the air somewhere over Saudi Arabia. We can use it as the link for forwarding the mid-course tracking data from the Peace Shield radars. The AWACS may even be able to acquire the missile on its own radar."

Bar-Tel considered for a moment. "Hmm . . . It has possibilities. It might be worth looking into."

The general still looked dubious. "I still don't think there's any way the Prime Minister would buy it."

"Why don't we explore it?" Tessler urged. "I know the top people down there. I can have them send one of their experts up, and we can lay it all out. Then you'll have something specific to take upstairs."

The general looked at Bar-Tel, who shrugged. "Why not?" Tessler already had his small notepad out and was leafing through it. "May I use the phone?"

He punched zero and got the operator. "I wish to place a call to the Boeing Airplane Company in Riyadh." He read off the number. "Yes, that's in Saudi Arabia."

He smiled at the operator's reaction, putting his hand over the receiver. "She probably thinks I'm a spy. This may take a while."

While Tessler waited for the call to go through, the general drew Bar-Tel away to one corner of the room. "Give me your honest appraisal of our chances if we don't get this AWACS tie-in, just use the satellite warning data and go it on our own. Ninety-nine percent? Fifty-fifty? Worse? I need a hard data point."

"It's too early to give you any hard numbers, general, until we put it on the computer. The chances are better than fifty-fifty—I feel safe in saying that. But how much better remains to be seen."

While they spoke, the call to Riyadh had been expeditiously consummated, much to Tessler's amazement and delight. He hung up the phone and approached, his face beaming.

"By a strange stroke of luck, one of their top AWACS experts is presently on his way to Tel Aviv. He's scheduled to arrive at Ben Gurion at nine-thirty tonight. His name is Richard Llewellyn."

Kiryat Shmona, with some eight thousand inhabitants, was the largest town in the upper Galilee. It stood a scant nine kilometers from the Lebanon border and the border crossing known as Ha Tovah, or Good Fence, so named because of the relaxed regulations exercised by the authorities on both sides of the fence in the interest of good relations. It was here that Lebanese Christians and Druze were allowed to pass through to obtain free medical service and to hold jobs in Israel.

On this particular sunny afternoon business was brisk in the open air cafes and falafel parlors along the highway just north of the main hotel and bus station. A Druze funeral procession from one of the nearby Druze villages had paused here to take refreshment, the hearse and a number of autos parked along the road. They were a colorful lot, dressed in their traditional costumes for the occasion, the women in ankle-length black robes with white shawls covering their heads, the men in long, white, shirt-like garments and distinctive black-and-white head scarves. A number of the older men sported thick moustaches and wore black *shirvelas,* low-hanging, bloomer-like pants dating from the Ottoman era.

The Druze were a fiercely independent Islamic sect whose beliefs set them apart from the Shiite and Sunni Muslims. Here in Israel they were loyal citizens who served in the armed forces, their youth called into service at the age of eighteen like most other Israelis.

One of the cafe proprietors struck up a conversation with a traditionally attired Druze man who had ordered coffee. "You cross into Lebanon?"

The Druze nodded, indicating the hearse parked down the street with a flick of his head. "Uncle Suleiman. It was his dying wish to be buried in his native village on the other side. We are making a *short* stop here while his remains are transferred to the burial casket." He looked significantly at the man sitting next to him, wearing a chauffeur's uniform.

The hearse driver gulped the remains of his coffee and stood up, wiping his mouth. "A quick comfort stop and I'm off to the mortuary."

As the chauffeur disappeared inside the cafe, a tall Druze man detached himself from the others and crossed the street to where the autos were parked. Arriving at the rear of the hearse, he reached up and unlatched the double doors, remaining in a crouch as he scanned the body of fellow mourners across the street. Reassured that he wasn't being observed, he scrambled inside and closed the doors. He crawled past the casket to the other end of the funeral compartment and flattened himself against the partition separating it from the front seat so that he couldn't be seen through the driver's small observation window.

A few moments later the driver of the hearse emerged, crossed to his vehicle, climbed into the driver's compartment, and drove off.

Northbound on Highway 90, a white, unmarked panel truck slowed in heavy traffic at the outskirts of Kiryat Shmona. In the back of the truck on its bare metal floor, still bound hand and foot, David Llewellyn sensed that they might be reaching their destination and redoubled his efforts to free his hands.

Shortly after their departure he had managed, by scraping his blindfold against the floor, to move it a bit higher on his forehead so that he could see out beneath it if he tilted his head backward. From his position on the floor, there wasn't a lot to see. His captors were hidden behind the front seat, their heads obscured by the headrests extending above it. There were no windows in the side of the vehicle, and he could only see out through the tops of the side windows in front, which from his angle had so far revealed nothing but patches of empty sky.

He had begun taking stock of the van's interior and his chances of escaping from it. The door handles on its side and rear were too high for him to reach. Besides, what could he do if he did manage to open them and fall out, with his hands and feet tied?

If only he could do something about the bonds on his wrists and ankles . . . Try as he would, he hadn't been able to budge them. With his restored sight, he had begun casting about the interior of the van for a sharp edge or metal ridge that he could saw them against. On the floor, halfway back toward the rear doors, he spied a pair of metal brackets, apparently for the attachment of a removable seat. He squirmed his way toward them, turning and twisting his body until his back made contact with one of the brackets. A few more wriggles and his hands, bound behind his back, contacted the cold metal protrusion . . .

For almost two hours—or so it seemed—it was as if the van were driving itself; there had been no conversation between his captors. He found it astounding that they had not checked up on him. He had been sawing steadily at the bonds on his wrists and could tell that the rope was weakening, but it still resisted his efforts to snap it.

The van had slowed to a crawl, the noise of congested traffic increasing. Now it braked suddenly and he heard its turn indicator clicking as it slowed almost to a stop, then swung sharply to the left. Was this the end of the line? Through the top of the driver's window he caught a glimpse of a sign high up on the side of a building whose grounds they were entering.

The sign was in three languages—Hebrew, Arabic, and English. No matter how you wrote it, it spelled MORTUARY.

The hearse driver turned into the funeral home garage and drew up to a loading dock where a shiny new casket was laid out, awaiting his arrival. There was no one on the dock to help him and he was running a bit late for his appointment. He tapped the horn twice, the two sharp blasts echoing off the narrow walls of the loading room. That should bring someone running. Alighting from the hearse, he walked around and opened its rear doors.

"Ma Salaami."

The hearse driver recoiled at the sight of the tall Druze seated next to the wooden casket. "What—what are you doing here?" he stammered.

"I swore an oath not to leave the side of my beloved father until he is laid in his grave. I will assist you in his transfer to the burial casket."

"You are Suleiman's son?"

"One of three, the eldest."

"Your assistance won't be necessary. The mortuary provides that service."

"Then I will see that it is done properly."

This was going to complicate things. He had to get rid of the man. But how? The driver's thought process was interrupted by the arrival of two burly funeral attendants dressed in black, who greeted him with a wordless nod. Hoisting the empty casket, they slid it into the hearse alongside the pine box that held the remains, then clambered in behind it, the tall Druze backing out of the way.

One of the attendants opened the burial casket, revealing a luxurious quilted lining of rose-colored satin, while the other pried the lid off the wooden coffin. It was not hinged to the coffin and he set it to one side.

"Uncle Suleiman" was dressed in his Sabbath best, looking at peace with the world, hands clasped over an ample stomach, his ruddy face closely shaven except for the prolific moustache that arched from beneath his nose to the bottom of his jaw. His tall son gazed fondly at his remains, wiping away a tear.

The attendants took positions at opposite ends of the box and bent over it. At a sign from one, they lifted the expired Druze patriarch and deposited him in his new satin-lined repository. Readjusting his arms to the folded position and smoothing his garments, they closed the lid of the casket.

"Does this stay or go?" one of the attendants inquired, indicating the now empty pine coffin.

"It stays," the driver replied. "That will be all, thank you."

The bereaved son replaced the lid on the pine box and sat down on it. It was apparent to the driver that he was not going to move the powerfully built giant without some help.

"I have to take care of the paper work," he remarked, then followed the funeral attendants through the door that led to the anteroom of the mortuary. But once inside, he detoured to another door leading to the outside parking lot.

There was the white panel truck he had been told to look for, parked in the far corner of the lot. He hurried toward it. As he approached, a heavy, muscular man wearing sunglasses got out of the passenger side, watching him warily.

"Are you the al-Rahmen party?" the hearse driver inquired. Al-Rahmen was the pre-assigned password.

"Yes. We are here for the Darwaza funeral." Darwaza was the countersign. The big man signalled his partner, who stepped out of the driver's side and joined them. He was slighter of build than his confederate, with a wiry body, and also wore dark glasses.

The hearse driver informed them of his problem. "He won't be budged."

"Then we must find some way to budge him," the man with the wiry build observed calmly, fingering a bulge in his pocket.

"He is a member of the funeral party," the driver cautioned. "If the funeral is disrupted, you will never get your—merchandise—across the border."

"Let us try to persuade him. If we are unsuccessful, I have something that will take the starch out of him. He will be taken ill, and the funeral will have to proceed without him."

It was becoming clear to the hearse driver that the spokesman was the leader of the twosome and was calling the shots. He addressed his larger, more muscular associate.

"I will tend to this problem while you take care of our prisoner. It is time for his sedative. I will take one of the back-up syringes with me."

The other man went back to the truck and returned with a blue plastic case. Inside were four pre-filled hypodermic needles resting on a bed of cotton, a pale yellow fluid visible inside the graduated tubes. The wiry man helped himself to one and placed it carefully in the pocket of his windbreaker.

"Get him prepared and we will bring the hearse around for the transfer." He strode off with the chauffeur of the hearse in the direction of the mortuary.

His partner watched the pair enter the mortuary, then slid open the side door of the van. The prisoner was lying on his back, motionless, just as he had been when they last checked on him. The big man took another of the hypodermic needles from the case and stepped into the back of the van.

"That's funny—he was here just a minute ago." The man in the chauffeur's uniform swiveled his head around in disbelief. Except for the two coffins, the hearse was empty. The tall Druze who had sworn not to leave his father's side was now nowhere to be seen . . .

"I have no idea what happened to him," the hearse driver observed, throwing up his hands.

"Never mind—it's good riddance. Start the motor and get us out to my truck, so we can finish this job."

"All right, but first there's the matter of the rest of my fee."

The wiry man scowled. "I don't have your money. You'll be paid the balance on the other side, after the delivery is made."

"By whom?"

"Whoever picks up the merchandise. Didn't they tell you it was C.O.D.?" He roared at his own witticism.

Llewellyn had heard most of the conversation between the men outside the van and had a pretty good idea of what was coming. In one last supreme effort to free his hands, he tensed his muscles and tugged for all he was worth. The frayed rope refused to give. The side door of the van opened and he froze.

The muscular kidnapper squatted on the metal floor beside his prisoner and squinted through his sunglasses, watching the needle of the syringe as he pressed the plunger to eject a thin stream of fluid. All set. The effect of the solution would be instantaneous and there was enough in the syringe to knock him out for twenty-four hours. Laid out in the coffin, he would have the appearance of a dead man, in case anyone at the border should look inside, which they seldom bothered to do.

He considered in what part of the anatomy to make the injection. Medical practice favored one of the buttocks, but he wasn't about to go to the trouble of removing the prisoner's trousers. The upper arm would have to do.

Llewellyn's head was tilted back and he could see just enough beneath the blindfold to realize what was happening. As the muscular arm reached underneath him to pull up his sleeve, he rolled his body on top of it, pinning it, at the same time raising his feet and knees in an attempt to dislodge the hypodermic in the other hand.

It worked! The syringe flew from his captor's grasp and out through the open door. With a howl of rage, the powerful man retaliated. A heavy fist slammed into the side of his jaw and then another, flush in his face, bloodying his nose. The blows kept coming as he tried to roll with them, weave his head so they wouldn't land solidly. But they had already taken their toll. His efforts to resist grew feebler, and he felt himself blacking out.

On his hands and knees, breathing heavily, his assailant looked around for the syringe. It wasn't on the floor of the truck. Peering out through the open door, he spied it lying on the pavement. It hadn't broken; it was plastic. He crawled to the door and reached down to retrieve it.

From out of nowhere a giant black boot descended on his hand, pinning it to the pavement. He screamed in agony, trying vainly to free it from the crushing weight, his bulging eyes raking upward over the black-clothed figure that towered over him, encountering a pair of fiery eyes that burned back at him from beneath a white *kaffiyeh*. His free hand reached for the weapon concealed in a holster under his jacket. It never made it—a hand more powerful than his own caught his wrist and twisted it like a stick of bread dough, propelling him out of the truck and slamming him against the pavement.

The dazed kidnapper stared up into the muzzle of his own gun. "Who—who are you?"

"Silence, scum of the earth! Move so much as a hair and you die." The "Druze" thrust his head inside the truck.

"Mr. Llewellyn? Are you all right?"

Llewellyn drifted slowly back into consciousness. Someone was calling his name. The voice had a familiar ring to it. He knew it, but it eluded him.

A hand ripped the blindfold away, and a face shaded by an Arab head scarf swam in front of his eyes. It still didn't register. Then its owner removed the Druze head covering and he saw the flashing white teeth and caught the inimitable twinkle in the eyes.

"Khalidy! How—?"

"Later. Right now we have to be going." The Palestinian's knife slashed through the stubborn bonds on his wrists and ankles. Moments later the wheels of the white panel truck squealed as Khalidy gunned the motor and shot off toward the exit.

22

LLEWELLYN HANDED THE phone back to the U.N. chauffeur, Ivar Hagstrom, the same driver who had performed so admirably during the Gaza terrorist incident. He had already called the police in Kiryat Shmona and put them onto his would-be abductors at the mortuary. Without their van, they couldn't have gotten far.

He and Khalidy had dumped the van a few blocks away, where the Druze funeral vehicles were still parked awaiting the return of the hearse, Ivar's limousine among them. As they sped south in the limo, Llewellyn told Khalidy that the man behind his abduction was none other than the man who had procured the sword amulets found hanging around the necks of dead terrorists. The same ones, he added, who on two occasions had tried to assassinate him. It was Malamud, he'd explained, who was bankrolling the terrorists' anti-peace campaign.

The Palestinian was astounded. "Malamud is a Jew, yet conspires with Islamic fanatics dedicated to driving his own people from Palestine?"

"Strictly business," Llewellyn had observed. "He's a wealthy financier. His firm has apparently got a big stake in West Bank real estate developments for Jewish settlers. A peace agreement between your people and the government abolishing such settlements might wipe him out."

Khalidy's sense of outrage mounted. "He would put such crass business interests above the welfare of millions of his fellow men?"

"His sense of values is pretty warped, all right, to say nothing of his sense of humor. Like these expensive trinkets he procured—the Arab sword with the Jewish shofar. All just to make a point."

"But to underwrite terrorism and destroy the peace process out of pure lust for money!" Khalidy fumed. "He is no better than the murderers he hires. In fact, he is far worse! If I could get my hands on him right now, I am afraid of what I might do."

Llewellyn grinned. "I thought that might be your reaction. Would you like to pay him a visit?" With Khalidy's concurrence, he instructed Ivar to head for Caesarea. Then he dialed Daniella's number.

Richard Llewellyn's flight would arrive an hour late, the airport advised. Daniella was glad for the extra time; she was running late. No sooner had she hung up the phone than it rang. She snatched it up again.

"Shalom, hello."

"Shalom, double shalom!" said the voice she most wanted to hear of all possible voices.

"David!" she cried. "Thank God! Are you all right?"

"Fit as a fiddle, except for a slight dent in the noggin. I'm going after the guy who put it there. But first I thought I'd better check in."

"Where are you? I've been frantic. What happened to you?"

"I'm in the Galilee. We're headed back. Sorry I couldn't call you sooner or get word to you, but I've been tied up." His chuckle was audible. "Literally. Since yesterday evening."

She gasped. "You were kidnapped, too?"

"Too? Who else was kidnapped? Not . . . you?"

"It's all right, David . . . I'm fine now. It happened while I was on the street yesterday, showing that picture around of the white-haired suspect. A man posing as an Arab street vendor chloroformed me and they drove me off in this van."

"I knew it!" he exploded, furious with himself for ever leaving her yesterday. "I knew I should have stayed with you instead of taking off after that guy when he bolted."

It took a moment for what he'd said to sink in. "Wait a minute, David . . . You mean you were *there?* You followed me?"

He could hear the slight irritation in her voice. "Well, I thought there might be trouble and I was right. I can't believe this Shmona guy! The least he could have done is give you some protection."

"You shouldn't blame Baruch. If it hadn't been for him, I might be . . . He chased the van and got me out. I owe him my life."

"You weren't hurt? I'd never forgive myself—"

She flung his own cliché back at him. "I'm fit as a fiddle, except for being worried sick about you. You say you were struck on the head?"

"By 'Whitey,' the man in that picture of yours, no less. It's too long a story to go into right now, but I'll tell you the happy ending. That guy I chased led me to him, and I know his identity. His name is Malamud. He's the head of a big investment syndicate and he's in bed with the terrorists up to his eyeballs. He tried to shanghai me, handed me over to some terrorists, then split. But I know where he's holed up. We're on the way right now."

"We?"

"You had your rescuer, I had mine. Out of the blue, just when I was about to buy it. It's my Palestinian buddy, Ibrahim Khalidy."

She finally laughed. "The man you were assigned to protect?"

"Yeah, isn't that a twist? Listen—this is important. We're in Khalidy's limo headed for Malamud's hideaway at Caesarea. I want you to alert your boss and have him meet us there. I have a hunch we can get Malamud and his assistant to crack, identify the terrorists. This may be the link we've been hoping for to a certain hijacked weapon."

"David!" she protested. *"Must* you go after this man yourself, after what you've just been through? Let Baruch handle it. Those head wounds can be nasty. It should be looked at immediately."

"Not to worry. My head's better already. And besides having a score to settle with these characters, I have a special club to help persuade them to talk. You've heard of a shillelagh? This one's a Khalidy."

Exasperated, she realized there would be no talking him out of it. "Where should Baruch meet you?"

"There's a country club in Caesarea—a golf clubhouse. Malamud's house is nearby; I don't know exactly where. Someone at the club must know him—he's probably a member. Tell Shmona to bring a copy of that portrait you were showing around."

"When will you be there?"

"We're about three hours away. He'll have plenty of time."

"I'll call him as soon as I hang up. David—"

"Yes?"

"When will you be home?"

"Sometime tomorrow, I hope . . . You're right about one thing. I'm pretty tired; I haven't had much sleep. I need to crash."

"*Please,* be careful. And hurry back. I miss you terribly."

She decided to try Shmona's office number first. He often worked late; she knew that on occasion he even spent the night there when the going got heavy. This must be one of those nights; he answered on the third ring. She brought him quickly up to date.

"Does David know where in Caesarea the suspect is holed up?" Shmona asked.

"No. He wants you to bring a copy of that portrait Sergeant Neff made to show to people."

"I'll do better than that. I'll access the computer for unlisted phone numbers in the area. If we come up with Malamud's address, we'll put his residence under surveillance immediately. I can't promise that we'll be able to wait for David to arrive before we make the arrest, but we'll try."

"Fair enough. I'll tell him if he calls back."

"Daniella? Don't hang up. There's something else . . . I have a new assignment for you. I hesitated to involve you while your husband was missing, but now that he's safe, I really have no choice . . .

"There's been a new development on the missile. I can't go into detail, but we're extremely shorthanded and running out of time. The director has laid this on my shoulders; it may be our last chance to track down the location of the missile before it's too late. I want you to go to Iran."

"Iran? The missile is in Iran?"

"We don't know that. But we have evidence that a terrorist courier en route to the missile site with certain critical supplies may be traveling through Iran. We have people along two of the possible routes but none in Shiraz. That's where I'm sending you. Your flight leaves at eight in the morning."

"Tomorrow morning? But Baruch—what about David? He won't be back by then. He expects me to be here."

"I'll explain it to him when I see him. Daniella, I don't have to tell you what this means. It's countless lives—our country's whole future."

"I know, I know . . ." She sighed. "I'm not trying to get out of the assignment. But if David's right and you can get Malamud to talk, he may provide you with the identities of the terrorists and their whereabouts."

"Fine, if it pans out. But we can't be certain it will, so we have to cover all bets. I want you in Shiraz, in position, by tomorrow night. Come to the office early tomorrow, on your way to the airport. There'll be a briefing tape in your safe with your tickets and new identity papers. Further instructions will reach you in Shiraz."

Llewellyn, Khalidy, and Ivar were now headed for Caesarea, as fast as the venerable limousine and the winding road descending from the mountains of the upper Galilee could carry them.

"Perhaps the two men who had you in custody can also be persuaded to talk," Khalidy suggested. "And the hearse driver. He was obviously in on it with them."

"Perhaps. But I doubt that those two belonged to the same fraternity as the ones we encountered in Jericho and Gaza. They apparently act as go-betweens for the Lebanon Hezbollah. That's where I was headed when you stepped in. How on earth did you do it, figure out what was happening and manage to be there?"

"It was not that difficult. After the ambassador called this morning, I said to myself, suppose it is another diplomatic abduction—how will they get my friend out of Israel without being caught? As I told the ambassador, I have certain connections, channels open to me, which are not available to others.

"I had heard rumors about the so-called 'Good Fence' in the upper Galilee—its suspected use in smuggling bodies across the border under the auspices of Israeli Druzes, who have special privileges that include rights of burial on the Lebanon side. I called a Druze acquaintance in an upper-Galilee village and learned that a funeral had been scheduled across the border for this very afternoon.

"The timing seemed too perfect to be coincidental. As you Americans say, I decided to play a hunch. And praise Allah that I did, my friend."

"Amen to that!" The thought of how close he had come to becoming a Hezbollah hostage made Llewellyn all the more impatient to get his hands on Malamud. "Can't this old crate go any faster?"

Ivar speeded up a bit, the tires squealing as the limousine took the next curve. "We'll be out of the mountains soon, sir. Then the road will straighten out and we'll make better time."

"How long till we're in Caesarea?"

"A good two and a half hours. We can't do much better than that."

"May I make a suggestion, my friend?" Khalidy had been watching Llewellyn intently. "You could do with a nap. It will help to pass the time. Why don't you stretch out here on the backseat?"

The Palestinian swung his long legs over the seat in front of him and climbed up beside the driver. Llewellyn lay down on his side, his head against the arm rest.

In less than a minute he was fast asleep.

A gentle rain had begun to fall as Daniella exited the express-way and drove into Ben Gurion International. Inside the terminal it was a mob scene, as usual. Somehow all the flights seemed to arrive at once. Daniella had met David's younger brother only once, at their wedding. She circled the crowd around the baggage dispenser, her eyes searching for the face she remembered that bore only a slight resemblance to her husband's. Could that be Richard, there in the corner, chatting with another passenger? Yes! She rushed up to him and threw her arms around him.

"Daniella!" His face was grave as he hugged her to him and kissed her on the mouth.

"Oh, Richard! I have the most wonderful news!" She wiped a tear away. "David's all right! He phoned me, just before I left for the airport. He's on his way home."

It took a second to register. "He's okay? He's safe?" A broad grin broke over Richard's face. "Didn't I tell you my big brother could take care of himself?"

Quickly, she filled him in on what had happened to David. "I guess I brought you here for nothing. I wouldn't blame you if you got right back on that plane."

"Not on your life." His grin came back. "This is a great excuse for a visit. I haven't seen you guys since the wedding. I'll stick around and help you celebrate Davey's homecoming."

She noticed that the man Richard had been conversing with, while pretending to be occupied with lighting his pipe, was taking it all in. Richy answered Daniella's inquiring look with an introduction. "This is Dr. Tessler. My sister-in-law, Daniella. It seems that Dr. Tessler also came here to meet my plane. According to his business card, he's a U.S. consultant on 'Strategic Weapon Systems.' "

"Charmed, Mrs. Llewellyn." Tessler made a slight bow before turning his attention back to Richy. "As I was about to tell you a moment ago, your consultation is needed on a matter of some immediate urgency to both the U.S. and Israel. If you can meet with us tomorrow morning, I can assure you that your trip here will not be wasted."

"I guess I need to make something clear, Dr. Tessler. I don't consider my trip here wasted. I haven't seen my brother and sister-in-law in several years and look forward to spending some time with them. If you want my participation on something that's classified, you'll have to contact the Peace Shield program office and file the necessary clearances. Then we can take it up back in Riyadh when I return."

"The clearance has already been taken care of. I spoke with your supervisor in Riyadh. It's being faxed to IDF headquarters here in Tel Aviv. The Israeli participants will be standing by in the morning."

"You have been busy, haven't you? Sorry to disappoint you, but I'm here to visit my family."

"But this is a matter of—" Tessler glanced sideways at Daniella. "Would you excuse us for a moment?"

Richard shook his head emphatically. "Dr. Tessler, this is not the time or the place—"

"It's all right, Richard." The look in Daniella's eyes suggested she might have an inkling of what this was about. "You'd better hear him out."

The two men moved off to a corner of the big room, standing apart from the crowd of new arrivals. Daniella watched Richy's reaction as the man with the pipe spoke earnestly to him at some length. She saw his eyes widen in disbelief and she felt certain she knew the reason.

They left the terminal and crossed to the parking structure, Richy lugging a small suitcase. Neither spoke. The rain had stopped but the pavement was still slick, presenting the appearance of a smooth black lake, the distant autos resembling boats skimming its surface, their light reflections weaving intriguing patterns.

In the car, headed back to Tel Aviv on the expressway, Daniella broke the silence between them. "Whatever he told you seems to have hit you right between the eyes."

"Sorry. I . . . I'm still trying to sort some things out. It's hard to believe that what Tessler said is true, it's so incredible. And yet it would explain a lot about what the Saudis have been up to. I wish I could discuss it with you, but Tessler swore me to secrecy."

"I think I already know. It involves something that was hijacked off a cargo ship, doesn't it? Something that represents a threat to Israel?"

Richy stared at her. "You *do* know! But if people here know about it, how can they go about their business like nothing was happening? I'd think there would be panic in the streets, a mass exodus out of here!"

"There may well be, once the news leaks out. Right now it's being closely held; the media haven't got wind of it yet. And even some of those who know, I think, still discount the threat. There's no proof, yet, that this—thing—is actually deployed, aimed at us. It's still just a possibility. But we have to be ready to defend ourselves, just in case. That's what they want your help on, isn't it?"

"Yes. Yes, it is." He was lost in thought again for a long moment. "Does my brother know?"

"Yes. David was instructed to start planning for a possible evacuation. He couldn't think of a way of doing that without starting a panic. Right now he's trying to help my government find out where the—where this thing is located. That's the unfinished business I spoke of."

Richy nodded. It all fit together now, the frantic search for a certain freighter over thousands of square miles of Indian Ocean, the subsequent involvement of the U.S. Navy in throwing up a hastily contrived blockade. The "contraband" carried by the freighter was not some load of narcotics or assault rifles or even the Stinger missiles he had suspected.

It was the ultimate weapon . . .

His mind backtracked over the missions he had flown in the Saudi AWACS, poring over radar imagery of shipping in the sea lanes between Singapore and the Gulf, trying to identify and eliminate each ship until things boiled down to a specific cargo ship of unknown origin and identity. Then the radar contact with the Lebanese freighter, the *Beirut Victory,* and his certainty that it was the one carrying the contraband. Until its boarding and search by a U.S. destroyer proved otherwise.

"What would you do—what would your country do—if you found out the location of this weapon?"

Daniella considered. "That would be up to the Prime Minister—and the military. The Air Force would probably bomb it, if it was reachable. Or we might send in commandos. Why do you ask?"

"Because I think I might know where it is."

23

It was almost dark when the United Nations limousine pulled into the outskirts of Caesarea and stopped at a service station for fuel and directions. Llewellyn hadn't considered that it would be nighttime when he had proposed to Shmona that they rendezvous at the golf clubhouse. What if it was closed?

They drove past the darkened, deserted fairways, a lone flagstick barely visible on one of the greens, silhouetted against the final glimmer of light on the western horizon. "I've heard about this place," Ivar, the chauffeur, volunteered. "Instead of the number of the hole, all the flags have the Star of David."

Approaching the clubhouse, they were relieved to see light emanating from it, a number of cars still in the parking lot. As Ivar pulled to a stop and switched off the motor, they heard lively music coming from inside. Some sort of affair was apparently in progress.

Llewellyn left the car to investigate. At Khalidy's suggestion he pocketed the pistol the Palestinian had lifted when he subdued one of the kidnappers. They were fifteen minutes ahead of the meeting time he had proposed to Shmona, but the Mossad agent would have had plenty of time to arrive ahead of them. There was no sign of him around the parking area.

Llewellyn walked toward the entrance, the crunching sound of his footsteps on the cinder path reminiscent of his ordeal the previous morning, locked in the trunk of Malamud's car. Stepping inside the entrance, he was suddenly conscious of the disreputable appearance he must present, unshaven and disheveled, wearing the same rumpled suit he'd had on since his abduction. His discomfiture was heightened when a major domo in a tuxedo appeared, looking him up and down.

"Can I help you, sir?" he inquired in English.

"Perhaps you can." He decided to try the direct approach. "This is kind of an emergency. I'm trying to find a certain gentleman, Nachman Malamud. I think he's a member here. Do you know him, by any chance?"

"No, sir, I do not, and the club is closed at present, except for a private wedding going on in the ballroom. But I will inquire if a Mr. Malamud is in attendance. Please wait here."

Llewellyn gave him a head start, then followed him at a distance down a long corridor leading toward the sound of increasingly boisterous music. The tuxedo-clad figure disappeared through a double swinging door. Llewellyn approached it and peered through the small window set into one of the doors.

Inside the ballroom the band was playing a hora, a ring of dancers cavorting to the lively strains of the folkdance, among them the bride, still in her wedding gown, and the formally attired groom. Other members of the wedding party were seated at tables surrounding the dance floor, clapping out the rhythm. The major domo was circulating unobtrusively among the tables making his inquiries. Llewellyn scanned the faces he could see and the backs of heads. None of them bore any resemblance to Malamud's.

It was then that he caught a fleeting glimpse of a man and woman disappearing through a side door. He was almost certain the man's hair was white!

"Is there another way out of the ballroom?" he demanded of a passing waiter.

"Only through the kitchen."

"Which way to the kitchen?"

The waiter pointed back up the corridor.

Llewellyn bolted back in the direction he had come from and down the side corridor. He burst through a pair of swinging doors. The kitchen was a busy place, cooks in white uniforms bustling about, engaged in putting the final touches on the wedding repast.

"Did someone just come through here?" he shouted.

One of the cooks pointed toward the rear of the kitchen. Llewellyn ran past him, almost colliding with two others as he dodged his way through the kitchen to reach the rear exit. He plunged through it into the almost total blackness outside.

Stopping to listen, he heard footsteps running away to his right but could see nothing. He followed in the direction of the footfall, running hard. If it was Malamud, he was headed for the parking lot and had a pretty good head start. Too good. There was the sound of a powerful engine firing up and headlights flared, tires squealing as a car shot out of the parking lot.

Llewellyn came around the side of the building and ran back to where the limousine was parked. "I think that was Malamud!"

He dove into the backseat as Ivar gunned the motor and roared off in pursuit. The taillights and headlights of the other vehicle were visible far ahead. It had a good lead and was moving fast. "Left! He just turned left!" Llewellyn shouted. Ivar came to the junction and skidded into a sharp left turn onto a side road.

But now there were no headlights or taillights visible. Ivar was mystified. "Where'd he go?"

"He's turned off his lights. Switch on your high beams!"

Twin shafts of light shot out to penetrate the blackness ahead, illuminating a thin ribbon of blacktop and the terrain immediately surrounding it far down the road. If another auto had been in the powerful beam, its tail reflectors would have glowed like beacons. There was nothing on the road as far as the eye could see.

"Looks like we've lost him," Ivar lamented.

"Keep going . . . we may still catch him. He can't drive too fast without lights."

But the only thing they caught up to was another auto that was moving much too slowly to be Malamud's and turned out to be an old pickup truck. After blowing past it, with nothing in sight beyond, Llewellyn had to admit defeat. "We might as well go back to the clubhouse and try to hook up with Shmona."

As the limo slowed in preparation for a U-turn, the staccato beating of helicopter rotors could be clearly discerned. The noise increased and a bright shaft of light plunged earthward to bathe the limousine in a sudden, blinding brilliance.

A police chopper. This was a stroke of luck; it could help them run down Malamud. Llewellyn jumped out and began waving his arms frantically, shielding his eyes from the intense illumination. The helicopter hovered directly over him for a few seconds, the wind blasting down from its powerful rotors. Then the searchlight swung off to light up an open field bordering the road, and the ponderous noise maker settled slowly onto it.

Llewellyn hurried toward it. The door opened, and a short, bearded man stepped out and jumped to the ground. Shmona! Llewellyn ran up to him.

"We were following Malamud!" he shouted above the din of the rotors. "We lost him. He's getting away!"

The Mossad agent only smiled, grasping Llewellyn's hand and shaking it vigorously. "I'm happy to see that you're all in one piece. You had us worried."

"Didn't you hear what I said?" Llewellyn shouted. "We've lost him! We need the chopper to—"

But the helicopter was already accelerating its motor again in preparation for lifting off. Shmona waved at it, then motioned Llewellyn toward the limousine. "I'll ride with you. I believe you have a phone in your car? Don't worry about Malamud. I know where he is."

Once inside the limo, the Mossad agent explained. "I was on my way in the chopper to meet you at the country club. We saw this car come speeding out of there, then your limousine in hot pursuit. We followed. When the other car turned off its lights, we used a night-vision device to keep track of it. It went straight to a house in a nearby development—a house we've had under surveillance for the last hour. It's Malamud's; we found an unlisted local number in his name. He and his wife just went inside. May I use your phone?"

Ivar handed the cellular phone to Shmona in the backseat and he punched in a number. "The couple who just arrived— they're still in the house? Good. We'll be closing in shortly. If anything changes, call me on this number." He read off the cellular phone code and number.

"We're going to carry out this arrest strictly by the book," he proclaimed, handing the phone back to the driver. "I have the local police standing by. We'll go in cautiously. We have to assume that he's armed."

"He's packing a pistol," Llewellyn volunteered. "I only got a glimpse of it before he bashed me on the head with it. But I don't think he'll get violent. Doing his own dirty work isn't his style."

"He got violent with you, didn't he? We'll take no chances. You are all to remain in the car; we'll let the police make the actual arrest. I'll accompany them, with the warrant."

Llewellyn exploded. "Shmona, for God's sake, you can't leave this up to the local cops! What if they shoot him? The man has information we have to have. He's our only source!"

"I'm perfectly aware of that, and I've already impressed on the police chief the imperative of capturing Malamud alive and unharmed. His men have been instructed not to shoot under any circumstances. Now I must insist that you cooperate and do not try to interfere."

"On one condition—that you give us a shot at him after the arrest is made, before the police interrogation begins. Khalidy and I both have a score to settle with this guy. When he comes face to face with the man he twice conspired to assassinate and the man he thinks is out of his life forever as a Lebanese hostage, it's bound to loosen his tongue. We need the identity of those terrorists *now,* not after some long drawn-out plea bargaining with his high-powered lawyers in the act."

Shmona regarded him shrewdly with his owl-like eyes. "Hmm. All right, it's worth a try. I'll arrange it with the police. We'll be listening in, of course, and recording everything. If it doesn't work we can always try some other kind of—persuasion."

He gave the driver some directions, and the limousine moved off in the direction it had originally been traveling. Shmona got back on the phone. "I am presently less than a kilometer from the house. The suspect is inside. He is believed to be armed with a small hand gun. It is now ten minutes to nine. We will rendezvous at the designated spot at nine sharp and close in to make the arrest. Remember, no shooting— under any circumstances."

• • •

The police were moving in. Llewellyn and the others watched tensely from the limousine, parked at the end of the block, as two squad cars without lights or sirens converged on the house from opposite ends of the street. Two uniformed men, their service pistols drawn, hurried to the front door, while two others ran to the back.

The drawn guns made Llewellyn nervous. Where in the devil was Shmona? He must have stayed in one of the squad cars.

He had promised Shmona to remain in the limousine, but his anxiety made that impossible. He got out of the car and stood beside it, craning his neck for a better view. Lights were visible inside the house. The policemen had reached the front door and apparently rung the doorbell. One was carrying a bullhorn. When there was no response, the bullhorn shattered the silence with a strident ultimatum. The police waited. Finally the door opened and they pushed their way inside.

From somewhere a shot rang out! Oh, God, no! Llewellyn began running up the block as Shmona charged out of one of the squad cars and rushed into the house. As Llewellyn reached the front door, the Mossad agent reappeared.

"You were supposed to stay in the limousine!"

"The shot— Did they—? Is Malamud—?"

"Go back to the limousine. You can follow us to the station. We have Malamud in custody. He had a bag packed. He was getting ready to run."

"They didn't shoot him?"

Shmona shook his head.

"But the shot—" Llewellyn read Shmona's eyes. "Zilbert?"

"Shot himself in the head. He's dead."

Llewellyn and Khalidy waited in a special room at the district police headquarters near Caesarea while Malamud was booked and fingerprinted. It was the same room used for police lineups, behind a two-way mirror through which witnesses could view suspects without being seen. It was completely wired for sound, with a video camera behind the disguised window.

While Khalidy sat calmly at a table, Llewellyn paced. He

was depressed over Zilbert's suicide. Malamud's crony would have been the easier of the two to break.

"What's keeping them? I don't trust Shmona. I'll bet they're doing their own interrogation first."

The Palestinian chuckled. "It's easy to see you've never been in an Israeli jail before. I have been in many. Their favorite form of torture is making one wait interminably. They are all the same."

There was a knock on the door and Shmona's voice. "Get ready in there. They're bringing him now." Llewellyn sat down beside Khalidy, facing the door.

Malamud's voice was heard outside the door addressing Shmona, his tone imperious, demanding to know why he was being held incommunicado, threatening dire consequences if he was not allowed to call his lawyer. "In due time," was the Mossad agent's soft reply.

"Where are you taking me now?"

"You'll see."

The door opened and the white-haired tycoon entered, his hands cuffed in front of him, his jaw set. The door closed again.

"Hello, Malamud."

Malamud's jaw went slack, his posture of righteous indignation shattered. "Llewellyn! How—?"

"How did I escape from those goons you handed me over to? With the help of a friend, one who's been dying to meet you. Almost dying, that is, on the two occasions your paid assassins tried to kill him. Permit me to present the chief negotiator for the Palestinians in the forthcoming peace talks, Ibrahim Khalidy."

Malamud's eyes showed terror as the giant Palestinian stood up from the table, towering over him. He couldn't face the withering gaze and looked away. Khalidy stepped closer and seized his jaw in one oversized hand, forcing it back.

"I have something to say to you and I want you to look at me when I say it. In the old days, when my people caught a thief, they would cut off his hands. You are the worst kind of thief. You would steal *peace* from the people, and for what? To line your own pockets."

With a disgusted thrust of his hand, Khalidy released his

hold, wiping his hand on his robe as though to decontaminate it. "Death is too good for you. I cannot think of a punishment terrible enough for what you have done."

"Perhaps I can," Llewellyn interjected. "Let me suggest one. To see family, friends, business associates—half of the city that you called home—wiped out by these same terrorists you've been bankrolling, your country and its economy crippled in the process; to know—and for everyone who survives to learn—that you were responsible *and* that you could have prevented it."

"What are you saying?" gasped Malamud, his question echoed by Khalidy's look. Llewellyn hadn't broached the subject to him.

"A ballistic missle that could wipe out half of Tel Aviv—in the hands of terrorists—*his* terrorists!"

Now it was Khalidy's turn to gasp.

"I tried to tell him about it this morning," Llewellyn went on, "but he dismissed it as a desperate ploy to get myself off the hook. Well, I'm not on the hook anymore, Malamud, am I? And I'm still saying it, because it happens to be true. You have one chance to atone, at least in part, for what you've done—by identifying the terrorists and telling us where to find them before it's too late."

Malamud looked shaken but was still not buying it. "How can you be so sure that the ones who have this weapon are the same group of terrorists—?" He stopped just short of incriminating himself.

"The same group of terrorists you've been sponsoring?" Llewellyn smiled grimly. "We have you to thank for that, Malamud. Those symbolic little items you ordered from a certain jeweler on Allenby Road, now deceased, to be worn by your mercenary 'soldiers.' One of them turned up at the scene of the hijacking after that bunch of terrorists took off with the missile."

Llewellyn watched the struggle going on inside a thoroughly deflated Malamud, saw the look in his eyes change as the truth sank in.

"I . . . I can't believe—"

"But you do believe, don't you? I can see it in your eyes." The financier's face went ashen. He looked close to collapse.

Llewellyn eased him into a chair. "How could such a thing happen?" he asked, his voice a barely audible whisper.

"Your Arab bedfellows are even cleverer than you thought. And better organized. Their operation has been superbly planned and orchestrated. And also well financed, thanks to you. They played you for a sucker. This is your chance to get even. Tell us, now—who are they? Where are they?"

Malamud shook his head helplessly from side to side. "I don't know."

Llewellyn banged his fist on the table. "You're in it with them all the way, aren't you? Why else would you be protecting these scum who are trying to blow up your country?"

"No! You've got to believe me! If I'd had any suspicion they were planning such a—"

"Then tell us! We need names, not pathetic excuses. The names of their leaders, descriptions, addresses—something we can use to track them down before—"

"I don't know *any* of those things," he whined. "I've purposely dealt with them at arm's length. All I have is a phone number."

"Give it to me!" Llewellyn shoved pencil and paper at him. "Write it down."

Malamud complied, grasping the pencil in the trembling fingers of his two cuffed hands and scrawling the number laboriously.

Llewellyn grabbed back the sheet of paper. "You never saw any of them face to face?"

"Only once, when he broke our rule, came to my office. I still don't know how he discovered my identity . . . It was the one in charge, the man whose picture was in the paper—the tall, thin one."

Llewellyn and Khalidy exchanged looks. "We've met him. When was this?"

"Three days ago."

"What did he want?"

"Money."

"You gave it to him?"

Malamud nodded. "He threatened to expose me."

"That should have tipped you off that things were out of control. How much?"

"Fifty thousand American dollars."

Llewellyn whistled. "What was it for? More anti-peace terrorism?"

"Not necessarily." Malamud's eyes were downcast. "There were no strings on it."

"He didn't tell what he was using the money for, where he was going?"

"Just that he was leaving town soon. He suggested I should do the same."

"Why?"

"He said that Tel Aviv wouldn't be a healthy place to stay much longer. I thought he meant—"

"Now you know what he meant. Did he happen to mention a time frame?"

"No."

"Did he look like his picture—the portrait we published?"

"Yes. I recognized him immediately when he took off his disguise."

"Disguise?"

"He was dressed like an ultra-orthodox Jew. He was wearing a false beard and a Hassidic hat with false side curls attached, and a long black coat."

Larnaca International Airport on the island of Cyprus might well have been termed Israel's doorway to the Arab world. Direct flights from Israel were banned by virtually all of the predominantly Muslim countries. The Cyprus airport, a scant two hundred air miles from Tel Aviv, served as a funnel for passengers bound for countries not serviced by carriers flying out of Israel. Tiny Cyprus Airlines capitalized on the state of affairs with two daily shuttles in both directions between Tel Aviv and Larnaca.

The pilot of this morning's shuttle got his final takeoff clearance from the Ben Gurion International tower and poured on the coal. The commuter jet roared down the runway and was airborne at 8:20. Daniella Llewellyn leaned back into the soft upholstery and tried to relax. She had been up and on the go since five in the morning, completing her packing for the hastily arranged trip, driving to Mossad headquarters for her new identity papers, and listening over and over again to the taped instructions on her new assignment prepared for her by her control before he left for Caesarea.

The details had been skimpy and she was still mostly in the dark on what was expected of her and what her role would be once she got to Iran. She was also nervous about masquerading as a Canadian jewelry buyer, the new identity selected by the Mossad to cover her stay in Iran. The jewelry part was okay; she felt well enough informed on that score to get by. But she had never been to Canada and scarcely knew anything about the country. What if someone questioned her on the subject?

Operating under cover in the friendly environment of her home town had proved hazardous enough. The thought of doing so as a Jew in a Muslim country terrified her. If only she'd been able to see David before departing. He was a source of strength for her, sorely missed at a time like this. But she knew that he'd have tried to stop her from going. Shmona had known it, too. He must have delayed telling her husband; there had been no call from him during the night.

She couldn't worry about David's reaction now. She had to concentrate on the job ahead of her. The real cloak-and-dagger stuff would start when she got to Cyprus. During the three-hour layover at Larnaca before boarding her Iran Air flight to Tehran, she would completely change her outfit and identity, becoming Jane Monpleasure of Ottawa, Ontario. The fake Canadian passport in that name with her own picture attached, hidden in the lining of the new purse she carried, had already been imprinted with the Larnaca entry stamp and also contained an Iranian visa. Her own Israeli passport, after she used it to get through customs in Larnaca, would be stowed with some of her other things in a locker inside the airport terminal, to be retrieved and used on her return trip.

Her mind went back over the taped instructions she had memorized. Her mission was to pick up the trail of a certain courier or couriers from Iraq, thought to be traveling through Iran, bound for a rendezvous with the terrorists in possession of the hijacked missile. She had no information on the identity of the courier, only that he was transporting bulky equipment that might weigh as much as a quarter of a ton. It didn't take much imagination to deduce that the equipment could be a special warhead for the missile. The courier would probably have entered Iran through Turkey to avoid the much stricter screening of entrants and baggage at entry points along the border with Iran's foe in the recent war, Iraq. A charter flight from northern Iran was considered the most likely means of transport. Daniella was to check into the airport hotel at Shiraz and await further instructions.

Jane Monpleasure. She repeated the name to herself several times, trying to get used to it, wondering where on earth the Mossad staffers had come up with that one. She knew a little French; Monpleasure had a definite French sound to her, an Anglicized version of *mon plaisir,* no doubt. The pleasure is all mine. How appropriate.

The gong chimed and the seat-belt sign went back on. The short flight was coming to an end. Daniella braced for the dash to be first in line at immigration and customs. The flight was packed; fortunately she was near the front of the plane.

She studied the other passengers in her vicinity. They were an eclectic group, from well-dressed businessmen to jeans-clad youths in western T-shirts. There was an Arab in the traditional robe and headdress, and sitting just in front of him a Greek Orthodox priest in his distinctive black hat and tunic. She had even caught a glimpse of a bearded Hassidic man in the back of the plane, fur hat and all, as she was taking her seat. Where were they all bound, she wondered? Would she encounter some of these same faces on the flight to Iran?

The jet made a quality landing and taxied to its berth at the main terminal in what would have been record time at one of the larger international airports. Daniella was one of the first to deplane through the only exit, at the front of the aircraft.

She had already descended the mobile staircase and was halfway to the terminal by the time the tall, bearded man in the wide-brimmed black hat of the Hassidim reached the front of the plane. From deep hollows above high cheekbones, smoldering eyes stared out to follow her progress across the tarmac, never once leaving her until she disappeared inside the terminal.

24

At the base of Old Jaffa's high promontory, just east of the clock tower, a cluster of tightly wound alleys comprised the Shuk Hapishpishim, Jaffa's memorable and venerable flea market. On any day of the week but Saturday the colorful conglomeration of open-air stalls could be found teeming with shoppers and bustling with activity, the air filled with the clamor of hawkers plying their wares and bargaining vociferously with customers. A wondrous array of assorted treasures and junk of all kinds lined both sides of the narrow alleys, jewelry and leather goods and Oriental rugs, glass, brass and copper creations, even giant nargilehs, the Middle-Eastern water pipes.

The sun was up, but the shuk had not yet come to life, its streets deserted and stalls still boarded up as the SWAT team moved in. Men in commando uniforms armed with assault weapons slipped silently in from several directions, converging on a ramshackle, single-story structure fronted by one of the larger stalls. When they were all in place, one blew a whistle. Windows on two sides of the house were broken and tear-gas cannisters thrown inside. The assault team waited for the occupants to emerge, their guns at the ready.

Nothing happened. They waited a few minutes more, then broke in the door. Donning gas masks, two of the special police detachment moved cautiously inside. In less than a minute, one came back out to report. The man he reported to ran into the alley and waved to a car idling at the end of the block. It pulled up in front of him. Baruch Shmona got out of the backseat. With him was David Llewellyn.

"Looks like your bird has flown," observed the SWAT team leader. "There's nobody home."

"Not again!" Shmona hurried toward the house, Llewellyn right at his heels.

"You can't go inside just yet," warned the SWAT boss. "We teargassed it."

Shmona got a whiff of the fumes coming out the door, coughed, and backed off. The second man emerged and ripped off his mask.

"The place has been cleaned out," he reported. "Doesn't look like they'll be returning. But someone was in there this morning. Coffee in a pot on the stove is still warm."

"Damn. We must have just missed him." Llewellyn's haggard and unshaven face betrayed his disappointment. Near exhaustion, he had still insisted on staying up and tagging along on the raid, sensing that they were close to capturing the tall, gaunt terrorist. But returning from Caesarea, tracing the number obtained from Malamud, and lining up the SWAT team had taken longer than he had bargained for. The delay had apparently cost them dearly.

Shmona refused to admit defeat. "He still might come back. I want this place staked out. And we'll get the crime lab people in as soon as it's aired out."

"A stakeout here? In the shuk?" The SWAT leader looked at him like he was mad. "Do you realize what this place will be like in another hour? Swarming with people, pure pandemonium."

Shmona was in no mood to argue. "Just *do* it."

The leader shrugged. "I'll tell the captain. I can't guarantee it."

"Never mind. I'll tell him myself." Shmona drew Llewellyn aside. "We'd better get you home—you look ready to drop. I'll send you in my car. I can ride back with the police."

"Thanks. I'd like to call Daniella first."

The Mossad agent consulted his watch. "I doubt if she's still home."

Llewellyn stared at him. "What do you mean? It's not even eight in the morning. Where would she—?"

Shmona avoided his eyes. "I was supposed to tell you. With

everything else going on, I forgot. She's on a new assignment. She had to catch a plane this morning."

"A plane? When I talked to her yesterday, she didn't say anything about . . ." Wait a minute. A new assignment? Her assignments came from one source.

"Jesus Christ, Shmona! You did this behind my back. Hasn't she been through enough?"

"She wanted to do it. And I needed her."

"What is this new assignment?" Llewellyn demanded. "Where are you sending her?"

"I can't tell you that. It's classified."

"Classified? Shmona, I've got news for you. I'm cleared for classified, especially 'Daniella Confidential.' Now I'm going to ask you once more, as nicely as I can, to tell me where you sent her before I choke it out of you."

"No. You'd try to interfere. That could put her life in danger."

"Put her life in—Shmona, where in God's name did you send her?"

The diminutive agent recoiled involuntarily, anticipating an onslaught from the exasperated American envoy. "You promise not to interfere?"

"I promise nothing. Except to ring your neck if you don't tell me."

"All right. It's too late for you to stop her now, anyway." Shmona had thought of a way to get out of his predicament without giving away the farm. "She's on her way to Cyprus." In a few hours Daniella would be aboard the Iran Air flight to Tehran. Without knowing her new identity, it would be almost impossible for Llewellyn to trace her.

"Cyprus?" Llewellyn was puzzled by the response. There was nothing life threatening about a Cypriot destination. Unless she was continuing on.

"An Arab country. You're sending her to an Arab country!"

The expression on the agent's face was all the confirmation he needed. He grabbed the other man's shoulders.

"For Christ sake, Shmona, she's no spy! She hasn't even been trained for undercover work. If they catch her, she's dead!"

"She'll be fine," he said, trying vainly to shake free. "It's *not* an Arab country. And she's not being sent there as a spy, just as an observer. We're trying to trace a courier to the missile site. I needed another pair of eyes in Iran."

He hadn't intended to mention the country. It had slipped out. "Where in Iran?" Llewellyn demanded. "What city?" He tightened his grip.

"Which city, Shmona?"

"Shiraz. Now let go!" Llewellyn set him free, and he rubbed his bruised shoulders, ashamed that he had allowed himself to be coerced. It didn't matter anyway, he told himself. There was no way that Llewellyn could follow her there. Iran was one Islamic country where American diplomats were even more unwelcome than Israeli Jews.

Promptly at eight in the morning an olive-drab staff car pulled up in front of the Llewellyn's apartment building in Jerusalem and honked its horn. Richard Llewellyn opened the window of the sixth-story apartment and waved to the driver. He finished penning a hasty note to his brother, left it by the telephone, and went down on the elevator. Five minutes later the staff car was on the Route 1 expressway, headed for Tel Aviv.

The meeting was at Hakiriyah, the Israeli Defense Forces enclave in central Tel Aviv. Dr. Tessler was standing by the entrance of the IDF Headquarters building waiting for him as the car drew up, puffing on his ubiquitous pipe. He shook Richy's hand warmly.

"I thought I'd escort you to the conference room. On the way over I'll fill you in a little on the Israeli players."

"A cast of thousands?"

"Quite the contrary. There will be only a handful. They had their big Anti-Ballistic-Missile bash yesterday and the day before at the Weizmann Institute, chaired by Dr. Bar-Tel, one of the finest minds in Israel. He is here this morning with two of his panel members, his working group leaders on radar and communications. General Tuchler, the IDF chief, who sponsored the ABM session, will be looking in on the meeting at some point in time, and some of his own experts are standing by in case we want to call on them."

"So it's basically just the five of us, to start with?"

"Yes. I think we'll get more accomplished that way."

"The radar and communications types—are they military or civilians?"

"Civilians. The radar man is from Ashdod—Elta Electronics. The communications expert is from ECI Telcom here in Tel Aviv."

"How do we proceed? Do they expect a briefing on AWACS?"

"Nothing formal. Let's play it by ear; let them ask questions. Bar-Tel will run the show. By the way, the security is squared away. Your IDF clearance came in, and I had the Peace Shield clearances phoned in this morning for the Israeli participants."

They arrived at the conference room and Tessler introduced Richy to Bar-Tel as though he had known his fellow American all his life. "Our top expert on the AWACS radar, one of its original designers. He's been involved in the program ever since and is over here to add some new modes to the Saudi version and do a flight evaluation of the new software."

"Welcome, Mr. Llewellyn." Dr. Bar-Tel gave him an enthusiastic handshake and introduced him to the two other Israelis. "This is Bernard Shiffrin, who heads up surveillance on my panel, and this is Shlomo Arens, in charge of the three Cs—Command, Control, and Communications. Shlomo's English is not the best, but I will translate for him, as necessary."

Richy shook hands with them. "Shalom."

"A pleasure," said Bernard. "Hi," said Shlomo.

Bar-Tel wasted no time getting to the point. "You know about our little problem. If we could locate this missile, we could snuff it out with our fighter-bombers. Since we can't, it becomes an exercise in ballistic missile defense. Not your classic BMD exercise, where the re-entry vehicle carries a nuclear warhead or perhaps several, independently targeted. We would have little defense against that at present, until our Arrow anti-missile system is developed and deployed. My panel has been working a much simplified problem, where the re-entry vehicle may indeed contain something very nasty, but it is non-nuclear, permitting us the luxury of an endo-atmospheric engagement at substantially lower altitudes, where the RV has slowed its speed appreciably.

"The computer simulations we have run using the East Wind III characteristics for the threat clearly show that both the Patriot and the Hawk have the inherent ability to counter this threat, provided that its re-entry trajectory can be predicted with sufficient accuracy. By the way"— Bar-Tel's eyes shifted to Tessler as he delivered an aside to the Peace Shield consultant—"Let's not forget your commitment to check with the Saudis on any possible changes to the East Wind configuration in this new shipment from the characteristics we modeled."

"I have it in my notes," Tessler assured him. "I'll tend to it as soon as I return to Riyadh."

"So the nub of our problem appears to be in early warning and tracking," Bar-Tel resumed, shifting his gaze back to Richy. "Warning of missile lift-off is available from several possible sources, including your country's DSP satellite. It is in the mid-course tracking requirement that we apparently have a serious shortcoming."

Richy nodded. "No surveillance systems deployed far enough up-range."

"Exactly. And to deploy airborne radar to the vicinity on continuous air alert for any length of time would be prohibitively costly, if not impractical."

"So you're looking at the Peace Shield assets and AWACS as possible 'gap fillers.' "

"Considering that, yes. But I must tell you that our commander, like virtually all of our leaders, is negatively inclined to place any dependence in so crucial an engagement on a country that is hostile to Israel's very existence. However, Dr. Tessler has pointed out that we could implement these assets, as you call them, by dealing with Americans, not Saudis."

Richy shrugged. "That's pretty much true. We control and operate the assets, at present, even though they're owned by the Saudis. Besides, it's my impression that the Saudis would be only too happy to cooperate. They'd face worldwide condemnation if one of their missiles created a holocaust."

"In any case you agree that we can at least assess the merits of employing these assets and work out the feasibility of doing so without involving their government?"

"That seems to be what I'm here for," Richy agreed.

"Good. Then let us proceed. First off, do you have any comments on what I've told you so far?"

"I have a suggestion about your approach on early warning. This function is so crucial to success that you might want to back up the satellite warning with AWACS. Satellite data goes through a long chain of command before it reaches you; there could be unforeseen delays. With AWACS we could data link the warning to you directly. I assume you'll be relying on our data link anyway to relay mid-course surveillance data from the Peace Shield radars."

Bar-Tel appeared surprised. "AWACS can detect a ballistic missile launch?"

"Not the launch itself, the way optical sensors do when they pick up launch signatures. But with a software modification I've already checked out on the U.S. AWACS, anything in the radar beam that registers a high enough Doppler shift—relative velocity—will trigger an alarm and set up an immediate track file. I call it a 'Doppler fence.' Anything that crosses this fence—that registers a velocity higher than a manned aircraft would be capable of—sets off the ballistic missile launch alarm. Within a minimum of two minutes after lift-off, we would have it in our sights."

Bar-Tel turned to his radar panelist from Ashdod, who had been following Richy's discourse with evident interest, nodding periodically. "You are familiar with this 'Doppler fence' mode? Do you see any problem with it?"

"Not at all. I have recommended such a mode for our advanced surveillance platform, the Phalcon. It should work beautifully."

"Well, I'm afraid I see a fundamental problem with it," Bar-Tel observed. "To use AWACS for early warning presupposes that you know where to point your radar to encompass the missile launch site, does it not?"

"Within certain limits, of course," Richy answered.

"How large an area can you keep under surveillance in this ballistic launch detection mode?"

"Our normal swath width—say a hundred by a hundred

miles. We would fly a race-track pattern to keep the same area under surveillance."

Bar-Tel grimaced. "We may not know the site location even that accurately. We certainly don't at present."

"I think I might," Richy offered.

Four pairs of eyes blinked at his extraordinary assertion. "Explain that," Bar-Tel challenged.

"Wait a minute," Tessler broke in nervously. "I think perhaps we're getting out of the realm of scientific fact and into the realm of guesswork. Let's get back to—"

"Let him answer." Bar-Tel sensed that there was more to the American's statement than idle speculation.

"I've done a good bit of flying lately aboard the Saudi AWACS," Rich explained. "We happened to be checking out an improved sea-search mode at about the time the hijacking of the missile occurred. The Saudis began diverting AWACS planes from other duties to check out shipping in the Indian Ocean and keep track of it. They hoped to eliminate legitimate cargo ships by cross-checking with maritime services and boil things down to a few questionable ships that would later be searched. They eventually called in the U.S. Navy and a blockade was set up.

"That's when I really got interested in the problem. There was this one suspicious freighter we'd been tracking that didn't show up on any maritime lists, finally identified as the *Beirut Victory,* of Lebanese registry. I felt certain it was the one. A U.S. destroyer was dispatched to intercept and board it, but then the Navy lost contact with it overnight. I found it on the AWACS radar the next morning and the destroyer sent in a boarding party. The ship was clean, no trace of the terrorists or their cargo."

"I fail to see how this—"

Tessler was silenced by a look from Bar-Tel. "Go on."

"The Navy continued to check out shipping headed for the Gulf; we continued to help. There were several more board-and-search operations, but the terrorists and their weapon never turned up. I think now I know why."

Tessler jumped to a hasty conclusion. "You think this Lebanese ship dumped the missile overboard?"

"Not overboard. Not in the ocean, anyway. I think they

dumped it on dry land. If the ship steamed at flank speed, it could have made landfall during the time the Navy lost contact with it, off-loaded its cargo, and steamed back to sea to the point where the AWACS re-detected it."

Bar-Tel got out of his chair and strode to a wall-mounted phone. "The general's got to hear this." He dialed a number, barked out a message in Hebrew that Richy couldn't understand, and hung up.

"He'll be along presently. Back to what you were telling us. Where did this happen? What was the location of this Lebanese ship when your Navy lost it—and when you found it again?"

"It was about twenty miles off the southern coast of Iran, not too far from the Pakistan border. Iran's most sparsely settled province is there, an isolated, desolate area with a few sheep herders, and that's about all. The province is called Baluchistan."

David Llewellyn stared at the bewhiskered face in the mirror, barely recognizing it. Funny how a couple of days' growth could change a person's appearance. Expelling a handful of lather from the dispenser, he spread it over his beard. As his hand prepared to draw the razor across his jaw, a sudden thought arrested it.

Perhaps he should keep the beard as a disguise. Would it be a help to him in entering Iran? He had returned that morning to the empty apartment and read the brief notes from both Daniella and his brother. Her note said only that she was leaving town on a short assignment, giving no clue to her destination or how he could reach her. He knew she had purposely been vague to spare him from worrying; she'd been right, he was worried sick. The very thought of her in that volatile hotbed of Shiite fanaticism drove him up the wall.

The minute he had wormed the truth out of Shmona he knew that he would follow her to Iran. The only question was how? He had crashed that morning before he could come up with the answer, had been dead to the world for six hours. In the quarter of an hour since the alarm had called him back to the land of the living, he still hadn't figured a way.

The razor moved again, emblazoning a pink trail across the

white-on-black terrain it traversed. A disguise would be no help; a disguise would be self-defeating. To get into Iran he would need new identity papers with his picture on them—a passport from some country other than the U.S. or Israel, one that had diplomatic relations with Iran, and a current visa. They would have to be forged. There was only one place he could turn to for such forgeries; the intelligence and clandestine afffairs section in the U.S. embassy, irreverently referred to by some as DDT—the Department of Dirty Tricks. But that would take the ambassador's approval. And there was no way Abrams was going to approve his chasing off to Iran after his wife.

A key sounded in the door, breaking his train of thought. "Anybody home?"

Richy! He wiped the residue of lather from his face and went to greet him.

"Sonny!"

"Daddy!"

It was a game they'd played since their pre-teens. The youngest in the family, Richard had inherited the nickname "Sonny" from his father, who had been called the same by his parents. Richy hated it, as David well knew. Whenever his older brother invoked it to needle him, Richy responded in kind.

The brothers wrapped each other in a bear hug. "Ouch, my ribs!" Richy pulled away. "You're not getting any gentler in your old age. Or any smarter, it seems. I thought you'd put aside all that spy stuff. What's the idea of getting yourself kidnapped and scaring us half to death?"

"I wondered why you were here. Daniella sent out a distress call, did she? And here I thought you were paying us a social visit."

"If I was, I'd be pretty insulted. I no sooner get here than your wife leaves."

David's expression turned serious. "What'd she tell you about that? Did she say where she was going, or why?"

"Just that something came up at work and she had to leave on a business trip." Richy read the concern in his brother's eyes. "Oh oh. *Monkey* business, right? She's back for another hitch in that Israeli 'secret circus'?"

"Circus is right. Her ringmaster cracks the whip and she jumps through the hoop. She's in danger, Rich. She took the assignment because Israel's facing this crisis situation from a bunch of terrorists—"

"Crisis situation? Her trip wouldn't be connected with—?"

"Sorry," his brother interrupted, "I shouldn't have mentioned that. I can't discuss it with you. The security is—"

"It's the hijacked missile thing, isn't it? Don't look so shocked. I'm cleared on it—that's what my meeting today at Hakiriya was all about. Hell, I've been helping the Saudis and the Navy search for these terrorists for weeks, tracking freighters halfway across the Indian Ocean. But it was only yesterday I found out what we were looking for, what it was they hijacked."

"You were at IDF headquarters? What for? What's going on?"

"Sorry, it's classified. I can't discuss it." With a straight face, Richy pulled out a chair and sat down at the kitchen table. "At least not till you pour me a drink. I've been here for fifteen minutes and you haven't offered me one."

"You miserable little brat." David broke out a bottle of Johnnie Walker Red and two glasses, half filling one. "You still take it the same way?"

Richy nodded. "Neat, no ice." He picked up the glass as David poured another. "Cheers."

They went on to debrief each other, their conversation largely focussed by the urgency of the situation on the missile problem.

"I think I know where it is, Davey. I think the ship that was carrying it was the one I was tracking on AWACS—that it put the missile ashore and went back out to sea."

"Put it ashore? Where?"

"Iran. The southernmost province, Baluchistan. I told this to the Israeli military types today. I'm not sure they totally believed me, but they said they'd forward the information to their intelligence people."

Iran! Now he knew he had to follow Daniella there. And suddenly he had the answer to how to manage it. "I have to make a call."

He punched out the U.S. ambassador's number at the embassy. "Sheilah, is the ambassador in? Yes, I'm fine. I'm at home. A meeting? Would you interrupt it, please? I think he'll take my call. It's an emergency."

In less than a minute Abrams was on the line. "Yes, sir. I'm fine, sir. It's a long story; I'll fill you in later. Yes, I did say it was an emergency—a good kind of emergency. That potential disaster we've been so concerned about? We may be near a breakthrough on the location; I can't go into it over the phone. Could I meet with you at the embassy—say in one hour? Good. And sir, to follow this up, I have to go to Iran. Yes, sir, I said Iran. Of course I know we don't have diplomatic relations. That's why I'm going to need a 'special' passport and visa. Could you please alert our people in the basement and get them started on it? I have to leave first thing in the morning."

The receiver sputtered with the ambassador's denial that such a thing was possible.

"Mr. Ambassador, you forget that I was once in that business. I know how it works; they'll do it if you okay it. I'll explain everything when I get there. Thank you, sir. Could you give me back to Sheilah?

"Sheilah, I need a seat on the morning shuttle to Larnaca. Could you get my secretary to make a reservation for me and get me a ticket? An open date on the return. Tell her I'll be in later today to pick it up."

"That's the same flight I'm on," Richy noted as his brother hung up the phone.

"Good. We can drive to the airport together and talk some more." He knocked down the rest of his whiskey. "Now I've got to finish dressing and get to my office to nail this trip down before everybody leaves for the day."

"So you're going to Iran. That wouldn't by any chance be where Daniella was headed, would it? No wonder you were worried."

"Okay, so you broke the code. Mum's the word." David disappeared into the bedroom.

"You don't have to worry about me, big brother." Richy remained at the table, sipping his scotch in solitude.

"Some visit. Everybody I came to see takes a hike."

• • •

The skies were already darkening when the Iran Air 727 climbed out of the Isfahan airport traffic pattern and turned south on the final leg of its flight from Tehran to Shiraz. The cabin was packed and overheated and the air was bumpy. Near the back of the plane where Daniella was sitting, the turbulence was amplified. In her narrow middle seat, wedged in between an obese Kurdish woman and a large-boned Irani man with a flagrant case of body odor, she was miserable, her stomach ready to heave. She fingered the paper air bag, expecting that at any moment she would have to use it.

The turbulence eased. An announcement was made in Farsi and the seat belt sign went off. Several passengers got up from their seats. Anything was better than sitting here, she decided, undoing her belt. She managed to squeeze past the woman, who refused to budge from her seat, and headed for the lavatory at the back of the plane. Perhaps some water on her face—

The water helped, along with decreased bumpiness and the cooler air entering the cabin. She felt almost human again. One good thing about the nausea—it had made her forget her fear for the moment. Less nervous and somewhat more at ease, she flushed the toilet and unlocked the door.

Emerging from the bathroom, she almost collided with a tall man in a white linen suit wearing sunglasses and a Turkish fez. "Sorry," she apologized. He didn't say anything, just stared at her rudely, though it had been as much his fault as hers. One of those businessmen who put women down, probably. Turkey was full of them.

The way some people wore sunglasses indoors had always amused her. It reminded her of Hollywood, where, she had heard, it was a common practice. Perhaps the Turkish businessman had been there, she mused, returning to her seat.

The man in the fez kept his eyes riveted on her as she resumed her seat—eyes that might have given him away, save for the dark glasses; eyes that had been captured in a portrait circulated throughout Israel. Kareem filled a paper container with water and washed down two aspirin tablets. He had developed a severe headache and was certain that the presence of the Llewellyn woman was responsible. Running into her on the short flight to Cyprus this morning had given him quite a start. But nothing like the jolt he received when she turned up on the Iran Air flight to Tehran, after he had changed his identity again. Had she recognized him, seen through his Hassidic disguise and followed him? No, he'd quickly realized, her trip, like his, would have had to be preplanned to gain entry into Iran. She must be traveling under a false identity also.

But when she again appeared on the connecting flight to Shiraz, it put an end to any speculation that her presence could be pure coincidence. Her connection with the Mossad had been known to him since the outcome of the last attack on her person, that had cost the lives of two of his men in the van that crashed into a Mossad vehicle. Was the Mossad on to him; had they learned, somehow, that he would be on this flight? Again he rejected the idea. She would hardly flaunt herself, expose her presence to him, if that were the case.

Then what was the explanation? He couldn't rule out the possibility that the Mossad had somehow penetrated their plan, learned of the merchandise being transported across Iran and its deadly purpose, and were sending in an agent to investigate. The same agent who had been an eternal thorn in his side, who seemed to have more lives than a cat, surviving his every attempt to snuff her out.

He would have loved to rid the world of her here and now, to find some way of dispatching her high above this ancient land that was a shrine to Islamic Fundamentalism. He could easily have slipped his knife into her, in their near collision moments before. But he couldn't afford to take the chance. Nothing must jeopardize the mission he was on, the all-important connection he would make in Shiraz.

No, he would have to be content with the passive form of revenge he now decided upon. On landing in Shiraz, he would send an anonymous tip to the Irani authorities. A Jewish agent was in their midst, a spy for the Israelis. He would supply them with her real name; her false identification and forged papers would be the only evidence they would need.

They would make short work of her. Justice was swift in Iran, where spies were hanged.

25

OUTSIDE THE ABANDONED rock quarry near the coast of
Iranian Baluchistan, a lone sentry huddled in the cover of a
clump of bushes and tried to stay awake. A skilled missile
technician, he resented having to pull guard duty, especially at
night when the desert-like chill set in, when he could have been
playing cards with his comrades in the relative comfort of the
portable stove that heated the makeshift quarters under the
camouflage net. Besides, this sentry business was a joke. In the
three days they'd been here, the only living thing that had
come within sight was a stray sheep that had wandered by.
The cook had shot it with an assault rifle and prepared an
Arab-style feast. He could have saved his bullets, the sentry
reflected. The meat was tough, with a strong mutton taste. It
must have been an old sheep.

In the quarry below him, beneath the camouflage net, the
banter and occasional laughter of the card players could be
heard. Their leader did not join in, sitting apart from the rest,
alongside the immense black cylinder that rose six stories
above where he sat in the deepest part of the quarry. He was
otherwise occupied, preparing to put pen to paper to generate
a message that would be sent as soon as certain missing ingredients were installed beneath the glistening white nose
cone. It was a message he had composed in his head a dozen
times. He knew it by heart.

Tomorrow. That was when the lethal, death-dealing ingredients were due to arrive that would give his gigantic
rocket its purpose, its *raison d'être*. All else was in readiness,
the liquid-fueled rocket motors checked out and prepared for

lift-off, the guidance computer programmed for the selected trajectory and destination. His chief engineer had assured him that the installation of the warheads was a straightforward process requiring minimal time and effort. The task could be completed as early as tomorrow evening. The next morning, at the very latest.

Lifting his eyes toward the heavens, he followed the contour of the missile skyward until its outline was lost in the darkness above. He visualized the manner in which it would come to life at his signal, imagined that he could hear the thunderous explosion as the flames shot out from its bowels, saw it lift itself off its haunches, imperceptibly at first, then ever faster, rising majestically toward the heavens to realize its destiny as avenging angel for the martyred Palestinians.

Was this how it would be? Would he witness it thus, a day or two hence, this inexorable agent of death and destruction set in motion by his own hand? No, it would not be by his hand, it would be by their own, the Zionist persecutors of his people. Was he not offering them terms? It would be their choice, not his.

But he was certain in his heart that they would never accept his terms. So be it, then. Vengeance would be his, and nothing would taste sweeter. Their acquiescence to his ultimatum would only rob him of that taste. Which way did he want it to end? *Insh'allah.* Let Allah decide.

He moistened the tip of the pen with his tongue and began to write. TO THE VILE USURPERS WHO SHAMELESSLY AND WRONGFULLY OCCUPY THE LANDS OF THE PALESTINIAN PEOPLE IN ABROGATION OF THEIR BIRTHRIGHT—

Baruch Shmona was beginning to get that feeling. It happened whenever one of his cases was going down to the wire, the sensation that he was on the verge of a breakthrough, that everything was coming to a head. His response was to do what he always did at such times. He marched himself down the corridor outside his office to an equipment closet, slid out a folded cot on wheels, and rolled it back inside his office.

Home sweet home. This would be it, for as long as it took. He had already missed one night's sleep; another would wipe him out. But to leave the office now was unthinkable—he had too many balls in the air. Daniella was due to call when her plane landed in Shiraz, and he had calls in to the two other Mossad agents in Iran. There was also the two-man night shift he had arranged at the director's behest, poring over satellite photos in another part of the building, with instructions to notify him immediately if they came up with anything.

The frenzy of activity had started with the mid-afternoon phone call from his man in Tabriz, whom he had assigned to check out manifests and flight plans on file for charter flights out of northern Iran since the warhead thefts in Iraq three days ago. His field agent had discovered two flights in which the cargo weights listed on the flight manifests met or exceeded the estimated weight of the three stolen warheads. One was a twin-engine Beechcraft operated by Omar Khayam Charters, Ltd., that had taken off from Tabriz two days ago with a single passenger accompanying the cargo. The flight plan had listed Tehran as the intermediate destination, with the final destination open. The Mossad agent in Tehran was checking it out at that end.

It was the other flight that had excited Shmona more, since it was clearly headed for the Gulf region, its listed destination Bandar Abbas on the Strait of Hormuz. Operated by Logan Air Charter Service, the plane had left Urmia airport in West Azerbaijan province this morning, carrying two passengers and some 280 kilograms of cargo. According to the flight plan, it was overnighting in Shiraz to pick up a third passenger before continuing on. This would give Daniella the opportunity to check out the plane and its passengers and hopefully get a look at the cargo. He had immediately reserved a seat for her on a commercial flight to Bandar Abbas tomorrow morning to continue her surveillance, in case her first look corroborated his suspicions.

Shmona unfolded the cot and smoothed out the folds in the minimal mattress so that it covered the metal springs. He rolled up his jacket to make a pillow and flopped down. The telephone was within arm's reach, close enough for its ring to awaken him, even from a sound sleep. The cot was reasonably comfortable, and his weary bones were grateful for the chance to stretch out on it. But he knew he wouldn't be able to sleep, not for a while at least. He was too keyed up.

The call from the director, coming on the heels of the Tabriz input, had been galvanizing. Shilo had just received a message from the Israeli Defense Forces chief that the missile was believed to be located in southern Iran, near the Baluchistan coast, somewhere between Cape Medani and the Pakistan border. At the director's suggestion he had immediately initiated an around-the-clock effort to scrutinize the available satellite data for evidence of any recent alteration in the area's topography that would signal the erection of a missile launch site.

Iran again! Now he was all the more certain that the missile site was the destination of one of the charter flights he was tracking. Did this mean the government of Iran was involved in the plot, was knowingly harboring the missile hijackers? He certainly wouldn't put it past them.

Since Israel had no diplomatic relations with Iran, there would be no delicate way in which such an inquiry could be pursued. But if hard evidence could be obtained of a terrorist missile launch site inside Iran, it would be a different story. Israel would have the ammunition to approach the Rafsanjani government head on, backed up by the threat of an immediate air strike to destroy the weapon. He wondered how the photo interpreters downstairs were coming along. He wondered the same about Daniella.

It was past time for her to have reached her hotel if her flight had landed on time. Upon arriving there she would find the message he had sent earlier waiting for her. It had been sent in the clear; anything in code would arouse attention and possibly throw suspicion on her. The telegram had originated in Canada and had been worded to appear as an instruction from her jewelry company's headquarters in Ottawa, directing her to contact the pilot of the chartered plane overnighting in Shiraz on the pretext of exploring a future charter on behalf of her company. It was suggested that she personally inspect the plane to assess its "passenger accommodations and cargo-carrying capacity."

Immediately on receipt of the wire she was instructed to call the number specified and verify receiving it. The dummy Canadian number was rigged so that his own phone would ring.

He looked at his watch again. Had something happened to

her? Why didn't she call? He knew he would never get to sleep until she did.

It wasn't exactly the Ritz, but the Shiraz Airport Hotel at least looked reasonably modern. The outside reminded Daniella of one of France's Sofitels—aluminum and glass, no nonsense, no frills. The interior proved to be even more spartan, the minimal lobby sparsely furnished with few places to sit, all of them occupied. The floor was choked with baggage, more on the way in from the airport bus she had arrived on.

She hurried to beat the other passengers to the registration desk, picking the shorter of the two lines. Both desk clerks were conversing in a language she didn't understand—Farsi, she assumed. Hopefully, someone on the staff spoke English. It was uncomfortable to be in a country where she didn't speak the language; she couldn't remember being in that situation before.

Her turn came and she presented her Canadian passport. "Mrs. Jane Monpleasure from Ottawa. I have a reservation."

The clerk flipped through the pages of her passport, frowning. Had he understood her?

"Canadian," he read, with a heavy accent. "You traveling by yourself, Mrs.?" His reproving look told her what he thought of women who did so.

"Yes. My husband was unable to join me." It sounds like I'm apologizing, she thought.

He consulted his reservation list, then thrust his hand into one of the mail slots behind him. "A telegram came for you, Mrs."

She tore the envelope open and hastily read the wire from her "company" in Ottawa, immediately recognizing it for what it was, a message from Shmona. It instructed her to contact a charter pilot named Logan at the Shiraz air charter terminal regarding a possible charter arrangement. The purpose was also obvious to her: to get a look at what his plane was carrying.

"Bad news, Mrs.?"

"No, on the contrary. Quite good, actually."

He pushed a thick book in front of her. "You will sign the register, please."

She picked up the pen and absently scanned the names on the page as she prepared to enter hers. Many were illegible; a few were in Arabic, which she could read. Hello. There was an Al Logan registered, his address listed as Logan Air Charters Ltd., Tehran.

Entering her Canadian name and address, she exchanged the pen for her passport and room key. "Room 406. You have luggage?"

"Just a small bag. I can manage it myself. There's one thing more. I believe you have a pilot staying here, a Mr. Logan of Logan Air Charters. Could you tell me his room number, please?"

"Is not permitted to give out room numbers, Mrs. If you use house phone, they connect you." He pointed toward the opposite wall, then impatiently waved her aside to permit the next in line to reach the desk.

"Thank you." She crossed the lobby and picked up the phone. It took three tries to communicate the pilot's name to the operator. The ring was promptly answered with an English-sounding hello.

"Mr. Logan?"

"Yes."

"My name is Jane Monpleasure, from Canada. I'm downstairs in the lobby. I'd like to explore a possible charter arrangement with you for my company. Could you perhaps meet me down here, and we could discuss it over cocktails?"

"Cocktails?" The pilot's booming laugh assaulted her eardrum, making her pull the phone away. "You haven't been in this country very long, have you? Miss Monpleasure, is it?"

"Mrs.," she corrected.

"You won't find liquor in any of the hotels here in Iran, Mrs. Monpleasure, except in private bars. It so happens I possess one of those—the traveling kind, that keeps me company on my trips. I'm in room 612. Would you care to join me?"

"You mean right now?"

"No time like the present."

"Well, I haven't been up to my room yet. If you'll give me a little time to unpack and freshen up. Say fifteen minutes?"

"Fifteen minutes it is."

She hurried toward a departing elevator, then halted abruptly. She had caught a glimpse of someone through the elevator door, someone she didn't relish riding up with. It was the rude Turkish businessman from the plane, still wearing his fez and dark glasses.

"Whiskey?" Lockjaw Logan inquired.

"Whiskey would be fine."

"It's not Canadian whiskey," he warned. "It's the only real whiskey—what you Americans erroneously call 'Scotch.'"

"It will still be fine. Not too much, please."

"You also erroneously call people from Scotland by the same name," he observed, pouring her drink.

"As you erroneously call Canadians Americans?" she quipped.

"Touché," he laughed. "I'm afraid I have no ice. And I wouldn't advise you to drink the water here."

"Straight will be fine." She accepted the glass. "I take it you are a Scotsman, Mr. Logan?"

"Born and bred. Clydebank, on the River Clyde, near Glasgow." He clinked glasses with her. "To the incomparable dew of the highlands."

Daniella was not much of a drinker. Scotch was David's drink and had always tasted like medicine to her, but she sipped it bravely without making a face. She rather liked this rugged, rawboned Scotsman with the lantern jaw. She had a feeling that he liked her, too. Just so he didn't get any ideas.

"I've never been to Scotland," she remarked.

"Nor I to Canada."

She was relieved to hear it; that makes two of us, she thought. "What brought you to Iran, Mr. Logan? Have you been here long?"

"Over twenty years. It was the flying. I came with a British company that serviced the oil fields. They pulled out when the Ayatollah arrived. I stayed on."

"You must like it here, then"

"You might say I was married to the country." He grinned at his own inside joke. "I married an Irani, you see. Never regretted it; started my own company. There were some lean years. But now I have to turn customers away."

"Not me, I hope."

"That depends. I'm booked solid for the next two weeks. How'd you get my name, by the way?"

"My company. They import jewelry from all over the world. They sent me a wire to check you out for some future charters. I'm supposed to inspect your equipment."

"Equipment, eh? I've just the one plane, but she's a winner. Bit dark to have a look now, though, and I'm out of here bright and early tomorrow."

"I'm an early riser. Perhaps I could meet you at the flight line and you could show me your plane before you take off." She used her most persuasive smile.

"You're on. Hangar two, seven sharp. If you're late, I won't be able to wait. I've three passengers and their gear to run down to Bandar Abbas by nine in the morning."

He got up from his chair and rummaged through a duffel bag on the floor. "Here. You'll need this gate pass to get in." He handed her a piece of flimsy cardboard with an official-looking stamp on it. She stuck it in her purse.

Three passengers and their gear. Her pulse began to quicken. She desperately wanted to get a look at them, particularly the "gear." "How many passengers will your plane carry?"

"Up to seven, depending on how much luggage they haul along. My Aero Commander doesn't have a lot of baggage capacity; extra gear overflows into the passenger space. You take these Turkish oil men I flew down here today—they must have brought half a pumping station along. Three special motors, they said. Takes two men to lift one."

Her heart was racing now. Three heavy parcels . . . "That won't be a problem, in our case," she commented, trying to cover up her excitement. "Jewelry doesn't take up much space."

"Are you prepared to talk schedules? It's best to book as early as—"

He was interrupted by a raucous chorus of sirens, reaching an abrupt crescendo just below the hotel room window. Logan jumped out of his chair and peered out between the blinds.

"Son of SAVAK!"

Herbert Crowder

Daniella misunderstood his outburst, taking it for some form of unfamiliar Scottish expletive. She joined him at the window and saw uniformed policemen pouring out of two squad cars and into the hotel. Terror seized her. She had an overwhelming premonition that it was her they had come for.

"Son of SAVAK," Logan repeated. "That's my name for the government's so-called security police. SAVAK was the Shah's secret police force. They had a reputation for ruthlessness and were hated by the people, and of course abolished by the Ayatollah. Now we have this new bunch, operating much the same way."

"I—I think I'd better return to my room, now. Thank you for your hospitality, Mr. Logan. Seven in the morning, then, at hangar two?"

"Must you rush off, just as we were getting on so well?" He looked at her more carefully and realized that the clamorous arrival of the security police had thrown a scare into her. "Don't let those bloody buggers upset you. They're probably after some hash smuggler."

"It's been a long day. I really must go. I'll see you tomorrow." She moved toward the door.

"Tomorrow, then." Opening the door for her, he watched her disappear into the corridor that led to the elevators. He closed the door and shook his head. Being a woman alone in a foreign country could be a frightening thing, especially your first time, especially a country like Iran.

Daniella pushed the down button. There was no indicator to tell her what floor the elevator was on. "Come on, come on!" She had to get back to her room and place the call to Shmona; she should have done it right away, instead of waiting until she had spoken to the pilot. She punched the button again.

Finally it arrived, the door opening on a crowd of people. She squeezed in with them and punched 4.

Her room was just down the hall from the elevators. The first thing she saw when the door opened on the fourth floor was a uniformed man standing by her door, the door ajar. She shrank backwards, pressing the door-close button. "Wrong floor," she muttered. She didn't think the policeman had seen her. But it occurred to her that they might be watching the elevators in the lobby.

She got off on the second floor and looked around for the stairwell. It wasn't near the elevators; where would it be? She found it at the far end of the long main corridor. Was it likely they'd be watching the stairs exit also? She stole down the staircase to the main floor and started to push the door open, then hesitated. The staircase went down another flight. There must be a basement.

Descending the last flight, she opened the door cautiously. The basement was half filled with parked cars. There was no sign of life at the moment. Oh, yes there was! She heard a car door slam and a motor start. Headlights flashed as the vehicle came racing toward her. She ducked behind the nearest car, as the fast-moving auto swung past her, turned up the exit ramp, and disappeared.

Warily, she followed the path it had taken. As she neared the top of the ramp she saw flashing lights and heard the static-filled sound of a police radio turned up to high volume, cutting in and out. The exit ramp opened out right where the police vehicles were parked. Had they seen her?

Running back down the ramp, she opened the door of a parked sedan and dove into the backseat. She flattened herself on the floor, holding her breath. Nothing happened; she heard no following footsteps. She began to breathe a bit easier.

What was she going to do? She couldn't go back to her room, and all of her things were there. All, that is, except what she had in her purse, which had her passport in it, thank God for that. Was there anything in her luggage that would incriminate her? She made a hurried mental inventory and concluded that there wasn't. The clothing supplied by the Mossad had labels from Canadian stores. They'd been thorough. There was nothing she could think of that would tip off her Israeli identity.

She began to feel a little less scared. If she lay low until morning, she might still be able to keep her appointment with Logan at the airport, then call Shmona, who would be beside himself that she hadn't called sooner. The telegram! Had she left it in the room? It would establish her connection with the pilot! She wouldn't be able to show her face—

Frantically, she clawed open her purse and rummaged inside. Paper rustled. There was the telegram, in one of the side pockets, neatly tucked back into its envelope. With a sigh, she laid her head back on the floor of the sedan. The garage remained silent, no vehicles moving in or out, no steps that would signal the approach of a driver retrieving his car. It was getting pretty late. She told herself the chances were good that the sedan she was in would not be needed until morning.

She got up cautiously and peered out through the window. The garage was deserted; the lights of the police cars continued to flash near its exit. She lay down on the backseat. It was nicely upholstered and much more comfortable than the floor.

Something that had been drummed into her as a little girl came back to her: When you're lost, stay where you are, so the people who are looking for you can find you. Unfortunately, the people who were looking for her were not the ones she wanted to find her. She decided to stay put anyway. She didn't know what else to do.

26

SOMEWHERE IN THE hotel's basement garage a car engine roared to life, and Daniella was suddenly wide awake. She watched its headlights trace a path along the far wall as it swung around, then shoot past the sedan she was in and on up the ramp toward the exit.

Following its progress, she made a heartening discovery. The flashing lights of the security police cars were no longer in evidence outside the exit; the only light visible was the first faint glimmerings of the morning sun.

Her watch read five minutes to six. What sleep she had gotten had come only in the last several hours, but she felt refreshed and less frightened, encouraged over passing the night safely and avoiding discovery. With the hotel coming to life, that situation could change abruptly, she knew. Her best chance to elude the Iranian security forces who had descended on the hotel would be to vacate the premises immediately, under cover of what little darkness remained.

Clutching her purse, she closed the car door as silently as possible and made her way cautiously up the exit ramp. The curbside no-parking zone where the two police cars had stood was indeed vacant. Warily, she thrust her head outside and peered back in the direction of the hotel entrance. A car was idling in front of it, the same car, she felt sure, that had just left the garage. There were no police visible and no other sign of activity outside the exit, nothing else stirring at this early hour.

She took a deep breath and left the cover of the garage, walking briskly along the sidewalk in the opposite direction from the entrance. How far was it back to the airport? She tried to recall from the trip on the bus the previous evening. It had to be at least several kilometers. An unescorted woman in western attire walking such a distance was bound to be conspicuous, to draw attention.

She was approaching the zone where taxis waited in line for customers to emerge from the hotel. Several were parked there, their motors off, their drivers nowhere to be seen. As she passed, she peered inside the dormant taxicabs. One wasn't vacant after all; its driver was stretched out on the backseat, apparently sound asleep. On an impulse, she banged on the window.

The driver opened his eyes, sat up, and saw her face. Scrambling out of the cab, he held the door open for her. She hesitated.

"Can you take me to the airport, hangar number two?" When there was no immediate response, she repeated her question, flapping her arms like wings and holding up two fingers.

The driver seemed richly amused, grinning from ear to ear. "I speak English, lady. Please." He nodded her into his taxi. They took off in the direction of the airport.

"You English, lady? American?"

"No, Canadian."

"Ah, Canadian. You fly home today? Where are luggages?"

"At the hotel. I am not leaving yet. I have a business appointment at the airport."

"Ah, business," he nodded.

It was a short ride. He pulled up in front of the main terminal entrance from which the bus had departed the evening before. "Airport. Hundred rial, please."

"This is not where I asked you to take me," Daniella protested. The charter flight hangar might well be accessible from the main terminal, but she wanted to avoid going in the terminal entrance; they might be watching it. "Hangar two!" she insisted, again raising two fingers. "The *charter* terminal, for *charter* flights."

"Ah, charter . . ." He started up again and turned into a parking area no more than a few hundred meters beyond the main terminal. Driving across the lot, he pulled up in front of a gate that opened onto a large building behind it and held up two fingers, mimicking her.

"Charter airport. Hundred twenty rial, please."

It was highway robbery, but she was in no position to haggle. She paid him out of the money she had changed in Tehran and left the cab, walking to the gate. A non-uniformed attendant was standing just inside; he wore an official-looking cap. She flashed the pass Logan had given her. The man barely looked at it; he was too busy looking at her legs. She hurried past him without looking back.

The entrance to hangar two opened into a small waiting room. There wasn't a soul inside. Where would the ladies' room be? Off a side corridor she found an unmarked door, behind it a closet-sized facility that apparently functioned for both sexes, containing one toilet of the most primitive sort and a tiny wash basin in dire need of a good scrubbing. There was no lock on the door and no door on the toilet, but she was too desperate to worry about privacy. Minutes later, after a good sponging down at the basin using the coarse toilet paper to towel off, she felt revived and halfway human again.

The waiting room was still deserted when she returned, with no sign of Logan. Walking back down the corridor, she opened the door at its end and found the interior of the hangar, its vast concrete floor covered with airplanes of every description. All appeared quiet, the only sign of activity at this hour a pair of maintenance workers in one corner of the sprawling hangar removing an engine from a small private jet. She wandered out among the planes, wondering which one was Logan's.

"You really are an early riser, aren't you?"

She spun around to see Logan grinning at her. The sight of him gave her spirits an enormous boost; it was like running into an old friend when you were lost and alone and friendless.

"Mr. Logan! Good morning." Her smile was radiant.

"If you're looking for my plane, it's parked outside on the ramp." He led the way out through the front of the hangar toward a white aircraft with blue trim that was somewhat larger than its neighbors on the flight line. "There she is. You can do your inspection while I run through my preflight check."

He unlatched the cabin door and held it open for her. As Daniella climbed up and stepped inside she was startled by the appearance of a bearded head popping up between two rows of seats.

"Oh!" She drew back and bumped into the pilot, who was entering behind her.

"Sorry. I forgot about him. That's one of my passengers. He insisted on spending the night here, to keep an eye on his cargo." Logan stepped back onto the tarmac, Daniella following suit, as the passenger came forward and descended the steps.

"Good morning, Nestor. Get any sleep?"

Nestor Rishad staggered sleepily out of the plane, stretching his limbs and back. "Yes, thank you, Captain," he responded cheerfully. He looked awfully young for a petroleum engineer, Daniella thought. She avoided his eyes but was conscious of them scrutinizing her. Logan must have noticed also.

"This lady's a future customer for my charter service, Nestor. She's here to inspect my equipment. You want to visit the loo? I'll keep an eye on your gear."

Rishad looked dubious, but his urgent need to relieve himself made the decision for him. He hurried toward the hangar, looking back periodically.

"Shall we try again?" The pilot indicated the open door to the cabin. "After you."

He followed her inside and indicated the copilot seat. "Sit down there and I'll run through the panel instrumentation for you."

"Thanks, but I'd like to see the seating arrangement first." While he settled into the cockpit, she made her way into the cabin, intent on getting a look at the cargo stowed there before Logan's passenger returned. If he had stayed up all night to watch over it, it had to be something pretty special . . .

The interior of the cabin reeked of gasoline. She understood why when she saw the bulky parcels stashed in the back, two long cylinders and one giant sphere, taking up several seats. They were wrapped in a heavy canvas that appeared to be permeated with oil. From their dimensions and the pilot's earlier comments about their weight, she had little doubt that these were the articles she'd been sent to find.

Logan was busying himself in the cockpit. She fingered the wrappings, than tapped on the side of one of the cylinders with her fingernails, eliciting a tinny, metallic sound. Metal cannisters. Her conviction increased that these were, indeed, the stolen Iraqi warheads.

She made her way back to the front of the plane. "What's that terrible smell in here?"

Logan wrinkled his nose. "Pretty bad, eh? It's that bloody petroleum gear in the back. Don't worry, we'll have it all aired out before your charter begins." He grinned. "We'll have the cabin smelling like a bloody bed of roses."

She was anxious to get back to the terminal and phone in her report to Shmona, but Logan insisted on sitting her down in the cockpit for a run-through on his plane's versatile instruments, including a multi-mode radar he had recently installed. While he was talking, she saw his passenger emerge from the hangar and hurry back toward the plane.

"Thank you, Mr. Logan. I believe I've seen enough. I'll have no reservations about recommending your service to my superiors." She rose from the cockpit and moved toward the door.

"Hold on, we haven't talked specifics yet. What runs are you considering? What dates?"

"I'll have to get back to you on that. It won't be for several weeks at the earliest. I have your number."

She opened her purse and withdrew one of the business cards the Mossad had prepared for her. "Here's my card if you wish to contact me." She thanked him, shook hands, and stepped down out of the plane just as the passenger named Nestor arrived back.

With a slight nod of her head she walked past him and set sail for the hangar. Nestor Rishad followed her with his eyes, appreciative of her full, shapely figure and the way her accelerated gait made her hips dance. Moistening his lips, he climbed back into the plane.

"Any sign of your fellow passenger?" Logan inquired.

"No, but he will be along presently, I am sure."

"Your third party arrived? He'll be flying with us as planned?"

Rishad nodded. "He checked into the hotel last night. Ish-

309

mael is bringing him." He smiled. "Otherwise, you might not be paid."

It was the second time one of the pair had made such a jest. Lockjaw Logan didn't see the humor in it. Until he was paid the balance due him, his Aero Commander wasn't taking off.

Daniella walked back through the hangar between its rows of planes, concentrating on the phone call she had to make. She hadn't seen a public telephone in the waiting room but maybe she'd missed it. She decided to check out the waiting room one more time.

She stepped through the door and found herself face to face with the man in the white linen suit and fez—the tall Turkish businessman from the plane who had stayed at her hotel last night. He seemed as startled by the unexpected encounter as she.

It was the first time she had seen him when he wasn't wearing his sunglasses. Those eyes . . . cold, unfeeling . . . eyes of pure evil, staring at her! *She knew those eyes.*

Pure fright seized her. Without a word she turned and bolted back through the door.

"Spy!" she heard him cry out. "Woman Jew spy! *Stop her!*"

She plunged through the corridor and out among the planes again, sprinting across the hangar floor in the direction she had come from. Her first thought was to turn to Logan for help. But even if he wasn't in on it with them, what could he do? His passengers were terrorists, unquestionably armed, and now reinforced by their tall, gaunt ringleader.

His shouting continued behind her but grew fainter; he was evidently not pursuing her. But someone else was. As she headed for the side of the hangar opening closest to the main terminal, she caught sight of him from the corner of her eye. It looked like the man who had been standing with "Evil Eye" in the waiting room. He must be the other passenger. And now he was coming after her.

She had a pretty good start on him and was a strong runner, but her high heels were slowing her down. She kicked off her shoes. Her pace increased. If she could reach the main terminal ahead of him, she would have a chance . . . It had been jammed with passengers when she came through last night. She could lose herself in the crowd.

Clearing the end of the hangar, she swung back toward the main terminal. But a chain link fence stood between her and the terminal. Was there some way to get through? She couldn't see any. Could she climb it? With every stride she took, it looked higher.

She could hear her pursuer's steps behind her now and glanced back. He had closed the distance between them. Her eyes searched desperately for an opening in or around the fence, but its uninterrupted expanse ran all the way to the wall that sealed the airport off from the street.

Then she noticed the wall was lower than the fence. She could climb the chain links to the top of the wall and get around the fence that way! She took another nervous glance to her rear. He was still coming, scarcely fifty meters behind her. She reached the end of the fence, threw her purse over, and attacked it, thrusting her fingers through the openings, her feet finding toe holds in the gaps between links.

Up she went, the metal tearing at her fingers, the fearsome pounding in her ears of the terrorist's footfall bearing down on her. She got one knee over the wall and pulled herself on top of it just as he arrived.

The force of his impact rattled the foundation of the fence she had been clinging to. He had a knife with a murderous-looking blade. Wild-eyed, he slashed at her with it, slicing nothing but air, as she scrambled out of reach along the top of the wall. She contemplated the drop to the ground on the other side of the fence, hesitating.

Repocketing the knife, her assailant launched himself at the chain link fence. That was all the incentive she needed. Sitting on the wall to reduce the distance of the fall, she sprang down, landing on all fours, turning an ankle and skinning her knee.

A passenger gate on the near side of the main terminal looked no more than a hundred meters off. Her foot hurt and she was limping. Please God, let it be open!

Footsteps behind her again, gaining on her. She couldn't make herself go any faster, her wind almost gone. Resisting the temptation to look back, she kept her eyes glued to the passenger gate and plodded on.

The door to the gate opened and a uniformed attendant came out. Passengers began to spill out onto the tarmac; a flight must be in the process of loading. The sound of her pursuer's footfall grew louder. She couldn't stop herself from looking back. He had closed more than half the distance between them, and he had drawn his knife again! If only the people up ahead would look this way!

She tried to shout to draw their attention, but only a hoarse croak came out. Were those people blind? Why didn't they see what was happening?

"Help me!" she cried, running into the terminal. Cries of alarm came from the passengers in her wake. Her pursuer must have entered the building behind her. They must have seen his weapon. If only someone would tackle him, trip him, slow him down. Where were the police? The airport had been crawling with them last night.

She raced up the stairs, toward the most crowded sector of the terminal with its check-in counters, shops, and restaurants. At the top of the long staircase she allowed herself the luxury of another look back.

He'd fallen down! He lay at the bottom of the steps, glaring at her, the knife still in his hand, onlookers shrieking and scattering. Racing on, she looked for some place to duck into.

The main area of shops was just ahead. She had explored it last night while waiting for her luggage. There was a large restaurant; she could hide in its ladies' lounge. Or in its kitchen—she might even find a knife or meat cleaver to defend herself.

Then she thought of the dress shop. It had several dressing rooms to hide in. She could alter her appearance, purchase a new outfit, so that once she did emerge he wouldn't recognize her. There it was, just ahead on her left. She glanced back down the corridor. She couldn't see the terrorist, too many bodies in the way. Slowing to a walk, she stepped inside the dress shop.

She must look a sight! In her stocking feet, out of breath, panting, her hair awry, stockings torn. Avoiding the salespersons, she hid herself between two racks of dresses while she caught her breath, pretending to look at the clothing, her eyes glued to the store window.

No sign of him yet. Searching the potential hiding places she'd passed might slow him down. Breathing easier, she kept one eye on the traffic outside the store window while she examined the dresses more closely. There were some colorful Kurdish smocks like the one the heavyset lady had worn sitting next to her on the flight from Isfahan. She found one in her size and took it to a saleslady.

"Do you speak English?"

"Yes, madame. You wish to try this on?"

Daniella nodded and was shown to one of the fitting rooms. She removed her suit with the Ottawa label. The dress fit somewhat loosely, but that was the style. As she was stepping back out of the fitting room, she saw him. He was standing in front of the dress store, staring in through the window!

She drew back behind the curtain and peeked out. He was still standing in the same place, his eyes searching the interior of the store. Could he have seen her enter? She couldn't see how, with all the people milling around outside. Remaining behind the curtain, she called her saleslady over.

"I'll take the dress. I'm going to wear it. I'll also need some other things. A new pair of stockings—there's a run in these. And would you please pick out a head kerchief that will go with the dress. Also a pair of Kurdish sandals."

"Your size, madame?"

"Six-A."

He was still there, but making no move to enter the store. Now he was peering around at some of the other shops. He had put his knife away. When the saleslady brought the other clothing, she replaced her stockings with the new pair, pulled on the sandals, and wrapped the kerchief around her head. Opening her purse, she withdrew a pair of sunglasses and donned them, inspecting the overall result in the dressing room mirror. She was satisfied with the disguise . . . except for her handbag. It was a dead giveaway.

Emerging from the dressing room, she found a purse that would do. "I'll take this also. And could you please wrap the clothing I was wearing so that I can take it with me."

"Of course, madame. Will there be anything else? If not, I will prepare your bill."

"Nothing else, thank you." She had already added the cost

of the items in her head and produced two hundred-rial bills. While the saleslady arrived at her own total and made change, Daniella transferred her possessions from the old purse to the new one. She handed over the empty purse. "Please wrap this with my other things. And do you have a telephone?"

"No, I am sorry. But there is one in the restaurant." While Daniella waited for her package, she checked up on the terrorist. He was no longer in front of the store. She spotted him across the way, in front of the restaurant, peering inside. A minute later, her package in hand and ready to leave, he was still there.

She waited for him to commit himself. Come on, come on! I have a call to make! He showed no sign of budging from the spot. She took another look in the mirror to reassure herself. Her disguise was perfect! Her own mother wouldn't have known her. She stepped out of the dress shop and walked determinedly toward the restaurant.

At eight o'clock sharp, with her customary punctuality, Baruch Shmona's secretary arrived at her desk and set about her daily chore of preparing the morning pot of coffee. The door to her boss's office was closed and it didn't occur to her that he might be inside until she heard a sound that was halfway between a groan and a wail. She opened the door.

The appearance of the office was appalling, the desk littered with paper cups and the remains of a half-eaten sandwich, cigarette butts everywhere. Shmona was in his undershirt, sitting in the middle of the cot he had dragged in, his head in his hands. He looked up at her with dull, bloodshot eyes totally devoid of their usual sparkle of intelligence.

"What on earth—?"

"They've got her, Rachel. They've got Daniella. I never should have sent her in."

"Mrs. Llewellyn? Sent her where? Who's got her?" Rachel hadn't been told a thing about Daniella's new assignment.

"Iranian security police, probably. Better them than the terrorists."

"You sent Mrs. Llewellyn to Iran?" Her homely face registered disbelief. Such a *meshuggeneh* country. "Well, I'm sure you had a good reason. How do you know somebody's got her?"

"She was supposed to call last night. She didn't. I was up all night waiting."

"But that doesn't prove—"

"Why else wouldn't she call? She knew that I was counting on it, that reporting in was crucial. They've got her, I tell you!"

Rachel was trying to think of something she could say to calm him when the phone rang. Shmona snatched it off the hook.

"Yes?" His look of hope dissolved as he heard the voice. He listened without comment for the better part of a minute, his frown deepening. He hung up shaking his head.

"That husband of hers! He's somehow found a way to get into Iran. He's going in after her."

"Good for him! If they've arrested her, someone needs to help her. Or were you planning on sending another agent?"

"No. There's no one available. At least Llewellyn has diplomatic immunity."

"And he also has counter-spy experience, I understand."

"Yes. Yes, he does." Shmona got up from the cot and sat down at his desk, deep in thought.

"Look at this place!" Rachel raised her arms in disgust. "I'll bring you some coffee, and then I'll clean it up."

When she had left the office, he picked up the phone again. Llewellyn would be taking the morning shuttle to Larnaca. There might still be time to catch him at the airport. What Shmona was contemplating involved a breach of Mossad security, as well as his own personal consumption of a large portion of crow. But he owed it to Daniella.

27

Lockjaw Logan remained blissfully unaware of the encounter between two of his passengers and the Canadian woman. Occupied in the continuing pre-flight of his Aero Commander, he had missed seeing Jane Monpleasure's headlong dash from the hangar and the subsequent pursuit by Ishmael. With the check-out completed and two of his passengers still absent, he had sent Nestor Rishad back to the hangar to look for them.

Nestor had returned shortly thereafter with the new passenger in tow, his attire a striking contrast to that of his two associates. Elegantly dressed in a white linen suit and sporting a fez, he was introduced as Mustafa Mafoud, an oil drilling executive from Ankara. The pecking order was apparent; Nestor was lugging his bag, as well as a long leather case that Mafoud insisted accompany him into the cabin.

Where was Ishmael, the pilot inquired? His planned departure time had come and gone. "A last-minute errand," was the response from the tall man in the fez, who didn't try to disguise his annoyance. "If he does not return within the next few minutes, we will leave without him."

Logan shrugged. "Seeing that we have to wait, let's use the time to settle my account and pay me the other half of my fee. Ishmael says you're the paymaster."

"That would be premature," Mafoud demurred. "I believe it is customary to pay on arrival. We have not yet reached our destination."

"You believe wrong," Logan replied bluntly. "The custom

is to pay in advance. I want the balance now, or we don't take off."

Mafoud glared at him, trying to stare him down. Logan held his ground, his eyes not wavering. He'd dealt with tough customers before, though this one had a look about him that suggested he could be the toughest. Oil drilling executive, eh? He looked like drilling holes in people might be more his style. Logan wondered what special drilling equipment might be hidden in that long rectangular case he'd been so insistent on bringing into the cabin.

The man in the white suit gave in. "All right, since it appears that you don't trust us—take your money. Two thousand rials, is that correct?" He removed the bills from a fat wallet and thrust them at the pilot. "Your impatience has just cost you a handsome bonus."

Kareem was seething inside. He'd deal with this money-hungry pilot later; now was not the time. Now it was time to get moving, get his act back on schedule. The morning had started off badly, the unexpected appearance of the Llewellyn woman, who he had thought to be in custody of the Iranian secret police, shattering his equanimity. She had been out looking at the airplane, the brother called Nestor had just informed him. How much had she seen? How much did she know?

He had sent Ishmael after her to dispatch her once and for all. It should have been a simple matter; Ishmael should have been back by now. What could have gone wrong? He couldn't afford to find out the hard way.

"Let us be on our way, Captain. I don't propose to wait any longer."

"But what of our brother?" protested Nestor. "What will—?"

Kareem silenced him with a look. "Do as I say, Captain. We depart immediately for Bandar Abbas. You will obtain clearance for take off, please. Now."

Ishmael was still inside the Shiraz airport terminal, searching for the woman Kareem had identified as an Israeli agent. Kareem had ordered him to kill her. The whole cause would be in jeopardy if she escaped and informed her countrymen, Ishmael's own brilliant coup at Mosul going for naught.

He stood in the center of the departure-level mall and let his eyes roam once more over the restaurant and surrounding shops, fingering the knife in his pocket. She was still here, somewhere, hiding from him. He could feel her presence.

Attired in her newly purchased outfit, Daniella strode determinedly toward the restaurant, bent on reaching the telephone that would connect her with her Mossad control. She stared at the back of the denim-clad knife wielder who remained planted in front of the restaurant, knowing there would be no way to escape his scrutiny when she entered. But he was looking for a tailored brunette in a two-piece suit. In her loose-fitting, brightly colored caftan, sandals on her feet, a kerchief covering her hair, she was no longer that person.

At first glance Ishmael paid her scant attention. Then the design on the shopping bag she was carrying caught his eye and rang a bell. It was a silhouette of a slender woman with an even more slender dog, a Russian wolfhound—the design he had seen on the dress shop in this same mall.

His head swung toward the dress shop, then back toward the woman in the kaftan now entering the restaurant, wheels beginning to turn in his head. At that very instant a noisy disturbance distracted him. It was coming from down the corridor in the direction from which he had entered the terminal. Belatedly, a bevy of uniformed airport police had converged on the chase scene and were marching up the corridor toward him, shoulder to shoulder, accompanied by a cluster of excited spectators. When the terrorist saw one of them point in his direction, he decided not to wait around.

In the restaurant, Daniella was unaware of this development. Still apprehensive that he might follow her inside, she found the telephone in the back of the place near the kitchen. Now the tricky part began, how to get a long-distance number in a foreign country where you didn't speak the language. She couldn't read the instructions on the phone, a rotary dial affair of uncertain vintage. Direct dialing was unlikely to work, but she decided to try it anyway. She had armed herself with a purse full of change at the dress shop. Inserting her largest denomination coin, she dialed 1 plus the international area code and number of the dummy line in Canada.

As she'd expected, the operator came on the line. Was the woman giving instructions or asking her for a number? Daniella had memorized the Farsi words for the numbers from one to ten en route to Iran, but under the pressure of the moment couldn't recall any of them. She read off the number in English, the only thing she could think of to do.

The operator repeated whatever it was she had said before. "I'm sorry, I don't speak Farsi," she replied, repeating the number in English.

Nothing happened. After a considerable delay, a different voice came on the line, speaking English. "You wish to make a collect call?"

"Yes, yes!"

"To where, please?"

"Ottawa, Ontario, in Canada."

"Who you wish to speak?"

"Anyone who answers."

"Your name?"

"Jane."

"Will take a few minutes. Hold, please."

When she finally heard Shmona's voice accepting the call, she broke into tears. "Oh, thank God!"

"Daniella, is that you? What happened to you? I expected your call last night. Where are you?"

She mustered all her will and managed to control her voice. "I'm at the Shiraz airport, in a phone booth. The security police came to the hotel last night to arrest me before I could call. I had to hide."

"Were you able to carry out—?"

"Yes. Those items you're looking for are here. I saw them in Logan's plane this morning."

"Now, Daniella, we must be absolutely certain. How can you tell—?"

"Because he's here, also," she interrupted again. "The man who ran me off the road—the one in the picture! He was on my flight from Tehran. He must be going on with Logan, with that cargo."

The line went silent for a moment. "Baruch? Are you still there?"

"Yes, Daniella, that's splendid news! This is the break we've been waiting for. But we can't lose their trail, now. We've got to—"

"Baruch, there's more. The terrorist saw me, recognized me. He tried to have me killed! One of his men chased me into the airport with a knife. He's still looking for me. What am I going to do?"

"You're going to get out of there, that's what you're going to do. I booked a seat for you on the morning flight to Bandar Abbas. It leaves in half an hour. You still have time to—"

"Baruch! Don't you understand? The security police are looking for me. If my Canadian name's on the passenger list, they're sure to be watching that flight. I'll be arrested!"

"Okay, okay, you're right. But we've got to get you on that flight. Do they know what you look like?"

"Not so far as I know. But anyway, I've bought some things, changed my appearance."

"All right, here's what you do: Purchase a ticket in another name. That flight was only half full. You should have no trouble getting a seat."

"But my passport . . . It won't be the right name."

"I doubt if they'll check passports on a local flight. If they ask you for it, you didn't know to bring it. Wait until the last minute to board. They're less likely to make a fuss if the airplane's waiting. You should be landing about the same time as Logan—your commercial jet is faster. I want you to find his plane; his flight plan ends there. We have to learn where they're headed next. Okay, Daniella?"

"I—I guess so." It was far from okay. She'd hoped that he would bring someone in to help get her out of this.

"Daniella, I know you've been through a lot, but you've got to hang on. We're so close, so much depends on what happens next."

"It's just that I feel so alone, so vulnerable. I've never been so terrified, Baruch. Isn't there another of your people in the area, someone who could help me?"

"I'm afraid not. There isn't time to get anyone there." He sensed that he had to give her something to cling to.

"But there's one thing you should know. Your husband learned about your new assignment. He's on his way there right now, on the same flight you took yesterday. I couldn't stop him. Maybe it's for the best, maybe he can help."

David, dearest David, worried about her, coming after her! Tears welled up in her eyes, her fierce pride that might once have resented such an intrusion in abeyance. He loves me. He'll protect me. He'll find a way to pull us through.

"Daniella, are you still there? Did you hear what I said?"

"Yes, Baruch, I heard." She dried her eyes and blew her nose.

"Now, if I don't hear from you, I'll assume you made that flight. I'll get word to your husband, so he can join you in Bandar Abbas. Call me from there as soon as you've made contact with the plane again."

"Goodbye, Baruch."

She walked to the door of the restaurant and peered out. The terrorist was no longer there, the reason apparent. The area was alive with police.

Fearlessly, she stepped through the door. They weren't looking for her. They were looking for a smartly dressed Canadian lady in a tailored beige suit.

Shmona had made it sound easy. Just buy a ticket to Bandar Abbas in somebody else's name. Waiting in line at the Iran Air ticket counter, Daniella kept thinking of possible hitches.

What name should she use? What would arouse the least suspicion on the passenger list? If the name sounded foreign, they were more likely to ask her for her passport. So perhaps she should pick an Iranian name. But then they would speak Farsi to her and she wouldn't understand.

She thought of the heavyset woman from Kurdistan who had sat next to her on the flight in. The Kurdish woman, though a native Irani, had not understood the flight attendant's Farsi either, had answered in a tongue that sounded a lot like Arabic. That was the answer; she could use a Kurdish name and fall back on her knowledge of Arabic.

What was the fat woman's name? It had been written on the boarding pass tucked into the pocket of the seat in front of her, had reminded Daniella of "stardust." Sardasht, that was it. What was a good Islamic given name? Faida. Faida Sardasht. She jotted the name down on the notepad she carried in her purse and tore out the page.

When her turn came, she stated her destination, Bandar Abbas, and held up one finger, enunciating the Arabic word for one, *wahad*. The ticket agent came back at her in Farsi with what was obviously a question. Assuming he was asking if she wanted today's flight, she nodded. That must have been the right answer; he punched his computer keyboard and checked the screen, as she pushed the page with the name written on it in front of him and laid down a hundred-rial note.

If he asks me for identification I'm in trouble, she thought, but he took the slip of paper without comment and copied it, punching the name into the computer and inserting a fresh ticket into the ticket printer. While it chattered away he wrote out a boarding pass and made change. Holding up six fingers for the gate, he pushed her change toward her and handed her the ticket and boarding pass. As she left the window she saw him point to his wrist watch. He was telling her to hurry; the flight was about to leave.

She rushed to Gate 6, at the farthest end of the terminal, only to learn that the flight hadn't even begun boarding yet. Taking a seat in the departure lounge with the other waiting passengers, she looked around warily. There were no police uniforms in evidence, no sign of any special surveillance of this particular flight. But that didn't prove a thing. If the security police had noticed her name on the passenger list and were laying for her, they would hardly advertise their presence and scare her away.

The ringing of the phone at the departure desk startled her. The attendant picked it up. Daniella was certain that the call had to do with her. She should never have exposed herself by sitting in the lounge, should have waited and watched from a distance until the loading began. She got to her feet, prepared to beat a hasty departure.

The attendant put down the phone and picked up the microphone. The announcement was in Farsi and was accompanied by groans from the assemblage of travelers, who began standing and picking up their carry-on baggage, complaining

loudly to one another. She followed the other passengers back
to the terminal and stopped at the information desk, where
English was spoken. The flight had been cancelled because of
equipment problems, she was told. There were no more scheduled flights to Bandar Abbas until the following morning.

Shmona would be crushed, she thought, as she headed back
to the restaurant to phone him. Contact with the terrorists
was in jeopardy of being lost, her Iran mission thwarted. She
should be feeling crushed also. Why wasn't she?

She knew why. Now she would be here when David arrived,
would be at the airport to meet him. Before the day ended she
would feel his strong arms around her and her ordeal would
be over. He would take care of her, he would know what to
do. At this point in time, her need for him outweighed all
other considerations.

The hop to Bandar Abbas was a short one, just over an hour's
flight time from Shiraz. The man in the fez and the white linen
suit had started the trip in the copilot seat, but shortly after
takeoff had moved back to sit beside the other passenger.

Logan's ear, used to filtering out the background noise of
the two engines, had no trouble picking up snatches of their
conversation, though he couldn't understand the language.
Clearly, they didn't want him to; both passengers spoke passable English. But he had heard Arabic spoken often enough
to recognize it. If these were really Turkish oil men, as adver-
tised, why weren't they speaking Turkish?

It confirmed his suspicions that they were something very
different than they pretended. He thought again about the
heavy objects in the back of the cabin that the passenger called
Nestor had felt compelled to sleep with. If they weren't pieces
of oil apparatus, what were they?

At the moment Kareem was not that concerned about what
the pilot might think. He was worried about the Llewellyn
woman, the Mossad agent who had somehow evaded the trap
he had set for her at the hotel. That woman had more lives
than a cat! Had she also managed to escape Ishmael's knife?
If not, why hadn't he returned?

He pumped Nestor Rishad for details. Had the woman set
foot on Logan's plane? Yes. Did she get a look at the cargo

in the cabin? She might have, while he was relieving himself in the hangar. What was she doing there; was she a friend of the pilot's? She was interested in arranging a charter flight, Nestor explained.

Kareem didn't believe that for an instant. Did she know the plane's destination, Bandar Abbas? Nestor couldn't help him there, suggesting that he ask the pilot.

Kareem couldn't think of a way to do that without arousing Logan's suspicion. He didn't know what the relationship might be between the pilot and the Llewellyn woman. She was the type that men found attractive, and he wouldn't put it past her to use whatever wiles she had to achieve the ends of her infamous organization. He decided that in the end it really didn't matter what she knew. Informing the Mossad would not really endanger him. Once he was out of Bandar Abbas they would never find him.

"Seat belts!" Logan had turned in his seat to shout above the roar of the engines. "Prepare for landing." He banked to the left so that they could see the Strait of Hormuz up ahead, the city of Bandar Abbas just below them. To call it a city might be stretching tl.ings a bit, he reflected. But it was the last town of any consequence from here east to the Pakistan border and had a halfway decent airport with a better than average maintenance facility.

It was not a busy airport and the clearance to land took no time at all. He turned from his approach leg to the final without having to go around again. A minute later they were on the ground, taxiing toward the private aircraft reception area.

"Which is your helicopter charter?" Logan inquired. "Jalal Brothers? A&R Helicopters?"

Kareem didn't want him to know. "Just unload us at the terminal. They will find us."

"There is no terminal for charters here. That must be yours, that Bell Ranger parked over there. It's one of A&R's."

He taxied toward the only helicopter in evidence, parked on the flight line in front of the maintenance hangar for private aircraft and charters. A short little man jumped out of the chopper and stood in front of it waving his arms. He was wearing a green flight suit and a beat-up pilot's cap looking several sizes too large that came down over his ears.

"Well I'll be jiggered if it isn't Hot Shot!" Logan knew just about everybody that flew planes for a living in Iran. He knew the diminutive chopper pilot better than most, dating back to the time they worked together before the return of the Ayatollah—or "Second Coming," as some irreverently referred to it. Hot Shot's real name was Jeremy Olds. The nickname had been bestowed on him by one of the American pilots, who was struck by his resemblance to a legendary cartoon character of yore named "Hot Shot Charlie," a Boston-bred World War II fighter pilot.

The American had also bestowed his own WW II Air Force cap, replete with its "fifty-mission crush." Jeremy, who was Canadian, not American, and had never been to Boston, nevertheless had accepted both the hat and the title that went with it and had been Hot Shot ever since. The ill-fitting cap became his lucky charm. He never flew without it.

Logan maneuvered his Aero Commander alongside the chopper and cut the engines, then jumped down to greet his old flying mate.

"Heard you were coming in, Lockjaw." They shook hands, Hot Shot grinning from ear to ear. He had to be pushing fifty, thought Logan, but with his heavy freckles and red hair he still looked like a kid.

"This your consignment, Hot Shot? Turkish oil personnel and oil rig gear for Qeshm Island?"

"Sounds like it." Hot Shot peered dubiously inside the Aero Commander's cabin. "But I was expecting three passengers. I only see two."

"One turned up missing. His nibs, the one in the fez, decided not to wait."

Kareem was already descending from the plane. He hurried over to put an end to the unmonitored conversation between the two pilots.

"You are the pilot assigned by A&R Helicopters? Captain Olds, I believe?"

"Yes, sir, at your service." Hot Shot saluted smartly. "Lost a passenger on the way, did we?"

"There will be just the two of us. Kindly see that the baggage and equipment are transferred. I would like to get started as soon as possible."

Logan opened the doors to his plane's two small baggage compartments and pulled out the passengers' three suitcases, setting them down beside the helicopter. "The heavy stuff's in there." He motioned toward the Aero Commander's cabin. "I'll give you a hand."

"That won't be necessary, Capain Logan," Kareem demurred. "Nestor will help him."

"Suit yourself." Logan had wanted a moment alone with his friend, out of earshot from the others. Clearly, the "oil executive" wanted to prevent this. He opened the loading door of the helicopter and began stacking the suitcases inside. Hot Shot came backing down the steps of Logan's plane, holding one end of a long, fat cylindrical package with Nestor at the other end.

"Damn, this oil rig gear is heavy stuff," he wheezed. "Let's set it down a minute, whilst I get a better grip."

As he bent down to release the load, Logan whispered in his ear. "Watch your ass, mate. There's something fishy about these birds. Better get your money up front."

Hot Shot showed no sign of having heard. "Let's get the other two. Then I'll decide where to stow them." The two re-entered the Aero Commander cabin and emerged with a second bulky object wrapped in oil-stained canvas.

"This one's even heavier," Hot Shot grunted. Setting his end down next to Logan, he straightened up and whispered back, "We were paid in advance."

"Do like I said—watch your bloody ass," Logan reiterated.

Though he couldn't hear what was said, Kareem knew that words had been exchanged between the two. As the final heavy parcel was being trundled out of the plane, he walked over to Logan.

"Mr. Logan, you have been paid. There's nothing further to detain you."

"Right. Well, then, good luck with your drilling." He gave Hot Shot a hasty handshake and a significant look. "Fly safely."

He climbed back into his plane and started the engines, then called the tower for his take-off clearance. As he released the brakes, he saw the man in the white suit run in front of the plane, waving his arms excitedly.

Logan reset the brakes and reduced the throttles, sticking his head out the cockpit window to hear what was being shouted. Something about a piece of luggage. He looked behind him. His passenger's long, narrow leather case had been left on board.

Nestor climbed back aboard to retrieve it, slinging it over his shoulder, and exited again, a bit too hastily. There was an ominous clanging of metal against metal as the object inside the leather case struck the side of the door.

Heavy-caliber stuff, by the sound of it, thought Logan. He wondered if his warning to his old mate had been strong enough.

28

QESHM WAS A skinny, sixty-mile-long Iranian island in the Strait of Hormuz. Hot Shot had heard that there was oil-exploration work going on near its southwest extremity but hadn't been down that way recently.

"Yours must be one of those new rigs down near the south end of the island," he remarked to the man sitting in the copilot's seat, as the eastern tip of Qeshm came into view. Kareem did not respond immediately, instead reaching for the long, rectangular leather case behind his seat. He unzipped it.

"We're not going to the island after all. That was just for your flight plan. We have a different destination planned. A secret one."

The steel snout of an automatic rifle protruded from the leather case, pointing at the pilot's stomach. Hot Shot's eyes bugged out of his freckled face. Christ! Lockjaw had been right about these birds . . .

"You're going to alter course without telling anyone. We will fly directly east, to the southern coast of Baluchistan. And you will stay off the radio."

For all his lack of stature, Hot Shot was a feisty one. He made no immediate move to comply, sizing up the situation.

"Make your turn," Kareem ordered. "Now!"

"You're not going to shoot me. Who'd fly the chopper?"

"You would," Kareem answered with icy calm, "with one less arm or leg. Which would you prefer to lose? A kneecap, perhaps? An elbow? A hand? A foot?"

The guy in the fez meant business. His eyes were cold as blue steel. Hot Shot considered his options. Bandar Abbas might still have him on their radar. If he turned now they might notice the departure from his flight plan and report it. He racked the helicopter up suddenly into a tight banking turn to port, pinning his surprised passengers against their seats.

Kareem bristled as the chopper pulled out of the steep turn, brandishing his weapon. "Don't surprise me like that again!"

"Just following instructions." Hot Shot's radio was still tuned to the Bandar Abbas tower. If they had seen him change course they should be calling at any moment. He leveled out on a new mag heading of 128 degrees, waiting for the call to come through. It didn't.

"If I don't call in soon, they'll know something's wrong," he warned.

"Not necessarily," Kareem rejoined. "Radios go out of order all the time. This one will go out of order permanently if you try to use it."

He pointed to the compass. "Your heading is still too far south. I told you to head due east, for The Baluchistan coast."

The pilot shook his head. "I'm afraid I can't do that."

"Why not?" Kareem demanded hotly.

"Not enough fuel." Hot Shot indicated the fuel gauge on the instrument panel. It showed half empty.

"I only loaded enough for the Qeshm round trip. If you want to get where you're going, we'll have to put down at Jask to refuel."

"You stupid———!" Kareem snatched up the map case lying between his seat and the pilot's, unfolding one of the maps. He found Jask on the Gulf of Oman, less than halfway to his chosen destination from Bandar Abbas. A full tank of fuel would easily have gotten them the full distance. He chastised himself for not checking on fuel before they left.

"How far can you fly on the fuel you have?"

"We could just about reach the Baluchistan border."

"Then why do we have to land at Jask?"

"It's the last place between here and where you're going that can refuel us." If it's open, Hot Shot added to himself. The bare-bones facility at the tiny airport was pretty independent, keeping its own hours. It closed down on any sort of Muslim or Iranian holiday, or just about any other pretext.

"How long before we land there?"

"About an hour."

Kareem forced himself to accept the situation. It wouldn't delay them that much; Jask wasn't that far off course. They could still make it to the launch site well before nightfall. Al Saif was not expecting him any sooner. It was his own impatience to be reunited with the leader that was feeding his disgruntlement.

He pictured his triumphant arrival in the helicopter, the unloading of the priceless warheads that would complete the brilliant coup he had helped to plan and engineer, the adulation of the leader and the others. It was going to be quite a reunion.

David Llewellyn was the first one off the evening flight from Isfahan that had just landed at Shiraz airport. Carry-on bag in hand, he plunged past the knot of bystanders waiting to greet arriving passengers, intent on getting to the street and hailing a cab to the hotel. Among those waiting was a woman in some sort of native costume, wearing sandals and sunglasses. He didn't give her a second look.

"David!"

He could scarcely believe his ears. He came to an abrupt stop and swung around. "Daniella?"

In the twinkling of an eye she was in his arms, hugging him for all she was worth and sobbing uncontrollably. He hugged her back and patted her consolingly.

"That's it. Let it all out . . . It's going to be all right now. I'm taking you home."

Her sobbing began to subside. Finally she regained her composure. "You wouldn't believe what I've been through. The same man who ran me off the road is here! One of his men tried to stab me! And the Iranian secret police are after me as a Jewish spy."

"We'll have you out of here before anything else can happen. We'll take the next plane back." Gently, he lifted her head off his shoulder to look into her eyes.

"Don't look at me, David. I know I look like hell." She found her purse and rummaged through it for a Kleenex, dabbing at her eyes.

"Not to me. You've never looked better. Do you have any luggage?"

"No. It's still at the hotel. I couldn't go back to my room; the security police were there."

"Never mind. You won't need it. We'll be home tomorrow." He took her by the arm.

"We'll go directly to the airline counter and—"

She held back. "No, David, wait. We can't. We have to talk."

Passengers were streaming by on all sides now. She drew him off to a secluded corner of the waiting room where they could sit and not be overheard.

"You know the reason I was sent here."

He nodded. "No thanks to that boss of yours; I couldn't get much out of him. But I've got most of it figured out. The terrorist missile is somewhere in southeastern Iran, isn't it? Your nemesis from the highway incident must have been coming through here to join up with his chums. You were supposed to follow him and locate the missile launch site. Am I right?"

She nodded. "But there's a little more to it than that. The terrorists are carrying warheads, David. I saw them, touched them! They fit the description of the warheads that were stolen from Iraq's manufacturing plant at Mosul."

"So that's what Shmona wouldn't tell me! Chemical warheads. Or biological. Either one could be big trouble. Where are they? Did they get away?"

"They were about to be flown to Bandar Abbas by this charter pilot, Logan. After I escaped I was ordered to take a commercial flight there this morning and find out where he was going next. But the flight was cancelled. There won't be another till morning."

Llewellyn was incredulous. "Wait a minute . . . Shmona ordered you to . . . After everything else he's put you through? I don't believe this guy!"

"He had no choice, David. I was the only one here, the only one in position to—"

"Well, it's too late now, anyway. They could be all the way to the missile site by now. You did your best and almost got killed doing it. What more can they expect? It's time to get you home and let the professional spies and the military handle this thing."

"Oh?" she bristled, suddenly sitting erect. "You don't think I'm professional?"

"I only meant—"

"I'm not a quitter, David. I was ordered to go to Bandar Abbas and try to pick up the trail of these terrorists. That's what I have to do."

Llewellyn groaned. "Sweetheart, enough is enough. Besides, you said there were no more flights until tomorrow."

"No more scheduled flights. But we might be able to arrange a charter."

"We? I came here to take you home."

"David, I don't think I can do this without you. You are going to help me, aren't you?"

Her bottom lip was protruding in that stubborn sign he knew so well. She wasn't going to budge. Could this be the same woman who had dissolved into tears a few minutes ago?

His conversation with Ambassador Abrams came back to him, before he had leaped off to Iran on the pretext of helping track down the missile hijackers. It had been more than a pretext; the safety of Tel Aviv's inhabitants was a major concern to both of them.

"Okay," he said simply, "I'm in."

They left the main entrance to the terminal and walked to the neighboring charter terminal, Daniella showing him the way. She still had the pass Logan had given her in her purse and showed it to the guard at the hangar two gate to gain admittance.

She had noticed on her previous visit that several charter services had small offices around the perimeter of the hangar. But it was after 8:00 P.M. The offices were all closed.

They walked out onto the hangar floor among the planes, where there was no one to be found but a mechanic, of little help. Outside, however, they found a floodlit charter plane on the flight line. As they approached, the door of the plane opened and a man stepped out onto the wing, a wrench in his hand.

"Do you know the pilot of this plane?" Daniella inquired.

The man in green fatigues looked down at them without

replying as he stepped along the wing toward the nose of the plane. Daniella was about to try another language when he spoke.

"Do I know the pilot? You might say so. I'm him."

Llewellyn took over. "We need to charter a plane. Is this one for hire?"

"That depends." He began removing lugs from one of the engine cowlings.

"We can pay, if that's what you're worried about."

The wrench slipped. The pilot cursed and set it down, turning around. "When, where, and for how long?"

"One day should do it. Flying east, to the coast of Baluchistan. And we need to leave right away. Tonight."

The pilot looked at him like he was crazy. "Baluchistan? Why would anyone want to go there? They don't even have airfields. Anyway, my plane isn't ready to fly. I couldn't possibly leave before noon tomorrow."

Llewellyn was on the verge of pressing him further when Daniella tugged on his sleeve. "David! That's Logan's plane, the blue one over there! I'm almost certain." She pointed to a twin-engine plane a few rows away.

The pilot overheard her. "Sure, that's Lockjaw's Aero Commander. You friends of his?"

"Yes—yes!" she answered. "Do you know where we could find him?"

"Probably at the hotel. Or he might still be at Flight Operations. He was headed up there when he left."

"Flight Operations," she repeated. "How do we get there?"

"It's on top of the hangar . . . You go up an outside staircase. You'll see it near the entrance."

They thanked him and rushed back to the hangar, Daniella filling her husband in on her assessment of Logan. "I'm sure he'll help us. But we may have to take him into our confidence."

"If we have to, we have to," Llewellyn agreed. "It's a little late to start worrying about security clearances."

After the termination of his charter in Bandar Abbas, Logan had put into Shiraz to refuel and overnight. Worried about Hot Shot, he had gone straight to Flight Operations to see what he could find out. He was on his third call to A&R Helicopters at Bandar Abbas, Hot Shot's home base, listening to the dispatcher's report. The pilot and his chopper had been expected back several hours earlier. He still hadn't returned, and there had been no radio contact with him since shortly after he took off for Qeshm Island.

"I knew it . . . . That bunch of slimeballs were up to no good. Probably hijacked him."

"We can't be sure of that," the dispatcher hedged. "He could just be down somewhere on the island with a bad radio."

"Isn't anybody out there looking for him?" Logan was getting exasperated at the calm tone of the dispatcher.

"A night search would be impractical. We'll have some planes out there as soon as it's light."

Logan made a hurried decision. "I'm coming back down. Tell the boss I'll be there to help."

He hung up the phone and stood there frowning down at the counter. There was now no doubt in his mind that his two former passengers had commandeered Hot Shot's chopper. Qeshm Island had never been their intended destination. Where were they really headed?

"Hello, Mr. Logan."

He looked up to see a face that was both attractive and totally unexpected. "Mrs. Monpleasure! What brings you—?"

"Something terribly urgent." She noticed several clerks, or whatever they were, within earshot behind the counter. "I have something to tell you in great confidence. Is there some place we can talk without being overheard?"

"Why don't we go down to the waiting room. There's no one there this time of night."

On the way down the stairs, she introduced the pilot to her husband.

"Llewellyn," Logan repeated. "Then your name is not really Monpleasure?"

"I am Daniella Llewellyn, Mr. Logan. And I'm not Canadian. I am an Israeli. My husband is a special envoy to Israel from America."

A light dawned in the pilot's eyes. "That Israeli agent the 'Sons of Savak' were looking for at our hotel! It was you?"

She nodded. "And the one who tipped them off to my whereabouts was none other than your passenger of this morning, the Turkish gentleman. Who is, of course, not a Turk at all, but a Palestinian, wanted by my country for numerous acts of terrorism."

"Does he know about your narrow escape of this morning?" David interjected. Logan's expression said he didn't.

"When I left your plane, I encountered this terrorist and recognized him, despite his disguise. The man who was with him chased me at knifepoint to the main terminal, where I was able to lose him."

"So that's what happened to Ishmael!" The pilot thought this had to be one of the pluckiest women he'd ever laid eyes on. "Palestinian terrorists? That explains a lot. That cargo of theirs—do you happen to know what it is, where they're taking it?"

"That's why we're here." David Llewellyn picked up the thread. "We have something to tell you in the strictest confidence—Al, is it?"

"Which stands for Aloysius," he confided. "Most of my friends call me Lockjaw."

"Al, we're going to trust you; we need your help. What I'm about to tell you will astound you. If the story were to leak out, it could panic an entire nation. So we must rely on your discretion"—he grinned—"and hope you live up to your nickname."

Llewellyn told the pilot everything he needed to hear—from the hijacking of the missile to the stolen warheads.

Logan blinked and looked from one face to the other. The story sounded more outlandish than the plots of some of the suspense thrillers he had read. But he could read in their eyes it was true. Which meant that his old pal Hot Shot was in even deeper shit than he had imagined.

"How can I help?"

It was Daniella's turn. "You can start by telling us who picked up your passengers at Bandar Abbas and where they were headed."

"The two passengers and their gear were loaded aboard a chopper chartered from A&R Helicopters, bound for Qeshm Island in the Strait of Hormuz. An old mate of mine was at the controls. I was worried about him, came in here to call Bandar Abbas and check on him. They haven't heard a word from him since he took off. He's disappeared."

The Llewellyns exchanged glances. "Hijacking is something they've gotten pretty good at," David observed. "You can bet they're headed for Baluchistan."

Daniella seized the pilot's arm. "We've got to find them! Can you fly us down there?"

Logan considered. "It's eight hours since Hot Shot took off. They've almost certainly reached their destination by now. Unless—"

He snapped his fingers. "Wait for me here. I need to call Bandar Abbas again."

He hurried back up the stairs. The call went through quickly. The A&R dispatcher's "Hello" was on the irritable side; probably trying to get some sleep, the pilot surmised.

"Logan again. I had a thought. How much fuel did Hot Shot load for Qeshm?"

"I already checked on that. Half a tank full. Qeshm's a short run."

"What's that figure out to in miles for a chopper like his?"

"A couple of hundred. Two fifty on the outside."

"If they were headed east, they'd have to stop at Jask to refuel. There's nothing beyond."

"You still on that hijacking kick? Hijackers would more than likely head south for the Emirates. If they landed at Jask, they're out of luck."

"Why's that?"

"The place was shut down tight all day today. Some kind of local religious observance."

"You sure about that?"

"Positive. We've been putting out advisories since yesterday. No fuel available until tomorrow, eight in the morning."

Logan came back to the waiting room beaming. "I don't want to get your hopes up too high, but I think we may have had a stroke of luck. It appears they've had to set down to refuel and encountered an unexpected delay."

"What are we waiting for?" Daniella was on her feet, ready to go.

Logan held up his hands. "We have a big day ahead. How

long since either one of you has had a good night's sleep?"
Two pairs of bloodshot eyes answered for them.

"I thought as much. Here's the plan. We spent the night at
the airport hotel. We take off at dawn."

"We'll lose them!" Daniella protested.

"I don't think so. It looks like these terrorists of yours will
be spending the night at Jask. They won't be going anywhere
until the fuel depot opens in the morning. We'll have a much
more comfortable night than they will.

"Jask is a dump. There's nothing much there but the air
strip and the fuel pumping station. One falafel stand, maybe,
if it's open. And not a single bed to be had. They'll have to
sleep in the chopper."

Kareem was fit to be tied. Stuck in this abysmal hole for the
entire afternoon and night because of some obscure Shiite
holiday celebration! He should already have landed at the site,
would already have been participating in a celebration of his
own amid his Sword of Islam brethren. He was too upset to
even think of sleeping.

Look at the pilot back there, stretched out on the floor of
the helicopter, sleeping like a baby! He felt the urge to take it
out on the man, administer a sound beating for his lapse in not
taking off with a full tank. It would give him satisfaction to do
so. But he thought better of it. He wanted the pilot in good
condition for tomorrow's flight and landing. After that he
would be totally expendable.

In the back of the helicopter, Hot Shot was only feigning
sleep. The realization of what a tight spot he was in had sunk
in with full force. These were clearly terrorists of some sort,
though he had no real clue to their identity or what their
business was in Baluchistan. Lockjaw had apparently known
something, had tried to warn him. But what good had the
warning been? What could he really have done to prevent
what happened? Nothing.

His only hope of escape seemed to be the possibility that the
tall one seated by the door with the assault rifle would fall
asleep. The other man would be no problem, his desultory
snoring proof that he was already out of it.

Hot Shot opened one eye and assessed the situation. The

man with the gun was motionless. His head seemed to have slumped forward. The pilot shifted his weight onto his side and got onto his hands and knees. Still no movement from the gunman. He began to crawl slowly along the aisle toward the exit.

The door had been intentionally left open to draw in the cool night air. If he could reach it without arousing the gunman, he could exit noiselessly. Still on all fours, he inched his way past the sleeping terrorists. Another few feet—

"What have we here? A slinking dog?" Using both hands, Kareem brought the butt of his weapon down on the back of the pilot's neck.

With a cry of pain, Hot Shot recoiled, scrambling backwards.

"That's it, slink back to your kennel, dog. And stay there, if you wish to live through the night."

Kareem smiled with satisfaction. He had been right. It felt good to strike the pilot. Now perhaps *he* could get some sleep.

They registered as husband and wife. The desk clerk who had checked Daniella in the night before didn't recognize her in her peasant costume and dark glasses. He handed Llewellyn the key. "Enjoy your stay, Mr. Svenson."

"Mr. Svenson?" Daniella whispered, as they headed for the elevator.

"My traveling name, Mrs. Monpleasure."

The sight of the bed was too much for Daniella. With a cry of ecstasy she flopped down on it, not even bothering to remove her sandals. When her husband returned from the bathroom after a quick shower, he found her fast asleep.

He slipped off her sandals, taking care not to wake her. Tenderly, he set about undressing her. The kaftan was a problem; it had to come off over her head. He lifted her hips to slide the dress beneath them, then lifted her back and drew the garment up around her neck. Gently, he raised her head and pulled the dress free, lowering her head again. He needn't have worried about waking her; she was dead to the world.

He stood there for a moment, just taking in the sight of her. He was married to a beautiful woman. Despite all she had been through, she had never looked better. The sight of her full breasts rhythmically rising and falling began to arouse him. They were cruelly constrained by the tight brassiere; he had to set them free.

He raised her head and back again and undid the catch on the bra. Her breasts escaped from it, their whiteness enhanced by the uniform tan on the rest of her body. The bra had left red marks on them; he couldn't resist massaging them a bit. She stirred but didn't awaken.

Thoroughly aroused now, he turned off the light and climbed in beside her. What a merry-go-round they'd been on, no time for each other. It had been days—almost a week— since they'd been in bed together. I'll just hold her for a minute, he thought, until I fall asleep.

He got an arm around her waist and drew her to him, kissing her lips tenderly. That was funny—they seemed to be kissing him back. Amazing, the unconscious responses of a woman's physiognomy. Her body, too, seemed to be pressing back against his. Could she still be asleep?

Her hands certainly were not; they were suddenly very busy, making exploratory overtures, then sliding off her underpants.

"Sorry," he whispered, "I didn't mean to wake you."

"Who's awake?" she answered, climbing on top of him.

Minutes later, the merry-go-round had finally begun winding down. It was going slower and slower and he was almost ready to get off.

"You're a great lover, Mr. Svenson," she said, giving his bare rump a good night pat.

"You're not so bad yourself, Mrs. Monpleasure." He returned her pat, then fell asleep.

The sun had not yet fully risen when the Aero Commander left the runway at Shiraz and poked its nose into the brightening sky. Logan leveled off and called the tower, requesting clearance to turn onto his new heading for Bandar Abbas and Jask, which was immediately granted. The twin-engine plane banked sharply, pulling out on a course that was almost directly into the rising sun.

"How far to Jask?" inquired David Llewellyn, seated in the copilot seat.

"About four hundred miles. Looks like good flying weather; there's even a tailwind. We should be there in well under two hours."

In the cabin behind her husband, Daniella sat stroking her gleaming black hair with a small hairbrush from her purse. She had finally had a chance to wash it that morning at the hotel. She felt rested and halfway human again, but now the tension was starting to build once more.

So much depended on their mission this morning. What if Logan was mistaken? What if the helicopter wasn't there after all, when they got to Jask? It was the key to discovering the missile launch site. Without it, what chance would they have?

"What are the chances the terrorists will still be there, Al?" she asked, seeking reassurance.

"Good, provided they went in there yesterday to be refueled. The dispatcher for Hot Shot's company told me the fuel trucks don't go out till eight in the morning. That gives us time to get there and orbit a few times before the chopper lifts off. We'll follow at a distance, out of visual range, using my radar."

And then what? he asked himself. Supposing everything worked out and they did find the location of this terrorist missile base? How would that help his mate? The Israeli response would probably be an immediate air strike to erase it. Poor Hot Shot. He was caught up in something a lot bigger than he'd bargained for. Even if he survived the terrorists, he was in danger of being erased along with his captors.

Logan had thrown himself into this affair with the notion of rescuing his friend. Now he wondered if there would be any possible way to save him.

A thick haze hung over the Strait of Hormuz, turning its blue waters to a dull, battle-ship gray color. Ahead they could just make out the brownish land mass of Ras al Kuh, the cape just east of Jask.

"Ten minutes to go." The Aero Commander made landfall briefly over the promontory, then broke out over water again, flying parallel to the shoreline that lay just to port. Another five minutes passed before a small peninsula came into view, thrusting southward into the Gulf of Oman like a sharp beak.

"There it is, on the tip of the peninsula," the pilot announced. "That's Jask."

Llewellyn had the pilot's binoculars. He trained them ahead, focusing on the two crisscrossing air strips. He could make out several planes parked near the far end of the longer runway. None of them looked like helicopters.

"I don't see them yet."

"Keep looking." Logan took his plane over the airfield at ten thousand feet. All three of them had a clear view of the entire area. The only planes to be seen were fixed-wing aircraft. There were no helicopters.

"Son of a bitch!" Logan looked at his watch. The dial read 7:32. "Looks like I got a bum steer from Bandar Abbas."

"Maybe not." Llewellyn felt the same letdown he could read in Daniella's face. "Maybe they were never here."

"Or maybe they were here and got refueled ahead of schedule," the pilot replied. "See that vehicle next to one of the planes? That's a fuel truck. It's already pumping fuel, and it's barely seven-thirty!"

He advanced the throttles and turned on his radar. The radar scope set into the instrument panel came alive, a bright green strobe line moving back and forth across its face as the antenna swept out its search pattern. No blips yet, Llewellyn noted. The pilot made some adjustments. Still no blips.

"We've got better than a hundred-knot speed advantage on Hot Shot," Logan observed. "Unless he had a huge head start, we have a good chance of overtaking him."

He corrected the heading a few degrees. They were still flying parallel to the coastline, a mile or two south of it, over the water. The haze was gone; Llewellyn had a perfect view of the terrain along the jagged coastline and the mountains jutting up vertically behind it. It was desolate looking, no cultivated land to be seen, no other sign of human habitation. He commented on it to the pilot.

"It's like this all the way through Baluchistan to the Pakistan border," Logan responded. "Some of the bleakest, most sparsely settled countryside anywhere in the world. A few shepherds and fishermen, that's about it. The sheer mountain range makes the coast virtually inaccessible, except by sea."

"Perfect."

341

"What was that?"

"I said perfect—for the terrorists—made to order. They couldn't have found a better place to hide their rocket."

They flew over another prominent headland jutting southward, which the pilot identified as Cape Meydani. "We're into Baluchistan now."

The terrain looked even wilder. Llewellyn continued to divide his attention between the rugged landscape and the radar scope, still blipless. They hadn't even passed another plane, the only sign of human activity in the region an occasional ship or smaller boat leaving its wake in the glistening waters below.

A sense of hopelessness began to set in. There was no real evidence that the helicopter they were searching for had spent the night at Jask, had even been there. Suppose it had doubled back yesterday, refueled somewhere else? It could have set down at its destination hours ago—yesterday. Without a clue on where to look, trying to spot it or the terrorist rocket in the kind of rugged terrain he'd been staring at would be an exercise in futility.

"There he is! There's Hot Shot!"

At the shout from the pilot, Llewellyn's eyes flew back to the radar scope. Sure enough, there *was* a faint blip near its upper extremity.

"He's still twenty miles ahead," Logan commented. "But we're gaining on him rapidly, about two miles every minute. When we get a bit closer, I'll throttle back. We'd best stay out of eyeball range so those terrorist blokes don't get onto us."

The blip became more prominent, moving steadily down the scope face. The pilot began to reduce the throttles. The blip closed to seven miles on the range scale reading and remained there as Logan stabilized the throttle setting at 150 knots air speed.

Following the path of their target, they had moved off the water and overland, the ocean still visible off to their right. Llewellyn looked back at the scope and saw that the blip was now moving again, its range dropping. The pilot saw it, too, and reduced throttle even more.

"He's slowing down. He must be landing!"

Staring out through the windscreen, Llewellyn could still

see no sign of the helicopter, though the range was down to four miles. "Shouldn't we be able to see him?"

"He's too low," Logan explained. "He's . . . the bugger's landed!"

Llewellyn jerked his head back toward the scope. The blip had disappeared.

29

KAREEM WAS AMAZED at how effectively the huge rocket had been hidden from aerial surveillance. Only by knowing its exact location in advance and using the wooden dock on the small inlet and the overgrown dirt road leading from it as reference points was he able to find it. And it was only when the helicopter had descended to within a few hundred feet of the quarry that his eyes were able to discriminate the mammoth camouflage net that covered it from the surrounding terrain.

The countryside that had looked so deserted moments before came alive as the helicopter touched down. From several different directions, men from the launch site crew converged on the chopper as its engine went quiet and its rotors slowed. The pilot was the first one out, emerging at gunpoint, Kareem just behind him holding his Kalashnikov. He raised his hand in a clenched-fist sign of victory, as the surrounding throng cheered wildly.

Al Saif limped up and the onlookers parted to let him through. Kareem turned the pilot over to one of the other terrorists, and the leader and his chief lieutenant embraced, to further cheers. It was al Saif who pulled away first.

"I must see what you have brought me."

"They're inside. Bring them out, Nestor."

Nestor took three others into the helicopter with him. They emerged shortly, carrying the two cylindrical warheads. The spectators went wild.

"Nerve agent," Nestor exclaimed, beaming proudly, as the cylinders were set down at al Saif's feet. "Ishmael and I took them right out from under the nose of Saddam Hussein." He regretted that his friend, who had masterminded the job, was not here to enjoy this moment.

"Get the other one, Nestor."

Next came the black sphere, still wrapped in its oil-soaked cover. "This one contains micro-organisms, every deadly plague known to man," said Nestor, parroting words he had heard from Ishmael.

There was more cheering, but it was short-lived. A man ran up to al Saif, gesturing excitedly.

"Aircraft approaching, Excellency!"

"You must have been followed!" the leader shouted at the dumbfounded Kareem.

Al Saif turned to the others, his eyes blazing with anger. "Get this vehicle to its hiding place, quickly, as we planned. Then get back under cover, all of you!"

Stout ropes were attached to the helicopter and it was dragged on its skids to a nearby grove of trees. Many hands and a great deal of rocking and jostling were required to settle it among the trees, where extra branches were used to conceal it. The job was no sooner finished than the droning of the approaching aircraft was heard.

Kareem and al Saif were hiding in the trees when the twin-engine plane came into view from out of the west, moving slowly and flying quite low—not more than a few hundred meters up, Kareem estimated. It was heading almost directly over them, and he recognized it immediately.

"That's Logan's plane!" Kareem hissed.

"Who is Logan?" al Saif snapped.

"The pilot who brought the warheads to Bandar Abbas. He was acquainted with the helicopter pilot. He may be looking for him." Kareem trained his AK-47 on the plane overhead.

"No!" Al Saif jerked the muzzle down. "He could not have seen us. Not with all this cover. We cannot take the chance of giving away our location."

They watched the plane until it disappeared, its engine noise no longer audible. Al Saif hurried over to another stand of trees a stone's throw away. Under the protective branches of a large spreading tree stood a contraption with two large black discs arrayed side by side, like giant Mickey Mouse ears.

It was a listening device of the type widely used before the invention of radar, crude, but a big improvement over the unaided ear. Manning it was the man who had spread the warning.

"It has turned around," he announced. "The plane is returning!"

The blue and white plane flew over again, this time somewhat higher and farther to the south. The launch site crew watched and waited, remaining in hiding until the plane had long since passed out of earshot and out of sight.

The "Mickey Mouse" operator removed his headphones. "Gone."

"Let us return to the aircraft." Al Saif led the way back to the clump of trees where the helicopter was hidden. Opening the door on the pilot's side, he peered into the cockpit.

"See that the radio is disabled," he instructed Kareem. "That will insure that no radio signals are sent from here to give away our presence. Where is the pilot?"

"One of your men is guarding him." Seating himself in the cockpit, Kareem reached beneath the instrument panel behind the radio set, jerking out several wires.

"That should do it. What do you want done with the pilot?" He made a slashing sign with his index finger across his throat.

The leader shook his head. "He might be useful to us again. Have him tethered somewhere out of sight and away from the quarry, where he cannot see into it."

They walked into the quarry and stood beneath the camouflage net, Kareem getting his first look at the captured rocket. It was in the process of being lowered on its launcher in preparation for the installation of the warheads. He stopped short and stared, overcome by the immensity of it, marveling at the feat of transporting such a monster thousands of miles across the sea to this hiding place without being caught.

"Where are my warheads?" al Saif asked one of his men.

"Over there. Khan is inspecting them."

The leader walked over to his chief engineer, the elder of the two Pakistanis who had defected from the Saudi missile base at Jabrin. With several helpers he was bent over one of the cylinders, which had been stripped of its heavy canvas wrapping.

"Are they what you expected?" al Saif demanded.

"They are everything we could have hoped for," the beaming Khan replied. "They are self-deploying. We have only to install them in their re-entry vehicle. Some of the existing brackets and adaptors can be utilized for that purpose."

"When will you be finished, if you begin now?"

"By late this evening."

"Then we are ready." Al Saif turned to Kareem and embraced him. "The hour we have worked for for so long is at hand. It is time to send the ultimatum."

The Aero Commander was over the Gulf of Oman again, headed back to Bandar Abbas, its pilot elated over his success in locating the helicopter piloted by his friend. His passengers were somewhat less euphoric.

For the Llewellyns, there had been good news and bad news. The good news was that the point at which the helicopter had disappeared from the radar, presumably close by the terrorist missile base, had been pinned down within a mile or two. The bad news was that in two passes over the area under conditions of ideal visibility, they hadn't been able to detect any sign of the base or the chopper that had set down there. Would a force of strike aircraft, without benefit of a prior reconnaissance, have any better luck finding it?

Daniella planned to call the information in to her control as soon as they landed. She wasn't sure what Shmona's reaction would be. The news that the terrorists had been successful in delivering the warheads to the launch site would certainly not be welcome. On the other hand, the military would now have a much better handle on where to find them.

"I can't wait to tell that A&R Helicopters dispatcher I was right about Hot Shot's chopper being hijacked," Logan exclaimed. "They were planning a search-and-rescue operation over Qeshm Island this morning. They can call that off now."

"What will they do then?" David Llewellyn asked.

"Notify the authorities, I assume."

"You mean the Iranian government? Could they really be expected to take action against Palestinian terrorists?"

"You can bet on it. They may turn their back on acts of terrorism elsewhere, but an unsanctioned crime against Iranis on their own soil is another matter. They'll probably send an army unit in to rescue Hot Shot and shut down the terrorists."

Llewellyn was disturbed. Any precipitous action that threatened the terrorists could trigger the launch of the missile, now that they had the warheads.

"I'm not sure you fully realize the kind of outfit we're dealing with here, Al. These people are pros, and they're also fanatics. If they sense that someone's closing in, they could shoot off their rocket at the drop of a hat."

The pilot shrugged. "The same thing can happen if the Israelis try a commando raid or an air strike. I'm worried about Hot Shot. At least if the Iranians go in, there's a chance they can get him out alive. And they know the territory. Maybe they can sneak up on the terrorists."

David caught the look from Daniella. Informing the Iran authorities could be a disaster. He had to talk Logan out of it. "If you were about to be on the receiving end of that terrorist rocket payload, would you trust the Iranis to do this right? I'm sure the people of Tel Aviv wouldn't. That's one reason the Israelis didn't broach the matter to Iran, even after there was strong evidence the missile was here. They were afraid that Iran's interference might precipitate the very disaster they're trying to avoid. It's the Israelis who have the most to lose here. We have to give them the opportunity to take charge of their own fate."

The pilot didn't answer immediately, mulling over what he had just heard.

"You're asking that I hold the information back, not tell Hot Shot's employer that we know what happened to him?"

"I'm asking you to honor the pledge you made not to divulge what we told you in confidence about the terrorist operation."

"But if I don't tell them the whole story, they could go barging in to Baluchistan on a rescue operation and get their tails shot off."

"Exactly. So it's better not to tell them anything, for the moment."

"And let them go on searching for him in the wrong place?"

"For the moment, yes."

"I'm not sure I can do that."

Daniella got into the discussion with a question of her own. "What does this search-and-rescue operation entail? I mean, how do they go about finding the downed plane?"

"The A&R choppers carry emergency radio beacons. They turn on automatically when the chopper sustains heavy Gs, like it would in a crash landing. Or the pilot can turn it on after an emergency landing."

"And anyone with a radio receiver can pick it up?" David asked. "You could pick it up on your radio?"

"Not on my radio, no. It takes a special Search and Rescue set with a directional antenna to determine the bearing. Most of the choppers in the A&R fleet have them.

"I hate to think of all those ships out there flying around for nothing," he continued. "And Hot Shot has a new family, a young wife with a baby. I have to tell her something."

"What would you say to her that would comfort her?" Llewellyn challenged. "That her husband is safe? You can't tell her that, can you? Would she feel any better to know that her husband is in the hands of a sect of ruthless murderers? Better to let her go on believing that he's only missing and may still be found alive."

"That was blunt enough."

"Sorry. But we've got to face facts. Maybe your friend will get out of this and maybe he won't, but his fate is not in our hands. It's in the hands of the same madman who has his finger on a button that can send sudden death raining down on a city two thousand miles away."

They left the plane and walked into the terminal together, the Llewellyns still unsure of Logan's intentions. Daniella had at least extracted the promise from him to let her make her call and touch home base before doing anything. She had the impression that he was still undecided.

The pilot led her to the phone and helped her put her call through, speaking to the operator and reading off the number she showed him in Farsi. It was the dummy number in Canada that would access the special hook-up arranged by Shmona.

Her control came on the line sounding somewhat breathless and more agitated than she was accustomed to. "Daniella!

We've all been waiting! What's happened? Did you have any success?"

"Yes, Baruch, some." She quickly related the circumstances of the morning flight into Baluchistan and the eventual radar contact with the helicopter carrying the terrorists and their deadly cargo. "We have the approximate position at which the helicopter landed. The pilot says it is accurate to within two nautical miles."

She read off the latitude and longitude Logan had written down for her. "But Baruch, in two passes over the area we couldn't see any sign of the missile base. They've got it very well hidden."

"Good work, Daniella. Hold on for a minute. I want to pass this along to some military people who are with me."

He left the phone and she could hear his voice in the background mingling with others. Within a minute, he was back.

"Daniella, you've done a great job. But we've got a problem here. My military people insist that they need a more precise location. You know, an actual sighting of the terrorist base. We need you to return and have another look. Can you do that?"

"I don't know, Baruch. I'm not sure the pilot will agree. And I can't promise we would have any better success."

"But you must try, Daniella." She could hear the strain in his voice; he had to be under heavy pressure. "And it must be done without delay."

"Just a moment." She relayed the order to her companions. Llewellyn reserved comment, waiting for the pilot's reaction.

"So they *are* planning an air strike," Logan surmised. "Tell them a return trip would be futile. We had a good look the first time, under ideal weather and visibility conditions. We won't see any more than we did before."

"Baruch, the pilot is unwilling to go back. He believes it would be futile."

"Daniella, you've got to make the pilot understand. Something has just happened here that puts us in a desperate time bind—an ultimatum has been received from the terrorists giving us twenty-four hours to evacuate the occupied territories; otherwise, the missile will be unleashed against one of our cities."

"Twenty-four hours?" Daniella was flabbergasted. "But Baruch, that's impossible . . ."

"Of course it is. And sending in a military reconnaissance plane, they tell me, is not advisable. It would take five hours to get there, and we're afraid a military plane might spook the terrorists into launching early. Now do you understand why you're being ordered back for another try?"

"Yes. Of course. May I repeat what you've just told me to the pilot?"

"Do whatever you must, just so you persuade him."

"Hold on."

Her companions had overhead her end of the conversation. "An ultimatum from the terrorists?" Llewellyn guessed. He saw her nod. "Twenty-four hours for what?"

"For Israel to evacuate the occupied territories."

"There's no way! So they're going to launch it. We're down to the end game."

He looked at Logan. "There's no choice. We have to go back."

The pilot just stared at him. "What's the point? We won't see anything more than we did before."

"Maybe we'll get lucky."

Logan shrugged. "I suppose we have to try," he said resignedly.

David grasped his hand while Daniella reported back to Shmona. "He wants to know when he can expect to hear from us again."

The pilot considered. "An hour to refuel, two hours each way. Five hours at the earliest."

She relayed the answer and signed off.

"We can get a bite to eat while the plane is being refueled," Logan suggested. "There's a cafeteria downstairs."

The A&R Helicopters office stood at the head of the stairs. The pilot paused in front of the office door. "I need to touch base with these people. I'll meet you in the cafeteria."

Daniella's concerned eyes sought her husband's. "I don't think he'll tell them now," David whispered in her ear. They descended the stairs and went through the cafeteria line. As they were setting down their trays on a table, Logan joined them. He looked troubled.

"The air-rescue operation is in high gear," he reported. "They've got four choppers out looking for Hot Shot."

"What did you tell them?" Llewellyn asked.

"Not a bloody thing. They thought I was there to volunteer my services. They offered to install an air-rescue radio set in my plane."

"That's not a bad idea." Llewellyn wondered why it hadn't occurred to him before, a way to pinpoint the location of the terrorists. The pilot was looking at him quizzically.

"Al, put yourself in your friend's place," he went on excitedly. "If he had to make a forced landing somewhere, he'd turn on his air-rescue beacon, wouldn't he?"

"Certainly. He'd know that his A&R mates would be out looking for him."

"So he's made a different kind of 'forced landing' in Baluchistan. Maybe he'll still turn it on."

Logan looked dubious. "I don't know why. Not much chance they'd be looking for him there."

"He could have seen your plane when we flew over. Does he know you *don't* have an air-rescue set on board?"

The pilot shook his head. "No way for him to know that."

"How long would it take them to install this gadget in your plane?"

"An hour or so, I guess. It could be done while they're refueling." Logan stroked his lantern jaw thoughtfully. "It's a long shot. But we'll give it a try. Long shots seem to be about all we've got."

The emergency meeting of his cabinet had been going on for more than an hour in the Prime Minister's West Jerusalem residence. He had just cut off the strident and at times emotional debate that had raged among them since his revelation of the terrorist ultimatum. The tight-lipped group now hung on his words as he presented his proposal for dealing with the emergency.

The Prime Minister was making a special effort to appear cool and unruffled. He had to set an example, make a statement with his behavior as well as his tongue.

"I have heard some panicky talk here this morning. Panic is our worst enemy at a time like this. Let us remember that our country has faced worse crises than this and pulled through.

"There is no real cause for alarm. Thanks to the preparations we have made for just such a contingency, the situation is under control. In a moment I will review with you the plan that the Defense Minister and I have worked out to cope with this crisis. But first I want to deal with what I think may be the most difficult challenge that we face: keeping the lid on this situation, preventing news of the ultimatum from leaking out and causing wholesale panic in the streets of Tel Aviv.

"We have been fortunate so far that the ultimatum was delivered to a single source, the Jerusalem *Post,* no doubt with the anticipation that it would be broadcast to the world. But recognizing the sensitivity and potential for mass hysteria, the publisher brought it directly to me and has agreed to sit on the story for twenty-four hours. I want the assurance from each one of you that you will not divulge this information to anyone when you leave here—not to your friends, not even to your families. Is this agreed?"

"What about the Knesset?" a cabinet member interrupted. "Will they be informed?"

"Telling the Knesset would be like telling a gossipy yenta."

The Prime Minister's quip broke the tension, eliciting laughter. He returned to his notes.

"Here, in brief, is our plan. Number one—I propose to go through the motions of complying with the demand that we withdraw our forces from the occupied territories. We will do this to buy time."

He turned to the Defense Secretary. "I want the Palestinians to see trucks filled with soldiers rolling out of every major garrison in the West Bank and Gaza before dusk today. See to it, please."

"No!" shouted a shocked cabinet member. "You can't leave our settlers unprotected. They'll be massacred!"

"I said 'go through the motions,' Eli. We will leave a skeleton force in place at each garrison. They will be ordered to remain out of sight. Number two—we will mount a preemptive air strike against the terrorist missile base in southeastern Iran, to depart no later than 0300 hours tomorrow, fifteen hours from now."

"That could be a mistake," another member of the cabinet objected. "If our planes are detected by the terrorists, they will launch their rocket."

"They will eventually launch it anyway if we don't stop them," the Prime Minister countered. "Which brings us to number three—ballistic missile defense. In the event that our air strike proves unsuccessful, our Patriot and Hawk missile batteries are prepared to deal with this terrorist missile. They have already been placed on indefinite alert. Before our strike aircraft are scrambled, the special ballistic missile defense network we have set up to handle this threat will be fully activated.

"Number four—we will announce a special one-day civil defense drill in Tel Aviv, starting at 5:00 P.M. today. All civil defense workers will be pressed into immediate service. Gas masks will be distributed, and the emergency treatment centers will prepare to receive casualties. It will be billed as a kind of dress rehearsal for the real thing. All available city police units will be placed on extended duty to take part."

Several cabinet members nodded in agreement. "Good cover story," enthused one.

"That completes my summary," the Prime Minister concluded. "Before taking questions, let me remind all of you, once again, of your pledge of silence on this matter. You hold the lives of thousands of our people in your hands."

The Defense Secretary excused himself from the group, alluding to the pressing tasks ahead of him. The Mossad director also rose and walked out with him.

"I'll be reviewing the air strike plan with General Tuchler shortly, Mordechai," the Defense Secretary remarked. "What are your chances of getting us a better fix on the launch site location?"

"We're sending one of our agents back over the area for another look," Shilo responded. "But I wouldn't bank on it."

"I keep wondering which of our options we *can* bank on," the other confided. "Let's hope the Patriot is one."

"There's no way we could saturation-bomb a four-square-mile area, even if we had B-52s!" General Barkai, the Air

Force chief faced his boss, General Tuchler, across the latter's desk in Akirya, Tel Aviv, Israel's "Pentagon."

"Then what are you planning do?" the Chief of Staff responded patiently.

"If we don't get an actual sighting of the target or a more accurate location, we'll have to rely on our night-vision equipment, our infrared sensors, to find the damn thing."

"Night vision? You're going in before sunrise?"

"It's our best chance to avoid detection. If they see us coming, it's all over."

"Won't they see you anyway, before you get close enough to drop your bombs?"

"Yes, if we relied exclusively on bombs. We're planning on using our new 'smart' standoff weapons—IR-guided air-to-surface missiles. Hopefully, they'll reach the target and destroy it before the terrorists sight our planes and have time to launch."

"What are the chances your infrared sensors will find the target?"

Barkai shrugged. "I wish I knew. We've never tested them against this kind of target, a ballistic missile launch complex. The missile itself can't be expected to be much of an IR target in its quiescent state. But the terrorists must have some heat sources around their missile—electric generators, that sort of thing. I've got some people looking at the East Wind launcher to see what kind of IR signature we might expect."

"How big a force will you take in?"

"We're planning on less than a full F-16 squadron—eight planes. That should be more than enough, except they may not all get there. It's by far the longest mission we've ever attempted, more than three thousand kilometers each way. We'll have to refuel them in both directions over Saudi Arabia. I understand that's being worked out with the Saudis?"

Tuchler nodded. "We're asking that a special air corridor be set up for us. A one-time arrangement. Do you have a departure time worked out yet?"

"10:00 P.M. With refueling and all, it's around five hours to target."

"I assume you'll be leading the strike personally?"

Barkai's eyes narrowed. "Is that an order, sir?"

"No, no, I just thought—"

"Colonel Shani will be leading the strike. He's the best, much better qualified than I."

"Of course, as you wish."

"I'll be participating in the planning and preparation, of course. And in the briefing of the pilots. I'm off to Ramat David as soon as we're concluded here."

"Do your pilots know what they're going after?"

"Not yet. They won't be told what their objective is until the final briefing before takeoff."

"Good, good. I'll let you go, then." General Tuchler stood up and held out his hand.

"I know it sounds trite, but good luck."

"It's not trite, sir. It's not trite at all. It's what this mission needs more than any we've ever launched."

30

IT WAS LATE afternoon when the procession of open army trucks issued from the gate in the barbed-wire enclosure surrounding the Israeli Military Command compound in Hebron. Moving slowly past the courthouse, they turned north onto Mailak Abdullah, bound for Route 60 to Bethlehem and Jerusalem. The soldiers filling the trucks were in good spirits, their jubilation evident over leaving this strife-torn corner of the West Bank and heading for the big city.

As they passed the town hall, people on both sides of the street turned and looked on in silence. A young boy who had just exited the museum stared after the trucks until they were out of sight, then ran to the corner and jumped on a bus.

Fifteen minutes later the same youth got off the bus at Kiryat Arba, the Jewish settlement at the outskirts of town, and ran all the way to his apartment. He burst through the door.

"Father! Father! The soldiers are leaving!"

His father looked up from the newspaper he was reading. "Leaving? Nonsense. What makes you think so?"

"I saw them! I counted seven trucks. There must have been eighteen or twenty to a truck. They were going north, toward Jerusalem."

His father put down the paper. "What you saw was only a rotation of forces, my son. They do it all the time. Soldiers based here are rotated to other locations periodically and replaced with other soldiers. The same trucks you saw must have already brought their replacements in and unloaded them."

He smiled reassuringly at his son. "Enough of this. Have you finished your homework for tomorrow?"

"Not yet." The boy gave him a rueful look.

"Then you'd better run to your room and get it done."

As soon as the youth had disappeared, his father picked up the phone and dialed a number.

"Yehoshua, what do you know about the troop pullout? Yes, my son saw them. Seven trucks, twenty to a truck. That's almost the entire garrison.

"There's been no hint that this was coming from our friends in the government, has there? I thought not. We'd better get the committee together, Yehoshua, and consider what to do. If they don't send replacements soon, we can count on big trouble.

"You weren't here in 1980, were you? It was a debacle. We can't ever let ourselves be caught by surprise like that again."

Al Saif had just awakened from a brief late afternoon siesta to find his chief engineer standing before him.

"Our work is completed, Excellency. The warheads have been installed and we are about to replace the nose cone. I thought perhaps you would like to inspect it before we do so."

"By all means." The terrorist leader rose and walked with the Pakistani to the far end of the trailer-launcher cradling the immense missile, which had been lowered to its prone position. Its massive white tip had been removed and was resting nearby. Climbing atop the trailer, al Saif stood on his tiptoes and peered inside the open end of the missile's forward fuselage. This was the "bus" that carried the warheads, Khan had explained, the payload end of the missile that would detach itself from the spent rocket after burnout and coast on through outer space, ultimately reaching the re-entry point and disgorging its cargo.

The interior of the "bus" was dark and there was little to be seen other than the blunt nose of a re-entry vehicle. But al Saif had earlier witnessed the installation of one of the yellow-green cylinders containing the ultra-lethal binary nerve agent into the RV and knew that the other two warheads had been similarly installed, including the black sphere housing the deadly strains of disease-imparting microbes and viruses.

"A varied menu—something for everyone." Kareem had joined the leader and was staring over his shoulder.

"Yes. But there is a missing ingredient—something to give it a personal touch." Al Saif removed a chain from around his neck from which a tiny gold and silver sword dangled, a replacement for the one he had lost during the hijacking. He handed it to his Pakistani foreman.

"I wish to return this to its owner in Tel Aviv. Can you find a place for it in your nose cone?"

Khan grinned and nodded, taking the item from him. "It will be sealed inside and deployed with the warheads."

Kareem also smiled at the leader's jest, appreciating its grim irony. He, too, felt only contempt for the Jewish financier who had unknowingly funded the terrorist rocket project. Malamud had acted out of the basest of motives, personal greed. The settlements in the West Bank that had enriched him were a cancer inflicted on its Palestinian inhabitants. Kareem was sorry he had warned the financier to steer clear of Tel Aviv. He deserved to die.

He fingered the sword amulet suspended from the chain around his own neck. Whatever its origins, it had brought him luck. He decided to keep it.

The radioman ran up with a message for al Saif. It had been sent in code from the Sword of Islam brother in East Jerusalem who had delivered the ultimatum that same morning. The leader read the message aloud.

"The Israeli Defense Forces appear to be pulling out of occupied Judea, Samaria, and Gaza. Our people report large truck convoys of troops departing from Nablus, Ramallah, Hebron, Jericho, and Bethlehem, as well as from garrisons in the Gaza Strip. These garrisons now appear deserted."

A loud cheer erupted from those within earshot. Kareem looked at them scornfully.

"Fools—don't you smell a trick? The message says nothing about settlers leaving."

"If the soldiers stay away, we can handle the settlers," al Saif observed. "But I am inclined to agree. The 'feint' is an old army trick, well known to our Zionist enemies. They can return as quickly as they departed."

He handed the message back to the radioman. "What has

been the reaction to our ultimatum? Wholesale panic in the Zionist city?"

"I have no report on that, Excellency."

"Send an inquiry, immediately. I—"

He was arrested by the beeping sound from the direction of the aircraft warning station. Al Saif limped out of the quarry toward the listening station, Kareem beside him. The operator met him halfway.

"A single plane approaching from the west, Excellency."

"Get everyone out of sight!" the leader shouted. He ordered the operator back to his post and returned with Kareem to the cover of the camouflage net, squinting through it at the bright western sky where the sun was preparing to set.

"There it is!" Kareem pointed to a speck silhouetted against the brilliant firmament. Their eyes followed it, unable to pick out any distinguishing features until it came closer and moved out of the sun's influence, on a course that would take it well south of the launch site. A crewman ran up with a pair of binoculars. Al Saif handed them to Kareem. "Your eyes are better than mine."

"It's Logan's plane again," Kareem spat. "He must have located our base."

"On the contrary." The leader smiled back at him, his voice calm. "If he had already found us, why would he return? He is still searching. The fact that he came back proves that he did not see us the first time. And he had several good opportunities, too, passing almost directly over us.

"He isn't going to find us. We are too well hidden."

Hot Shot had recognized Logan's plane immediately, without any need for binoculars. The venerable Aero Commander with its high wing was unique. He had seen it fly over the first time that same morning, and had instantly known that his old friend was out searching for him. It had given him a ray of hope to cling to. If Lockjaw had spotted the terrorist base, a rescue operation could be underway.

He had immediately set about trying to find a way to free himself. When al Saif had instructed his men to put the helicopter pilot on a tether, they had taken him literally. Hot Shot was in a small stand of trees not far from the one where his chopper was hidden, his wrists handcuffed behind his back and a rope tied around his neck, its other end secured to the trunk of a tree at a point too high for him to reach. His feet were free; he could walk around, but there was no place to go. The rope was scarcely a dozen feet long.

He reminded himself of a dog tied up in its yard. Except that nobody had showed up to throw him a bone, or even give him a bowl of water. They seemed to have forgotten about him. He was quite a distance from the opening into the quarry, where most of the activity seemed to be centered, too far away to see inside of it. Watching workers move in and out of the quarry, he sensed that something nefarious was going on there, though he had no clue to what it might be. Something they didn't want him to see; something life threatening, he felt sure—especially to him.

Almost from the first moment, he had cast about for a way to escape from his dog leash. The rope that held him was not that heavy; winding it several times about his wrist to take the pressure off his neck, he tried to break it by stretching it taut and leaning all his weight against it. It refused to snap. After falling down three times in the process, he gave up on that approach.

He walked back toward the tree, letting the rope go slack, and inspected it. It was composed of three strands. If he could somehow saw through two of them, the other could probably be snapped. He thought of something that might work.

Walking around the tree, he wound the rope around its trunk. It took him several tries to master the technique of allowing just the right amount of slack so that one of the windings encircled the trunk at the same level as his hands. With his back to the tree, he began to rub the rough metal ring that joined the two bracelets of the handcuffs against the rope, rocking his wrists up and down with a sawing motion.

It was slow, hard work; before long his wrists began to ache. While he rested them, he turned around to inspect the damage done to the rope. He could see the beginnings of a notch in one of the strands, and it gave him the incentive to continue.

It seemed to take forever before the first strand parted. He continued to saw away at the one behind it. This one went faster, the groove formed by the parted strand helping to keep the pressure focussed at a single point. He felt the second strand give and continued sawing into the remaining one. When he sensed that he was far enough through it that his weight would snap it, he unwound the rope from the tree, again winding it around his wrists, and walked away from the tree until the line was taut. The minute he leaned against it, it parted.

His first thought was to get to the helicopter. He realized that there was no way that he could escape in it; he was incapable of dragging it out of the woods, let alone piloting it with his hands cuffed behind him. But if he could manage to turn the radio on, he could send out a Mayday signal.

Glancing around to make sure that he wasn't observed, he ran across the short span of open ground to reach the helicopter. His hands made the blind connection with the door latch and in a flash he was in the cockpit. From countless hours of flying, he could have found the radio switch in the dark. His back to the instrument panel, he groped for it with his fingers and switched it on.

There was no response, the characteristic hum of the radio not audible. He turned and saw that the pilot light had not come on. Then he saw why—wires hanging down from the instrument panel that had been pulled out of the radio unit. Reconnecting them with his cuffed hands was out of the question.

What if he was discovered here? Suddenly feeling very vulnerable, he left the cockpit and hurried back to his tether tree. He matched up the two loose ends of rope and sat down on top of them so that anyone passing by would not see the break. He needed time to catch his breath and think.

The idea of trying to escape into this wilderness with his hands cuffed behind him and no food or water was not attractive. He was already dying of thirst. Surely they would bring him some water soon. And some food. He could smell something cooking. It must be close to dinnertime.

He was still sitting on the rope when he heard the commotion around the quarry, then the sound of the plane. When he saw that it was Lockjaw again, his first reaction was disappointment. There was no rescue expedition on the way. His friend had come back to do some more searching.

He watched Logan's plane fly past, farther away than it had been on the previous passes. His first impulse was to run out into the open and wave his arms, but the plane was too far away to see him. Like they said in blindman's buff, he was getting colder.

His company must be looking for him too, Hot Shot realized, mounting an air-rescue effort as they always did for one of their downed pilots. They would have started their search at Qeshm Island, but Lockjaw would have told them—

The thought hit him like the impact of a bullet, and he kicked himself for not thinking of it sooner. Now was the time, while the terrorists were preoccupied with the plane. He bolted back across the space between the two groves of trees.

Inside the cockpit, he backed up to the instrument panel again, his hands finding a different switch. He flipped it on.

This time his ears were rewarded with a distinct though subdued hum. He turned around. A pilot light on the instrument panel glowed red. The decal beside it read: AIR RESCUE BEACON.

Logan banked the Aero Commander sharply to begin another pass over the area where Hot Shot's helicopter had disappeared from his radar hours earlier. He was feeling discouraged. On the flight here he had persuaded himself that his newly installed air-rescue device would detect the beacon in Hot Shot's chopper and give them its precise location. The direction-finding radio was turned on and tuned to the proper frequency, but there had been no response from it.

The first pass over the area had been no more successful than its precursors in spotting the terrorist launch site. Craning their necks to help find it, the Llewellyns had also come up empty. The second, four-hour round-trip from Bandar Abbas was turning into a classic example of a wild-goose chase.

He leveled out and started back across the area again, using his binoculars to try to pick out what they were looking for. The Llewellyns were using binoculars, too, this time; they had brought along two extra pairs. The trouble was that their field of view was too small; you had to know just where to look to find anything with them. And the vibration of the aircraft made them shake; it was hard to keep them trained on the same point.

"Nothing?" he asked, as the pass was completed. They shook their heads and he saw his own disappointment reflected in their eyes. It was questionable in his mind whether they should continue this much longer. If the terrorists were, indeed, down there, the overflights were certain to make them nervous. He had discussed this with the others on the way out. If it made them too nervous, they might conceivably launch the missile ahead of the schedule laid down in the ultimatum.

"How much longer . . . ?" Logan never finished the question. A buzzing in his headset had told him that the air-rescue device had detected a radio source in its frequency band.

"Hot Shot! There he is! Good lad!" He went into another banking one-eighty and leveled out again, fiddling with the dials on the air-rescue unit control box clamped to the underside of his instrument panel. A small cathode-ray tube set into its front panel showed a bright strobe line extending from its center outward, at about the eleven o'clock position. This was the relative bearing to the radio beacon, the length of the strobe a measure of its distance from his aircraft.

"We'll make one more pass. Last chance to spot the rocket base." He corrected his heading so that the strobe line pointed to twelve o'clock. This would bring him directly over the beacon. His passengers had their binoculars trained on the terrain ahead of the aircraft. "You take the right side," Llewellyn suggested. "I'll take the left."

Logan confined his attention to the air-rescue display. The length of the green line grew progressively shorter as the range to the beacon continued to drop. He switched to the minimum-range scale and it doubled in length, then began to shrink again.

"I see something!" Adjacent to a large outcropping of rock, Llewellyn's binoculars had picked up an anomalous patch of terrain that was neither rock nor sand and did not quite match any of the surrounding vegetation. He kept the glasses trained on it as long as possible, moving back into the cabin to follow it through a side window until it disappeared under the left wing, just as the pilot called "Mark!"

The plane had passed directly over the beacon, the strobe

line on the display reversing itself, now beginning to stretch out at the six o'clock position. Logan had entered a fix in his navigation computer at the instant the strobe swung over.

"What was it?" he asked Llewellyn. "What did you see?"

"I'm not sure. Something man-made, I think—not natural. Can we go back for another look?"

The pilot concurred. "It's on our way back anyway. But we don't want them getting trigger-happy. I'm going to delay turning for a few minutes so they won't think we're on to them. When we do go back, I'll overfly the beacon again. I want to estimate the distance of this man-made thing of yours from the beacon. I'll try to get a look at it, too."

The pilot performed another one-eighty, lined the beacon up at twelve o'clock, and put the plane on autopilot. Llewellyn pointed ahead, off to the right of the plane. "See that huge chunk of rock sticking up? Look just on the other side of it." Three pairs of binoculars focussed on the area as the plane flew past.

"I see it!" Daniella shouted excitedly.

"Camouflage!" Llewellyn and Logan spoke the word simultaneously.

"How far off do you make it?" the pilot asked.

"You'd be the expert on that, but it's less than a football field."

"Seventy to eighty yards due north of the beacon," Logan agreed. "That's important information if your lads are going to try to bomb it. An eighty-yard miss with an iron bomb is as good as a mile."

Logan had learned a bit about weapon delivery from a stint in the Royal Air Force. He was pleased with the turn of events. If Hot Shot was in or near his chopper, as the sudden turning on of the beacon suggested, his chances of surviving a bombing attack would be considerably improved if the bombers were aiming eighty yards away.

But he also knew that the position fix he had taken on his navigation system was not good enough to bomb from. Short of sighting the target visually, the Israeli strike force would need a rock-solid reference point. They'd better pray that the beacon was still turned on when they went after the terrorist rocket.

• • •

The briefing room resembled a college lecture hall, the F-16 pilots sitting in wooden chairs with writing arms, pencils poised to take notes. But none of the pencils were writing at the moment. The pilots looked stunned, staring wide-eyed at their wing commander, Col. Dov Shani. He had just revealed to them the nature of their hastily scheduled mission, where it would take them, and the target they were going after.

General Barkai remained in the background. This was Shani's show and he had every confidence in the colonel's ability to handle it. Shani had planned the entire affair and would personally lead the strike, having picked seven of his best pilots to fly with him. If anybody could get the job done, he could. But from the beginning, Barkai hadn't liked the odds.

True, the chances had improved with the input received several hours ago from the Mossad, if it could be relied upon. According to the advisory, agents searching the target area in a light plane had seen what they believed to be the camouflaged launch site of the terrorist missile. They had reported its approximate position with a presumed accuracy to the nearest mile.

That news in itself was not that electrifying; the one-mile accuracy was not good enough for a blind weapons run. The F-16s would still have to rely on their night-vision equipment to find the target when they got there, and the study Barkai had ordered on the IR characteristics of a quiescent East Wind missile on its launcher had been disappointing. It was apparently not a very promising infrared target.

But there had been another more promising part to the Mossad message. An air-rescue marker beacon in a downed helicopter had been observed some seventy meters due south of the target. If the distance was accurate and if the beacon remained on the air, it could be used by the F-16 pilots to put their ordnance right on the money. Barkai's materiel man had been able to lay his hands on some compatible air-rescue radio sets and Col. Shani had installed them in his F-16s, tuned to the frequency reported by the Mossad. He was presently briefing his pilots on their use.

Barkai only hoped that it wasn't all for nothing. Three

thousand kilometers was a long way to fly to discover that the beacon was no longer functioning and the night-vision equipment incapable of acquiring the target. And there was the frightening added possibility that the terrorists would detect the approach of the bombers and get off their shot before the attack could be pressed home.

To minimize the chances of the latter happening, the plan was to utilize standoff weapons that would reach the target well ahead of the attacking aircraft, before they came into visual range. A "smart" air-to-surface missile, an improved *Have Nap* standoff weapon, relatively new in the Israeli inventory, had seemed ideal for the purpose. Its imaging infrared head recorded the picture of the target area as seen by the missile; a data link relayed the image back to the aircraft, where it was displayed to the pilot. By moving cross-hairs on his display, the pilot could send commands to the missile to correct its aimpoint, achieving delivery accuracies comparable to iron bombs, though launched from ten miles away. Each F-16 would carry one, in addition to its back-up supply of bombs.

Col. Shani was now covering this in his briefing, Barkai saw. At least Shani's pilots had all had training in the use of the new weapon. What they hadn't had training in was flying a ten-hour mission, with two in-flight fuelings along the way. Few if any fighter pilots in the world had done that. There were going to be some bone-weary fliers in tomorrow's debriefing—*if* they made it both ways without aborting.

The meteorologist was on now, giving his weather brief. It would be Barkai's turn next, to have the final word, tell the pilots something inspiring before sending them on their way. What would he say to them? What could you say to those from whom you were asking the impossible?

You could level with them. When he was called on, he began his speech with that as his theme.

"Gentlemen, we are asking the impossible of you tonight. It is not the first time that your country has asked this of its front-line defenders. Israel's short, beleaguered history is one of being underdogs, facing overwhelming odds, somehow achieving the impossible. From the War of Independence down through all the other wars in our continual struggle for survival, a few brave men have made the difference. Now it is your turn.

"Our country can never yield to blackmail; it never has, it never will. But these terrorists mean business, and they are professionals; let us not underestimate them. If you do not find this rocket and smash it, it will be sent crashing into our biggest city, to unleash its unspeakable chemicals and pestilence on our people. We know for a fact that its nose cone contains cylinders of the most lethal nerve gas known, plus a bacteriological weapon with strains of deadly disease that could leave our city contaminated for years and spread to other parts of Israel. The lives and welfare of thousands upon thousands of our people rest on your shoulders.

"You have one important advantage; the terrorists will not expect you to come calling. They believe they are safe from our planes, that our air power could never reach so far. Are they in for a surprise?"

"Yes!" shouted the pilots, to a man, fired up by the general's words.

"Are you going to accomplish the impossible tonight?"

Another chorus of yesses, louder than the first.

"Your mission this night will make history," he concluded. "God be with you. God guide your way."

31

AL SAIF AWOKE and looked at the luminous dial on his watch. It was not quite three in the morning. He lay back but he couldn't sleep. He had an uneasy feeling that something wasn't right.

Slipping into his army fatigues and boots, he limped out of the quarry. His first stop was the command post hidden in the rocks on high ground behind the quarry. This was the control station from which the missile would be launched, a safe distance away from the rocket blast. It was kept manned at all times. His chief engineer had the early morning watch.

Khan was alert and wide awake, using a pen light to illuminate a sheet of figures he was poring over.

"What are you doing?" al Saif demanded.

"Just re-checking the inertial guidance instructions programmed into the missile."

"They were in error?"

"No. They check out perfectly."

"Everything is all right, then—nothing amiss?"

"Nothing amiss here, Excellency."

The only other night watch was at the location of the aircraft listening device. Al Saif went there next. The equipment was operating; he could tell by the rotation of the giant black "ears" as they slowly swept out a search pattern centered at a generally west direction. But the operator had fallen down on the job. His headphones were in place, but his chin was resting on his chest. He had nodded off.

Al Saif drew a knife from the pocket of his fatigues, its long blade flashing in the moonlight. He held the point of the knife to the operator's throat.

"Wake up," he hissed.

The man awoke, terror-stricken, recoiling from the knife, his hand clutching his throat. "A thousand pardons, Excellency! It will not happen again!"

"If it *does,* you will feel more than just the point of my blade. Your blood will stain the ground red."

His route back to the quarry took him past the stand of trees where the helicopter was hidden. As he walked by, he heard a faint but unmistakable humming sound that seemed to be coming from the flying machine. He walked over to investigate, unlatching the door.

The red light on the instrument panel hit him right in the eye. In the dark, he couldn't read the words written on the plaque alongside it, but he knew it was trouble. He threw the switch next to the light. It went out, and the humming ceased.

"That accursed pilot!" He left the helicopter and drew his knife again, limping toward the nearby grove of trees where the pilot was tethered . . . But he wasn't there. The moonlight revealed the rope still tied to the tree, its frayed opposite end lying on the ground. The pilot had escaped . . .

Before he could sound the alarm, the man he had awakened at the controls of the aircraft listening device came running up.

"Excellency, come quickly!"

"What is it?"

"Planes approaching!"

"Planes? More than one?"

"I think so, Excellency. I will know after further listening. There could be many!"

In the lead F-16, some fifty miles from his target, Col. Shani rejoiced when he saw the strobe line pop onto the monitor of his newly installed air-rescue radio set. He had been warned not to count on the ground beacon, but there it was! It should make his job a lot easier.

The standoff air-to-surface missile attached to the inboard pylon of his F-16 packed a real wallop with its 750-pound high-explosive warhead. The *Have Nap*'s rocket booster gave it several distinct advantages over the glide bombs it was replacing in the Israeli and U.S. inventories: it could be launched from much farther away, at lower altitudes, and the launching aircraft could continue on toward the target without overtaking it.

But Shani was worried about how strong a heat source the unlaunched East Wind rocket would turn out to be, or whether it would even show up on his electro-optical display, where the picture generated by the imaging infrared sensor in the nose of his *Have Nap* missile was presented. Now the beacon not only told him where to look for the target; it could be used as an offset-aim point for his standoff missile as well as his bombs, in case no usable infrared image of the target materialized.

He set his mode selector switch to the offset position and instructed his fellow pilots to do likewise. The seventy-meter offset between beacon and target reported by Israeli intelligence had been programmed into the weapon delivery computer; a cursor now appeared on his display at the predicted target position. There was still no sign of any imagery at this spot, even though the infrared head of his missile was up and operating. Hopefully that would change as they got closer.

Shani corrected his heading to move the cursor into the center of the display, aligning it with the boresight of the standoff missile. Range to target, measured off the ground beacon, was now down to thirty miles. The plan called for the standoff missiles to be launched at twenty miles, whether the target image appeared or not. To approach any closer would risk visual detection of the *Have Nap* launch plumes. As the missile closed on the target and the amount of irradiance increased, there was a good chance the infrared image would eventually show up. If not, the missile would continue to be guided to the cursor offset position and they would have to pray that the information provided by the Mossad had been accurate.

When the range dropped to twenty miles, Shani released his missile.

"Fox One!"

A chorus of echoes ensued in his headset as his seven companions acknowledged they had followed suit.

• • •

Awakened by a nearby footfall, Hot Shot had witnessed the man with the limp entering the helicopter and knew what was coming. He immediately went into hiding, scurrying off into the cover of some nearby shrubs, where he could observe what happened next.

The limping man came out of the chopper really steamed, and Hot Shot pushed further down into the weeds as the man headed in his direction, brandishing one of the biggest knives he had ever seen. When he heard a shout, he raised his head and saw another man run up, then the two of them run off together. He came out of his hiding place and moved toward the helicopter.

The humming was no longer audible. The beacon had been turned off. He opened the door and clambered inside, backing into the cockpit and straddling the seat with his legs, so that his hands could reach the instrument panel. His fingers felt the beacon on-off switch. He turned it back on.

Backing out of the helicopter, he pushed the door closed with his head, hearing the latch click.

"Miserable dog!"

He swung around to see the terrorist leader standing there, his face contorted with rage, his right hand poised to deliver a blow with the giant blade.

"Die, dog. *Die.*"

Al Saif slashed at him with the knife. Hot Shot tried to dodge the blow but wasn't quick enough. The blade entered the right side of his abdomen, just below the rib cage, and he went down.

Kareem arrived on the run. "What is going on?"

"This miserable infidel has given away our position! We are being attacked by a host of planes!"

Al Saif rushed back to the command post. Despite the leader's disability, Kareem could barely keep up with him.

"Fire!" the leader shouted to his chief engineer.

The Pakistani looked at him in disbelief. "But Excellency, the men have not had time to clear the area. We must wait for—"

"No! We will not wait another second! Fire, I command you!"

SCIMITAR

The terrorist leader still held the knife in his hand with the pilot's blood on it. Khan swallowed and reached for the master arm switch. It took both his hands to activate the series of switches that set the final swift countdown in motion.

A klaxon screamed its warning into the night. Terrified crewmen, bedded down beneath the camouflage net stretched over the top of the quarry, scrambled to their feet and rushed headlong toward the road leading out of the enclosure, knowing they had a scant ten seconds to separate themselves from the violent explosion the rocket's ignition would trigger. In the confusion aggravated by the semi-darkness, several fell to the ground, quickly regaining their feet and scrambling on, except for one unfortunate, either too stunned or too paralyzed by fear to do so. He lay there, cowering, and waited, only at the last second making the pathetic gesture of covering his ears with his hands.

With a brilliant flash of light, the unstable mixture of lique-fied gases ignited. The solid rock floor beneath the immense black cylinder began to shake as though in the grip of a major temblor, as a giant fireball erupted from the rocket nozzle and spread out, completely engulfing the interior of the quarry. As the thunder of the blast reverberated through the enclosure, loose rock from the sheer sides of the excavation split off and tumbled downward like layers of a giant glacier loosened by a sudden burst of sound, shattering in showers of white dust as they struck the bedrock below.

So fearful was the effect of the fireball that al Saif was certain his weapon had exploded on the launch pad and self-destructed. He threw up his arms, shielding his face, unwilling to gaze on the sorry end of his audacious enterprise. But moments later, when he dropped his arms again, the behe-moth was miraculously all in one piece and rising majestically above the inferno that raged beneath it.

His heart almost burst with triumph. *Allah be praised!* He must tender his gratitude. But he could not take his eyes off the instrument of his retribution. Nor could he think of it as just a thing, an inanimate object. It was vibrant, alive, a magnificent beast he had unleashed, roaring off to do his bidding and unarrestable. Not even he, its master, could call it back.

The fire subsided quickly, but the smoke and dust took longer to settle. Some of the bravest of the crew ventured back to look for their fallen comrade. Al Saif didn't see them. He was still gazing raptly at the dwindling plume of light that began to move westward as the missile commenced its programmed tilt toward its target. He turned and prostrated himself in the same direction, for that was also where Mecca lay.

When the beacon response suddenly disappeared off his monitor, not long after the standoff missiles were launched, Shani was shaken. There was still no sign of an infrared target image on his display, and he had been keeping its cross-hairs centered on the cursor, offset seventy meters from the ground beacon position, causing the missile to receive guidance commands that would drive it to impact at that spot. The cursor still appeared on his display, but now its location was based on computer memory. This would gradually degrade with time, Shani knew, and cause significant error buildup that could turn a hit into a miss.

He fussed with the control knob on the air-rescue panel, but the beacon strobe failed to reappear. His earphones began to buzz with reactions from his pilots, requesting instructions. "Keep tracking the cursor," he admonished. "Keep looking for a target image."

The time-to-go window showed twenty seconds to missile impact. His eyes strained to discern some image from his missile's infrared sensor head constituting the actual target that he could use to refine his aim point. Nothing!

The cursor under the cross-hairs took a sudden jump sideways. What the . . . ? The explanation dawned as his eyes jumped to the air-rescue set monitor. The beacon was *back*. Alerting his pilots, he corrected the cross-hairs, watching the time to go continuing to drop.

When it reached ten seconds, his electro-optical display suddenly bloomed with a tremendous infusion of input. He raised his eyes to the windscreen. A plume of light flared up out of the darkness ahead, growing larger and more brilliant by the second.

The terrorist missile. Shani's heart sank. By a scant ten seconds, his preemptive strike mission had failed.

Minutes before the launch of the East Wind, Richard Llewellyn was sitting at his operator's station as the AWACS orbited over the Gulf of Oman, its radar scanning out a hundred-mile swath of Iranian Baluchistan. The radar plane had taken off from Riyadh shortly after the Israeli strike force was scrambled.

Richy had received only a cursory briefing from Tessler on the impending air strike, but when the procession of moving targets appeared on his scope, he knew immediately what they were.

The F-16 fighter-bombers were approaching their target.

He announced their presence to the rest of the crew over the intercom.

Would the preemptive strike succeed; would they succeed in trapping the huge rocket on the ground and destroying it? His "Doppler fence" mode was activated to give him his own launch warning if the ballistic missile came exploding out of the sector of ground his radar was illuminating. If this happened, "bells and whistles" would sound in the audio piped into his headset. He hoped and prayed he wouldn't hear any.

Though he didn't know the exact location of the terrorist missile site, he sensed that the fighter-bombers must be nearing their target. That was confirmed when several new moving target blips suddenly sprouted on his display. He pressed his intercom button to alert the crew to this latest development.

"The F-16s just launched standoff missiles!"

It would be only a matter of minutes, now, or less. Richy watched the gap grow between the F-16s and their standoff missiles and held his breath. So far so good. When excited shouts from the flight crew erupted into his headphones, he thought at first they must be witnessing the explosions as the standoff missiles arrived on target. But no—the missile blips were still visible on his scope. With a sinking feeling, he realized that what the crew must have seen through the windscreen was the fiery departure of the East Wind.

• • •

The first of the standoff missiles belatedly arrived. It plunged deep inside the quarry and detonated, creating a second holocaust in the charred environs still smoking from the East Wind's searing departure. Two of the crew, attempting to extricate the body of their comrade, were obliterated by it. Others near the perimeter of the quarry were knocked to the ground by the concussive force of the blast. As they struggled to their feet, a second missile exploded just outside the exit to the quarry.

At the command post a hundred meters from the quarry, the elder Khan watched in horror, his "brother" Khan among those who had been standing there moments before. More and more explosions rocked the area in and around the quarry that had housed the East Wind, as the remainder of the standoff missiles continued to arrive, the scene now totally obscured by smoke, dust, and debris.

The barrage ended as suddenly as it had begun. When the debris settled, there was nothing left but a smoking, rock-strewn wasteland and no sign of life.

The noise of the approaching fighter bombers was audible now, descending on the survivors like a swarm of angry hornets. Back at the command post, Kareem and Khan helped al Saif back to his feet and the trio ran toward the stand of trees where the four-wheel-drive vehicles were hidden. They were almost there when the full fury of the Israeli attack broke over them, the entire area deluged by clusters of iron bombs. Under the feet of the running men the earth rose up and took them with it. The grove of trees they were trying to reach disintegrated from a direct hit, parts of the hidden vehicles flying in all directions.

Two minutes after it had begun it was all over. A pair of F-16s zoomed over at treetop level on a strafing run, but there was nothing left to strafe. Fires from the burning trees and vehicles illuminated a stark landscape in which nothing moved or breathed.

A stone's throw from the totally engulfed cover they had been trying to reach lay the Sword of Islam leader, his chief lieutenant, and his chief engineer. Al Saif's body rested on its stomach, his head turned downward, as if in prayer.

Kareem lay only a few yards away, on his back, his sightless eyes staring at the heavens as if pondering how they had unleashed such a sudden, all-consuming onslaught. The article attached to the chain around his neck had spilled out of his shirt and lay atop his chest, its gold and silver surface burnished to a reddish shade by the glow from the rampaging fires. The sword amulet. It had brought him anything but luck in this ultimate engagement.

High over the Indian Ocean, in geo-synchronous orbit 22,300 miles above the equator, a Defense Support Program satellite's twelve-foot infrared telescope stared down at the landmasses surrounding the Persian Gulf. The sudden flare-up of light intensity at a point near the southern coast of Iran registered on its six-thousand-cell detector array. The spectral characteristics of the light flare were duly recorded by the DSP satellite's dual-wavelength processor as the IR telescope continued to monitor the brilliant light source.

Data-linked to the ground, the early-warning information was processed by ground-based computers, comparing the satellite's real-time data with stored rocket plume characteristics. When a match registered, a ballistic missile launch warning flashed over the satellite relay network to the Israeli Defense Forces headquarters in Tel Aviv.

It only confirmed what they already knew. The spectacular night-time launch of the East Wind had been witnessed by the F-16 strike force pilots and duly reported. Notification of the launch and the coordinates of the launch site had just been sent to all Israeli ballistic missile defense units and also relayed to Peace Shield headquarters in Riyadh via the AWACS data link. Israel's civil defense headquarters had also been notified, with strict injunctions against leaking the news to the media or general public. Mass hysteria would be counter-productive; there was insufficient time for any sort of an evacuation.

In fifteen minutes the encounter with the giant missile would be history.

In Tel Aviv, the Patriot and Hawk missile batteries had been put on alert at the time the strike force was launched from Ramat David. The self-test routines had long since been activated and all systems were go. Then came the hardest part, the waiting, more than two hours of it, while the strike aircraft cruised out over the North Arabian Desert and across the Persian Gulf to engage their distant target.

When the battery commanders finally received word that the terrorist missile had been launched, the atmosphere in the Hawk Battery Command Post and the Patriot Engagement Control Station turned electric. In a scant quarter of an hour, the fate of Israel's largest city would be decided. The personnel manning the batteries were helpless to affect the outcome until an up-range radar began tracking the East Wind and forwarded trajectory information that would tell them where to look to acquire the re-entry vehicle with their own relatively short-range radar. They had a further agonizing twelve minutes of sweating to go through before it would be their turn.

Even the powerful ground-based radar in the Negev Desert would be unable to detect the threat until it had traversed four-fifths of the distance to its target from its launch point. In an attempt to pick up the threat somewhat sooner, an E-2C Hawkeye was loitering over the Israeli-Jordan border along the predicted path of the terrorist missile, its radar scanning the eastern skyline. But it was the AWACS and Peace Shield radars in Saudi Arabia that would have the first opportunity to acquire the target. Without timely inputs from these sources on the terrorist missile's trajectory, the Israeli radars might never find it in time.

With no window to look out of, Richard Llewellyn had missed seeing the launch of the East Wind. But less than a minute later his headset registered the alarm he had instrumented; a moving object in the radar beam had exceeded the Mach 3.5 threshold he had set on Doppler-derived velocity. It had to be the terrorist missile. Now his radar had the missile isolated from all other radar reflectors and could lock onto it and set up a track. He found the image on his radar display, ran a target designator over it, and depressed the lock-on button.

"Got it!" A six-parameter track file was now established in the AWACS central processor, registering the target's range, closing rate, azimuth and elevation angles and angular rates, the measurements of these variables updated every second as the AWACS antenna re-scanned the target vicinity. After a dozen or so scans, a first cut at the missile's boost-phase trajectory was derived. It was far from being accurate enough to predict the weapon's impact point. But with the refinement of more track up-date measurements it would be more than adequate to hand off the missile's projected path to the Peace Shield radars in Saudi Arabia, already alerted to the fact of the weapon's launch and waiting for it to come within range.

He punched the command into the computer that would initiate the message to Peace Shield headquarters and IDF headquarters in Tel Aviv over the long-range communications channels linking them to the radar plane. The recorded track history and predicted path of the target would be repeated after each new scan until the East Wind flew out of range of the AWACS radar. A data-link status light blinked on to verify that the message was being sent. A few seconds later another light acknowledged receipt by the Saudi command center.

Richy watched the parameter printouts on the track file sub-display, marveling at the East Wind's acceleration, its velocity reading already above Mach 10. It was now abreast of the AWACS and in less than two minutes would be out of range, his own role in the crucial intercept operation over with. Knowing that gave him a helpless feeling. All those people back there in the big city he had only just returned from, the military bunch at IDF headquarters, people he had seen on its streets, in its airport, their lives hanging in the balance. Would the Patriot get the job done? There was no guarantee. The success of one canned demonstration didn't prove a thing; so many things could go wrong. Thank God his brother and sister-in-law were no longer in Tel Aviv!

The East Wind velocity topped out at Mach 15. Its huge rocket motor must have already separated. The weapon was now more than a hundred miles downrange from AWACS. Richy watched the blip on his display grow fainter until the track drop-out symbol appeared, then called the pilot on intercom.

"Let's go home."

"Mission accomplished?"

"Our part, at least. In another ten minutes we'll know the rest of the story."

It was going to be a long ten minutes.

• • •

In the wee hours of the morning there would normally have been only a skeleton crew on duty at Riyadh's Peace Shield headquarters. But this particular night was an exception. The word had made the rounds that a dramatic live "test" of the emerging defense network might be in the cards, and most of the day-shift personnel had stayed on, even those who were not participating. Many were Saudi personnel, not directly in the loop on this exercise but intrigued, nonetheless, with what was transpiring.

Dr. Tessler stood with a large group of other Americans clustered about one of the computer consoles that was gushing forth hard copy. His habitual air of studied calm had been preserved despite the frenetic circumstances, his pipe clamped between his teeth as he pored over the printed data. It had gone out some time ago, but he didn't appear to have noticed.

It had been just minutes ago that the DSP satellite launch warning had been flashed to Peace Shield over the NORAD hookup Tessler had helped arrange. The electrifying news had set the place on its ear. When, a minute or so later, the AWACS tracking data had begun to pour in, a cheer had gone up from the Americans. The Peace Shield satellite radars were immediately put on alert and supplied with track extrapolations of the big missile's predicted position when it reached their zone of coverage.

"Burnout!" Tessler announced, pointing to one of the columns of data on the printout. He tore off the data sheet and hurried to his office. A phone line was being held open for him to Israeli Defense headquarters in Tel Aviv. The Israelis would already be getting trajectory information over the AWACS link. But Tessler had promised Tuchler a personal call to pass along burn-out data that would enable his analysts to make a first prediction of the missile's impact point.

"Dr. Tessler, if I could have a minute . . ." It was the Saudi liaison officer, Captain Hammudi, intercepting him at his office door.

"Not now, Captain." Tessler brushed past the uniformed Saudi, making for the phone.

"But Dr. Tessler, it is the material you requested. It just

arrived by special messenger." He held up a slim, tightly wrapped packet.

The information on configuration changes in the new shipment of East Wind missiles—what a time for it to finally show up, with the East Wind already in flight! Tessler had requested it several days ago, had given up on ever getting it.

"I'm too busy to look at it right now. Why don't you open it and have a look." Tessler had already picked up the phone.

"I shall be happy to. But you must sign for it first." Hammudi held out the document receipt and a pen.

Tessler tucked the phone under his chin, scrawled his name on the receipt, and promptly dismissed the matter from his mind. The call to Tel Aviv went right through.

The solitary F-15 Eagle had been sitting at the end of the runway at Tel Nof for twenty minutes, ready to roll. Inside the cockpit, Lt. Gen. Chaim Barkai got the take-off clearance from the tower and rammed the throttles forward. Halfway down the runway, a double-barreled explosion shook the air as the twin afterburners cut in, and the Eagle rocketed upwards at a sixty-degree angle under full military power.

The general had heard about the startling outcome of his air strike through his headset only minutes before. Though bitterly disappointed that the missile had not been caught on the ground, he was far from surprised. He had regarded the long-range strike mission as something of a long shot from the beginning. At least it had dealt swift justice to those murderous maniacs. But now the terrorists' legacy of vengeance was hurtling toward his country and had yet to be dealt with.

The expectation that this might happen had been precisely the reason that Barkai had been disinclined to personally lead the strike mission. If there was to be an end game on which might hinge the salvation or destruction of Israel's major city, he was determined to be around to participate. There was no way he was willing to delegate the defense of his home to the exclusive purview of the Army's Missile Command. Patriot and Hawk were unknown quantities in the ballistic missile defense role. He didn't trust them.

Several weeks before, knowing the Chief of Staff might not approve, he had secretly organized an Air Force back-up effort on ballistic missile defense. His Air Force panel of experts had concurred with Dr. Bar-Tel's panel that one of their own air-to-air missiles had the capability to execute a successful intercept of the East Wind re-entry vehicle if it caught the RV at lower altitudes where its speed would be way down. But there was a catch; the RV's incoming trajectory would have to be predicted with great accuracy a full minute ahead of its arrival time, so that the aircraft launching the missile could be steered to a precise launch point at a specified time. In terms of launch tolerance, the launch "window" was only a few seconds wide.

Though admittedly hairy, the concept had appeared workable to Barkai. It fit in nicely with the "defense in depth" plan the Army had adopted, which called for the only three available Patriot missiles to be launched in salvo while the RV was still at relatively high altitude. Thus, on the off chance the RV contained a nuclear warhead after all, it would be intercepted at sufficiently high altitude to minimize blast damage and radioactive fallout. The Hawk missiles would be held for backup in case the RV somehow eluded the Patriots. Again, a salvo of three missiles would be used to maximize kill-probability.

Barkai planned to be in position in case both missile salvos failed. His F-15 would be under close control by an Air Force controller using inputs from Tel Nof's own high-powered radar. His plane carried two of Israel's own infrared-homing missiles, the Python 3, one under each wing.

Python 3 was Israel's third-generation IR-guided air-to-air missile, bearing a close resemblance to its progenitor, the Shafir 2. A bigger missile than the Shafir and the American Sidewinder, it carried a considerably larger warhead than either, designed to cause catastrophic damage to its target, the principal reason Barkai's advisory panel had recommended it for this mission.

The general was flying under voice control. He had rehearsed the mission several times under simulated conditions, flying the same profile he was flying now, working with the same controller. Amos's familiar voice now told him to level off at an altitude of twenty thousand feet and throttle back to a speed of 450 knots.

"Twenty thousand and 450 it is." He pushed the stick forward and reduced the throttles. When he had leveled out and adjusted his speed he reported again.

"Come to a new heading of zero-six-zero," Amos directed.

"Zero-six-zero. What's happening up-range, Amos? Has Peace Shield reported contact with the rocket yet?"

"Negative, General. There's been nothing on the voice channel since the initial AWACS data came in."

Barkai had arranged a UHF voice channel hook-up between his intercept command center at Tel Nof and IDF headquarters, which was tied into the Peace Shield Command Operations Center in Riyadh by both voice and data link. "We should have gotten word by now. Patch me in to that IDF voice channel. You can interrupt when necessary for your vectoring inputs."

"Can do, General. It's a bit noisy, though."

Amos had understated the case. The Peace Shield signal being piped in from IDF headquarters filled his headset with nothing but background noise. He turned down the volume, impatient to hear an announcement of the acquisition of the target by the Peace Shield radar. What was taking so long? The highly touted American-built radars of the new Saudi defense network were reputedly the latest state of the art.

They had better work.

At the base of the Persian Gulf's Qatar peninsula, just outside the small Saudi village of Salwa, a giant radar platform hummed like an electric substation, emitting powerful packets of electromagnetic energy into the chilly night air. The FPS-117 three-dimensional surveillance radar was one of seventeen supplied by General Electric to provide sensor coverage of the entire Saudi Arabian defense perimeter as part of Peace Shield. It was radio-linked to the Riyadh Combat Operations Center and to a localized Sector Command Center, one of five.

Inside the concrete enclosure at its base a technician was staring in disbelief at the prominent blip on a large vertical display. Between successive scans the blip was taking giant steps across the scope face. The operator had never seen a target move so fast. He called his supervisor.

Within seconds, the position fixes obtained by the radar were being flashed to Riyadh, where the time-indexed range, bearing, and elevation measurements produced a time history of the object's path through space. The voice channel to Tel Aviv announced the successful radar contact and apprised the Israelis that more complete trajectory data would be transmitted momentarily by data link.

At IDF headquarters, primed and waiting, a team of analysts read out the trajectory data and used it as input for their own computer program. With the rocket burn long since completed, the remainder of the missile's path was totally predictable up to the re-entry point, which the program would shortly yield.

The group of onlookers gathered excitedly around the printer as the printout began, several high-ranked officers among them, scrutinizing the lines of print as they emerged.

"It's Tel Aviv, all right, and it's right on the money!" The group leader ripped the first page off the tractor feed and pointed out the latitude and longitude of the re-entry point to the colonel at his elbow. "The next page will have a predicted re-entry velocity profile and time line."

"See that they're immediately faxed to the Patriot and Hawk batteries," the colonel told a subordinate, "and hand deliver a copy to the Command Center upstairs. I've got to call General Tuchler."

He picked up a nearby phone and started to dial, then stopped. "What time does the RV reach the re-entry point?"

"3:57:22," the analyst read off the computer printout. "Just under seven minutes from now."

32

SOMEHOW, THE WORD had gotten out. The streets of Tel Aviv, normally quiescent at this early morning hour, were suddenly teeming with vehicles and panicked citizens, all trying to exit the city at once. The major arteries leading out of town were already clogged, the Route 1 expressway to the airport and Jerusalem jammed with cars and moving at a slow crawl. Derek Haifa, leading north to Route 2, was in even worse shape, gridlocked by vehicles attempting to enter from choked side streets.

City police did their best to cope with the massive pile-up, but they had only a skeleton night crew and were grossly undermanned. The clamor increased, auto horns blaring incessantly. Drivers and passengers trapped in stalled autos started abandoning them, many strapping on gas masks as they rushed back to where they'd come from or looked for shelter closer at hand. Civil defense officials with arm bands circulated among them, trying to calm them and get them off the streets.

At Ben Gurion International Airport it was bedlam. The parking compound was already filled, with a steady stream of cars still coming in. Illegally parked cars were piling up everywhere, and the access road from the expressway was backed up all the way to the eastbound offramp.

Inside, the departure terminal was jammed, would-be passengers queued up in long lines at the ticket windows, only to be turned away. All available seats were booked on every flight scheduled to depart in the next forty-eight hours. El Al officials, called out of bed to deal with the unforeseen glut of customers, scrambled to line up more equipment from the charter lines.

Here and there an hysterical outcry was heard, but the crowd was surprisingly well-behaved under the circumstances, their spirits apparently bolstered by the sight of so many others in the same boat. There was much conversation among them concerning the threat that had prompted their hasty exodus. Everyone, it seemed, had heard a different rumor; no two stories were the same. An A-bomb had been smuggled into Tel Aviv by terrorists. No, a chemical bomb. It came from Qadaffi. No, from Saddam Hussein. *Mishegoss!* It wasn't a bomb at all. It was an ultimatum from Syria. Hafez Assad had a horde of missiles poised just over the border, ready to reduce Tel Aviv to a pile of rubble.

Civil defense representatives went around dispensing gas masks to those who were without. They only shrugged when asked to explain what was going on. The gas masks were just a precaution; there was no real danger. It was what they had been told to say. The truth was that they knew nothing more specific than anyone else.

And it was true. Those already at the airport were not in any danger. But for those in the city it was another matter. Their fate was yet to be decided.

The Patriot missile launching station was located in an open field near the northern part of Tel Aviv. Within fifty meters of one another, firing cannisters for three Patriots were canted up at a sixty-degree angle, trained a few points south of due east. These were the same cannisters the missiles had been stored and shipped in. A radio stick antenna projected vertically from each firing cannister to receive pointing and launch commands from the Patriot Engagement Control Station at a separate location.

Mounted on an M-814 truck, the Engagement Control Station was the operational command and control center for the firing unit. Its two large display and control consoles, computer, and communications terminals were manned by a crew of four. One of the displays monitored inputs from the multifunction phased array radar mounted on the M-860 semitrailer parked nearby. At the moment, the radar was scanning out a small sector about the expected re-entry point of the East Wind's payload, based on earlier inputs from IDF headquarters. The display showed no blips and the ECS crew expected none for another two minutes or more. What they did expect, momentarily, was an update on the predicted re-entry point, based on inputs from one of Israel's own long-range radars.

The crew went about their work coolly, but inside, each had his own anxieties to contend with. Only the Israeli major, the Tactical Officer, had been in any form of combat before. The radar operator and missile launch operator were American Army non-coms, sent over to help train the Israelis in the use of Patriot. The communications operator was an Israeli noncom. The group had worked well together during the Patriot test firing three days earlier. They hadn't imagined they'd be shooting off more missiles so soon, especially against a live, highly lethal threat.

"Here it comes." The communications man read off the new coordinates on the computer printout. "That's over two degrees different. And the ETA is twenty seconds earlier. Just over a minute to go!"

He tore off the sheet and handed it to the American manning the radar, who punched the updated re-entry point into his control panel. The Tactical Officer, in command of the unit, did not try to interpose himself. His men knew their business. A former Hawk battery commander, he was still learning about Patriot. So far, he was greatly impressed with both its technology and its tactical advantages over Hawk. His main role was to coordinate with the Missile Command through the IDF command center and make sure their orders were carried out.

His prior instructions from that quarter left him little latitude. Once the re-entry vehicle had been acquired by the Patriot radar and had entered the missile's launch zone, his three missiles would be fired in a single salvo to bring it down. He was not in the least familiar with RVs as targets or with how their behavior might differ from the aircraft targets he was accustomed to, except that they were less maneuverable. It seemed reasonable that this should make them easier to kill.

The UHF voice link from headquarters blared through the

loudspeaker. "We show thirty seconds to re-entry point, Patriot. Do you have radar contact yet?"

The major saw the radar operator shake his head. "Negative," he reported into his hand-held mike.

"Please advise when you have radar contact."

The major started his own countdown, watching the second hand of his watch tick away, surprised by the sight of the beads of sweat on his arm and wrist. He couldn't remember being this tensed up as an army corporal in the Yom Kippur War, when the Egyptian bombers came over. He counted off thirty seconds. There was still no sign of a contact from the radar operator.

As more seconds ticked by, doubts began to assail him. "Re-check your aim point!" he shouted to the radar operator. "Are you looking at the right spot?"

"Yes, sir," the American snapped. "I double-checked. Triple-checked."

"Go to an expanded frame!" commanded the major. "We've got to—"

"Wait! There's a blip!"

"Contact!" the major shouted into the mike.

"Range?" the loudspeaker queried.

"Fifty-six miles," the radar man responded. The major repeated the number into the mike.

"Be advised that the target will enter your launch zone in twelve seconds," the loudspeaker announced. "Prepare to salvo missiles."

"Major!" the radar operator shouted. "Now I see two blips!"

"Control, we have two targets!" the major reported over the radio link. "I repeat, *two targets!*"

"Acknowledged, Patriot. I am advised that one must be the rocket booster, accompanying the RV upon re-entry. It will shortly burn up. Prepare to launch missiles."

"Range thirty-one miles," the radar operator reported.

"We're in zone, sir," the missile launch operator advised. "Shall I launch?"

"Prepare to launch on my command," the major instructed. He wiped the sweat from his forehead. The target had closed twenty-five miles in fifteen seconds! It had been expected to slow down much faster. He couldn't afford to wait much longer.

"Fire!"

At the remote launch site, the three firing cannisters flashed fire and were immediately enveloped in clouds of white smoke as the sixteen-foot missiles rocketed out of them and up into the sky, powered by their solid-fueled boosters. They were presently under command guidance but would shortly transition to semi-active homing when their radar target seekers locked onto the illumination from the Patriot radar reflected back by the re-entry vehicle. This would provide the accurate steering required to bring them into sufficiently close proximity to the target for their blast-fragmentation warheads to destroy it.

But which target? Back at the Patriot Engagement Control Center the radar operator made a startling announcement.

"The second blip is still there! And now there's a *third* one!"

Dr. Tessler was still on the open line to Tel Aviv, waiting tensely for news of the engagement of the East Wind re-entry vehicle by Patriot, when Captain Hammudi knocked on his door, then burst in without waiting for an invitation.

"Doctor, I must speak with you!"

"Not now," Tessler hissed. "Can't you see I'm busy?"

"This will not wait!" Hammudi thrust a document under his nose, several of its pages folded back. His forefinger traced an underlined sentence.

"There was a block change. The East Wind has been MIRVed!"

"What?" Tessler pulled the phone away from his ear.

"The new shipment of missiles were all of the new configuration. They have provisions for three independently targeted re-entry vehicles!"

"Oh, God . . ." Tessler put the phone back to his mouth. "Colonel Elon! Colonel, are you there? Listen! This is critical—there may be three independently targeted re-entry vehicles coming your way! Inform the Patriot and Hawk batteries.

"Do you understand? *Three* RVs, not one. Three separate targets that must be destroyed!"

• • •

"Sir, what should I do?" The Patriot missile operator stared at the Tactical Officer, who had just reported the existence of three targets to headquarters and was waiting for instructions. "Should I reassign targets and try for all three, one on one?"

"Our orders were very explicit. Three on one." The Tactical Officer was sweating profusely. "Unless they're rescinded I can't—"

"But sir—there's barely time! We need a decision now, or—"

The loudspeaker blared again. "Patriot, we have just received confirmation that all targets are real. I repeat. There are three separate re-entry vehicles. They must all be intercepted."

The TO's decision had been made for him. It wasn't necessary for him to repeat the instructions; the missile operator had heard and was already working frantically to reprogram the three missiles he had in the air. Unlike Hawk, which could only handle a single target at a time, Patriot was designed for multiple targets. But the operator was used to much slower targets—aircraft targets. While the RVs had slowed appreciably in the denser air, they were still approaching at six times the speed of sound. With better than triplesonic speed, the Patriot missiles were closing on the RVs at a rate of nearly two miles every second!

The missile operator had already set up new track files on the two additional targets. Now he had to unslave the guidance heads of two of his missiles and redirect them to different look angles that would bring their new targets into their capture zone. He managed to get only one Patriot reprogrammed before time ran out.

Ten miles up, the first Patriot missile, which had been homing on the same target all the way, approached the glowing, white-hot re-entry vehicle at nine times the speed of sound. Its proximity fuze, redesigned for the high-speed ballistic missile encounter, was never triggered. With a solid track on the non-maneuvering target and more than ample guidance time, the Patriot struck it dead center. The contact fuze took over, unleashing the force of the modified Patriot's specially augmented blast fragmentation warhead, designed to assure weapon kill against ballistic missile payloads.

This particular RV carried one of Saddam Hussein's yellow

cylinders containing the binary nerve agent. The g-force of the collision was sufficient to trigger the device within the cylinder that would cause the contents of the two pressurized containers it housed to combine, form the deadly viscous nerve agent, and deploy. But before this could happen, the walls of the cylinder and its containers were penetrated by high-speed metal fragments, ripping the containers to shreds and spilling their contents harmlessly into the atmosphere. A second or two later another Patriot missile arrived and detonated on the debris.

From the ground, the effect of the double-barreled explosion was spectacular and awe-inspiring. In every part of the city the thunderous reports could be heard and the brilliant, multicolored fireballs seen, as thousands of anxious citizens trained their eyes skyward. In the vicinity of the Patriot batteries a resounding cheer went up from the military sky-watchers.

Inside the Patriot Engagement Control Station there was no cheering. Two targets remained on the scope face as the major and his team sweated out the fate of the last Patriot missile. When its warhead detonated, painting another vivid burst of color across the night sky, a second cheer went up outside the control station enclosure.

It was an uninformed response. Gathered around the radar scope, the Patriot crew saw that both target blips were still there and knew immediately what had happened. The reprogrammed missile had had insufficient guidance time to overcome the transient induced by the new target instruction. It had come within range of the proximity fuze, detonating its warhead at the point of closest approach. But that point had not been close enough to kill the target.

It had missed.

"One target destroyed," the major announced to headquarters. "The other two are still coming!"

The Hawk missile battery he had once commanded would now be taking aim. He knew the system like the back of his hand. It might be able to handle one RV; it certainly couldn't manage two. The battle of Tel Aviv had been lost.

• • •

In his F-15 Eagle, General Barkai had been following the Patriot engagement over his UHF radio channel and had witnessed the brilliant plumes of the three Patriot missiles as they plunged upward into the night sky. With the electrifying revelation that there were three separate warheads, of which two had eluded the Patriot missiles, his worst fears were realized. The Patriots were gone! Hawk was a single-target-at-a-time system; it would have time to handle only one of the two remaining warheads. It had come down to him and his Eagle, going one on one, against the other.

But his own radar scope still showed no targets. Though relatively small reflectors compared to aircraft, the two RVs should have been in range by now. Was he looking in the right place? His radar was scanning a narrow sector along the sight line indicated by the ground-based radar and computer at his home base of Tel Nof. He expanded the elevation coverage, adding two more rasters.

There they were . . . As the antenna scanned the upper bar, two blips popped onto the scope. Which should he pick? Which one would the Hawk select? The danger was that they would both pick the same target and let the other come through.

"Amos, I have them!" he announced to his controller. "Transitioning to self-steering. What's your estimated time to minimum launch range?"

"You have less than twenty seconds. Good luck!"

Only twenty seconds, then his launch window would shrink to zero. He didn't have time to coordinate with the Hawk battery. They didn't even know he was up here. He would have to pick one target and hope for the best. He moved the cursor over the left-hand blip on his scope and hit the lock-on button.

His mode selection switch was already set on lead-collision steering, and a steering dot appeared on his head-up display. He moved the control stick to bring it inside the circle and hold it there, his eyes flitting down to the radar scope, where target range was displayed next to max and min launch ranges for his Python 3 weapon. The range was shrinking rapidly, had almost reached the max launch range index.

His missiles were armed and ready, their IR tracking heads

slaved to the radar line of sight. When they picked up sufficient infrared radiation from the target, they would lock on and send a distinctive tone into his headset. It should happen soon. The re-entry vehicle was an ideal IR target, superheated by the friction of its hypersonic collision with air molecules as it made its way back into the atmosphere. So hot, it might even glow in the dark. But his eye could make out nothing through the windscreen, only blackness ahead.

His earphones sang with the tone from missile number one, under his right wing. He flipped the selector switch for missile number two to ON and heard an echoing tone immediately, slightly lower in pitch. Both missiles were now locked on to the same RV. He could fire at any time; his display showed the target halfway through the launch window. But he held off, his finger on the control stick trigger, one eye watching the scope, the other the windscreen. What was taking Hawk so long to engage? The fiery trails of Hawk missiles should already be arcing through the night sky.

When they finally did appear it was too late for him to wait any longer. He was almost out of launch window. He squeezed the trigger and prayed that the target the Hawks were streaking toward was not the same one he was shooting at.

His F-15 was jolted by the fiery separation of the first Python missile, its orange-yellow rocket plume dazzling his eyes as it danced across his windscreen and shot off into the black void ahead. He'd forgotten to close his eyes in time, his night vision destroyed for the moment. His finger still on the launch trigger, he flipped the weapon select switch to missile number two. He had planned to ripple-fire his two Pythons in a single salvo to maximize the likelihood of getting a kill. In a second or two he would be out of zone. Still, something held him back from squeezing the trigger.

His vision readjusted, the Python's plume now only a bright pinpoint ahead. A few seconds more and it would reach its target. His eyes again picked up the trails of the Hawks mounting ever higher and recorded the sudden culmination of one in a white-hot burst of light.

His eyes leaped back to the radar scope. His target was *gone!* The Hawk had splashed his target! The observation was immediately confirmed by his earphones, the aural tone from missile number two no longer audible. The source of radiation the second Python had locked onto was no longer there. His first missile was gone, wasted, hung out to dry!

His hand jumped to the radar-mode selector switch and he flipped to SUPERSEARCH. The radar commenced to scan a small region about its last track position. His eyes flew back to the scope. There it was, the last RV! Feverishly, he adjusted the cursor over it and hit the lock-on button.

Again the steering dot appeared, far outside the circle. He adjusted the stick and brought it back, a voice in his ears telling him he was a fool, it was too late. A glance at the scope confirmed this, the range on the new target well below the minimum range mark on the display. It was hopeless. He was out of zone.

As the steering dot neared the circle center the tone came back in his headset. The missile was locked onto its new target. What did he have to lose? He squeezed the trigger.

In the War Room at Israeli Defense Forces headquarters in Akiriya, Tel Aviv, General Yigal Tuchler sat with some of his aides and subordinates in front of a giant situation display, following the progress of the engagement with the terrorist missile. The War Room was in a concrete bunker buried three levels below ground, safe from every kind of threat with the possible exception of a nuclear direct hit or near miss. Its recirculating air-conditioning unit even had its own oxygen supply to avoid the intake of air that might have become contaminated from chemical or biological weapons.

Tuchler had been here since the departure of the F-16 strike force and had been joined an hour later by Mordechai Shilo, the Mossad director, who had driven in from Jerusalem. It was Tuchler, through his aide, who had just received the belated message from Dr. Tessler about the multiple warheads and had passed the word to the Missile Command. But not in time to help the outcome of the Patriot engagement, unfortunately. Now he and Shilo listened tensely to the voice channel in the Hawk battery where the final scenes of the drama were being played out.

The giant backlighted situation board showed one dead

target, whose light had been extinguished, and two live ones, still blinking their way downward, the projections of their trajectories impacting at two different points within the city. Both men knew, as did everyone in the room, that the best Hawk could do was account for one of them.

"We've lost . . ." Shilo murmured bitterly. It had been an act of faith for him to come to Tel Aviv tonight, faith in the defensive umbrella his old friend Tuchler had implemented in response to his persistent proddings. It had been he, Shilo, who had uncovered the existence of the threat, who had highlighted its urgency and spearheaded the effort to deal with it. How ironic that it should end this way, that the failure to counter the threat should fall into his own lap, a clear lapse of intelligence. For the Mossad should have found out about the MIRVing of the new shipload of Chinese missiles; it was their responsibility to do so. He had let his old friend down. And his country.

"Hawk got another one!" Cheers from the Hawk voice channel mingled with those from the War Room as one of the two threat lights on the situation board blinked out, its extrapolated trajectory into Tel Aviv erased. Shilo noted that Tuchler was not among the cheerers. His eyes were glued to the remaining threat light, winking its way inexorably along the path that descended toward the heart of the city.

"God help us if it's nuclear," he muttered.

Shilo raised his eyebrows. Hadn't he assured the general that there was no real chance of this, no intelligence that the terrorists possessed such a warhead? He started to protest, then thought better of it. Why should his friend believe him, after his failure on the other East Wind warhead particular?

A nerve gas warhead would be a bad enough alternative, he reflected. Even with all the gas masks handed out, there were bound to be numerous casualties. One tiny whiff and you'd never breathe again. Tel Aviv would have to be evacuated, for how long, no one could tell. The Israeli economy, already shaky, would be devastated.

But it was the biological weapon he dreaded even more. The latest descriptions he had seen of the virulent strains of organisms and viruses being developed in Iraq had been terrifying. Cholera, diphtheria, new strains of deadly influenzas. They could wipe out the population of an entire city, leave it contaminated and uninhabitable for months, years.

Exclamations from the other onlookers roused him from his morbid reverie. His eyes darted back to the situation board. The last re-entry vehicle . . . it was *gone*. The light had gone out. Its extrapolated trajectory was being erased!

"What happened?" he gasped.

Tuchler appeared as mystified as he. "Somebody playing games with the equipment. I'll have his—"

"General Tuchler, this is General Barkai." The strong voice of the Israeli Air Force Commander was coming in through the speakers over the UHF voice channel. "You can scratch that third terrorist warhead. Chalk one up for the Air Force. That's a confirmed kill; I just saw it with my own eyes. And it wasn't made by some American-supplied weapon. It was one of our own Python missiles."

Tuchler seized the microphone from a speechless communications officer. "General Barkai, where are you?"

"About four miles above you." Barkai's voice was exultant. "I'm looking at the most beautiful sight I've ever seen through my Eagle's windscreen. The lights of Tel Aviv, still burning brightly."

"General, I don't remember authorizing—"

"You didn't, sir." Barkai's chuckle was audible over the loudspeakers. "I'm afraid I forgot to ask permission."

Epilogue

THE SUN WAS scarcely a half hour from setting as the evening shuttle flight from Cyprus approached the coast of Israel and the city of Tel Aviv. Seated together on the left side of the plane, David and Daniella Llewellyn strained to catch their first glimpse of the threatened city. Stuffed into the seat pockets in front of them and overflowing onto the floor were newspapers they had bought at Larnaca airport and read en route. But it was one thing to read about the survival of Israel's largest city in the near catastrophe—it was another to see it with their own eyes.

Approaching from the northwest, the pilot initiated a broad, sweeping turn to the left to line up with the main runway at Ben Gurion International, leveling out as his jet made landfall just south of Jaffa light. The Llewellyns were treated to an incomparable view of Tel Aviv on a perfect sunny afternoon—a Tel Aviv that was alive and well, its beaches speckled with swimmers and sunbathers, its streets teeming with cars and pedestrians.

"Hot damn, what a sight!" David found his wife's hand and squeezed.

Mesmerized, Daniella could not speak or tear her eyes away. When at last she turned from the window to embrace him, he heard a sob and felt her warm tears on his cheek.

"It's finally over," he said, patting her back gently, realizing how much she needed this release. All the way back from Shiraz she had kept it together, had steadfastly refused to crack, even after hitches developed in their departure—escape—from Iran.

After the Israeli warplanes struck Iranian Baluchistan, the roof had fallen in. The outraged Iranis had thrown out a dragnet for Israeli agents, closing all commercial flights out of southern Iran to foreign nationals. Eluding a police net at the hotel in Shiraz where they had overnighted, the Llewellyns had hitched a ride on Logan's plane to his home town of Tehran.

It was a tired but happy Logan who had dropped them at Tehran International Airport, about to be reunited with his wife and young son after two weeks on the road. Contributing to his good spirits was the news he had received en route that his buddy Hot Shot had survived the raid on the missile base, rescued by an Irani commando unit and taken to a Shiraz hospital by a med-vac helicopter.

Logan had not foreseen any further problems for the Llewellyns this far from the scene of the bombing, as they said their goodbyes. They held reservations on the next flight to Cyprus and passports from countries not on Iranian black-lists. But when they stepped inside the terminal, it became apparent that it wasn't going to be that easy. The place was swarming with soldiers and police.

They had split up to appear less conspicuous. Almost immediately Daniella, still in her outlandish Kurdish costume, was stopped and interrogated. But she had kept her cool, explaining that the airlines had lost her luggage with her entire Canadian wardrobe. The soldiers had joked with her and given her back her passport and ticket. There was further questioning of both of them when they went through immigration prior to boarding, and they hadn't felt safe until their plane was in the air.

There would be some, Llewellyn reflected, who might consider what they had just been through a glorious adventure. Adventure or ordeal, it had taught him a lot about his spouse. What nerve it must have taken to plunge herself into that unknown, alien Muslim world, alone and unprotected. And when that world had predictably turned hostile, threatening her first with arrest, then death, she had managed to survive, living by her wits.

Maybe Shmona was right, maybe Daniella did have a rare talent for undercover work. But he hoped she'd had enough of it to last her a lifetime; he couldn't stand the strain of having her constantly in danger.

The wheels touched down, putting an official end to their Iranian caper. He squeezed her hand.

"We were quite a team, weren't we, Mrs. Monpleasure?"

"We *are* quite a team, Mr. Svenson, and don't you forget it!"

A light, early morning mist hung over the placid waters of Bahrain's main deep-water harbor as the bedraggled freighter slid silently toward its berth. One of the busiest ports on the Persian Gulf, Mina Salman, harbor to the nearby capital city of Manama, was just awakening to a typically warm and humid day, the long pier the ship was approaching seemingly deserted at this early hour. Deck hands from the freighter's own crew sprang onto the pier to man the lines that would secure it to its mooring.

The bearded captain of the *Beirut Victory* stood on the bridge, personally directing the docking operation. He was anxious to get ashore, find the freight agent, and get his cargo unloaded. An opportunity for his tramp steamer to pick up a new cargo had just opened up, for a destination that would take him through the Suez Canal and back into the Mediterranean, with a chance of putting into his home port of Beirut and spending some time there. But he would have to make port in Muscat within four days to seal the bargain.

The mooring operation completed, the crew were preparing to lower the gangplank when the first signs of life appeared ashore. An open jeep drove onto the pier and headed for the ship. As the captain watched, the driver, wearing some kind of uniform that was either police or military, parked his vehicle and stood beside it, waiting for the gangplank to descend. As soon as it was in place, he scrambled onto it and handed an envelope to one of the seamen manning it, returning immediately to the pier. But instead of driving away, he remained standing there.

The envelope was brought to the bridge posthaste. The captain tore it open. On official Bahrain government stationery, the message said simply that the *Beirut Victory,* its cargo, and its crew were being placed under indefinite quarantine. No one would be allowed ashore and no cargo could be unloaded until the quarantine was lifted.

The captain was furious. "They've slapped us with a quarantine? Outrageous. And no reason given." In all his days at sea this had never happened to him before.

"Take over," he told his mate. Leaving the bridge, he hurried down the ladder to the deck, striding to the gangplank and down it.

"What is the meaning of this?" he demanded of the jeep's driver, waving the envelope in his face.

"It is a quarantine, Captain."

The captain could barely understand him, the Bahrain dialect so different from the Arabic spoken in Lebanon. "There is no disease aboard my ship. Why am I being quarantined?"

"Something to do with your cargo, Captain. That is all I have been told."

"My cargo? There is nothing dangerous about my cargo. It is heavy machinery, packed in wooden crates."

The uniformed Bahraini shrugged. "The harbor master will arrive shortly. I'm sure he will explain."

"Shortly? What does that mean?" The captain had visions of a protracted glitch in his schedule.

"He has already departed. It should be no longer than—" The Bahraini's eyes shifted to the water. "I think that is his launch now."

Following his eyes, the captain saw a motor launch a few hundred meters off, speeding toward them. He could see that there were three men aboard, in addition to the helmsman, all wearing different kinds of officers' uniforms. As the launch drew closer, he recognized two of the uniforms, and drew in his breath sharply. One was the Royal Saudi Arabian Navy, the other the American Navy. What in the name of Allah were they doing here, in the independent sheikdom of Bahrain, descending on his ship?

The motor launch tied up to the pier and the trio made their way up the ladder. First over the top was the officer in the uniform he hadn't recognized. That would be the Bahrain harbor master. Next up was the Saudi officer, a distinguished-looking older man wearing the two stars of a rear admiral.

The last to emerge was the U.S. naval officer, a three-striper. The captain blanched. He knew this man!

"Well, Captain Atawi, we meet again." The skipper of the USS *Lawrence* saluted but did not extend his hand.

"Commander Spooner, isn't it?" Atawi did not return the salute. "To what do I owe this unexpected visit? Are you behind this attempt to quarantine my ship?"

"Why don't we let the harbor master answer that? We're on his turf."

The Bahrain official introduced himself to the *Beirut Victory*'s captain and also introduced the Saudi admiral. "We have had to place your ship under quarantine, Captain, because of a complaint from our brother nation and close neighbor. I will let Admiral Khateeb explain the charges against you."

"Charges? I do not understand."

The Saudi admiral produced some notes and proceeded to read from them. "You are charged with knowingly loading and transporting aboard your ship, the *Beirut Victory,* cargo stolen from the Royal Saudi Arabian government. You are further charged with unloading such cargo at a port in Iran, leading to its subsequent destruction. The loss of this cargo is valued at 350 million rials."

The horrified captain made a quick mental calculation: 350 million rials—that was over a hundred million dollars! "These charges are preposterous! How do I go about getting them lifted?"

"Lifted?" The harbor master appeared mystified.

"Surely you will not just take his word against mine. Is there no justice in Bahrain?"

"Ah, justice." The Bahrain official's face brightened. "Of course there is justice here. The *majlis* is conducted regularly. You will plead your case before His Royal Highness, the Amir, himself."

That was better news to the captain. At least there was no talk of extradition to Saudi Arabia. He stood a better chance having his case tried by the powerful sheik who ruled Bahrain than by King Fahd and the House of Saud.

"When will this *majlis* take place? I have a cargo to unload and a fresh cargo to fetch in another port. How long must my ship remain in quarantine?"

"Justice is swift in Bahrain," the harbor master replied. "It will be a matter of a few days at most. But your cargo must remain on board until your case is decided. It is considered part of the collateral, along with your ship."

"Collateral?"

"To reimburse the House of Saud for damages, in the event the decision goes against you. The 350 million rials I spoke of."

They were talking about attaching his ship and cargo! The cargo of heavy machinery was worth a fortune and would be unpaid for until unloaded on the dock. He and the other owners of the *Beirut Victory* would be liable!

"Witnesses. Will I be allowed to bring witnesses?"

"Of course, within reason."

"Then I will bring this man, the American Navy commander. As captain of the U.S. destroyer *Lawrence,* Commander Spooner boarded and searched my ship. He can testify that there was no such stolen cargo aboard her." He repeated the declaration in English so that Spooner would understand.

Spooner smiled broadly. "I have every intention of being at this trial—as a witness for the plaintiff. And I will be only too happy to testify that the two lighters containing the hijacked missile and its launcher were not aboard your ship, at least not at the time I searched her. You had already unloaded them, in a small inlet along the coast of Iranian Baluchistan."

"You have no proof of this!" the defiant Atawi shouted.

"Oh, but I have." Spooner pulled some papers out of his coat pocket and waved them in the Lebanese captain's face. "I have a deposition here from an Indian naval officer who commands an Indian Coastal Patrol boat operating out of Bombay harbor. The Indian lieutenant and his crew boarded your vessel and searched it a week before I did."

The dismayed captain stared at the papers in Spooner's hand, knowing full well what was coming.

"The Indian officer's testimony proves, beyond the shadow of a doubt, that the two lighters were aboard the *Beirut Victory* when she left India's territorial waters. Captain Atawi, I ~st my case."